BOOKS, BALLS, AND CUTE BUTTS FOR CHRISTMAS

Cameron D. James & Cali Kitsu

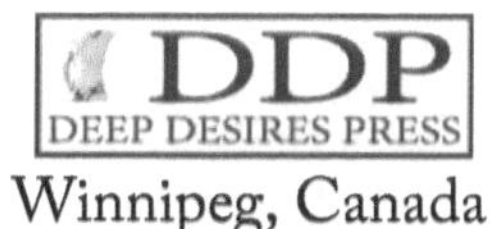

DDP
DEEP DESIRES PRESS
Winnipeg, Canada

Published November 2025 by Deep Desires Press, an imprint of Story Perfect Books.

Deep Desires Press
PO Box 51053 Tyndall Park
Winnipeg, Manitoba R2X 3B0
Canada

Visit deepdesirespress.com for more great reads.

Books, Balls, and Cute Butts for Christmas is our second co-written book, following *Cookies, Candles, and Cute Butts for Christmas*. We are best friends who love Christmas, books, and our husbands' cute butts. We also love having fun together, which is exactly what we did when writing this book.

This book is a high heat, super sweet, and very low angst opposites-attract MM romance.

If you don't like reading explicit sex between men, we can think of twelve scenes that you might wanna skip, including a super spicy one featuring a corset and candy-cane-flavored felching, but we'd recommend finding another book.

We hope that the story and characters we created make you feel happy, festive, warm, and maybe a little slutty, too.

Throughout this series, we use several names for stores and books that we've made up—it's something we enjoy immensely. The sillier the better. They are in no way meant to refer to or endorse specific stores or products that may currently exist or exist in the future.

As always, we would like to thank the Professor and the Pig for their support of our endless shenanigans.

If you like this book, please check out our podcast *Cali & Craig Talk...* where we talk about books, butts, and writing.

<3, Cameron & Cali

TABLE OF CONTENTS

BOOKS, BALLS, AND CUTE BUTTS FOR CHRISTMAS

Chapter One
The Wolf Takes The Mouse

   JACOB   

"He deserved it," I mutter to myself, and turn the TV off. Every single sports network is still talking about my suspension. Is it my fault that my team has lost three games in a row since I punched a ref? Technically, yes. Is it my fault that they can't score without me? No, not really. Either way, there's nothing I can do about it now. At this point, all I can do is ride my suspension out and enjoy my new life here in Frosty Bottoms. It's nothing like the life I have back in Miami, and even though I'm the most famous soccer player in the country, this break away from the media and soccer has been more refreshing than I expected. You wouldn't think going from a ten-bedroom beachside mansion to a four-bedroom home in a small gated community, in the middle of nowhere, would be an easy change, but, really, it's fine.

All I've ever known is soccer, it's been my entire world. But now, I don't have my security guard with me, no daily press conferences, no sponsorship appearances, and there's no screaming fans…except for the locals, and they keep it to a minimum—usually. Just me, here, running a contracting business. Life couldn't be any simpler at this point.

The comfort I feel when I sink into my new couch is quickly interrupted by my phone vibrating inside my pocket. Every time I look at it, I'm afraid it's gonna be my agent, Linley, telling me the media has figured out where I am. It's been two weeks, though, and no one has said anything, so maybe my dad was right—the people of Frosty Bottoms *do* know how to keep a secret. Of course, it could just be because my dad is the mayor that no one has told the press that I'm here. The whole town has been really welcoming, and, sure, some of them may take the flirting a bit too far, but still, they've respected me for the most part. Honestly, as long as none of them tell the press where I am, I can deal with whatever else comes my way.

When I unlock my phone, I see it's a text from my dad.

I hope you change your mind and come to the Halloween party tonight. There's no party like a party at Bottoms Up.

I text him back quickly: *I don't think so, Dad. The last place I need someone to find me is at a gay bar in the middle of Frosty Bottoms.*

Aaaand my father just sent me a picture of his costume. He is the most ridiculous man in the world. But the party does sound fun, and I have a mask that would hide my face… If I wear a long-sleeved turtleneck and a sweater on top, all my tattoos should be covered.

I text him back: *Nice costume. I'm not going to the party. I have four projects I have to deal with tomorrow, I can't afford to be hungover. Have fun. No more pics, please.*

That's only a half lie. Tomorrow, I do have to repair a shelf, install a showerhead, fix a sink handle, and I can't even remember what the other person wants. I'm glad I got my contractor license in college; it's really paying off here.

Let me know if you change your mind! he texts back.

I have no idea how I'm actually related to him. We couldn't possibly be more different than we are. Except for the fact that we both like men. Before I can put my phone down on the couch beside me, I see a text from Linley.

Call me.

Hmm, no, thank you. I'm gonna ignore that for a few minutes. The oven should be preheated soon. After I put my food in, I'll call her back.

Now my phone is ringing…of course, it's my mom. I take a deep breath and exhale before I answer. "Hello, Mother."

"Your father texted me that you don't want to go to the Halloween party at the gay club!" she shouts. Her voice is naturally loud, but it's even louder than normal today.

"Volume, Mother. You're screaming in my ear. Maybe turn the vacuum off while you're talking to me, or call me after?"

I don't know why she bothers pretending to care. She doesn't. I was so relaxed in the shower, then that stupid coverage of the soccer game pissed me off, then my dad's ridiculous costume, Linley trying to get in touch with me, and now the cherry on top, my mother. The woman who feels my entire reason for being born was so that I could play soccer and make her rich. I lean my head back against the couch and massage my temple.

"I can't stop vacuuming, Jacob, because *I* am still trying to fix the reputation of our family after your little incident. Wait, wait, I didn't call to talk about that, so don't hang up on me."

"How can I help you, Mother?"

"Stop calling me Mother!" she giggles. "Don't you want to go hang out with your father? He sent me a picture of his costume. Seems like it would be fun. You should go."

"I don't think so, Mom. Hanging out with my father, the mayor, at a gay club, while hiding out from the press is not really on my list of things I want to do tonight."

"Honey, you can't hide forever. Sooner or later, the press will figure out where you are. You gotta just live your life. Just like me. My son, whom I adore, punched a full-grown man, and narrowly escaped charges, then abandoned me, to hide from his problems in Frosty Bottoms, Vermont, but am I letting it get me down? No, no, I'm not. I gotta keep going, so that when you come back it will be like you never left."

She's stopped talking for the moment, but I still hear the vacuum going, so I don't know if this is just a dramatic pause or... "Mom, is this why you called me? To guilt trip me about leaving? I'm twenty-five, I haven't lived at home since I was eighteen. Don't say I abandoned you."

"Well, of course, you did. You've always been nearby, now you're all the way in Vermont, and I'm here all alone... You know, your father still has one hell of an ass after all these years. Whooee. I wonder if he can still dance, too?"

"Mom, please. I can't—please don't talk about his ass, or anything actually. Also, the flight from Miami isn't that long. You can always come for a visit whenever you want."

There's another long pause; she's probably texting my dad.

"Oh, Jacob, darling, I have to go. I'm getting another call from Gia Fernazzi, she's supposed to let me know what movie we're going to see tomorrow night. Talk to you soon."

Just like that, the caring mother act ends. It's always the same with her.

I need to get my dinner ready, the oven should definitely be preheated by now, but I didn't hear it beep. Walking into the kitchen, I can see that it's not quite ready yet. I take a seat on one of the barstools, placing my phone on the counter, and it immediately starts to vibrate.

Shit, it's Linley, again.

Jacob, don't forget that you need to start on your community service. I can line some things up for you with a few places. How long are you actually planning to stay there for?

She knows how I feel, but she doesn't listen. The incident with the referee aside, I was growing tired of South Beach, anyway. It's so nice being in a small town.

I bought a house here; I'm planning to stay here. We've been over this. I'm not going back to Miami.

You keep saying that and I don't believe you. What will you do next season? You have a year left on your contract. You're gonna travel between Vermont & Miami?

I have no idea. I'll figure it out.

You have responsibilities. You can't run away from them just because you did something wrong.

And now she's not getting a response. I might not be able to run away from my problems forever, but I'm sick of constantly feeling like my life isn't mine to live. Screw this.

Maybe it's time to finally have an anonymous hookup in a club. Scott is always going on about how sex with a stranger is so much hotter. I haven't used Grindr before, but I've popped on a couple of times just to check it out. I've always been too nervous that someone would know who I was and spread it on social media, and if that happened, I would become a distraction for the team. I'll never understand why people are so obsessed with who someone else has sex with. That's half the reason I won't ever be able to have a real relationship. I put that wall up a long time ago—the invasion of privacy is hard enough on me, but for someone who isn't used to public criticism—it's even worse. So, no relationships for me. Anyway, if I'm gonna go to the party, I can't let my dad know. I can't imagine a more embarrassing scenario than being at a gay club with my dad, the mayor, in the costume that he's wearing.

Alright, I'm gonna do it. I stand up from my couch and head for the closet in the largest of the guest rooms. There are still boxes everywhere. I could just make this the box room. Then I won't have to unpack everything. I slide some of the boxes around until I find the one labeled *Stuff I don't need.*

A few months ago, Derek hosted a *Twilight* themed party for Scott's birthday. All of us dressed up as vampires and werewolves. I was Team Jacob, obviously, no way in hell was I going dressed as a vampire. Pretty sure my mask is in this box. Quickly, I open it and dig through until I find it. Oh, wow. It's so hairy, I don't remember it being this hairy.

Time to download Grindr. Scott always finds guys that are traveling or just visiting, so I'll try that. When I get to the party, I'll see if there are any non-locals; that's safer than hooking up with someone that I may run into again.

Once I set up my profile, Grindr notifications start rolling in. Wow. So many options. There are a lot of guys close by. I need to get dressed and head out. I walk back into my room and grab a black turtleneck and sweater from my closet and quickly get ready, spraying myself with cologne and ruffling my hair up a bit. I'm not used to the cold here yet, so I'm kind of glad I can wear a few layers. Alright, I'm doing this. I'm not going to worry about anything. I'm just gonna go and have a good time.

I arm the security system and step outside. This is fine. I can do this.

I just need to keep repeating that to myself. Shit, wait. I forgot a condom. I head back inside and grab two condoms, and two packets of lube. Maybe I shouldn't do this… Someone may recognize me… No, I can do it. People hook up at these parties all the time. I re-arm the security system and head back outside, making my way to my car. Before I even unlock the door, I drop my head back, realizing that I forgot to turn the oven off. I step back inside and walk into the kitchen. As I turn the oven off, I feel my phone vibrating in my pocket. I'm not even going to check it at this point, because whatever it is will only make me stay here longer, and I really want to go. I'm gonna have fun tonight.

EDWARD

I pull my rusty car up to the curb in front of Chad's place and kill the engine. The heater in this car barely works, so it never got really warm, and it's already chilly again with the car off. When I get out of the car, I'm immediately assaulted with a brutal wind. This place is so much more wintry in late October than back home, even though "back home" is only an hour down the interstate.

I yank open the back door and pull out my backpack full of weekend gear—toiletries, a few changes of clothes, and a handful of smutty novels—and then lock my car and head over to Chad's building. As he'd promised, he'd left the key under a rock just to the left of the door.

It feels weird coming into someone else's apartment when they're not home. Yes, Chad is my half-brother, but we're not exactly close, we're just getting to know each other. Even though we have the same dad, our paths never really crossed.

"Come to Frosty Bottoms for your birthday," Chad had said on our video call last weekend. "Relax, put your feet up, check out the bar, maybe meet a guy. You know, just have a good time."

"I dunno," I had said. I played it kind of low-key because I didn't want to get my hopes up. The gay scene in Twilight Hollow is pretty much non-existent, with the local guys on Grindr limited to maybe a dozen blank profiles and headless torsos who just want a quick blow-and-go behind the Burger King.

"Besides," Chad said, "it'll help you close that chapter and move on. Get your head out of it for a bit."

That "chapter" was the closing of my bookstore. It had done fine as a business, though Twilight Hollow isn't much of a romance town—if I'd run a horror bookstore on the other hand… But it just wasn't meant to be; my landlord had sold the building to a developer and I had to close up shop.

Before I could get mired in what could have been, Chad's husband Lucas had slid next to him in the video call. "You have to come…and then we'll find a guy to make you come," he said with a wink.

And so now I'm here in Frosty Bottoms on my birthday weekend, which also happens to be Halloween. To kick off the weekend is the costume party at Chad and Lucas's bar, Bottoms Up.

I take a moment to check out their apartment. I hadn't known what to expect, but a rather modern-looking and very clean place somehow hadn't been at the top of the list.

"Awrk! Dirty boy! Dirty boy!" The harsh yet musical voice startles me, but then I remember the parrot Chad had warned me about.

"Hey, Petey, I'm Edward," I say to the bright red and green bird in the massive cage inside the living room.

"Dirty boy! Dirty boy!"

I giggle at the thought of what this bird has overheard, if this is what he's saying.

Spotting the door Chad had texted me about, I cross the nice living room and step inside. The bedroom is perfect for a little weekend getaway. The bed is a double mattress with red pillows and comforter, and there's a dresser with a mirror along one wall and a small window above the bed with fabric curtains.

I lay my backpack on the dresser and sit on the edge of the bed. My phone buzzes with a text from Chad: *Bro. You in town yet?*

I tap out a quick reply: *Just got to your apartment.*

His reply is instantaneous: *Hurry up and get down here. The place is crammed full of hot men.*

Unzipping my backpack, I dig around for my costume.

"Damn it," I mutter, pulling *everything* out. No costume. "Where is it?"

I text Chad again: *I forgot my flipping costume!! What do I do??*

We have a box of masks and costumes in the hall closet by the bathroom on the top shelf. Pick what you want.

I hurry through the apartment and find the box with masks sticking out of it. A hairy wolf mask sits on top, which instantly reminds me of Jacob from my favorite movie *Twilight*. As much as I love Jacob, I'm obviously Team Edward. Next to it are a sequined bunny and a gray mouse. Since my hair is one of my best features, I don't want to cover it up with a full-face mask, so I choose the mouse; the gray fur on it will contrast nicely against my black hair.

Returning to the bedroom, I sort through the clothes I piled on the bed, looking for what goes best with the mask. Since I dress entirely in emo black, none of it really goes with the gray mask, which also has pink accents. I put on a pair of slim-fit jeans and a tight short-sleeved shirt, which highlights both my biceps and the tattoos down my arms.

I try flipping my hair over the top of the mask, and then pull it back, testing what looks best. In the end, I go with my hair over the top because it maintains a bit of my style while dressed as a mouse.

Suddenly, I have this rush of anxiety about this costume party. I want to go so badly and just enjoy the night, but it's all so overwhelming. I haven't been to a gay event this big before. I wonder if Chad is exaggerating about the number of hot guys there or if it's really like that. While the idea of hooking up with someone isn't entirely out of the question, the romantic in me is always hoping for something more. Years of reading romance novels made me this way.

I pull off the mask and collapse onto the bed, seeking just a few minutes to be by myself in the silence of the empty apartment. Even though the drive wasn't that long, I feel a little exhausted, so a quick rest should help.

Sitting next to my backpack is one of the trashy novels I brought. I grab it and open it. *The Lumberjack's Massive Wood.*

My bookstore had a wide selection of straight and queer titles. Most people went for pretty tame things, but I've always been drawn to the more erotic. The guys that start out as the biggest jerks in these books end up being the most passionate lovers in and out of bed.

My *Boys Kiss Boys Or I'm Out* bookmark takes me to the page I'd left off on and I read a few paragraphs.

"Oh," I say to myself. The characters had just finished having sex out in the woods and the top offered to set up a campfire to whip up a quick batch of pancakes. "That's sweet."

I dig through the stuff on the bed until I find a little tattered notebook and open it. It's my BBL—my Book Boyfriend List. I add "makes pancakes after sex" to it. This is a lengthy list of all the sweet and romantic things boyfriends in my favorite books do.

I've had such awful luck with guys back home that I started making up this dream list for the right man. Beside a few items are checkmarks from guys who matched some of the criteria, but the most any guy ever had was three checkmarks. Of course, none of this really matters, because I always end up getting dumped after the first date.

I close the book and the BBL and get up. After all, I didn't come all this way just to read.

Shoving the BBL in my back pocket, I grab the mask, my keys, and my coat, and head out to my car. The parrot shouts "Dirty boy!" as I exit the apartment. In the car, I say a little prayer to the smut gods that it will start and, after a third try, it does. I prop my phone up on the dashboard with Google Maps open to help me navigate this tiny wintry town. It takes no more than a few minutes to get downtown and then a few more minutes to find parking. I could have walked here.

When I get out of the car and wander around the corner to the main street, I slow my pace to take a good look up and down the block. This place is so different from Twilight Hollow. Whereas back home it would be customary to see skeletons and pumpkins as décor all year round, especially at this time of year, this place already has Christmas trees and fairy lights everywhere, and I get the sense they're year-round decorations. Part of me thinks it's weird, but then I realize my downtown has a giant witch's hut as a tourist attraction in the town square.

There's a large selection of businesses down both sides of the street. Next to my half-brother's bar is a cookie shop, there's a candle shop across the street, and it looks like a new pizza place opening two doors down.

The sidewalks are packed with people, and in between them my eyes catch a sign with two words in giant font—FOR LEASE. I eye up that storefront, trying to get a sense of the size of it and estimate what it might cost, but then I shake my head. I can't just leap at the first "for lease" sign I see. I need to make smart decisions, not impulsive ones.

I head to the bar and slip my mask over my face before I enter. Just inside they have a coat check set up, so I hand over my coat, and they give me a ticket.

Before I step further into the place, I take in my new surroundings. The bar has a quaint classic wood paneling vibe to it, but the sheer number of disco lights clearly make this a queer space. That and Cher blasting from the speakers. The place is crowded, packed wall to wall with hot guys. Chad wasn't exaggerating.

There's a lot of skin showing. Even a few ass cheeks. The costumes range from fully elaborate to even less effort than *I'm* currently putting in.

And then I finally spot my half-brother across the place. He's behind the bar wearing a pair of boxers and has his hair all wild. I make my way through the crowds and find a stool in front of the bar.

"I know that mask!" he says as he comes up. He gives me a hug across the bar. "Great to see you, little brother!"

I flip my mask up briefly so I can look him up and down and give him the full expression on my face. He is, indeed, wearing only boxers and a pair of flip-flops. His hair is even wilder than it had looked from across the bar. "What are you supposed to be dressed as?"

He backs up and puts his hands out in an *isn't it clear* gesture. "I'm a guy whose house was destroyed by a tornado before he got fully dressed. Obviously."

"Obviously." I flip the mask back down. "Does this meet health requirements? I better not get armpit hair in my drink."

"The health inspector is that dude over there in a thong, dancing on the table."

I follow his pointed finger and see a hairy, muscular man wearing a bikini and platform heels dancing on a bar table, earning hoots and hollers.

"Who's that other guy?" I ask. Dancing on the next table over is a man who must be in his forties, at least, wearing a glittery silver skin-tight body suit that goes down to his waist, leaving his ass and thighs exposed, and then matching knee-high boots. "And is he dressed as…"

"Lady Gaga from the 2017 Super Bowl halftime show? Yeah," Chad says. "That's Mayor Dick."

I blink a few times, trying to clear what had to be a brain aneurism. When nothing changes, I realize I'd heard right. I turn on the stool, swiveling back to Chad. "Your *mayor* is dancing on a tabletop in a gay bar with half his ass hanging out?"

"That's nothing," Lucas says as he sidles up to Chad. He's clearly heard what we were talking about. "If you head into the bathroom later, you might see what he's really known for."

"Too much," I say. "That's too much."

"Too much what?" Chad asks.

"Information, maybe? There are things I'd rather not know."

"Just to be clear," Chad says, "when I suggested you come here for a fun weekend and maybe get laid, I didn't mean Mayor Dick." He winks at me. "But no judgement if you're into guys like him."

I hold my hands up. "First of all, you said 'meet someone', not 'get laid,'" I say. "Second of all, that guy is definitely not my type."

"So, he's not your type, but are you opposed to getting laid?"

"I didn't plan on it, but looking around—*not in that direction*," I say, gesturing to the mayor and health inspector, "I might be on board with it."

"See anything that could fully convince you?" Chad asks. "There are bears, daddies, twinks, jocks, otters, and more."

I swivel around to face the crowd again. It's then that I spot a wolf across the room; he's wearing a tight sweater that shows just how fit he is. Even though he's fully covered and masked, he's freaking hot. My gaze follows him for a moment, and when he dips out of sight behind some people, I take in the rest of the crowd.

I turn back to Chad; Lucas has gone off to the microphone at the other end of the bar to announce the costume contest is beginning soon.

"I don't know," I say to Chad. "It's like there's too much choice, too much pressure; I'm not used to it. Plus, they're all wearing masks or costumes."

"You've got Grindr, right? Pull it up and I'll help you sort through the riff-raff. There are a lot of cute butts in Frosty Bottoms."

I pull out my phone and open Grindr, swiping down to refresh the feed. Admittedly, before I left Twilight Hollow, I'd updated my profile to say I was visiting here, so that guys knew I wouldn't be around for long. So if they were looking for relationships or liked to talk for three weeks before meeting up, I wasn't the guy for them.

The feed is filled with mostly photos and the occasional picture-less profile. I hope that the wolf pops up as nearby, but I don't see him—not that I'd recognize him, of course, because of his mask.

After a few minutes of searching and Chad pointing out a few different guys—none of whom catch my interest—I swipe down to refresh the feed.

A new profile appears near the top. The pic is of a very nicely defined set of abs. I turn my phone to Chad. "Who is this guy?"

Chad's eyes go wide. He grabs the phone from me and zooms in on the pic. "I wish I knew! Fuck, those are some nice abs."

"You haven't slept with him?" I ask.

"Not yet," he says.

"Nice abs!" Lucas says as he comes up beside Chad. He takes the phone from his husband and also zooms in on the pic. "We should invite him back to our place and have some fun with him." He taps around, then frowns. "No married guys, it says. He's boring." He gives the phone back to Chad, who gives it back to me.

"Worth a shot," Chad says, "though I can't guarantee a good time with him since I haven't personally sampled the merchandise."

I lock my phone and put it face down on the bar; I'm not ready to jump into the often-disappointing world of a Grindr conversation. Chad passes me a drink, and I take a long sip. The "for lease" sign I saw on the way in suddenly pops up in my mind. "What's the deal with that place across the street that's available for rent?" I ask Chad.

"Beside Kellan's candle shop?" Chad says. "That's Jack's old place, Rub One Out Massage Parlor. He's retiring and moving out to the countryside."

"So, nothing's wrong with the place?"

Chad shakes his head. "Not that I'm aware of, and I haven't heard anything from Kellan either and they share a wall."

"And what's the rent around here like?"

"Surprisingly cheap, all things considered." He suddenly smiles. "Are you thinking of setting up shop there?"

I wave my hand dismissively. "I don't make business decisions when I'm drinking," I say. Really, though, I'm kind of considering it, but setting up shop in a new town that I know nothing about might not be the smartest move. It feels odd to even be thinking about it, but opportunity seems to be laying itself out—my shop closes, I get a payout for my landlord ending the lease early, and a potential spot opens up in a town with a more vibrant scene than I currently have in Twilight Hollow.

Suddenly, my phone buzzes loudly on the bartop. I pick it up and check the notification.

"Mister amazing abs messaged me," I say to Chad.

   JACOB   

I park my car in the back of Dip Your Wick, it's across the street from the bar. I'm not gonna park behind the bar, I'd rather this hookup be completely anonymous. Besides, I don't need someone seeing my car there and telling my dad that I'm inside. I like the downtown area here, there are always places to park at night, unlike the city, where I always had to park in a parking garage or by valet. I pull my phone out and put my mask on, quickly scanning the area before getting out.

Deep breath, I tell myself, as I step outside and walk around to the front of the building. The bar is packed inside and out, even the sidewalk is full of people in costume, despite the freezing temperature. It kind of feels weird going to a party by myself. Not having security with me, or friends around me—that hasn't happened for the last seven years.

I step inside and pull my phone out. Woah. I'm having trouble seeing with this mask, but there are at least forty notifications. There's an open spot by a back wall, and I slide in between people dancing, making my way toward it, so I can check things out. Even though I feel nervous, I know this is all totally normal and fine. There's nothing wrong with me looking for someone else who just wants to have sex. Although, I'm certain my agent and security team would disagree.

"Oops, excuse me, Wolfie," a gruff voice says behind me. I turn and see a bearded man in a construction worker costume. "You got a nice ass. You looking for some fun?" he asks, lifting his chin toward the neon restroom signs.

Shaking my head, I wave him off, continuing toward the back of the room. Oh my God… As I turn around, I'm faced with the horrific sight of my father, who is currently dancing on a table. Coming here was a bad, bad idea. I can't unsee that. Not to mention, that table does not look sturdy. Can't imagine being brave enough to dance on a table.

The music stops for a moment, and I hear Lucas announce the costume contest from behind the bar. My father just gave a loud cheer, he's definitely going to enter. I'm not gonna stand out here and watch my dad dance.

Once I finally reach the back wall, I swipe down and refresh my Grindr feed. There are so many profiles for me to sort through… Threesome, looking for oral, looking for a daddy, ooh, this one says he's just visiting. Looking for fun. He's got a nice body, can't see his face. His tattoos are sexy… Hmm. Which guy is this? I'm looking around the room, but everyone is so close that it's impossible for me to tell which guy this is. Fuck it. Let's do it.

I send my first ever, Grindr message.

Me: *Hey*

The reply is almost instantaneous.

Him: *Hey*

Me: *Are you having fun? Your profile says you're visiting.*

Him: *Yeah. Just here for the night. HBU?*

Fuck, what do I say? I'm sure it's fine if I say I live here.

Me: *I live here.*

Him: *At the bar?*

I chuckle at that. Before I reply, I notice a few people looking down at their phones. Which one is he?

Him: *Jk. I just wanted to know if you were having fun.*

Me: *I'm not having fun yet. But maybe you can help me with that.*

Me: *Where are you?*

Him: *I'm at the bar.*

Me: *What are you dressed as?*

Him: *If you can figure out which guy I am, I'll follow you into the bathroom and we can have some fun.*

The whole time I've been messaging him, my eyes keep finding their way to a guy wearing a gray mouse mask. He's been chatting with Chad and Lucas a lot, though. It's probably not him. I start walking over and notice the mouse's left arm tattoos. It's him. What do I do?

"You want a drink?" Chad asks me, as I stand beside the mouse. I shake my head no and place my hand softly on the mouse's shoulder. I don't think Chad would recognize my voice because it would be too muffled, but with the way he and Lucas are always checking me out, there's a chance he could figure out that it's me.

The mouse looks up at me and taps his phone bringing up the profile picture of my abs. I stick my hands in my pockets and shrug at him, then take a seat beside him at the bar. I don't know what to do here, but Chad is keeping a close eye on him. I need to make sure there's nothing going on there first.

I send him a quick message.

Me: *Are you friends with Chad?*

Him: *Kind of. I guess.*

Me: *I'm not looking for a threesome.*

He laughs beside me and shakes his head. That damn mouse mask covers his face perfectly. I can't see what he looks like, but I really like his tattoos and his ear piercings. In any other setting, I'd really try to talk to him. But not now.

Him: *I'm not interested in Chad, but have you hooked up with him before?*

I pull my head back and scoff. I would never fuck around with a married man. Besides, Chad is not my type.

Me: *No. I haven't hooked up with anyone in this town.*

Shit, I shouldn't have said that. This is why I shouldn't be talking to him.

Me: *I meant to say I haven't hooked up with anyone yet.*

Him: *Are you nervous or something? Kind of feels like you're stalling. I told you I'd follow you into the bathroom, but you sat down. Do you want to actually talk? Or can I see those abs up close and skip all of this?*

I stand and grab him by the hand. Pulling him toward the bathroom with me. He giggles a bit. I'm half holding his hand here, and it feels weird. His fingers aren't intertwined with mine, but he's latched on tight. Holy shit, it's my dad. I release the mouse's hand and turn to the side, so my back is facing him. Please don't grab my ass, please don't notice me.

The mouse grabs my belt. And pulls me toward him. "Not getting away, that easily," he says.

My father is right behind me. I grab ahold of the mouse's hand. "I'm not trying to get away," I say, pulling him the last few feet into the bathroom behind me.

"Thought you were trying to leave me for Lady Gaga," he says.

"Sssh. No." I open the last stall in the bathroom, which thankfully isn't absolutely disgusting, and we both step inside. "You wanna do this with masks on?" he asks me.

"Yeah. And I don't really want to talk."

"Fine with me," he says grabbing my belt and unbuckling it. He lifts my shirt and looks at my abs. "Fuck. What are you a model or an athlete?"

I'm gonna pretend he didn't ask that. He palms my abs, rubbing across them slowly, then drops to his knees, tugging my pants and underwear down. He's already got me so fucking hard, even though that mouse mask isn't really doing it for me. His voice and his tattoos are, though. He grips my cock and licks the head, looking up at me. I can see his dark brown eyes through the holes in his mask, they're pretty. He takes all of me into his mouth and starts sucking slowly.

"Mmm…" I moan, lightly threading my fingers through his thick black hair.

"I like the way you taste," he says.

I drop my head back and grunt as he works my cock using his hand and his mouth. I want to fuck this little mouse. When I pull back from the warmth of his mouth, he seems to know exactly what I want. He stands and pulls his pants and underwear down, turning his ass toward me. I lean down and grab the condom and lube out of my pants, bringing my face right next to his juicy round ass as I start to stand back up. I have the urge to eat him out, which I rarely do, but his ass is fucking gorgeous. I'm not taking my mask off, though. Besides, I shouldn't waste time playing with him. Once I'm standing, I grip him by the waist, turning him in the stall. He leans over the toilet bracing himself against the wall. I rip the condom open and cover my dick with it, then squeeze some lube from the packet onto his hole, and my cock. "Mmm…" I trace his rim with the head of my dick, then stick one finger inside. He's tight, but not too tight.

He lets out a light moan of approval as I start to finger him. "You don't have to go easy. Use me."

Fuck, that's hot. I slip a second finger in, stretching him out, my fingertips graze his prostate, and he lets out a tiny squeak, and scratches the wall.

It's getting hot with this mask on, and I really can't see all that well. "Hey. I want to take my mask off, but don't turn around, okay? It's too hot to fuck you like this."

"I won't look, just fuck me."

I pull my mask up on top of my head and press my cock firmly against his knotted flesh, then slowly work my way inside. Fuck, he feels good. His hole is clinging to every inch of my cock. He pushes back against me, and I fuck into him harder, and faster, gripping his waist while my balls smack into him. I'm ramming full force into him and he's panting and moaning, head down, eyes closed.

More. I need more, I need to come…and I'm close. I grip the sides of his ass—I'm pumping and grinding into this filthy little mouse, whose breaths are getting louder, and are kind of high pitched, too. It's fucking driving me crazy. I can tell he's on the verge of screaming, and I kind of want him to do it. "I'm gonna come," he cries out, then repeats himself, "I'm gonna fucking come."

And at that moment I come, hard and fast, and he does, too.

Chapter Two
We Don't Say
Hello Like This

Edward

"All ready for your big day?" Chad asks me as I walk out of his guest bedroom.

"Of course," I say. "I'm so excited!"

After that fateful Halloween weekend where I got the railing of a lifetime, but also saw the opportunity of a lifetime in that storefront for lease across from the bar, I had decided to dive in head first.

Within a week, I had the keys to the place and started doing weekend trips between Twilight Hollow and Frosty Bottoms, carting over boxes and boxes of books, along with all the other retail equipment and supplies I'd had in my old shop. I wasn't sure my car would survive all of that, but it pulled through.

"Awrk!" Petey screeches. "Bend over! Bend over! Awrk!" I'd learned Petey likes gentle neck scritches, so I poke my finger through the cage and give him a little loving.

"What time do you meet Jacob?" Chad asks.

I glance at the time on my phone. "In a couple hours."

Chad had been a major help in getting this new shop off the ground. While I had been tying up my life in Twilight Hollow so I could pack it all up and move here, he had arranged for a contractor to start on the renovations. I needed to change it from the massage parlor it used to be into the romance bookstore it's meant to be.

I haven't had a chance to meet Jacob in person yet, although we've spoken a lot on the phone, sometimes several times a day. I sort of feel like I already know him and it's kind of like I have a new friend with a very sexy voice—and according to Chad, Jacob is "fucking hot" and a sports star or something. Might've been table tennis? Something like that.

When I'd pop by on the weekends with carloads of books and supplies, I got to see the progress he was making, but the timing never worked out for us to meet. I like how he works; he's efficient and very good at what he does.

"Thanks again for your help with everything," I say.

"Of course," Chad says, "it's what half-brothers are for."

I eventually manage to make and eat a quick breakfast and throw myself through the shower. I get into my car and drive over to my shop— Hot for Plot, I had decided to call it—and pull into a tiny space in the lane behind the building.

Now that I'm alone again and not in a rush anymore, I pull out my phone and open up Grindr. I swipe down to refresh the feed, searching for that set of amazing abs. They're nowhere to be found.

Clicking into my chat history, I scroll down until I find our DMs. I tap his profile and search for the date he was last online. It simply reads *offline*, which is what it's said since the week after we hooked up, meaning he hasn't logged in again since that night.

At least, not from that account. That's why I check the local profiles frequently. He might've lost his login and created a new account. But, once again, I don't see anything; the only places those abs exist are in my DM history…and my dreams.

After shoving my phone into my pocket, I pull out my BBL from my other pocket and flip through it, rereading the notes I'd made that night after our hookup. It was the only time I added notes based on a real person and not a fictional man.

I close my BBL and let out a little sigh of disappointment, then put it back in my pocket and get out of the car. I don't have a key to the back door of the store yet, so I hunch my shoulders and make sure my neck is fully covered as I walk around the block to the front of my shop. Pride swells in my chest as I approach my storefront and slip the key into the lock. I swing the door open and let myself in. After turning off the alarm, I turn on the lights and just smile as I take it all in.

Jacob had painted the place in bright pinks and complementary colors, and he'd even painted quotes from some of my favorite romance novels onto the walls. But the impressive part is all the bookshelves lining the space. While they're all easily reachable from someone of average height, I'd gotten Jacob to install one of those rolling ladders attached to the wall, and the railing stretches around half the room.

In the front corner by the window stands the register where I'll process the transactions, and in the middle of the room are half a dozen vintage mismatched chairs and end tables for people to relax while they browse, as well as some smaller shelves. In the middle of the arrangement of chairs and tables is a fake fireplace that also doubles as a space heater for days where it gets extra cold.

The store is nearly done, there are just a few finishing touches to put in place, like stocking all the books on the shelves and attaching the lighting fixtures to the ceiling, but this definitely feels like the right decision to me.

I glance at the time on my phone; my meeting with Jacob isn't scheduled for another hour and a half. I look around the room and start planning for how to fill the shelves.

Stacked near the chairs are the last batch of boxes I'd brought here; the rest are piled precariously in the miniscule stock room behind the back wall, next to what will be my office. I open the top box and find classic romance books from my vintage section. They're mostly gently-used, though I'd found some reprints of popular titles a little while back.

I try to dig up my memory of the stocking outline I'd sketched a few weeks ago, of which sections would go where. The classic romances are going to go on the bottom shelves against the back wall, if I'm remembering right.

Tugging off my zip-up hoodie, I sling it over a chair, pop in my earbuds, blast some My Chemical Romance, and haul the heavy box of books to the back of the store. I sit down on my heels and start unpacking the box. I wish I could say that past me planned for future me and that the box is organized…but it isn't. Everything is out of order.

After emptying this box, I grab the second one, which also has romance classics, and I return to my spot. I start emptying it as well and making little piles all around me as I sort through them. I get into a good rhythm with it, rocking out to the music in my ears and totally in my element as I start getting my shop in order and ready for the grand opening…which is only two days away. I really didn't plan this very well. At this point, I should've been putting the last two boxes of books on the shelves, not the first two.

When I reach the halfway point of emptying this box, I'm suddenly aware of the passage of time. Jacob will be here any moment.

I dust off my hands, and both rise and turn at the same time…

…and end up face first in a man's balls. He grunts, but doesn't move. I'm frozen in what feels like a mix of terror and anxiety, but all I can focus on is that this man is very well hung, if what's pressed against my face through the thin polyester of his track pants is any indication.

   JACOB   

"Thank you, Ms. Hyung," I say, as she taps her card against my phone for payment.

"Of course," she replies, giving me a playful wink. "Added a little extra in there for you, too."

"You didn't need to do that. It was no trouble at all. Though next time, I'm pretty sure you could do it yourself and save some money."

"Oh, no, I don't think I could. I can barely hold that screwdriver. My hands are too small for that."

I give her a smile and get inside my car. As I reverse out of the driveway, I realize I'm a few minutes early for my meeting with Edward. I'm excited to finally meet him, but also a bit nervous. He's really nice and easy to talk to, but people change when you meet them in person.

He doesn't seem to have any idea who I am, or he's really good at pretending. Being a professional soccer player, there are definitely people who don't know me, but the media does tend to focus on me, so I rarely come across anyone who watches sports that hasn't at least heard of me.

One of the most refreshing things about working with him is that he gives me actual jobs to do at the store. It's been kind of amazing working on it since day one. Unlike the rest of the jobs I do in town, like the one I just did—tightening a screw on a light switch plate. That was the most asinine thing I've ever been paid for. No, I take that back, I've been paid for even stupider things.

I'm also a bit leery of Edward because he's Chad's brother. I like Chad and Lucas well enough, but they're both always real flirty, and I'm not into that. I doubt I'll ever get married, but if I do, whoever I marry will be the only person I flirt with.

Once I pull into the back of the bookstore and park my car, I check my reflection in the mirror and try to decide if I should put my beanie on or leave it off. My hair is doing weird shit today... On, I'm definitely putting the beanie on. I tug it over my ears and step into the parking lot.

There's only one other car parked back here, and the bumper is covered in stickers. Some of them are pretty funny. *Book Boys Have The Best Butts.* Okay, I think that one is my favorite.

Walking around toward the front of the store, it's obvious that the tourist season is in full swing. It's starting to get busier every single day, especially at Dip Your Wick and BJ's Cookies, those two places are always swamped. It makes me slightly nervous seeing all these tourists walking around, but hopefully none of them will recognize me. I'm pretty much used to the temperature here now, but since it's cold, I can stay covered up for the most part. Although, I swear there's a permanent wind tunnel near the front of the store. I always get blasted with cold when I'm headed inside. I look through the door before opening it, trying to sneak a peek at

Edward, but I don't see him. "Hello," I say, looking around the front of the shop when I step inside. I still don't see him anywhere.

Walking around the large bookcase on the far side of the store, I finally see him. He's sitting on his heels, putting books on shelves. He's really cute…and he has tattoos. Dark hair, but I don't think he's noticed me, which is crazy because I'm like two feet away. "Hey," I say, stepping closer. But nothing happens. Nothing. He still hasn't looked at me. Is he pissed about the work I did? No. I seriously don't think he's noticed me. I'm gonna suggest he get bells for the door.

There we go, he's turning toward me. Oh my God. His face is pressed against my dick… And for some reason this feels kind of familiar. The top of his hair, his piercings, and his tattoos…I've seen this before. Exactly this, same position, same top of the head. Holy shit. It's him…the guy from my Halloween hook-up, and he still hasn't moved his face. My dick apparently hasn't forgotten him either. I need to step back, but I'm frozen in place.

"Uh…we, um, don't say hello like this where I'm from," I finally say.

"Technically, I haven't said hi yet," he says, against the front of my pants.

The vibration from his voice sends shockwaves straight to my dick. Oof. I take a step back and thankfully he stands up.

"Hi, I'm Edward," he says, giggling. His cheeks are slightly red, and if I weren't sure that this was the guy that I railed in the bathroom on Halloween, mine would be, too.

But at this moment, I'm more curious than embarrassed. "Have we met before?" I ask him.

He shakes his head. "Nope. I can say with one-hundred percent certainty that I've never met you before, although I wouldn't be opposed to a do-over if you wanted to go outside and come back in. We can just do the whole introduction over, but this time I'll say hi like a human, and I won't put my face in your balls."

I laugh at that and point toward the door. "So, I'll go outside, walk back around the corner, then come back in, and this time, you'll actually hear me coming in, and greet me with a handshake instead of motorboating my dick?"

"I can try, but I can't promise anything," he says, tilting his head at the door.

Following his eyeline, I see a few regulars walking over from the other side of the street. Shit. "I'm gonna lock the door. Cool?"

"Uh, just to be clear, you said we're gonna re-do the intro and I'm not motorboating your"—he gestures toward my dick—"that, but you're locking the door?"

I walk quickly toward the door and lock it before the few people outside reach the entrance. "Yeah, I'm locking the door because this is the time I usually start working in here, and if I don't lock it, people will come in and bother us."

"What do you mean?" he asks. "Do they want to buy books? I've been here for a few hours, and no one has come by."

He's either a very good liar, or he truly has no idea that we've had sex, and that I'm famous. But judging by the way he's looking through the door at the crowd walking over, I kind of think he's just unaware. I should have the same conversation that I have with every person that I meet here, and ask him not to take any pics of me, or talk about me to anyone, but for some reason, I feel like I don't need to do that with him.

He holds his hands out toward the door. "Should I let them in so they can tell me what they're looking for? I should make sure I have the books they want for opening day," he says.

How do I say that they're here for me, without sounding like a self-absorbed asshole? Ah, never mind. One of the women, I forget her name, is staring through the door. Her hands are cupped against her face. "Well, why don't you find out? Open the door a little and ask that woman what she wants," I say. "But don't let her in. I'm gonna go in the back. After you talk to her, close the blinds and that should do it."

"Okay, seems weird, but I'll do it."

I watch as he walks to the door, opening it just a bit. He listens well. Just like that night in the stall, he never turned around or looked at me once.

"Hi, I'm Edward, this is my—"

He's interrupted by the woman who was looking through the door. "Where is Jacob?" she asks.

He tilts his head in confusion. "Do you need him for something?"

"I just want to look at him, haha. But, for real, I wanted to see if he needed anything, like a tea or a snack." She's looking around him, and he's furrowing his brow at her. His face all squished up like that is kind of adorable.

"He's in the bathroom; I think he has a stomachache. He's probably going home for the day," he says and shuts the door. He looks over his shoulder at me, then closes the blinds.

"That your girlfriend?" he asks.

"No. Definitely not. Thanks for the cover," I chuckle.

"Well, nothing sexy about being in the bathroom. I figured that would work."

"I don't know, bathrooms can be sexy…"

He drops an eyebrow at me and sticks his hands in his pockets, giving me a little shrug. "I really love everything you've done here. I told you that on the phone, but everything is just exactly the way I imagined it, well better than I imagined it."

"I'm glad you like it. I'm gonna get these light fixtures installed today, and tomorrow I'll try to get the hammock chairs up. Do you want to point out the other stuff that you'd like done? According to my list there's not too much left, but I want to be sure we get everything finished in time."

Edward leads me around the store pointing out the few things that still need to be finished. I keep catching him staring at me, but he doesn't look like he remembers me at all. I think he's just staring at me, but it's a different kind of look than I'm used to, and I can't quite explain it.

"If that's everything, then I'll get started," I say. I head into the back room and pull my hoodie off, leaving it on the table then wrap my tool belt around my waist. It feels weird having it wrapped around with my track pants on, but it's fine. I grab the ladder and walk out toward the light fixtures in the center of the shop.

Edward is staring hard at me as I walk past him. "Do you need me to hold the ladder for you?" he asks, slowly looking me up and down.

I shake my head at him. "Nah. Thanks, though." Once I'm on the top of the ladder, I reach up toward the fixture, stick my drill into the hole and tighten it up. I do the same with the eight screws around the light. I hear a soft "Mmm" from below me and realize that my shirt is raised a tiny bit. Edward's eyes are glued to me, well, to my abs, is probably more accurate. Maybe my abs will jog his memory. I stretch higher hoping to give him a better look.

"So, you're staying with Chad?" I ask him, while continuing to tighten the screws.

He doesn't answer, but I can feel him checking me out. I talk a bit louder, hoping he'll hear me this time. "Or do you have a place of your own already?"

He shakes his head. "Huh? What? Chad?"

I step down from the ladder and lift my shirt, pretending I'm just rubbing my own abs. He *has* to remember my abs, he was obsessed with them. He's entranced for sure but doesn't seem like he's making the connection. "Yeah, Chad. Are you staying with him and Lucas?"

"Oh, right. Yeah, I'm staying with them, just until I find a place."

"Lots of changes for you. And you're here just as Snowflake festivities are starting to kick off. I still think it's kind of crazy to be opening a business this time of the year here."

He grabs a stack of books out of the box and heads over toward the rolling ladder. "It is kind of crazy. Normally, I overthink things, but something about this just felt right, so I went for it. Kind of like hiring you just because my half-brother said you were really good at what you do." He climbs up the ladder, then adds, "Chad trusts you, so I trust you. No questions asked. Anyway, how do you like it here? You said you moved in sometime in October, right?"

He doesn't look super sturdy on that ladder, but it's definitely secure because I installed it. "I like it. It's a lot different than Miami. I have a good amount of privacy here, and business is great. Trusting Chad is a wild concept. Between him and Kellan, I don't know which one is the bigger flirt."

"My brother flirts with you?" he asks.

"Ha. Your brother flirts with everyone, it's probably just from years of being a bartender."

"I'm really just getting to know him. We weren't raised together, so it's interesting hearing what other people think of him. I probably would have met him sooner, but my parents travel a lot, they always have. But he's said a lot of nice stuff about you."

"I bet he did. Is that weird for you just getting to know him at this age? You're probably the same age as me, right? I'm twenty-five."

"Yeah, I actually turned twenty-five the last time I was here. I came for my birthday."

Uh yeah, he *came* and that was because of me. I laugh at myself. He has to know, right? I'm trying to cover my smile, but I can't. "So, you *came* on your birthday?"

"Yep."

I chuckle a bit. "What did you *come* for? Did someone make you *come*? Or you just had the urge to *come*?"

"It was my birthday and I was looking for some fun. The landlord had just sold the space I was leasing. I really was just looking for a good time. So, I came."

Nope. He has no idea. No idea what it sounds like he's saying, and he really has no idea that we had sex. "Well, I'm glad you *came*." Last one, I couldn't help myself.

"Me too," he says. He lines up some of the books on the top shelf, then looks down at me. "Damn. I grabbed the wrong box. Can you pass me the box right beside that shelf?"

"Of course. But I don't think you can balance the box and the books. I can just pass you a few at a time. Are the rest of the boxes lined up in front of the right shelves?"

"Yeah, I have a system. The boxes should fill out the shelves they are in front of. I just grabbed the wrong one, I think I was distracted by your abs...abs-olutely wonderful craftsmanship."

I knew he was checking me out. I stand behind him and pass him a stack of about five paperback books, and he quickly shifts them to the shelf. He smiles awkwardly. "Thanks. Now do I want the really dirty stuff up high, or should that be in a different spot?"

He said that out loud, but I think he's talking to himself. I'm just looking up at that gorgeous ass while he moves the books around.

"So? What do you think?" he asks.

"Fucking spectacular. Probably the best one I've ever seen."

"What? Is this shelf that much better than the others?"

"Wait, what were you asking me about?" Oh my God. I am such an idiot. He meant the books, not his ass. Of course he didn't mean his ass.

"What did you think I was asking ab—"

I have no idea how, but he slipped, he actually slipped, and his ass is currently resting on my face, while I hold his waist. I went to catch him but since he wasn't up that high, he just kinda fell backward onto my face. I have never been so afraid to move or speak or breathe.

After a few seconds, I press him forward toward the ladder and look up at him.

"Oh my God," he says. "First my face is in your balls, now I just sat on your face. These aren't things I normally do until someone has at least bought me dinner."

"Pfftt. Are you okay?" I ask, trying not to laugh. "Sorry. I tried to catch you and you just kind of landed there."

He waves me off and steps down the ladder. "Totally fine. Thanks for catching me. I don't even know how that happened. I'm so embarrassed."

I hear two knocks on the door and see Braden and Kellan standing outside. I like these guys, but they're also my next-door neighbors. They're always asking me to hang out with them, and I don't really want to. Braden is cool because he still plays rugby occasionally, so we've hung out during workouts a few times, but Kellan really embraces the "everyone is family" motto in Frosty Bottoms. I'm not really into that. They're both nice guys, though. "Have you met Braden and Kellan?" I ask Edward.

"Yep." He waves at them and walks toward the door. "I met them a couple of times. Chad wanted me to be sure to pick an idea for the

Snowflake Festival before I saw Kellan, so I've already had the idea for a few days. He might be here for that."

I really don't feel like hanging out with Braden and Kellan right now, besides, I have Tony's thing I have to get ready for. I want to stay here and talk to him a little longer, but not with them here. "I think I'm gonna head out. I actually have somewhere to be in a little bit. I can definitely get the hanging chairs up tomorrow. Does that work?"

He gives me a look that makes me think he's disappointed that I'm leaving, but he opens the door for Braden and Kellan anyway. "Hi, guys!" he says as they enter.

I watch as they greet each other. They haven't noticed me, and I could just slip out, but I feel weird not making plans with him. Was there something else he needed from me? Should I just leave?

"Jacob!" Kellan says, walking toward me holding a red box of what I assume are cookies. "The place looks great. Minus all the books that aren't on shelves yet."

I nod at him and look around the room. Braden smiles lifting a drink carrier up. "We brought cookies and cocoa. I would have brought tea if I knew you were gonna be here."

"Thanks, I'm on my way out anyway." I look at Edward, trying to read his expression. Maybe he doesn't like being around people? "You good?" I ask him. "Did you need me for anything?"

Edward smiles and shakes his head, looking around the room. "Nope. I think I'm good."

"Alright," I say, as I give the group a wave and head outside.

CHAPTER THREE
DON'T CALL ME DADDY

EDWARD

I watch as Jacob hastily makes his exit from my store. My whole body feels like it's fluttering with anxiety and horniness all at the same time. How the hell is it that the man I've been talking to on the phone for a month and a half is this god among men? I'd instantly thought his voice was sexy, but I had no idea how much everything else about him would align with that sexiness.

Just two minutes ago, I'd fallen off the ladder and landed ass-first on his face. That was horrifying. But the fact that he was strong enough to catch me? Horny-fying.

And those glimpses of abs he kept giving me? Extra-horny-fying. That man is well-built.

But I get this weird feeling he might be straight, so I'm just going to have to jerk off to thoughts of him tonight. It's a shame he's straight, though, because I have a feeling he'd check off a number of items on my growing Book Boyfriend List. He'd already done a few BBL things. Saving the damsel in distress? He caught me off the ladder. Fucks like a porn star? Well, he has the dick of a porn star; it was at least as long as my face when I was pressed against it.

I can feel myself getting hard, and this isn't the time and place for it—*down*, I urge my dick. I divert my eyes back to Braden and Kellan.

We'd met a few times when I would come up here to drop off boxes of books and supplies. I mean, I couldn't not visit my retail neighbor, Dip Your Wick, and BJ's Cookies has the best coffees and really good snacks. It hadn't taken long for me to learn that they were married and that Kellan was the Snowflake Princess, whatever that means.

"What brings you gentlemen to my store?" I ask. I wave toward the vintage chairs, and we migrate there and sit down. Kellan opens a small box and puts it on the table between us, showing off some of the baked goods from Braden's shop. And Braden hands out travel cups from the cardboard tray he's carrying with him.

"We wanted to see how things are coming along for your grand opening in two days," Braden says.

I look at all the bare, empty shelves around me. "I'm, uh, on track."

Braden and Kellan share a look, then Kellan says, "It's okay to say if you're a little swamped and behind."

I wave my hand dismissively. "It's putting books on shelves. I can handle that." I lean forward and snag a cookie from the box. It looks like a snickerdoodle, and when I bite into it—yeah, it's a snickerdoodle—it's kind of bland. Definitely my least favorite of Braden's cookies so far. I give my best smile, though. "So good," I say.

Kellan leans in like he's about to share a secret and we're twelve. "So, what's it like working with Jacob?"

"What do you mean?" I say.

Kellan glances at Braden, then says, "Well, he's super hot..."

I can feel my cheeks burn with a bit of a blush at the memory of face-mashing his dick and then falling off the ladder and shoving my ass in his face.

"...and he's a famous athlete."

"Oh, right," I say, desperate to move my mind off his super hotness. "Like, rugby or something, right?"

Braden gives me a wide-eyed look. "Do you not know who Jacob Rizzo is?"

"Is it not rugby? Was it golf?"

"Jacob Rizzo," Braden says, "is one of the hottest soccer stars in the world. He's the reason we won the world championship last year."

"Soccer? Are you sure?"

Braden's eyes narrow. "Are you pulling my leg?"

I hold my hands up defensively. "I honestly know nothing about sports and they're all the same to me. Look at me, you think I know anything about sports?" They make eye contact with each other again in the way that couples do. I'm not going to say that working with him is like having my own personal supply of eye candy. I play it low-key and say, "But working with him is fine. He's good at what he does."

I flip open the top of my travel cup and take a sip. Okay, this is *actually* good. It's hot chocolate with a salted caramel drizzle on top.

"Alright," Kellan says, "now for the ulterior motive of why we're here. I'm the Snowflake Princess." He says that like it's supposed to mean something to me other than conjuring up visions of Kellan in a glittery white princess dress.

"I've heard," I say. "I don't know what that means, though."

"The Snowflake Festival starts in a few days," he says, "and I'm in charge of it."

"Ah, that I've heard of. Chad explained some of it to me. He told me since I'm a new business owner, I have to pick an event to host for the festival. It lasts a week or something, but I only need to do my event for one day, right?"

Kellan says, "Way to suck the Christmas spirit out of it, but, yes, that's basically it."

I take another cookie. This one is, thankfully, not a snickerdoodle. "I don't mean to, but I come from Twilight Hollow and it's like this but Halloween instead. So it sounds pretty similar."

"Do *thousands* of people come from all different states for Twilight Hollow's Halloween festivities? I don't think so," Kellan says. "The Snowflake Festival is the *biggest* Christmas celebration there is. It's the most exciting thing that happens in the town all year."

"The Festival has a way of getting you into the Christmas spirit," Braden says, looking lovingly at Kellan. "Or at least the people do."

"Well, it sounds nice that all the businesses participate. Given I run a romance bookstore, I was thinking of a Book Boyfriend Auction. It's basically a date auction but book-themed. If you win, you get a date with a hot guy. The money would go to charity."

There's a sparkle in Kellan's eyes. "I love that idea! There are lots of hot guys in this town. Can I email you with details on the Festival so we can get your event scheduled and start promoting it?"

"Sure," I say and I give him my email address.

Kellan side-eyes Braden. "Do you think Jacob would participate?"

Braden pffts. "Not a chance in hell."

"I could ask him," I say.

They shrug. Then Kellan says, "I wouldn't get your hopes up."

Shortly after that, they head out and return to their businesses. I like them; they both seem nice and supportive. Nothing like the business community back in Twilight Hollow.

I lock the door behind them and set to unpacking more boxes. Within a few hours, I'm a sweaty mess. The middle of the room holds a big pile of empty boxes, and a third of the shelves are full of books. When I glance toward the door again, I see through the glass that the sun has set, and we're now into the evening.

I glance at the time on my phone. It's already six and Chad and Lucas invited me along to dinner for seven. I'm so sweaty and disgusting and exhausted. "Maybe a shower will help," I say. Checking that everything is fine to leave overnight and the coffee pot is unplugged, I throw on my coat and head out the door to my car and then drive back to Chad's.

After showering and changing, I wander out into the living room to find Chad and Lucas sitting on the couch, quickly separating from each other. I clearly walked in on something. Petey the parrot looks like he's paying attention in the hopes of picking up new lingo.

"So, where are we going?" I ask them as I sit in the chair next to the couch.

"The Twelve Inch Italian," Chad says.

"Sorry," I say, "I thought we were doing dinner, not a Grindr hookup."

At the mention of Grindr, Petey makes the classic Grindr notification sound. I know it's Petey, but both Chad and Lucas pull out their phones to check.

After they shove their phones back in their pockets, Chad looks at Lucas with a look I've seen them share before, then he says, "I wouldn't mind sucking Tony's Italian sausage, but that's the name of the Italian place next to your bookstore. It's his grand opening today and since we're neighboring businesses, we got invited to the exclusive friends and family opening. We closed the bar for the night and we're dragging you along."

"Free pizza?" I say. "You don't have to drag me there, I'll go willingly."

"I didn't say it was free, little bro," he says. Lucas slaps him on the chest. Then Chad says, "I mean, I'd love to pay for your dinner."

"Pizza! Pizza!" Petey shrieks. I feel kind of relieved he knows words other than sexual phrases.

"We should head," Lucas says as he stands up. We all get our coats on and head to Chad's car. He drives us downtown, parking in a spot behind the building.

Earlier, I had come around the block from the other direction, so I hadn't passed The Twelve Inch Italian, nor seen the flurry of activity within. I remember this place from when I was here on Halloween. This had a giant "Coming Soon" poster in the window. It's kind of cool that we're opening within days of each other.

Chad opens the door for us. Lucas goes in first, and Chad gives him a little pat on the ass. Thankfully, he doesn't do the same for me.

"Chad," a loud voice says. From across the room, a very attractive man wearing a flour-covered apron comes striding toward us. He embraces Chad in a too-long hug that has Lucas smiling weirdly.

"Tony," Chad says as they break from their hug, "congratulations on the big day! You know my husband Lucas; he works in the bar with me."

"Ah, yes," Tony says, shaking Lucas's hand, "I was there for the Halloween party. I thought it might be a good way to make some friends in this new town."

"And this is my half-brother, Edward. He's opening the bookshop next door."

Tony grabs my hand and shakes it firmly. "It's so good to meet you, and congratulations on your store! I have a feeling we'll get to know each other very well. It's kind of fun our openings are so close together. I'll definitely come in your opening—I mean, come *to* your opening."

"Uh," I say. "It's good to meet you too. Congratulations to you too."

"Good, good," Tony says. Then he puts a hand on Chad's lower back and points us toward a three-seater round table in the front corner of the restaurant. I take the seat in the corner, which gives me a good view of the place. It's crowded in here with lots of little tables, and it has an open concept kitchen, so I can see Tony and a couple sous-chefs at work preparing all the food.

"Why is this place called The Twelve Inch Italian?" I ask Chad and Lucas.

Chad wiggles his eyebrows. "I believe that's his sausage size."

"That," Lucas says, "or he's apparently famous for his twelve-inch Italian subs. But it's likely the sandwich thing."

"I kind of want to try one of those sandwiches if he's famous for them," I say.

"You'll have to come back," Chad says, "because tonight is all pizza."

"I will never complain about pizza," Lucas says. Then his attention gets caught by something on the other side of the room. "Is that Jacob Rizzo in the kitchen?"

My gaze shoots toward the kitchen and, yes, Jacob is there. He's dressed a little nicer than what he wore to the shop with a fitted button-up shirt and a backwards hat. He's spinning pizza dough in the air like a seasoned pro.

Every time he raises his arms to spin pizza dough, the fabric of his sleeves tightens around his muscles, and the collar at his neck opens a little wider. God, I'm getting hard again.

"What's he doing there?" I ask.

"Jacob helps with a lot of things around town," Chad says. "I wish he would help with my orgasms. But, alas, I think he's straight."

We're interrupted as a guy Chad's age comes up to introduce himself to me—Geoff, owner of the Pump 'n' Go gym. I do the polite handshake and greeting and then he goes and sits down. And because he did it, a few other business owners come and introduce themselves, as well as a few members from the Chamber of Commerce. Kellan and Braden see me from across the room and wave, but don't come over.

When the visits calm down, I glance at Jacob in the kitchen and find him watching me with a look of amusement. He must be able to tell that this is already way too much socializing for me. But there's another look in his eyes too, and it's one I can't quite decipher.

"Do you think..." Chad says, his words drifting off. He glances over his shoulder at Jacob and then looks back to me. "Your mystery abs guy...do you think it could be Jacob? Maybe he's not so straight?"

"Jacob?" I say. "No..."

I look at Jacob again and try to match him up to the memory of the men's room pounding, but it can't be him. Sure, he's about the same height and build, from what I can remember, but it seems way too good to be true.

"Why not?" Chad says. He leans in closer, like he's whispering a secret. "I bet he's mega-hung and he's definitely a top."

I keep to myself that I know face-first how hung he is. I roll my eyes, then say, "It's not Jacob. I've been with him half the day and I've gotten zero vibes like that. If he was the bathroom hookup, don't you think he'd be flirty with me?"

"Maybe it's him and he doesn't know it's you because of your mask. It might go both ways. Just like Jacob."

"I'm telling you," I say, "it's not Jacob."

"Or maybe it's Tony," Lucas says.

At this, we all turn our attention to the lead man in the kitchen. Tony is about the same height as Jacob but a bit more built muscle-wise. But he's also very hairy; there are tufts of it poking out the collar of his shirt, and the backs of his hands had been furry when we'd shaken a few minutes ago.

"He's clearly gay," Chad says. "If a bit dumb sometimes."

I try to picture Tony as the guy from the men's room, but it just isn't working. "He looks too hairy. The wolf didn't have any hair on his abs when he lifted his shirt." As I reflect back on those abs at the club, I'm reminded of seeing Jacob's abs earlier today—those were effing nice.

"Maybe he shaved before the club? We know he was there; he said so," Lucas says.

"And I don't remember seeing him," Chad says, "so he could've been the wolf, because the wolf never took his mask off."

"If we're going by that logic," I say, losing my temper a bit, "then it could be nearly any man in this room that I don't recognize!"

"Okay…" Chad says, "not either of them. Got it."

A new person comes up to the table to presumably meet me. He's older and has a glass of wine in his hand, but it's clearly not his first glass because he's not exactly steady on his feet. He looks vaguely familiar.

"Hi, you must be Edward," he says, extending a hand. His words are slightly slurred.

I shake it; his grip is a bit clammy. "I am, good to meet you. And you are…"

Lucas leans close and whispers in my ear. "2017 Lady Gaga at the Super Bowl halftime show."

My eyes widen. "You're Mayor Dink?"

"Dick," the man says. "Mayor Dick."

"Sorry, *Dick*," I say, correcting myself. "Good to meet you."

"Welcome to Frosty Bottoms," he says, throwing his arms wide in a grand gesture, wine sloshing over the rim of his glass. "The most Christmassy town in all of America, where you're guaranteed to have the gayest time. Gay in the old sense of the word, of course."

"And the new," Lucas mutters under his breath, just loud enough for me to hear.

I giggle-snort, then smother my laughter. "I'm so glad to be here. I'm looking forward to meeting the town and seeing their businesses throughout the Snowflake Festival."

"The Snowflake Festival is our pride and joy!" He swings his arms again, and more wine sloshes out of his glass. "I especially enjoy the Christmas masquerade party at Bottoms Up!"

"Oh?" I say. "It's a good party?"

Mayor Dick puts his glass down on the table and then leans forward conspiratorially. "Let's say people are in a *festive mood* that night, and if you play your cards right, you can get some action in the men's room—"

"Okay," Chad says, "it was great seeing you, Mayor Dick. Why don't you head back to your seat? I'm sure the pizzas are going to come out soon."

"Pizza?" he says, sounding bewildered. He looks around the room.

"Maybe Mayor Dick was your mystery men's room Romeo," Lucas whispers, barely containing a laugh.

"You know, you might be right," Chad whispers, playing along, "he could be the wolf! Except…the wolf wasn't dressed as Lady Gaga."

Mayor Dick turns back around to face us. "Oh, right, pizza." He picks up his wine glass, then pauses like he's having a thought. "Oh, I wanted to ask how my son is getting along…"

"Your son?" I ask. "Who's your son?"

Mayor Dick half turns and points with his wine glass toward the kitchen. "Jacob. Is he handling things at your shop? Are you satisfied with the work he's done?"

I look across the room at Jacob. How is this Jacob's father? They look nothing alike, and they're definitely completely different personalities.

Jacob's gaze alternates between looking at me with a frown and staring lasers into the back of his dad's head.

I finally tear my eyes away from Jacob and say, "I'm very happy with the work he's done."

"Good!" he says, raising his glass in salute and tottering back several steps.

   **JACOB**   

Tony elbows me. "You like that new guy better than me?"

"What?" I laugh.

He slices the pizza in front of him then slides it down to one of the other servers. "Take that to table twenty-two," he says. "But, you, your eyes have been glued to Eddie. Does he owe you money or something?"

I scoff and pull my head back. "Who the hell is Eddie?"

"Chad's brother," he says, flipping dough in the air. "Isn't that his name?"

Shit. Have I been staring at him? No. I'm sure I haven't been that obvious. "What are you talking about? You just met him a few minutes ago. You forgot his name? It's Edward, and my eyes are glued because my moron of a father is over there talking to him right now."

My dad is so unpredictable; who knows what he's saying to Edward. After what I saw at the Halloween party, I wouldn't be surprised if he starts dancing on a table, and if that happens, I don't know what I'll do. I need to get over there.

"Nice try," Tony says. "Your dad just walked over there. You were staring long before that. So, what is it? Did he have a problem with the work you did at the store?"

"Why would he? Did you have a problem with any of the work I did here?"

Tony flips the pizza dough again. "Nope. But maybe *he* did."

I'm not gonna stand here and explain to Tony that we hooked up at the Halloween party. I don't talk about things like that with anyone. I should be more careful, though. If Tony is picking up on me staring at Edward, it must be really obvious, because Tony is just about the most oblivious person I've met since moving here. He's really nice and he seems to fit right in, but he also seems to be completely unaware when men flirt with him.

He kind of reminds me of someone else I spent the day with. I know Edward was checking my abs out when I was on the ladder, and he definitely got a face full of me when I walked in, and *I* got a face full of his ass... That ass is a work of art. Maybe I should message him on Grindr. I haven't opened the app since that night, but I wonder if he has. I'm curious if that was normal for him—a bathroom hookup with a stranger.

Oh my God. My father is still standing over there, he looks drunk, or at the very least, really tipsy. I need to break this up. I slice the pizza in front of me, and instead of passing it down the line like I'd done with the ten other pies that we'd made so far, I grab it and head for Edward's table.

"Jacob!" my father says, holding his arms wide toward me.

"You're gonna spill your wine all over Tony's floor!" I tell him.

My dad downs the rest of his glass and smiles at me.

He taps my cheek, and I pull my face and the pizza I'm balancing back. "What are you doing? Don't touch my face." I chuckle.

Edward is looking over at me, as is everyone else in the room. This is so embarrassing. When I moved here, I knew my dad was over the top, but I didn't realize how comfortable he is around the people of Frosty Bottoms. I think a part of me is envious of that, but not right now—right now I'm mortified. I see Edward looking at his phone. I really can't tell if this guy is into me, but with my father here, I'm not gonna find out anytime soon.

Edward looks up from his phone and gives me a soft smile. "Do you need help?" he mouths silently to me.

"I'm looking forward to seeing your mom and nonna on Sunday," my dad says.

"Yeah, yeah, Dad. Sure thing. I can do that on Sunday." I pat him on his shoulder and head for Edward's table. I have no idea what he asked me for, because I was lost in Edward's big brown eyes.

I place the pizza in the center of the table. "Hey, guys. Extra cheese, because that's what Tony decided everyone is getting tonight."

"Wow," Chad says. "Did you make this one personally?"

"No idea," I say, with a shrug. "I've made probably ten pizzas tonight. So, there's a fifty percent chance that I did. Does that matter?" I turn my attention to Edward. I want to sit down and talk to him, but I know Tony really needs my help.

Lucas is smiling at me while he elbows Chad in the side. "Are you gonna serve us tonight? Wasn't expecting you to bring our food out."

I point at the pizza. "You can just use the—Ah, shit. I forgot the pizza server. I'll be right back." As I turn to leave, I notice that Edward's drink is half full. "What are you drinking?" I ask him.

"It's just water," he says with a smile.

"I'll be right back." I quickly make my way into the kitchen and grab a pizza server, then fill up a new glass of water. I noticed that he had a lemon in his glass, so I wash my hands, then pull a fresh lemon from the pile and clean it, then slice it and drop it into the glass.

Tony eyes me suspiciously and raises his chin. "That for Eddie?"

"Shut up…and stop calling him Eddie!" I shout as I leave the kitchen.

I place the drink down and Edward looks shocked, as do the other two at the table. "Thank you. That was so thoughtful. I still have half a glass left."

"I need more water. I'll take it," Chad says.

I tilt my head at him. "I got that water for him. You want to take water from your brother? Who does that?"

"How are you even hotter when you're acting like a jerk?" Chad asks, looking me up and down.

I point at myself. "Me? I'm not acting like a jerk. You're trying to steal his water. If you need water, I'll tell a server. I brought that for him."

"Far be it from me, to ask the great Jacob Rizzo this, but aren't you holding a pizza server in your hand?" Lucas asks facetiously.

"Yeah, so?"

Lucas holds his palms out. "Then aren't you our server?"

"I'm ready to be served," Chad chimes in.

I tilt my head at Edward. "You're one-hundred percent sure that Chad is your brother, right? I assume there was a test or something?"

Edward laughs and holds his hand out for the pizza server. "I can do it. You probably need to get back there to help."

"Nah. I got it." I slide the long sleeves of my shirt up, and I notice Edward's eyes lock onto my forearm tattoos. I reach forward and lift a piece of the pizza for him, then put it on his plate. "You need parmesan or red pepper? I can grab it from the kitchen."

"Nope. All good. Looks great. Thanks!"

I place the pizza server onto the tray and put my hands on my hips, while Chad holds his plate toward me. "I'm hungry, too, Daddy."

"You're older than me. Why are you calling me Daddy? Besides, I think your husband can do it for you."

Lucas snickers, "Oh, I can definitely *do* it for him, but you could probably *do* it for him faster."

"I don't serve men who call me Daddy," I say, shaking my head at the two. As I start to leave, I realize that I didn't even ask Edward anything about tomorrow. I walk backward a few steps.

"Hi again," Edward says with a mouthful of pizza.

"Jacob! I need your help back here!" Tony shouts.

I give him a playful salute, then turn back to Edward. "Do you want to meet up at the store at nine tomorrow morning? I can get there earlier if you want to get started before that."

His eyes are wide as he looks at me, still chewing his pizza. "Nine is good."

"Great. I'll see you then." I jog back into the kitchen and take my place beside Tony at the counter. "What are you shouting at me like that for? Did you forget you aren't my actual boss?"

Tony gives me a hearty chuckle. "I don't know who the boss was in the situation I just watched. Looked to me like you were really going out of your way for one person at that table. Chad's water was empty. You didn't want to bring him water, or give him pizza?"

I tilt my head at him. "He called me Daddy, I didn't like that."

"Who called you Daddy? Chad? Don't know what your problem is, but I like being called Daddy. My ex used to do it all the time. You really don't like it?"

I hold my hands out. "Why would you need to know if I did?"

"You're so sensitive sometimes. Aren't we friends? Friends talk about this stuff." He slices through a pizza and slides it down the line, then immediately slices the next one.

I pat him on the back. "We're friends, big guy, or else I wouldn't be here helping you for free."

"You gonna tell your agent about this? Could use it as community service hours."

I do need the community service hours, but I'm not reporting this to Linley. As soon as I tell her I've done anything, she'll be up here with a camera crew looking for a photo op. Even if I tell her not to, the second the press finds out I did any community service, people would know where I was. I have a sort of a perfect scenario here right now, since only Linley and my parents know I'm in Frosty Bottoms, and I don't want anything to change that.

"Thanks for your help, Jacob. Couldn't have gotten through the night without you," Tony says across the parking lot.

"Anytime." I sit inside my car and close the door. Leaning back against my headrest, I close my eyes. This day was wild. I was not expecting Edward to be the guy from the Halloween party. I don't know if it's right that I don't say anything to him, but I also feel like it might be wrong if I do. We have a professional relationship right now, so until that's over, maybe I need to relax. That sucks though, I'd rather just be honest with him. But what would I even say? *Hey, remember yesterday when you put your face in my balls? That wasn't the first time you did that...* Or I guess I could say, *Remember when you sat on my face yesterday? Can you do that again? Preferably naked?* I can't say either of those. Well, there's only one thing to do. I need to work harder on the store, so I can make sure everything is done by Friday. Then I can ask him out once I finish the job.

After the parking lot is empty, I get out of my car and go in through the back entrance of the bookstore. I can't do much because I don't want to put the lights on. The last thing I need is for someone to see me here alone at night.

What can I do to help him? I look around the room and see a bunch of boxes full of books that still need to be placed on the shelves. He told me earlier that they were all in front of the shelves he wanted to put them on. There's enough light on this half of the store coming in from the top of the window that isn't covered by blinds. I won't be able to finish it all, but this should make things easier for him tomorrow.

Chapter Four
Can I Touch?

 Edward

I'd gotten to Hot for Plot nice and early this morning. While I'm certain I can get everything done in time for tomorrow's grand opening, I also know that old saying that whatever can go wrong, will go wrong. So to prepare for the unpreparable, I got here well before sunrise with the plan of unpacking boxes of books.

When I got here, it took me a few moments to realize what was different since I'd left the night before. A bunch of books had been stocked on the shelves. Someone—obviously Jacob—had come by late last night and emptied six boxes of books, placing them correctly on the shelves. He had done a *considerable* amount of work last night. And the care and attention he'd put into it, and the fact that he'd done it at all, touched my heart. Almost made me want to touch my dick.

So when I got over the touching gesture (double entendre intended), I moved to the back of the store and started unpacking the dozen or so remaining boxes. The first shelf of today was a personal favorite, with a bunch of bad boy romances. I'd added a lot to the BBL from these ones, especially *Bottoming for the Alpha*.

Now that it's approaching the time Jacob said he'd come by, most of my shelves are full, and I'd located a couple boxes of stuff for the register—

bookmarks, buttons with funny slogans, the reader for processing credit cards, and a few other things.

I'd been thinking about him all night and, yes, I did indeed jerk off to thoughts of him like I knew I would. How could I not after seeing those abs of his and feeling his long and thick dick pressed against my face?

And those tattoos…

When he'd come up to our table at The Twelve Inch Italian last night, he'd rolled up his sleeves and I'd seen tattoos on the inside of his forearms. They were *very similar* to the tattoo I remember seeing on the wolf's forearm at the Halloween party when he'd briefly tugged one of his shirt sleeves up. It was almost enough to convince me that Chad's insane theory was right, that Jacob was my mystery man. *Almost.* Problem was that since I had a mask on, I hadn't gotten a super clear look at the tattoo—and, besides, my attention was focused on other things at the time.

While Jacob *could* be my wolf, I'm not certain, so I can only sit back and watch him for the day…and maybe jerk off to him again when I get home.

The teasing from Chad and Lucas certainly hadn't died down after Jacob had served our table.

"That wolf is very protective of his mouse," Chad had said. "All I wanted was some water."

"And pizza," Lucas had said. "But maybe he only serves mice who serve up their ass for him."

"Guys, I barely know him," I had said. "I spent the day with him. Trust me, it's not him. I've gotten no such vibes whatsoever. I haven't even gotten an 'I'm into dudes' vibe off him." Then again, he lifted his shirt an awful lot to show off his abs. But I wasn't about to say that to Chad and Lucas.

"That whole display of dominance we just witnessed over your water glass doesn't scream 'this mouse is my man'?" Chad had asked.

There's a rattle behind me that pulls me immediately back to the here and now. I made sure not to wear my earbuds again and blast music, because I didn't want a repeat of yesterday's greeting. Well, I *did*, but one that was consensual.

I stand and turn around. So far, so good, no dicks in my face. Jacob has a light jacket on to match today's warmer weather, which he takes off after he locks the door, and drapes it over the back of one of the antique chairs.

"Good morning," I say.

"Morning," he replies. "Do I smell coffee?"

A slight blush hits my cheeks. "I thought it might be a better way to say hello than motorboating your balls."

"Well, the day's still young," he says.

What the hell do I say in response to that? *We can do it now, if you want?*

Instead, I follow him to the back room.

"Want some coffee?" I say, offering him a full cup.

"Oh, thank you, but no. I have to be careful about what I eat or drink."

I keep the full cup of coffee for myself and take a sip. "Thank you for what you did."

"Oh? What did I do?" he says. I can tell he's teasing me a bit; he wants me to say it.

"The books. You put them out, right? I mean, it had to be you, no one else has a key."

He gives me a mischievous smile, but doesn't say anything. After I get really flustered from the heat of his gaze, he finally says, "So, on today's agenda…the hanging chairs, helping you with whatever you need help with…and then you're ready for the store opening tomorrow?"

I turn around in the doorway and take in the sight of my shop, letting out a long, slow breath. "I think so? I've only done this once before." I look at the place once more. "I've been thinking it might be nice to get a vintage lamp or two to put near the chairs, in case it's a dark day."

He comes up beside me in the doorway, and I can feel the heat of his body, almost as strongly as if he were pressed up against me. I also smell his scent—clean and fresh, very similar to the man in the men's room, if I'm remembering right—and it seems to make my neurons fire improperly and thoughts don't seem to form coherently.

"There's a cool little vintage shop across town, near my neighborhood. We could make a plan to go there at some point today."

I take another sip of my coffee, hoping the caffeine hits immediately and makes my brain work again. I'm a little afraid to open my mouth and talk. "Sounds. Sure good." Damn it. "I mean, sure, sounds good."

There's just the slightest chuckle from him that seems to rumble deep in his chest. "Why don't I get started on the hammock chairs and you keep stocking your shelves?"

This time I don't try to talk; I simply nod. I walk to the center of the room and put my coffee cup down on one of the end tables set up there, then turn to one of the bookshelves that need stocking. Behind me, I hear Jacob rummaging about and the clattering of him bringing out the big ladder he has stored in the back room. He goes out to retrieve something from his car and comes back.

After a few minutes of us doing our own things, he comes up beside me. I slowly, *and carefully*, look up at him.

He has his hand behind his neck and looks kind of apologetic. "So, uh, some bad news and some good news…"

I clear my throat before speaking, and this time I'm pretty sure I can put words together, or at least trust myself with a single syllable response. "Oh?"

He hitches a thumb over his shoulder, pointing toward his stuff. "I forgot to bring along the right anchors for those hammock chairs. They need to be extra secure so they're safe. The anchors are at home, so I need to run there quickly. That's the bad news."

"That's not so bad. What's the good news?"

"Since the antique store is on the way and you've got most of your store set up, I thought I'd bring you along and we could get a couple lamps, then pick up the anchors, swing back here, and finish setting up your store for tomorrow. What do you think?" He gives me a megawatt smile.

The chance to spend more time with Jacob has my chest feeling warm. "I think I can step away for a bit," I say.

We take a quick moment to unplug the coffee maker and turn off the lights before we head out. I follow him outside to the little lot in the back.

"We're taking your car, right?" I ask. "Because mine is, well…" I point at it.

He whistles. "So, you're the car held together by bubble gum and a prayer. I like your bumper sticker. *Book Boys Have the Best Butts.*"

I blush at a memory of where my butt had landed yesterday. It doesn't escape my notice that he commented on a fairly gay bumper sticker, but I avoid that topic and focus on the car. "Yeah, it's gotten me around a lot, but I really need to upgrade. It's just a bad time with opening the new store and all." I look around; there are a handful of cars here from the various businesses. "Which one is yours?"

He pulls out his key fob and hits a button and a car chirps behind me. I turn around and look at the *nicest* car I've ever seen in person. It's sleek and powerful-looking and black with darkly tinted windows.

It's my turn to whistle. "That's some car. I didn't realize sports paid that much."

He gives me a funny look like he can't decide if I'm joking or not. I then realize I must have vastly underestimated how much professional sports pays.

"Hop in," he says.

I open the door and sit in the firm leather seat. This is worlds different than my car. It's not even in the same universe. He slides in to the driver's seat, and the car starts with the push of a button, roaring to life. I'm suddenly feeling very close to him, and it's making me nervous. We're sharing the same air and sitting only, like, eight inches from each other.

"Buckle up," he says. Then with a smile, he adds, "Unless you need help…?"

While the thought of Jacob reaching across me to grab the seat belt, and ultimately putting his plump, kissable lips near mine, is enough to make me squirm, I buckle myself in.

"So, where we headed?" I ask.

He pulls out of the spot, using the backup cam to help navigate, then smoothly takes us down the lane and out into traffic. "I live in Sticky Pines, and there's an antique store I pass everyday just outside the community. I think it's called Older is Better or something like that."

"Cool," I say, suddenly feeling at a loss for words. "Sounds good."

After driving in silence for a few moments, Jacob glances at me, then says, "So, are you getting all settled in?"

"Well, as settled in as I can be since I don't have a permanent place to live yet. Once the store has a few successful months of operation, then I should be able to apply for an apartment or something. They generally don't rent to people who don't have stable employment."

"I'm sure the business will do fantastic," he says. "The store looks great and you have a clear vision for it."

His words make me feel all warm inside. "Thank you," I say, smiling.

He turns a corner and then a moment later turns into a parking lot. "Here we are," he says. He leans forward to look up at the sign. "Ah, it's not Older is Better, it's Dusty Balls."

We climb out of his car and then head into the antique store. The place is kind of small but absolutely packed full of all sorts of old furniture, décor, and knickknacks. I pause to flip through a few records in the music section.

"Edward?" I hear Jacob call from somewhere in the stacks of antiques. "Lamps are over here."

"I'm coming," I say back. "If I can find my way, that is…"

I do eventually find him, and he did find the lamps. There's a mix of floor lamps and table lamps of various styles and vintages—and various price tags.

"What do you think of this one?" he asks, picking up a table lamp with a stained-glass shade.

"It's pretty," I say, "but I'm not sure if it would match."

"I disagree. The reds in this shade would match that chair with the rose vine pattern on it. I bet this would really help make the colors pop."

It makes me smile that he remembers the furniture better than I do. But then again, he's spent more time in my store than I have. "You're right," I say. "I forgot about that chair. This would be perfect."

"See any others you like?"

I take a step back to take in all the other lamps. "What about this one?" I pick up a small lamp that's meant to look like an old oil lamp but contains an incandescent bulb. "Kind of has a Victorian romance feel to it."

He gives me a half smile. "I don't quite understand that sentence, but sure."

I laugh. "That's my line for when the mechanic tries to explain the new thing that's wrong with my car."

As we head to the till to pay, I pause by the Christmas section of the store.

"I want to get something here. We didn't really do Christmas in Twilight Hollow," I say. "I used to put up a little black Christmas tree with Halloween decorations in October and leave it up till the end of January, but I've always loved the Christmases I'd see on TV and movies with bright decorations. When I was a young kid, I did the more traditional Christmas things with my grandparents. I really miss that."

"You should buy an ornament then," he says. "You could start a little collection to bring Christmas back into your life."

"I don't have a tree to hang it on," I say to him.

He shrugs. "You can worry about a tree later. Whether you get one or not, that shouldn't stop you from buying a Christmas ornament." He looks at the selection set out on the display table in front of us.

"I don't know…I have no idea why I'm being so hesitant, but I don't know…"

"Would it help if I bought one for myself? I don't have many Christmas decorations for my house. Maybe this is something we can do together." He looks at me with something like hopefulness in his features.

It kind of makes my heart race a bit. It also makes me pause because this exact thing—buying Christmas ornaments together—is on my BBL; I added it after reading a really sweet Christmas romance a few years ago.

"Okay. Let's do it."

I pick up a glass ornament of a rosy-cheeked Santa on a toboggan, and he gets one of a snowman with a corncob pipe and a top hat.

After the store owners fawn over Jacob and his sports record, we pay for our merchandise and we're back in his car, and heading through the security gate into the Sticky Pines development. He pulls into the driveway of a two story house with lots of windows to let in sunlight.

"Wow," I say, "you've got a *nice* house."

"It's my home sweet home," he says. "Come on, let's go get those anchors."

I get out of the car and follow him to the front door, and he lets us in. While the house is big on the outside, it somehow looks even bigger on the inside.

"Do you live with someone else?" I ask.

He gives me an odd look. "No. Why?"

I shrug. "Seems like an awfully big place for one person. But, like, keep in mind, I've been living in a studio apartment for the last few years."

"I like my space, I guess," he says. "Come on, I've got my office upstairs and the anchors should be there."

I follow him up the staircase to his office. There's a wooden desk with a computer on it, a filing cabinet with papers stacked on top of it, a bookcase with baskets and boxes filled with various things, and a small couch along the wall.

Jacob rifles through the stuff on the bookcase until he finds the right box. He pulls out what I assume are anchors and holds them up for me. "These should do, don't you think?"

I give him the biggest shrug I can muster. "There's a reason I hired you to do this instead of doing it myself. I didn't even know what an anchor might look like until just now."

He chuckles. "Alright, I've got what I need, we can head back to the store."

He exits his office and brushes past me, getting incredibly close. His heat and clean scent both have my head in a tizzy.

I follow him down the stairs. At the bottom, he kind of looks over his shoulder at me for a moment. "Want a snack or something before we go back? I haven't eaten anything since breakfast."

You can snack on me, I want to say. But I don't. Because he's off limits or something. My hormone-addled brain can't keep it straight right now. Oh, right. I think he's straight, that's why. "Um…I'm okay."

"Come on," he says, leading me around a corner to his kitchen. He puts the anchors on the island and opens the fridge, pulling out a container of grapes. It looks like it's pre-portioned. He pops a few in his mouth, then holds the container toward me. "Are you sure you don't want some?"

Reluctantly, I pull one out. As he puts the container down on the counter, I catch a glimpse of that tattoo I'd noticed at the Italian place, just peeking out of the sleeve of his shirt.

"I've been meaning to ask about your tattoo. Is that a vine?" I say as I point at his wrist. I angle my own arms forward a bit. "I'm sure you've noticed I have some ink too."

He tugs the sleeve cuff up. "Yeah, it starts as a simple vine here, but then twists around my bicep and goes over my chest."

I'm trying to imagine him without a shirt, and I'm getting lost in those hormones again. "Oh…really?"

"Do you…wanna see?"

"Like…what do you mean?"

He grabs the hem of his shirt and pulls it over his head. Holy fuck.

Those abs he'd been teasing me with yesterday are on full display, as is his tightly toned chest and biceps. His body is incredible, he's hotter than a cover model. He steps closer, bringing that heat and clean scent again.

He holds his arms out to give me a better look at the tattoo. It goes across both arms, as well as over his chest. It's much more ornate and artistic than I had envisioned. But my vision is cloudy from the rush of being this close to one of the hottest guys I've ever met, and he's half naked.

Automatically, my hand starts moving, bringing my fingers to his wrist where the tattoo starts. I trace the vine up his arm where it swirls around his upper forearm and bicep. When my fingertips reach his chest, they slow down.

I'm so turned on. My brain is mush.

Jacob steps closer. I look up at him, and he's looking down at me. My gaze focuses on his lips—his full, kissable, plush lips. Acting on some level of desire I've never quite felt before and with a boldness that is completely unlike me, I bring my mouth closer to his for a kiss. And he doesn't seem to be pulling back or looking at me with disgust. If anything, he's leaning in closer, he's bringing his mouth to mine. We're just a couple inches away, just a second more and we'll—

We're interrupted by a musical chime blaring through his phone.

Chapter Five
Adorable, Aloof, and Bangable

   Jacob   

My doorbell sounds loudly, and my phone chimes with the same notification. I pull my face back from Edward's. I was just about to kiss him, and I think he was going to kiss me, too. I bite my lower lip and hear Kellan shouting through the door. "Jacob! It's a Snowflake Festival emergency! I know you're here; I see your car in the driveaway! Open up!"

Edward backs up a few steps and looks down at the floor. He's avoiding eye contact with me. Damn it. My dick is so hard right now. I don't want to deal with Kellan. What the hell is a Snowflake Festival emergency anyway? "I'm coming!" I shout.

I open the door, and Kellan's eyes almost fall out of his head. He's staring right at my chest, couldn't be any more obvious. "What's up? What the hell is a Snowflake Festival Emergency?"

"I, um." He blinks his eyes hard. "First time you've answered the door shirtless. I actually forgot what I was here for."

He leans to the side, looking around me. "Is that Edward in there?"

I shrug and move to block his view of Edward. "You're here because there's some kind of an emergency, right? So, what is it?"

"Oh, the emergency! Yes! Santa's sleigh needs repairs. Bray says he can help, but he's not sure about the side piece. He seems to think there is something you can do that he can't. Also, your dad was there when we found the damage, and he said you need community service hours. So, I thought since you're licensed, maybe you might feel like knocking out some hours? It would really help me out."

"Ahhhh," I groan. "I have to help Edward get the shop ready for the grand opening tomorrow. I don't know how soon I can deal with that."

"Are you guys pulling an all-nighter? Maybe you could stop by tonight and you and Bray could try and get it fixed up?"

I look over my shoulder and see Edward in the same place I'd left him. He's still staring at the floor.

"I can do that. I don't know if I can fix it, but I can try. No community service, though. I can just help."

"I would like to hug you right now," Kellan says.

"No."

I shut the door and turn back to Edward. His cheeks are bright red. Is he embarrassed? This is torture. If he only knew everything we'd already done. "Sorry about that. Told you he was kind of annoying." I walk past him toward the kitchen. I don't want to crowd him if he's uncomfortable. One thing I hate is people getting in my space when I'm trying to think something through.

"You shut the door in his face," he says, following me into the kitchen. "Didn't he just ask if he could hug you?"

I open the fridge and grab out two bottles of water. "I don't like when people touch me."

"Oh sorry, I…your tattoo… I touched it. I shouldn't have."

I walk toward him with the bottles of water and pass him one. "Why would you apologize for that? Do you think I disliked you touching me?"

I twist the cap off my bottle and take a long drink. He's just staring at me. It's like he's trying to figure something out. I *am* being pretty fucking obvious here. I'm shirtless with him in my house, and I think our mouths were maybe four inches apart before Kellan got here.

"I don't know. Did you?" he asks.

My phone is vibrating on the counter. It's Linley. "I have to take this," I tell him, then answer the call on speaker.

"Yeah?"

"Jacob! Listen. Marco is getting antsy over the community service. Said to tell you that he's understanding of your situation, but if you don't work to repair your image, he's gonna need you to come back to Miami."

"What? I'm not his fucking dog. He can't just order me around."

Edward's eyes are wide looking at me. Everyone in the town knows I got suspended for punching a ref, but I don't know if he knows that.

"Are you serious? Whose name is on your paycheck? He owns you, whether you like it or not."

"No, he doesn't."

"Funny. The twenty-five-million-dollar contract you signed says otherwise."

Edward coughs loudly. "Are you okay?" I ask him.

"Don't get cute, Jacob," Linley says. "Can't you just do the hours and get this over with? Your mom said she's coming for a visit soon… Maybe I should tag along."

Edward nods covering his mouth. "Sorry. Didn't mean to interrupt. Swallowed wrong."

"Who are you talking to?" Linley asks. "Are you working?"

She doesn't need to know who Edward is. "Yeah, I'm working. But, wait, my mom isn't coming here? Who told you that?"

"Your mom told me that. I don't know which day she said she was coming. I can't keep up with her. What kind of work are you doing today?"

"I'm installing chairs today and tonight I have to fix Santa's sleigh."

Edward is looking down at his phone. It looks like he's texting someone. I can't help but feel a little nervous. I don't think he'd take a picture of me or anything.

"Gabriella was asking about you again," Linley says.

"I don't care. You better not have told her anything. I'm not even joking."

"Do you think I'm stupid? She said she just wants you to know that what happened wasn't her fault. You should just talk to her."

"Are we done? Like I said earlier, I'm working. If I do any community service, I'll let you know, but I don't see that happening anytime soon."

"I don't know…Santa's sleigh work sounds like it could be community service…" she teases.

"Bye," I say and end the call.

"Fuck," I mumble, raking my fingers through my hair. For a moment I forgot that Edward was standing there. He must be wondering what all that was about, but he's probably too polite to ask.

I turn toward him and put my phone in my pocket. "Go ahead, ask me whatever you want. You can't not have questions after hearing all of that."

He blows air from his mouth. "Hmm. Well, I don't really feel like it's any of my business. I'm good with not asking anything. But if you want to tell me, I can listen."

I shake my head. "I don't enjoy talking about myself, despite how it may seem. But out of all that, I just—I got fined for punching a ref during a game. He gave me a red card right before I punched him, so I should have left the field, which would have just resulted in me being suspended for a game, maybe two, but instead I punched him in the face." I shrug.

"I don't know anything about sports," he says, toying with his water bottle. "So, I didn't understand most of that. How come you have to do community service? Is that a normal punishment?"

"Nope. Special just for me. Basically, the team owner didn't like the example I was setting for younger kids or younger players. He said I was too important to the future of soccer to have acted the way I did. I got suspended for the remainder of the season, fined, and I have to do the community service. I was also supposed to issue an apology, but I refused."

He looks like he's considering what I said, or maybe he's just trying hard not to say the wrong thing. "Why wouldn't you apologize? You didn't think you should?"

"Nope. He deserved to get punched, so I did it. I don't regret it. If I could do it again, I would." I toss my bottle into the recycle bin under my sink.

"So, it's not that you have a problem apologizing to people, just in that situation you didn't want to apologize?"

"I apologize when I do something wrong. But let me ask you, if you got punished, suspended, forced to do community service, and fined $10,000, would you feel like you needed to apologize too?"

"I've never punched anyone, so I would probably apologize. I also make a shockingly less amount of money than you do. Wait, that's my question, actually. Do all athletes make as much as you? That was the most money I've ever heard of someone being paid."

"I'm definitely on the higher pay scale for professional soccer players. I also helped win the world championship, so unless I get hurt, I'll earn more than that when I sign my next contract. There are guys that make way more than me, but most make less."

"Soccer is the one where you're just kicking the ball, right?"

I'm not sure if he's being serious. "Uhhh. Yeah? But I mean, I have to score, so it's not as easy as just kicking the ball around. You've never watched soccer, or even played? Not even in school?" I walk out of the kitchen, and he's following me toward my room, but stops before following me inside. He's just standing in the hallway. "You can come in," I say. "I won't bite. Just grabbing a clean shirt."

He looks around nervously. "I'm good out here. But about what you asked, I think I may have played in school. Why do they call it soccer instead of football if you're using your feet? I've always thought football was the one where you kicked the ball around."

I pull a shirt over my head and check my hair in the mirror. "Well, you aren't technically wrong. All other countries call it football, but here it's soccer. I don't know why. What I do know is that my hair is doing weird shit lately. I don't know if it's the change in weather." I grab a hat off my dresser and turn it around backward on my head.

He's just staring at me. Maybe he's finally figured out that I'm the guy from the bathroom? Wait…there's a chance he's not thinking about that at all. Maybe he hasn't even thought about it since it happened. I just need to get his shop set up, then I can ask him out.

"We should probably head back to your shop," I say. "I want to make sure we get the chairs installed and get everything looking perfect for tomorrow. You ready?"

He smiles and nods at me, almost like he wants to say something, but is too afraid to. What's holding him back?

I grab the anchors from the kitchen counter, and we get ready to leave. "Your hair is really shiny," I blurt out when we reach the door. Oh my God. What am I doing? What normal person says something about another guy's hair for no reason at all?

"Thanks. Sometimes I think I want to cut it, but I like it this length. It's funny that you said your hair is acting crazy because it seems to look good—I mean normal, it looks normal, no matter what you're doing. It's humid in Miami, right?"

I open the door and set the alarm while he walks outside. "Yeah, it's crazy humid. But for some reason my hair is fine there. It should be the opposite, but it's not. This warm weather would be considered a cold day in Miami."

"The past few days have been warmer than I expected," he says. "I was hoping for a snowy Christmas, especially with all the Snowflake Festival stuff that's planned."

"Yeah. It's strange, it's freezing one day, then warm the next. I'm pretty sure I saw that we're expected to get snow next week, so you should still get your white Christmas," I say, getting inside the car.

After he buckles in, he picks up the bag with the ornament in it from the antique store and pulls it out as I start to drive. "Oh, whoops," he says.

I lift my chin at him. "What's wrong?"

"I brought the wrong ornament in your house. This is what happens when I try to help," he says with a giggle.

He's got a really sexy kind of giggle. Edward is a cross between adorable, aloof, and very bangable. I also like that he's a bit sassy sometimes. I smile and shrug at him. "No worries about the ornament. Just means you'll have to come over again to pick it up."

He puts the ornament back inside the bag, then ruffles his hair, looking out the window. In these moments, I feel like he's not interested in me, but maybe he just doesn't know how to reply. He was so flirty that night at the bar, though. I was the one that was nervous, not him. And with that almost-kiss we just had…did I actually misread the situation?

"I…I would. I could do that," he says.

EDWARD

Jacob is trying to talk to me in the car, and my phone keeps dinging with notifications. When Jacob was on the phone with his agent, Chad had texted to ask where I was, and I'd foolishly replied that I was at Jacob's house. And now he won't leave me alone.

He's already tried calling half a dozen times since we got in the car. I can't deal with Chad right now because my head is still spinning from that moment in the kitchen where we nearly kissed. At least, I think we almost did. His lips were so close to mine, and my fingers were on his chest. It was a moment that seemed frozen in time but passed so quick. I can't help but wonder what would have happened if Kellan hadn't come banging on Jacob's door.

When I think Chad's finally given up on getting through to me, I let myself relax. And then he calls again. Only this time, because of where I've got my phone, it rings and Jacob looks down at it.

"You're getting a call," he says.

"Um…yes," I say. I silence the call and chastise myself for not just turning off my phone when Chad started harassing me.

"You gonna answer it? It might be important."

"It's not."

My phone rings again with a new call.

"Sounds like someone's being persistent." He pulls to a stop at a red light. "You should answer it."

"It's alright," I say, silencing this call too. Before the light turns green, my phone rings yet again.

"You can answer it," Jacob says. "I don't mind."

I hesitate for a few moments, but then I do as he says. I swipe to unlock the phone, and before Chad can say anything, I angrily say into the phone, "God, Chad, what do you want?"

"Holy shit!" Chad shouts into the phone. I yank it away from my ear because he's so loud. I glance over at Jacob and I see the faintest ghost of a smirk on his lips as he proceeds through traffic. "What the ever-loving fuck were you doing with a shirtless Jacob at his house?"

I glance over to Jacob again and that ghost of a smirk is still there, but also a crinkle at his eyes that looks like displeasure. I remember him saying something about Chad and Kellan being too gossipy.

"How did you know that part?" I ask quickly, looking out the passenger window and avoiding Jacob.

"Kellan called me as soon as he left Jacob's place," Chad says.

Jacob exhales with something that sounds like annoyance. I glance over my shoulder, but he's concentrating on the road.

"We were just looking for something," I explain.

"Like a condom?" Chad asks.

"Listen, I can't talk right now," I say.

"Is he there?" he asks. When I don't respond right away, he says, "Are you naked in bed with him?"

"Chad, I'm hanging up now and I don't want you to call back," I say. "I'll catch up with you later."

"Just tell me how long his—"

"Goodbye, Chad," I say, cutting him off, then ending the call.

I put the phone down between my legs and lean back in the seat, letting out a long breath in a raspberry. "Sorry about that," I say to Jacob.

"It's alright," he says.

"I have no idea what's wrong with him."

"From what I've seen, he doesn't seem to have much of a filter, probably from years of being a bartender." He looks at me with a little smile. "Besides, we just hung out for a bit. Nothing happened."

Except for me feeling you up and us almost making out, I think, but I don't say it out loud.

Then Jacob pulls into the parking space behind the shop. We head into the store, and for some reason, I take the ornament with me—*his* ornament since we'd accidentally swapped. I don't realize that I have it in my hand until I'm digging my keys out of my pocket and opening the shop.

"I should have left this in your car," I say, holding it up.

He gives me a smile. "That's okay. We'll sort it out later."

Once inside the shop, we set to work. I continue unpacking the last of the boxes, and he sets to the task of the hammock chairs. It doesn't take me too much longer to empty the last of the boxes, then I break up all the cardboard and shove it in the back room to take out to recycling later. While Jacob continues his task, I get out a broom to sweep, and then follow it up with a mop.

With that done, I wander over to Jacob. He's on one of the top rungs of the tall ladder, and when I look up at him, I can see inside his shirt—if I look past his bulge, that is. It looks like he's now screwing the anchors into the ceiling.

He glances down at me, then says, "All done setting up?"

"Pretty much," I say. "I'm sure I'll be in a panic tomorrow morning over something I've forgotten, but right now I'm feeling confident."

"I'm sure it'll be fine," he says.

He screws the anchor into the ceiling and grunts with the effort. It's a deep, guttural grunt that sends a weird jolt to my crotch. I look up at him. *It can't be...* Then he grunts again. I've heard that grunt before. The wolf who was rutting me in the men's room at Bottoms Up on Halloween had grunted just like that. Suddenly, I feel like I'm back in that stall, bracing myself against the wall, getting the fucking of a lifetime.

"Edward?" a voice says, cutting through the fog that had wrapped itself around my brain. "Edward?" I realize it's Jacob.

I look up at him. "Uh, yeah?"

"Can you pass me that?" He points at a pile of braided rope. I hand it to him, and he finds the metal loops in the center of it and attaches it to the hook he's installed on the ceiling. He secures everything in place so it won't come apart on its own.

I watch as he comes down the ladder, and I try to envision him as the man who had ravaged me and realigned my guts. I'd been flirting with the idea that it could be him, but I'd always dismissed the idea for one reason or another. But this one? The grunting? This seems a little harder to dismiss.

Then again, it's a grunt. Lots of people grunt. And a lot of grunts sound the same. But that one…that one triggered something primal in me.

When he steps down off the ladder, I back up and give him space and watch as he attaches the hammock chairs to the dangling ropes he'd installed.

I eye the chairs, and my gaze travels up the ropes to the ceiling. "Are those really that strong?" I ask, wondering if the whole thing would hold up if Jacob railed me in it.

"It's fine," he says. "I anchored it into a solid beam and it's rated to hold five hundred pounds before there's any risk."

"Five hundred pounds?" I look at the braided ropes again. "Those things look more decorative than sturdy. I can't have people breaking their asses by falling on the hard floor."

Jacob huffs and sits in the hammock chair between us. "Sit with me," he says.

"What?"

"Sit with me. I'm one-eighty and you're, what, one-forty?"

I scoff. "I may be slim, but I'm not *that* slim. Not anymore anyway. I'm one-sixty."

"Even better. That makes three-forty combined. Sit with me."

I look at the hammock chair. Of course, with it being made of fabric, there isn't a spot next to him. When he seems to clue in to what I'm thinking, he pats his lap. That same lap that I had my face buried in on day one. Why is my heart beating so hard?

"Are you sure?" I ask.

In response, he pats his lap again.

Somewhat reluctantly, I move toward him and gently perch myself on his knees.

"That's not going to do it," he says. He grabs my hips and yanks me back. I fall into him with a yelp and put my full weight on him. The chair swings us back and forth. He wraps his arms around my waist. His hands are *very close* to my achingly hard dick. "Relax."

I try to force myself to release the tension in my body and just be comfortable on top of this gorgeous man who I clearly have a crush on…and who may or may not be my mystery men's room hookup. I wish I could just ask him about that, but how would I even go about it? If I ask and it's *not* him, then that question might give him the wrong impression of me.

"It's nice," Jacob says. He plants a foot on the floor and gives us a few more swings. "What do you think?"

I lean my head back against his shoulder. "I like it. It's very comfortable." My eyes go wide at the words that have come out of my mouth. I'm also now *fully* aware of every inch of muscle beneath me. Including the muscle I got to know face-first yesterday.

Before I can put my foot in my mouth again, or gather up the balls to offer my mouth for something else, Jacob leans in toward me, his lips slightly parted. Before our lips meet, a harsh knocking at the glass door startles us both.

"Oh shit," I say when I see two people hunched against the door, faces pressed against the glass.

"For fuck's sake," Jacob says.

We quickly get out of the hammock chair, and I stumble and almost fall face-first, but Jacob catches me before I do. Once I'm steady, he passes me and goes to unlock it.

"What do you want, Dad?" he asks.

Mayor Dick and Braden both come in, looking wide-eyed.

"Did we interrupt something?" Mayor Dick asks.

"No," Jacob says. "Now, what can we help you with?"

I briefly step behind Jacob and adjust my pants so things are less obvious.

"I wanted to see if you were available now for that sleigh repair," Braden says, hitching a thumb over his shoulder to indicate his truck parked in the loading zone. "I've got the old piece with me and we could stop off at Morning Wood for a new piece, then take care of it all at my place."

"And I'm tagging along because the Snowflake Festival is our premiere tourist attraction," Mayor Dick says, "so I want to make sure everything goes well."

"We're busy," Jacob says. But then he must realize he's being a bit too harsh because his expression softens and he adds, "Braden, I could probably come by in a couple hours, if that would work?"

He nods. "That'll work perfectly. I'll head to Morning Wood now, then get set up at home. Come by anytime—I'm free the rest of the day."

"Sounds good. I'll text you before I head over," Jacob says.

Braden heads out, leaving me with Jacob and his dad. I still have trouble believing they're related, but now that I get a good look at them side by side, there's some similarities around the eyes and the general facial structure, but other than that they're so different.

"You're not going too?" Jacob asks. Thankfully, the harshness from before was still softened.

"Nah, I was only tagging along if the work could be done right now, because I have a city council meeting tonight," he says.

"So, what happened to the sleigh?" Jacob asks. "Kellan was being dramatic and it seemed like the end of the world, but from how Braden talks, it seems like it's just one piece."

Mayor Dick nods. "It is. The panel on the side fell apart, so it needs to be replaced, but it needs an artistic touch that you're the best suited for. You could make it part of your community service, you know."

Jacob shakes his head. "I don't want it to be community service. I'm just helping out. So, what happened to it? It just fell apart?"

"Powderpost beetles, we think. They just ate right through it."

I feel a sudden chill go up my spine, and I let out a "G-g-gu-bl-l-llll…" sound with a shiver. When my eyesight comes in focus again, I see Jacob and his dad looking at me.

"You okay?" Jacob asks.

The heat of a blush hits my cheeks. "I have a big fear of spiders and the beetles triggered that." Even as I say the word "beetles", I feel another chill crawl up my spine, but thankfully I hold back from shuddering.

They continue to just stare at me.

"What?" I say to Jacob. "Don't you have a fear?"

"Clowns," they both say at once. Then his father repeats, "Jacob is scared of clowns."

"Don't—" Jacob warns, but he's cut off.

"At his fifth birthday party," Mayor Dick says, "his mom told me—"

"Dad!" Jacob says. He has his face in his hands.

"Okay, okay," Mayor Dick says. "Can I tell him the story about the Easter Bunny?"

"Dad!" Jacob says. He puts his arm around Mayor Dick's shoulders and spins him around, leading him to the door. "Don't you have something better to do?"

Mayor Dick looks over his shoulder at me. "While I'm here, I should ask how things are going with the new store. All set for tomorrow?" Jacob stops ushering his dad to the door and just stares at the floor in defeat. Mayor Dick comes back toward me. "Do you need help with anything tomorrow?"

"I think I'm okay, but thanks. I just have to set up a few more things and I should be all set to go. I used to run a bookstore out in Twilight Hollow, so I should find the rhythm of it again pretty quickly."

Mayor Dick holds out his hand, and I shake it. "Well, let me be the first to congratulate you on your opening. I'm sure you'll have a beautiful opening that everyone will enjoy."

Jacob lets out a little snort of laughter.

"Thank you, Mayor Dick, and I hope I'll see you at my Snowflake Festival event too. I'm having a Book Boyfriend Auction—guys will be auctioned off for a night on the town. I just need to find some eligible bachelors. The raised funds will go to an animal charity."

Mayor Dick's eyes go wide, and his head swivels around to stare his son down. "You should auction yourself up—it could be your community service! You'd raise a ton of money for a good cause!"

"No, Dad," Jacob says. "Absolutely not. Stop bringing up the community service. I'll get it done on my own time."

Mayor Dick looks back at me and shrugs. "I tried."

I give him a smile. "Thank you."

Mayor Dick looks at the time on his phone. "Well, now it's actually time for me to head off. It was a pleasure talking with you and I look forward to enjoying your opening tomorrow." As soon as he says those words, Jacob is at his side again, guiding his dad out of the store.

When he locks the door behind his dad, Jacob's shoulders slump and he lets out a sigh. When those shoulders raise again, he turns back around.

"I'm sorry about him," he says.

I can't help but chuckle. "I like your dad, no worries. I can see how being his son can feel like a bit much, though."

"He means well, but…yeah." He straightens his posture and comes closer to me. "So, what do you have left to do? I'd love to help you and we can finish this."

I feel like the floor drops out from underneath me. "Uh…it's okay. I can do the last thing myself."

Jacob looks past me. "Does it have something to do with that corner that you've strangely left empty this entire time?"

I refuse to turn and look at the corner. "It's just, uh, some decorations I've got in a box. That's all. It'll be really quick and I'll be done in ten minutes."

"I can help," he says, stepping even closer. "It'll take half the time if we do it together."

"Uhh…it's really okay. I can do it."

"Edward whatever-your-middle-name-is Kane…" he says in a scolding voice, "what are you hiding in that box?"

I hang my head in shame. Then I mumble, "It's the stuff for my *Twilight* shrine corner."

"Your…what?"

Staring at the floor and unable to look at him, I shuffle to the back room and pull out a very tall and very thin box. I rip the tape open and pull out life-size stand-up cardboard cut-outs of the main characters of *Twilight* in their full moody personas.

Jacob seems frozen in place. I still can't look at him because it's too embarrassing. Then he slowly crosses the room, his footsteps echoing all around us. He's got his hands on his hips and his head drops forward.

"I won't judge you for this," he says, "if you won't judge me for being afraid of clowns."

I feel some of the embarrassment melt away. "Deal."

We take a few moments to arrange the three cut-outs in the corner.

"There," Jacob says, "perfect."

I turn and look at my shop and find it's exactly as I'd envisioned it, right down to every last detail.

Jacob looks at me with a big smile. "So, that's it? We're officially done?"

I nod. "I'm all set for tomorrow. Are you going to stop by the opening?"

"Definitely. Plus, I know where everything is in this place, so I'll come in the morning to help out. If you need me to, I can stay for the whole day."

"I'd like that."

"So...to be clear..." he says, "I'm no longer your employee?"

I feel a little weird about how he's asking that; it almost feels like he can't wait to get away. Like his commitment to me is over. Was I misreading what had happened today? But how do I misread two almost kisses?

"Yeah. I mean, I guess I didn't quite think of you as an employee, but yeah. You're free to go," I say, trying to keep the disappointment out of my voice, but failing.

He gives me a quirky smile and says, "So, now that I'm no longer your employee, I was wondering if you might want to hang out tomorrow night...? We could go to my place and have a drink to celebrate your opening and exchange those mixed-up Christmas ornaments."

"That sounds nice," I say. "I'll be there."

He smiles and says, "I'm looking forward to it."

I decide to prod a little bit. "Sounds kind of intimate."

He smirks, then says, "No more intimate than the men's room at Bottoms Up."

"What?"

Before I even finish that one word question, he's turned around and is walking toward the door. He raises his hand over his head in a farewell wave. "See you tomorrow, Edward!"

I want to call out after him to ask him what he meant, but he's already out the door. "What the hell did that mean?" I ask the empty store. "Oh my God. Does that mean he's the mystery man? Or is that coincidence and he just pulled out a really random example?"

Sometimes I can be oblivious. Is this one of those times? He made that crack about the men's room, he has abs like the mystery man, a similar tattoo, and he grunts in a distinctive way. It could be him. It really could.

But…it could also be a total coincidence.

"God, I need a drink." I shut off the lights, set the alarm, and head out to Bottoms Up.

Chapter Six
No, Neither, and Yes

When I walk through the door, I find the place is pretty packed. Not quite as busy as the Halloween party, but definitely the busiest I've ever seen it otherwise. But it's Friday night, after all. I press through the crowd and approach the bar and find an empty stool there.

As soon as I sit down, Chad comes up and throws a cardboard coaster down in front of me. "First drink is on the house if you tell me absolutely everything you did today. Include all the lengthy, girthy, sweaty details."

I pick up the coaster and slide it through my fingers. "There's nothing to share. We spent the day together and it was completely platonic."

He blows a raspberry. "What was relayed to me was *not* platonic. What'll you have?"

"Surprise me."

He reaches beneath the bar and pulls up a bottle, uncaps it, and puts it on the coaster. "The cheapest beer we have since you're giving me the cheapest details. Give me something better and I'll serve you something better."

"Well, it's my lucky day because I like beer that tastes like water." I take a swig and barely manage to smother the intense look of distaste that is threatening to cross my features.

"Did he cross things off in your little notebook?"

"My *little notebook* remains untainted by Jacob."

When I put the bottle back down on the coaster, Lucas sidles up next to Chad. "You get any details yet? Or, better yet, any pics or vids?"

Chad never takes his eyes from me as he shakes his head. "He's tighter than a virgin bottom."

"So, what's his body taste like?" Lucas asks me.

I shrug.

"I don't have time for this," Lucas says, then heads across the bar to tend to customers.

"So, what happened?" Chad asks. "I'll give you another drink—a better one—if you give me something."

I mull that over. Normally, I don't want to air my dating affairs, but Jacob and I aren't dating. I'm not even sure if we're friending. I'm not sure what this is all about. "He finished all his work and so he said he's going to hang out at the store with me tomorrow and then we'll celebrate with drinks at his place afterward."

"Drinks?" Chad says, almost shouting the word.

Lucas hurries over. "Drinks? There are drinks involved? What kind of drinks?"

"Does it matter?" I ask.

"A beer is for friends," Chad says. "Wine is for someone you want to sleep with. Champagne is for lovers. What did he offer you?"

"He just said drinks," I say. "And we bought Christmas ornaments and got them mixed up so I have to exchange ornaments with him."

"Exchange ornaments, huh?" Lucas says. He looks at Chad. "Has he explained the shirtless thing yet?"

"No," Chad says. "Why was he shirtless? What were you doing?"

I take a swig of beer to delay answering and to make them antsier. When I put the bottle back down, I say, "He was showing me his tattoos."

Chad and Lucas look at each other and then at me. "Then what?" Chad asks.

"Then…your buddy Kellan came over and concocted some salacious story about what he *thinks* was going on in there."

"Ugh, you're impossible," Lucas says. He picks up a rag and starts wiping down the bar, heading away from us.

When he's out of earshot, Chad leans a little closer and says, "Your face is telling me more happened than you're letting on."

"I don't know what you're talking about," I say.

   JACOB   

I ring the doorbell outside of Kellan and Braden's house. I hope this doesn't take too long. Whenever I stop by, they always try to get me to stay and hang out with them. I'm really looking forward to tomorrow, so I'm gonna try and fix whatever is wrong as quickly as possible.

The door opens and Kellan greets me. "Hey, Jacob! Thanks for coming over," he says as he looks around me. "You didn't want to bring Edward along?"

I pull my mouth to the side. Why the hell is he asking me that? I don't want people talking about us. "No. Why would I bring the guy from the bookstore here?"

He pulls his head back, while gesturing for me to come inside. "Guy from the bookstore? Is that what you call him? That *guy from the bookstore* was in your house earlier and you were shirtless. Not to mention I've never even—"

His words are mercifully cut off by Braden. "Jacob, I didn't hear you come in. The piece we need to fix is out back. I'm sure you're busy, so we can get started right away," he says.

The whole house is flooded with Christmas, top to bottom, left to right, it's all Christmas. It feels so warm and cozy. The fireplace is lit, and their two cats, Mr. Fluffykins, and Senator Tunacan are cuddled together under the Christmas tree. It honestly looks like something straight out of a Christmas movie. It even smells like a perfect mix of Christmas in here. The smell of the tree mixed with the scent of freshly baked Christmas cookies is more than enough to make me kind of wish I had my own cats and someone to sit in front of a cozy fire with.

"Don't let him off the hook!" Kellan shouts playfully. "I told you he was shirtless, and Edward was just standing in the background, didn't even say anything to me." He turns back to me. "That tells me two things. Two very new things about you."

I exhale and look at Braden, who gestures toward the back door with his chin.

"I'm glad you learned two things today. Happy to have been a part of that," I say with a smile.

Kellan's mouth is hanging open, while Braden slides open the door. "Leave him alone. He's not gonna tell you anything."

I walk past Kellan and follow Braden outside. There is a large piece of wood, next to what looks like the side of the Christmas sleigh. It looks worse than I imagined. "What the hell am I looking at?" I ask.

Braden picks up the red siding piece. "This is the side of Santa's sleigh, it has been chewed straight through by powderpost beetles. So, what I need from you, is to cut this piece exactly the same as this one was before it was chewed apart.

I throw my hands up. "How do you expect me to do that? I don't even have the other side to measure it from. I can't use this piece, it's missing half of the bottom."

"Thought of that," Braden says, turning the new wood piece around to show me a terrible shape drawn on the back.

I see the faintest outline there. "What is that supposed to be? A pattern? I can't..." Truthfully, I can make it work, but I'll have to go home. It's not like I have a saw here. Oh, but if I say I need to run home, I fear Kellan will try to tag along.

Braden is tracing the pattern with his finger. It's such a small piece of siding. "If you can't do it, I can try, but my woodwork is not great. The guy that originally made the sleigh doesn't live here anymore."

"People actually leave this town?" I joke, taking the piece from his hands. "I can probably do it, but I'll have to go home." I look around the backyard. "Can I just sneak out of your gate? No offense to your husband, but I don't really want to be bombarded with questions. I want to try and get this finished. I have to help Edward with the opening tomorrow, and I need to make sure my house is clean." Shit. I'm stupid. I shouldn't have said that.

Braden's eyebrows raise, but before he can say anything, the sliding glass door opens, and Kellan is headed toward us. So much for escaping through the gate.

"How's it going out here? You guys need anything to drink? We have beer, wine, cocktails…basically whatever you want," Kellan says.

"We're just headed over to Jacob's house to try and cut the piece out," Braden says, as Kellan hugs him from the side.

I roll my eyes. There's really no sense in me telling Kellan that he can't come. He'll definitely follow us, even if I say no. And if I say he can't come, it will turn into a long string of jokes about cum or coming.

"You were gonna leave without me?" Kellan asks Braden.

Braden shakes his head. "No, but Jacob was just telling me that he needs to hurry because his house has to be clean tomorrow, for after he helps Edward with the grand opening."

Kellan's eyes go wide. I can almost see him holding in a squeal. "Oh. Okay. So, should we head over? I've never been inside, so it would be nice to see the difference in the two models," Kellan says calmly.

What the hell is his angle? He's not gonna say anything about Edward coming over?

Kellan starts walking toward the glass doors, holding Braden's hand. Braden drops an eyebrow at me and shakes his head silently. It's a look that makes me nervous for some reason. What's the worst that could happen, though?

I follow them back inside their house, and the cats are waiting by the doors for them. Kellan reaches down and pets each one on the head. "Now, you two can't come to Jacob's, besides, you're not even on a first name basis with him, the guy from the bookstore is a different story, as am I, of course."

I drop my head forward. "I do remember your cats' names. People names I forget, but cats, never. Also, I was going to sneak out and leave you because I don't feel like answering tons of questions about what you thought you saw and relayed to Chad earlier."

Braden lets out a chuckle and walks past us toward the front door. "Kellan would never tell Chad that he saw Edward in your house, and that it looked like he interrupted something. He also definitely wouldn't have mentioned that you slammed the door in his face when he asked you for a hug."

"Hey! If he would have let me hug him, I probably wouldn't have told Chad about that," Kellan says to Braden.

"Yeah, right," I say, following Braden out of the door with Kellan behind us. "Before you say anything else, that is not an offer for you to hug me, or an offer for me to hug you. I don't really like people touching me."

I place the piece of wood down and unlock my door with the keypad. "Please don't judge me," I say, bringing the piece inside. "Yes, I've been here for a few months, no, I haven't finished unpacking."

"You haven't finished unpacking and you invited a guy over for a date?" Braden asks me.

"I didn't invite anyone over for a date. You two invited yourselves over when I said I needed to cut this piece with my saw."

Kellan is looking around at everything. "This is the first time I've been in a famous person's house. It's decorated pretty nice. Did you pick all the stuff out yourself?"

I lean the sleigh piece against the garage entry door. "Yep. My mom is big into interior decorating, she taught me how to pick out furniture to fill a space."

"Can we see upstairs?" Braden asks.

"Yeah, but it's just my office up there." I walk up the stairs with the two of them following closely behind me. "This is it; I don't use this space that much. I try to keep work separate from the rest of the house. If I have to work on something, I'll only do it upstairs."

"It's nice," Braden says. "When Edward was here, did you guys handle business upstairs or downstairs?"

"Good question," Kellan says.

I groan, leaning my head back. "Oh my God. Okay, out, out. Into the garage. Come on. You two, you're perfect for each other. So nosy. Besides, we actually were upstairs because we came here to get anchors," I say, walking downstairs.

Once we reach the garage door, Kellan elbows Braden. "Did the guys at Morning Wood take their shirts off when you went there to get this wood? Or do shirts only come off of contractors when someone buys anchors?"

I open the door and gesture for Kellan and Braden to go in first. "You *can* leave, you know that, right?" I say to Kellan. Why the hell *was* my shirt off? I don't even remember why I took it off. Oh right, I was showing him my tattoos. I think he picked up on the bathroom joke I added before I left. He's surely realized that I'm the guy from the Halloween party by now.

"Why would I leave?" Kellan asks. "This is so fun. You don't look embarrassed at all, though. Do you not get embarrassed? You're secretive, but you still seem unfazed. How is that possible?"

I place the wood onto my work bench and put my gloves and safety glasses on. "What would I be embarrassed about? Edward was here, we came to get the anchors, I showed him my tattoos, and you rang the doorbell, then my agent called, and we left. I don't see anything to be embarrassed about."

"Well, you asked him over for dinner, right? So, like a date?" Braden says.

I put a hand up. "Shhh. No. I need to cut this without you guys distracting me. Go look at boxes or something. Actually, it would help if you could find the box that says Christmas on it."

"I was gonna ask why you didn't have any Christmas decorations up," Kellan says.

I shrug at him. "I only have one box of stuff and it's just a bunch of things that my nonna gave me, or random fans have sent. It's not a really big box. I don't normally decorate too much for holidays. Please don't lecture me. If you want me to cut this, I really have to concentrate."

I turn the saw on and flip the light above the bench. I can see the outline that Braden made pretty well. My mind is spinning right now. Why do I want the Christmas decorations out? Do I really want to impress

Edward? Why would he care if the house was decorated? But I think there's a small tree in there that I can bring tomorrow and put near the register if he wants it. I start cutting the piece and hear the two of them moving boxes, but I resist the urge to look up and continue cutting. After a few minutes, I turn the saw off and look up to see Braden and Kellan digging through boxes. I take the goggles off and give the wood a wipe.

"All done," I say, holding it up. "I can't paint it tonight, or sand it, that's all you."

Kellan takes a magazine out and holds it up while Braden starts walking toward me. "Don't you find it weird that your face is on magazines that are in people's houses? Maybe like in their bathrooms? Or bedrooms? This *Men's Fitness* one…"

"Well, that magazine is in *my* house, so not really. Honestly, I don't think too much about what other people do. Other people seem to be very interested in me, though."

Braden takes the piece from my hands. "This is great. You did a good job. Thanks. I really do wish you'd let me tell your agent that you helped us with this. It would be good for your image if people knew you were actually doing the community service you were told to do. Especially in such a small town."

Kellan starts walking toward me, holding a box. "All-Star Soccer Player Jacob Rizzo Singlehandedly Saves The Snowflake Festival By Fixing Santa's Sleigh. It's a good headline," he says, passing me the Christmas stuff.

"Thanks for finding this." I take the box and place it down by my workbench. "It would be a disaster if anyone knew I did community service here. As soon as one person finds out I'm here, I'll have to leave. This town couldn't handle the amount of chaos that would come with that. Why do you think I keep insisting that no one says anything? The media still has no idea where I am, and it has to stay that way. I can probably pay my way out of the community service once my suspension is up. The team owner has a soft spot for me. Well, he did before the suspension, he might not anymore."

"You dated his daughter, right?" Kellan asks.

I grab the box off the floor and shrug. "I don't think so."

"What do you mean you don't think so?" Braden asks. "You don't think you dated her or you don't want to remember dating her?"

"Hmm…which one makes you stop asking? I really gotta clean in here, so the sooner you two go, the sooner I can get to it."

"We'll leave after you tell us if you asked Edward over on a date. Then we won't ask any more questions," Kellan says.

I really don't like talking about this stuff. Besides I have no idea if Edward is okay with people knowing, or if Edward even knows that I asked him out. I think he does, but I really can't assume that. I gesture toward the front door and shoo Kellan and Braden toward it.

"Come on…just tell us. We won't say anything. I just really want to know," Kellan says.

"Step outside and I'll answer all three questions. But you can figure out which questions I answered when you get home. Deal?"

They walk outside and look at one another. "Deal," Braden says, while Kellan's mouth hangs open.

"First one, no, I didn't. Second one, neither because I didn't. Last one, yes, I did. Thanks guys, see you around." I shut the door.

"What the hell did any of that mean?" Kellan shouts.

Man, I'm tired. How can two people exhaust me so much? I grab the box of Christmas stuff and bring it into the kitchen. There isn't much in here, but the little tree is here, and it's perfect for beside Edward's register. I should get a real tree. That would be kind of fun. It's too late to do that tonight, though. I was thinking I might cook for him tomorrow night, but I don't know him well enough to know what he likes. I can just order something when he's here. Not really date like, but that's better because if he gets here and for some reason doesn't see it as a date, I won't look stupid for cooking him dinner. I know he's single and I'm sure he's into me, but I'm not sure if he realizes I'm into him. I can step up the flirting now that I'm not working for him.

I dig into the Christmas box and grab the red cabinet ribbons out that my nonna made for my house in Miami. The cabinets are much smaller here, but these should still work, since they're Velcro on the back. After attaching the bright ribbon onto the white cabinets, I take out the few remaining Christmas items. I'm gonna text Edward. I need to let him know that I still have the extra keys for the store.

Hey, I have three things for you tomorrow.

Almost instantly the message is read, and he's texting me back. It looks like he keeps changing his mind about what he's texting, though.

Who is this? JK Jacob. What do you have for me? Is it a big package?

I pull my head back. Is he flirting? He was like this on Grindr, too. Maybe he's just flirtier through text, or he was holding back until I finished doing the work for him.

Hmm…Idk what to say to that. I might have a package for you. If you think you're ready for it again. But that's not what I was talking about.

He replies with the thinking emoji. What am I supposed to do with that? I wait a few seconds, but he doesn't send anything else.

I have your keys, a small tree for the register, and bells for your door so you don't accidentally motorboat anyone's balls on the day of your grand opening. Lol

Damn. Even yours are off the table?

My eyes widen. He's definitely flirting. What else could he be talking about? I'm not holding back anymore either. These past few days have felt like torture.

I text him back: *Don't know how much time we'll have for that in the morning, but I'm really looking forward to tomorrow night.*

Chapter Seven
Do You Two Want To Kiss?

EDWARD

What has to be one of the tightest turnarounds—from seeing a space for rent on Halloween weekend to having a grand opening at a fully renovated store in a new city six weeks later—has finally come to fruition. It's day one of Hot for Plot.

Behind me, Jacob pours a coffee from the maker and passes the hot mug to me. "You alright?" he asks.

I wrap my hands around the mug to absorb the warmth. Though it isn't cold in here, my nerves have made my hands feel like ice.

"I'm a bit nervous," I say.

I hear a soft chuckle from behind me. "That's why I asked. But you've done this before."

I turn and lean my hip on the counter and look up at him. "But it was different there. I knew everyone. Here, I know no one. I don't even know if this town likes romances."

"Something tells me this is a romance town as much as a Christmas town," Jacob says. "You can see the line forming outside, so you know you at least have those customers coming in. More will come throughout the day."

"I hope you're right."

"I know I'm right," he says with a smirk. "You're going to do amazing today. I'm right about that, too. Besides, even if today goes rough, we're celebrating either way with a drink at my place tonight."

I feel a little flutter through my chest and also some blood flowing south. I still don't quite know what drinks at Jacob's place entails. I mean, it's pretty clear there's some flirting going on between us, especially with those texts last night. I just wish I'd get clear signals from him, so I don't accidentally make a fool of myself.

"I'm looking forward to it. It'll be a good way to cap off the day," I say once that flutter has dissipated. "We better open the doors. It's ten and people have been waiting in the cold." I take my coffee with me to the checkout desk and place it next to the cute little Christmas tree that Jacob had brought with him this morning. I still had his ornament from the antique store here, so he hung it on the tree, but facing me so I could see it all day.

I take a deep breath and look around the space. Everything is perfect. Jacob is standing in the middle of the store, giving me a big smile. I really couldn't have done all this without him.

"Ready?" I ask him.

He salutes me and says, "You're the boss. You've got this."

I take another deep breath, struggling to smother the nervousness. I glance at the glass door and see a friendly face first in line that I hadn't realized was there when I'd looked earlier. It's Chad and behind him is Lucas.

"I can do this," I whisper to myself. Then I circle around the checkout desk and approach the door. Jacob had also brought bells with him that we'd tied to the door this morning. It will be helpful when things get busy and people are coming and going.

I put on my bravest smile and unlock the door. "Come on in," I say loudly to the crowd of ten or so people lined up.

"Congratulations, brother," Chad says, giving me a handshake as he passes me by. Lucas gives me a clap on the shoulder. The rest of the crowd gives me a mix of congratulations and hellos as they filter into the store.

With the people in, I wander around casually, getting the vibe of the crowd and seeing how they take in the space. Chad and Lucas have taken seats in the hanging chairs; they might buy a book or two to be supportive, but I don't think they're really the reading type.

A few of the women have flocked to Jacob and are asking him questions like he's the owner of the store. I head over to them, but Jacob catches my eye and gives me a subtle cue that tells me not to bother intervening. I slow my pace but get close to them.

"I re-watched your game against France yesterday," one woman says, "you were amazing, especially in those shorts. Are you single?"

"I meant questions about books, ma'am," Jacob says. "I'm helping out for the day here and can help you find something."

"Hmm," the woman says, "then do you have anything about a soccer star who falls in love with a stay-at-home mom?"

Now I decide to swoop in. This is ridiculous—not so much showing up at my opening to talk to someone else, but more that the man can't have an ounce of privacy. "I believe you're looking for *Scoring in Her Net*," I say. I gently guide her away from Jacob. "Here, I'll show you the sports romance section."

When I return to Jacob, I see he's managed to shed one more woman and is left with a final one. "You should be a cover model," she says. "I've seen your abs online; you'd sell books. I'd buy whatever you're on."

He gives her a smile that doesn't reach his eyes in the slightest. "Thank you. But if you want hot covers, I think Edward has the extra spicy section over here," he says, pointing to his right at the shelves near the register. They are, indeed, the extra-spicy books. He paid attention while helping me stock the store.

Before I can say anything to Jacob or thank him or whatever, another woman comes up to him. "Can you help me reach something off the top shelf?" she asks.

"Sure, I should be tall enough," he says, following her across the store to the rolling ladder.

"You really should climb the ladder," she says. I watch as he gives her a strange look, but then he does indeed use the ladder to reach the top shelf, which he could've done without even standing on his tippy-toes. But when the woman backs up to take a good look at his ass, I realize what she's done.

And with that ass looking that great even from here, across the room, I silently thank her for the ruse.

The door jingles, and I look toward it to see an older woman coming in. Her excitement is clear as soon as she enters. I watch as she pauses and takes in the place, a brilliant smile coming to her lips. When she spots me at the register, she comes straight to me, extending her hand over the counter. I shake it and find she has a surprisingly strong grip.

"Welcome to the neighborhood," she says. "My name is Leora."

"Good to meet you, Leora, and thank you. My name is Edward."

"I've been watching the renovations from my condo—I live just above BJ's Cookies. The place looks amazing; you and Jacob have done an amazing job."

"Thank you, I'm really proud of the place. I had a bookstore in Twilight Hollow and had to give it up, I wasn't sure I'd have a place I loved as much—but now I love this one ten times more," I say.

"Oh, right, Twilight Hollow, Chad was telling me about that."

"You know my brother?" I ask.

"Dear, I know everyone. Maybe more context is needed," she says. "I used to run BJ's Cookies until I gave it to my grandson, Braden, a few years back. So, my shop was neighbors with Chad's bar, Lucas used to work for me, I became very good friends with Kellan, your store neighbor, and, most importantly, until I handed the title to Kellan, I was the Snowflake Princess."

"Oh, wow," I say, genuinely meaning it. "I hadn't remembered your name, but Chad was telling me all about you, about how you're the hub of the local business community and that I need to become friends with you."

She chuckles. "I don't know if I'm *that* important, but I'll take the compliment. Now, can you recommend a book for me? I'd like to be an opening day purchase for you."

"Sure, what are you looking for?"

She pauses to look over her shoulder, and I follow her gaze. Jacob is still up on the ladder, with a crowd of people around him, all of them asking for books off the top shelf. Doesn't Jacob realize he's being used for eye candy? But even as I'm thinking all this, I find my gaze locked on his tight round cheeks too.

"I'm looking for a book about a man built like that, with an ass made of cement."

I clear my throat, forcing myself to bring my attention back to Leora. "Sure, I've got a few in mind. Are you looking for MF or MM books?"

"Today, I'm looking for MM," she says. "Unless you have any MMM?"

"I think I have the perfect book for you." I lead her a couple bookcases over and squat down to reach off the bottom shelf. I pull out copies of *Debriefing the Lawyer* and *Seducing My Swim Instructor*. "I've read both of these…*multiple times.*"

"No further details required," Leora says. "I'll take them both."

I lead her back to the register and process her transaction—my first of the day. After chatting a little longer and earning an invitation to some Christmas party at her place, she soon heads off to get to reading her new books. Others start coming to the register. I don't know if this is the glow of love for a new business's opening day or if this is what the reading public is like in Frosty Bottoms, but either way I'm here for it.

A little while later, Chad and Lucas come to the desk with a few of the dirtiest MM romances I carry. I can't help but wonder if they're going to use them for inspiration. I just hope I move out before they do, because if they mimic what's in the books, it'll get *really messy.* Plus, Petey's language will get even more colorful.

A lot of my day from here on is spent processing transactions. By early afternoon, I realize I'm going to have to do a stock order first thing Monday morning to refill several of the shelves. While it gets a little quieter in the afternoon, it never quite empties out.

I'm so thankful for Jacob being here because I simply wouldn't be able to do this on my own, not today. Even with both me and him helping customers, there are still others waiting for their turn with both of us.

About mid-afternoon, a couple teen girls come in. They're definitely our youngest customers today—at least our youngest customers without their parents. They both walk in and look around, almost in awe.

Since there's a slight break in the customer flow, I come around from behind the desk. "Welcome to Hot for Plot. My name is Edward. Can I help you two find something?"

One girl looks to the other and they both giggle, then she looks back at me. "My mom sent me here to look for a classic romance she read when she was my age. She said it's really good and I'll love it too."

"Of course. If we don't have it in stock, I can always order it in for you. What's the book?"

"It was like *Moonlight* or *Midnight* or something like that," she says.

I rifle through the catalogue of books in my brain but I'm not coming up with any good matches. "Are you sure of the title?" I ask. I head toward the register so I can type it up on the computer. I can think of a few books that have those words in the title, but they're not exactly books I'd recommend to teens.

The second girl whispers in the first's ear, then the first says, "It's about a vampire and a werewolf or something? Like, maybe they kiss or people want them to?"

"*Twilight*?" I ask.

"That's it!" she says. "She told me to buy the whole series because she knows I'll love it. I think she really just wants to reread it but is too embarrassed to get it or something."

"I love *Twilight*," I tell her, leading them across the room to the back corner. I try not to look at Jacob because he's watching me, and I can't take the heat of his gaze right now. I pause in front of the cardboard cut-outs.

"It's the new *Batman* actor," the girl says.

"Um…this is Edward," I tell her, "from *Twilight*. He's the vampire."

"Uh…aren't you Edward?" she asks. "Did your mom name you after *Twilight*?"

I run my hand through my hair, feeling kind of nervous for some reason. "I was born before the first book came out, so no. But I'd consider it an honor if she did."

"Who's that guy?" the second girl says, speaking up for the first time.

"That's Jacob, the werewolf."

"Did you call me?" Jacob asks, stepping over. "Hi," he says to the girls, "my name is Jacob."

I shake my head. "Definitely did not call you over." I'm getting increasingly uncomfortable with us all crowding around my *Twilight* shrine.

"Wait," the second girl says, "did *your* mom name you after *Twilight*?"

Jacob looks at me, confused. To the girls, I say, "He's older than *Twilight* too, so no."

The first girl laughs, then points at the cut-outs. "And these are the two that my mom wishes would just kiss? Edward and Jacob forever?"

The second girl looks at us. "Do you two want to kiss?"

I look at Jacob, a hot blush burning my cheeks and another one making his face super red. Do I want to kiss him? Of-fucking-course.

"Uh, no," I say. Jacob smiles, but shrugs and walks away.

The girls look at each other and giggle.

"So…" I say, pointing at the shelves just to the right of the cut-outs, "here are the *Twilight* books. I'll just be at the register if you'd like to purchase them."

I watch Jacob as he circulates through the customers on the far side of the store, checking in with them and seeing if he can help. Do I want to kiss him? Of course. But preferably while he's wrecking me.

Almost as if he can read my thoughts, he looks up and makes heated eye contact with me. His gaze has me captive; I can't look away. Moments later, when he finally breaks eye contact—because a customer has come up to him—I'm struggling for breath.

When I finally regain it, the girls come to the register with all four *Twilight* novels. I quickly process their transaction, and they leave, giggling all the way.

I realize then that the store is kind of empty, with just Jacob and I and a couple customers browsing through the shelves. When I see the time, I realize that we're twenty minutes out from closing, so that explains the near emptiness.

Jacob is wandering around the perimeter of the room and eventually makes his way to me at the register. He looks at me kind of shyly, but then says, "I hadn't made the Edward and Jacob connection until then."

I chuckle. "Since I'm a Twihard, I made the connection pretty quick. I may be Team Edward, but I'm always on the lookout for my Jacob."

"Your Jacob?"

I glance away, embarrassed. "Well, yeah, he cared about her so much."

He looks like he wants to say more, but then one of the customers comes to the desk, and I process their transaction. And by the time they're out the door, the last customer comes to the desk too. As they head out, Jacob locks the door for me and flips the open/closed sign.

"You did it!" he says. "Day one! I'm so proud of you!"

I smile broadly at him. "Thank you so much for your help today. I'm not sure I could've done that all on my own. I'm sure that was all opening day buzz but if it's going to be busy regularly I'll need staff or something."

"See how it goes," he says. "This place can be really good at supporting local businesses, so it might be busier than you think."

I come out from behind the register and sit in one of the hammock chairs. It swings slightly under my weight. "It's good to be off my feet."

He sits in the hammock chair next to me. "Still up for coming over for a celebratory drink?"

I stretch my legs out, trying to ease the sore muscles. "Yeah. I just need to shower, I think. I'm kind of sweaty and gross from all that." Plus, if this is in fact a date I'm walking into, I'll want to be fresh and clean. But if it's not a date, I still need a shower anyway.

"I should shower, too," he says as he stands up. "I'll let the gatehouse know you're coming. Do you know how to get to my place?"

I nod. "I think I remember, but I'll text you if I get lost."

We grab our jackets and head out.

"See you soon," I say as we part ways in the parking lot. As I start up my car and drive away, I let out a long exhale of breath. I'm either about to have an awkwardly unsatisfying evening or amazing sex with the hottest guy I've ever met—and I'm still not sure which one it's going to be.

   # JACOB   

Edward will be here any minute. I'm so nervous for some reason. When has a guy ever made me nervous? I have to remind myself that I've already had sex with him. It's different, though. Because he had sex with a stranger at the Halloween party, not *me*. We didn't know each other then. I need to talk to him about it, even if it doesn't come up naturally. I can't have sex with him and pretend it's our first time, something about that feels wrong.

We didn't talk about what we were gonna do tonight, just that we planned to have drinks and exchange the Christmas ornaments back. I didn't remind him to take the ornament off the tree, but, honestly, it's okay if he keeps it.

The doorbell rings, and I see Edward on the camera outside. "Be right there," I say through my phone.

I open the door and see his adorable face. I kind of want to pull him inside by that tight-ass black shirt he's wearing, not just because I want to touch him, but because I don't want Kellan or Braden to come over. I'm sure they're staring through their front window right now. Do I hug him? Or just kinda move out of the way? What the hell is wrong with me? "Come in," I say and move to the side.

"Christmas!" Edward says, looking around. "This stuff wasn't up the other day. It looks great in here. Nice and cozy. You're missing something, though. Unless it's upstairs or in one of the other rooms…"

"What's that?" I ask, leading him into the kitchen.

"A tree. You're letting me borrow the little one, but now you don't have one. I feel bad, should we go get yours from the store now that the opening is over?"

"Nah, you can use that one. My mom isn't here to nag me about getting a tree, so I'm not worried about putting one up."

He sits on a stool at my kitchen bar. "Does your mom really like Christmas?"

"Mmm." I pull my mouth to the side. "She likes all things traditional.

So, Christmas decorations should be red and green, trees should never be artificial, you have to kiss under the mistletoe, the list goes on. If she were here, she'd already have pushed me into getting a real tree."

I pull out two bottles and hold them up to him. "Red okay, or would you rather have champagne?"

He pauses, staring at both bottles, looking like he can't choose. After a few moments of what looks like an internal struggle, he finally says, "Red is good. I'll take whatever you give me."

I tilt my head at him. He says things that sound flirty, but maybe I just have a dirty mind when it comes to him. I grab two wine glasses from the black hanging rack and start to fill them.

"So, are you close with your mom? Does she live in town, too?" he asks.

"I'm close with her, but I mean she's kind of terrible sometimes. She's always been mostly worried about how well I'm playing, and if I'm gonna make her look bad somehow. She's a good mom; she's just kind of not nice to other people. But she lives in Miami. One of the perks of moving here is the distance between us now."

"My mom is pretty absent for the most part. Uh…I'm sorry. This is bad conversation, right? I'm bad at this," he says, looking down at the bar.

I pass him a glass of wine. "I don't drink too much, but I do find that wine helps to make conversation a little easier for some people." I hold my glass up to his, and we clink them together. "Cheers. Congrats on a successful first day."

"Thanks. I don't know what I would have done without you there. It was much busier than I expected. I never had a day as busy as today at my old shop. Your presence might have had something to do with that."

"Nahhhh. They were there for you. And you helped so many people. It was fun seeing you in your element. You know so much about books. I like reading, but I don't have much time for it. This break has been the most time I've really had to myself since high school. How about you? Is reading what you've always done for fun?"

"Yeah, I've always loved reading. I like the idea of transporting to a fictional place and just losing myself in a good book. I learned everything I need to know about life from books."

"Like werewolves being better than vampires?" I say, trying to impress him with the little knowledge I have of *Twilight*.

He shakes his head and puts his glass down. "Werewolves are not better than vampires. Come on. You can't really believe that? Right?"

I sip my wine while staring at his bright white smile. He gets so passionate when he talks about books. I really want to kiss him. "I absolutely do believe werewolves are better. How could vampires be better?"

"Are we talking about vampires versus real werewolves, or are we talking about Edward and Jacob from *Twilight*? Those are two different arguments."

"I'm talking about whichever one makes you the most passionate. I like the way you look when you talk about books. So, for arguments sake, tell me why Edward is better than Jacob."

He takes a sip of his wine and stares me up and down. I know the look in his eyes. He wants me just as bad as I want him. "Well, in this room, I don't think Edward is better than Jacob, because I think Jacob is very…" He shakes his head and looks away. "I don't know what's okay for me to say sometimes to you. I'm not good at talking to people, as I'm sure you've noticed."

"You can say anything to me. You don't need to be afraid to be yourself. What were you gonna say? Jacob is very…what?"

"I don't know what I was gonna say." He sips his wine again, looking down at his glass. "I'm just not sure that I'm reading things right. I didn't realize what a big deal you are and that doesn't matter to me in the way that I think it should. Well, at least in the way it seems to matter to others."

I don't really know what he means, but I think he's trying to determine if I'm interested which I really can't dance around anymore.

"What are you trying to say? You don't care that I'm famous?"

"Yes. I just—I think it's cool, but you're Jacob. I don't see you as Jacob the soccer star. You're just Jacob. Does that sound shitty of me to say?"

I shake my head at him. "I think that may be the second sexiest thing a man has ever said to me."

"I'm flattered," he chuckles, "but I have to ask, what was the sexiest?"

I take my phone out of my pocket and open my Grindr app. I haven't opened it since the night we had sex. I pull up our messages from the bar and type out a message to him.

Hi. You wanted to know what the hottest thing that any man has ever said to me was. See, there was this mouse, and I fucked him in the bathroom at a Halloween party. Before we had sex, he took my dick in his hand and licked it. He told me he liked the way I tasted. Hottest thing ever. His big brown eyes were just looking up at me. Makes me hard just thinking about it. I've been desperate to take that little mouse into my bedroom and fuck him properly.

"What are you doing?" he asks.

I press send and put my phone on the counter. "I just answered your question."

He tilts his head to the side, and I hear his phone vibrating inside his pants. "You texted me?"

"Check your phone."

I watch as he pulls his phone out, and his eyes widen, while his face instantly lights up. He drops his head forward then looks up at me.

"Which way is your bedroom?" he asks, standing up from the stool.

Chapter Eight
Scream My Name

   **JACOB**   

I drink the rest of my wine and walk around the counter in front of him, taking him by the hand and leading him toward my bedroom.

"This feels familiar. Should I have brought the mouse mask?" he asks.

"No. Definitely not. That reminds me, I didn't get to do a few things last time." I pull him inside my bedroom and leave the lights off.

"What things didn't you get to—"

I pull his face close and crush his lips with mine.

"Mmm—" The faintest of moans escapes his lips, as I kiss him harder than I've ever kissed another person in my entire life. His mouth tastes sweet like wine, and, fuck, he really knows how to use his tongue. I'm trying to lead the kiss, but his tongue is wrestling mine for dominance, while his hands are fumbling with the button on my pants.

I shake my head at him, and break from the kiss. "No, not yet," I say, taking his hands in mine.

He's panting, just looking at me. "Why—why not?"

I pull his face close to mine again and kiss him, rolling my tongue around his. He reaches down again for the button on my pants. I pull back and bring my mouth near his ear, then lick his soft, small earlobe, flicking the piercing with my tongue, and whisper, "Because I haven't had my dinner yet, and I'm hungry. I want you to get into my bed and let me taste you. The last time we were together, your ass was right in my face, and it took all my willpower not to eat you out. I've been thinking about it non-stop. Just the thought of your ass pressed against my face like it was the other day, was enough to make me come last night." I reach around and squeeze his ass. "Do you want that? Do you want me to eat your ass?" I kiss the soft, smooth skin on the side of his neck.

He nods at me and quickly unbuttons his pants, dropping them to the floor along with his underwear. I lift his shirt over his head and turn him toward the bed, applying pressure to the middle of his back, urging him to bend over.

"You want me here?" he asks looking over his shoulder.

I nod at him as he rests on his elbows, then kneel behind him and lightly squeeze both cheeks. Fuck, what is it about this man's ass that makes me so fucking desperate? I press my lips against one cheek and massage the other, kissing slowly toward the center, dragging my tongue toward his crack, giving him goosebumps as I tease him. He's pushing back against me, and it's making me even harder. I grip both halves in my hands and spread him wide open. "You want my tongue in your ass?"

"Fuck, yes, Jacob. Eat me."

I trace his rim with my tongue, then attack his hole with long flat licks—fuck, he tastes sweet.

He's pressing back against my tongue, while I lick him over and over. I'm lapping at his hole desperate to taste more. "Mmm—fuck—fuck yes," he moans.

"You like that?"

"Mmhmm," he mumbles while grasping at my sheets.

He's grinding against the bed so hard that I'm losing my grip. I lightly smack both sides of his ass and pull him closer. He lets out a little squeak like he did when I fucked him at the bar.

I lick around his rim, then press my tongue inside his tight, warm hole.

He's softly moaning and panting, rubbing himself against my comforter, while I fuck him with my tongue. I'm so deep inside this man, sucking and swirling, while pressing my tongue in and out. I squeeze the sides of his ass, moving my face side to side, burying myself even deeper, sucking and slurping on this juicy fucking hole. His breaths are so ragged that he lets out another tiny squeak; it's a noise that triggers something ravenous in me, some fucking urge to claim him—I don't know what it is, but I need to fuck him now. "Don't move," I say, then quickly grab the lube and a condom from my nightstand.

He looks over at me, while I undress, seemingly trying to catch his breath. "Damn, you're hot."

I smirk at him. "You're not so bad yourself." I rub some lube on his hole and slide a finger inside, pumping slowly. "The last time I fucked you, I said I didn't want to talk. Do you remember that?"

His breaths are heavy, he's still pretty tight. "Haah—haah—yes—I do."

I slide my finger out then trace his rim with two fingers. "This time"— I press two fingers inside—"I want you to scream my fucking name."

His head drops onto my bed, and I feel his knees buckle. "Fuck me— fuck me, Jacob," he whimpers.

He loosens up pretty fast, after a few minutes of stretching him out. "You want to be fucked like this, or do you want to lie down?"

"I—I want to kiss you, but—"

I pull my fingers out and turn him around, yanking his body against mine, and kiss him softly. Edward deepens the kiss, and the feeling of his tongue moving around in my mouth knowing that my tongue was in his ass moments ago is such a turn on for me. His hard dick, sticky with precum, is pressed against mine.

Our mouths are slipping off one another, unable to contain the ferocity of our tongues, it's sloppy, wet, and definitely the hottest kiss I've ever had. I press him backward onto my bed and kneel in between his legs. He reaches forward, stroking my dick and cupping my balls, massaging them in a way that makes me drop my head back. "Fuck, yes." I grab the condom and pass it to him. He tears it open and slides it onto my cock, then watches as I slather the lube on my dick and his hole. I spread his legs open wider and press my cock teasingly against his entrance. "You want me inside of you, little mouse?"

He turns his head to the side and lets out a soft squeak. "Mmhmm."

"Your cute noises really turn me on, but I'm gonna need more than that." I press the head of my cock inside. He feels absolutely incredible, but I want to hear him say it before I give it to him. I pull myself back out, watching his eyes widen, then I press back inside. "Let's try this again. Do you want me inside of you, little mouse?"

"Yes, Jacob—please put your dick in me. I want it so bad."

"That's better," I say. I'm working my cock slowly inside him, but I can feel him tensing up. "Relax for me, let me inside." I push the rest of the way in until we're fully connected. "Fuck. You feel even better than I remember."

I lean down and start rocking slowly, then kiss him, rubbing our tongues together. He moans into my mouth sending some kind of a signal straight to my dick, and I start pounding into him harder.

"Yes—" he says, then covers his mouth with his forearm.

I move his arm. "Don't cover your mouth. Let me hear you." His hole is clinging to my cock so tightly, while I fuck him harder and faster.

"Haah—haah…" His breaths are heavy when I bite the side of his neck—I can't help but to bite him, his skin tastes so fucking sweet. I pull back, rising onto my knees, and toss his legs over my shoulders.

"Yyess—so—deep, you're so deep," he whimpers.

I keep pounding into him, over and over, until I hit his spot. A squeak louder than the others escapes his mouth. "Fuck, Jacob," he says in a voice barely above a whisper.

"That was it. That was your spot. I'm gonna make you come now. But I want to hear you. I want to hear you scream my name, little mouse."

I shift my hips to the right, and I know when I hit it, because his breath hitches. I drive harder and faster, ravaging his hole until he scratches down my chest. "Holy fuck, Jacob, Jacob, Jacob—I'm coming." His cum shoots all over his abs, and I keep pounding into him, grinding harder because the way his hole tightens on me as he comes is enough to push me over the edge. "Fuck—fuck—yes—" I say, as my cum shoots into the condom, and Edward scratches down my back.

My body collapses on top of his, and I tuck my face into the crook of his neck, giving his sweat-covered skin a soft kiss. I feel his fingers lightly tracing my back, while his heart beats beneath mine. There's something in me that's breaking—I don't know what it is. But I can feel a pull that I've never felt before, he's doing something to me, this connection with him—it feels so different. How can I feel like something is breaking when he's holding me so close and squeezing me so tight. I can't understand it. I should move—but I don't want to. Whatever is happening to me, if he's breaking it—I'll let him smash it to pieces, just to stay here in this moment for a little longer.

"I want you to stay like this, but you probably want me to leave," he says.

I lift my head, bringing my face in front of his. "What? Why would you think that? I don't want you to leave…unless you want to?"

He tilts his head at me like I was the one who just suggested he leave. "You don't want me to go?"

"If I didn't have to slide out at this point, I wouldn't want to move for the rest of the night." I kiss him quickly, and shift my hips backward, then stand from the bed. I look down at him, he's still in the same position, arm draped across his forehead. "What is this crazy stuff you're saying?" I ask him, while walking into the bathroom. I toss out the condom, then grab two washcloths from my bathroom linen closet.

"I'm just used to leaving after—I guess. I don't know, it's embarrassing," he says.

I turn the faucet in the bathroom on and allow the water to warm up. What kind of an asshole would make someone leave immediately after sex? What kind of guys has he been sleeping with? The thought of anyone treating him like that really pisses me off. I get the washcloths nice and warm, wipe myself down with one, then walk back into the bedroom with the other. "I can wipe you down, unless you'd rather do it yourself?"

"Are you real? Is this real?" he asks. I watch him lightly smack himself on the face. "Wake up, Edward."

I wipe his cum from his abs. "What are you talking about?" I chuckle, while wiping. "Sorry if it's cold."

"No, it's actually pretty warm, but, uh—you are doing all kinds of things to me for the first time tonight. I'm sorry if I seem a little out of it. It's all just a bit surprising."

I finish wiping him down and look over at him. "Which part is surprising?"

"That list is a bit too long and, as previously mentioned, very embarrassing. I don't think that the first night I sleep at a guy's house I should be talking about all the shitty things other guys have done to me."

"Agreed," I say. I toss the washcloth into the hamper, then grab a pair of sweatpants and T-shirt from my dresser and throw them on. "But, admittedly, I'm curious. Wait, did you just say the first time you're sleeping at a guy's house? Like ever?"

He sighs. "Yes. Like ever. I didn't even have sleepovers when I was a kid. And as an adult, the guys I've slept with were all just hook ups, or casual guys I went out with. I didn't stay the night."

I feel the makings of a plan in my head, but I should probably let him rest for tonight. Then again, he's gotta be hungry. "Well, those guys sucked. But I have a fun idea. How are you feeling right now? Hungry, tired, want a shower? Actually, let me get you some water. You can tell me how you're feeling when I get back."

"I can tell you how I'm feeling now," he shouts after me, with a giggle.

I walk into the kitchen and grab two bottles of water out of the fridge and scan the inside. It's all prepped meals, there's nothing workable, which is okay, I planned on this being a cheat day for me. I walk quickly back into my bedroom. He's sitting against my headboard now; his gorgeous chest is on full display. "Tell me how you're feeling," I say, passing him a bottle, before I sit on the bed beside him.

He gives me a nervous kind of look as he unscrews the cap and brings the bottle to his lips, taking a quick sip. "I feel like, for once, I'm glad I brought extra clothes with me, and I'm a little hungry."

"I didn't see you carry a bag in… Is it in your car?"

"Of course it is. I had no idea if you'd want me to stay over, but with Chad and Lucas making such a big deal about me coming over here, convinced this was a date—half of me packed that thinking I'd just go to a hotel tonight when you inevitably told me it wasn't one. You know, to avoid the walk of humiliation and the freaking foul-mouthed parrot."

I'm trying to wrap my mind around everything he just said. I need to get a few things straight with him. "First, I didn't know they had a parrot. Second, are you still wondering if this was a date? Because the way you just said that sounds like you're still not so sure."

He shrugs at me and takes another sip of water. "I don't—I don't know, Jacob. I'm pretty sure it was, but, like, why? You're obviously this huge star that people are just dying to be near, so why would you even want to go out with me? Seems like you could have anyone you want, and when I saw people around you today—I think I started to really question if I was misreading things."

"There are so many things that you just said that I need to respond to, but did you actually not realize it was me? I knew you were the guy from Halloween as soon as you motorboated my balls. When did you figure it out?"

"I really had no idea. I thought you could be, and Chad and Lucas definitely thought so, but I didn't figure it out until yesterday. That doesn't really—"

I interrupt him, "Wait, no. It doesn't matter, what matters is that I like you and I did ask you out. I took my shirt off in my house and invited you to basically touch my tattoos, why would I do that if I didn't like you? I mean, I do—I really do like you. I just—I couldn't really say anything until I wasn't working on your shop. I didn't want you to be embarrassed once you realized we'd already hooked up. Of course I want you to stay the night, which reminds me, we need to go get your clothes out of your car. Kellan and Braden are definitely watching, but they'll know you're spending the night anyway, since your car is in the driveway. Before you ask if you should leave or move your car—the answer is no. One of the reasons I like it here in Frosty Bottoms is because despite being nervous that someone could tell the media where I am, at this point, the person that I like—you—aren't really in any danger of being criticized or harassed, so no—leave the car where it is."

"Why would I be harassed? Because my car doesn't fit in with the neighborhood?"

I tilt my head at him. "I really like this innocent kinda thing you have going on for you. Has nothing to do with your car. If we were in Miami and you, or anyone aside from my mother, was parked outside of my house, there's pretty much always some asshole outside of the gate with a camera, looking for a story. And I take that back, there would be an asshole taking a picture of my mom, too. The headline would be like, *Jacob Rizzo Distraught Over His Suspension, Turns To His Mother For Support*, or some shit like that. That's why I came here when I was suspended, no one knows where I am, and it has to stay that way until next season starts."

"That sounds crazy. Don't people know who your dad is? How has the media not figured out where you are?"

"My dad's name isn't even on my birth certificate. He and my mom weren't really together, so my mom didn't put his name on it. My dad was fine with it. I—don't think it's right, but at this point, no one has any way to track me, only my agent knows where I am. I have nothing that would connect me to Frosty Bottoms. Even the contractor business, I have a license, but the business is in my dad's name. The mortgage, my cars, my agent took care of everything."

He's rubbing his arms and pulling the blanket up a bit higher. I think I made him uncomfortable. "I'm sorry, I didn't mean to dump all that on you. You asked and for some reason I felt the need to be completely honest with you. I'm sorry. I can run out to your car and grab your clothes if you want to take a shower."

"Don't apologize. I'm just cold. I think I will take a shower, though, if that's okay. I can just throw my clothes on and grab the bag. You don't have to do that." He stands from my bed completely naked, and I swallow hard at the sight of him.

I shake my head at his suggestion and my own dirty thoughts. "Come on, let's get you into the shower, I have an idea for after. Do you like Chinese food?" I ask, flipping the bathroom light on before opening the linen closet.

He follows me into my bathroom and looks around. "You weren't kidding, this *is* better than the bathroom at Bottoms up." He giggles. "Your bathroom is as big as my old apartment was. This is crazy."

"This one is smaller than the bathrooms at my other house," I say, passing him a towel and washcloth.

He nods at me. "So, you still have the house in Miami, too?"

"Yep. I'll probably spend most of my time there during the season and here during the off-season. Haven't figured it all out yet. Can I have your keys so I can get your clothes?"

He slides the large glass shower door open and looks at me with the most confused face I've ever seen. "Why would you need my keys?"

"Uh…to open the car door? You said your bag is in there, right?"

He laughs and turns the shower on. "My car definitely isn't locked. Jeez, Jacob, if I tried to lock the door it probably wouldn't ever open again. Just use the passenger door, it's on the front seat. The driver's door is kind of hard to close."

I give him a salute and turn to leave. "Oh, wait, is Chinese food okay? I'm gonna order dinner for us and set some stuff up."

"Ooh, I love Chinese. Ginger Beef is my favorite. What else are you setting up?"

"It's a surprise. I'll grab your stuff. Be back in a few." I toss my hoodie on and a pair of socks, then head outside. It's dark and clear tonight, and the stars are extra bright. The driveway is cold even through my socks, sending a chill right through me. I open Edward's passenger door and grab his backpack from the seat. There's a small blue notebook underneath it. I don't know if I should bring it inside. Nah. I'll just leave it. If he wants it, I can come back out for it. I close the door quickly and jog back inside my house.

The shower is still running, which is good because I still have time. I order Chinese delivery through an app, grab some blankets from the hallway closet and toss them onto the couch, then dim the lights. I quickly walk toward the bathroom, the door is open, so I shout inside, "Hey, I grabbed your stuff, delivery will be here in thirty minutes! I'll leave your backpack on the counter here. Oh, and there was a little blue notebook—"

"Aaaah!" he screeches. I widen my eyes looking at him through the shower door. He's covering his face. "Jacob, please tell me you didn't look inside that notebook."

"Ew. No. It's not mine, why would I look inside it? I just wasn't sure if you needed it. But why did you scream like that?"

He tilts his head back and rinses his face under the shower, then turns it off. The glass door slides open, and he steps out. "Because it's a stupid notebook, I would be embarrassed if you saw my notes in there."

"Like a diary?"

He wraps the towel around his lower half. "No, it's worse than a diary, but can we just not talk about it? I swear it's just an embarrassing thing, nothing terrible."

He's dripping wet and looks so fuckable right now. I really can't help myself, his tattoos are so sexy. I step toward him and hold the back of his wet head, pressing our mouths together. His mouth is so warm and inviting, I swirl my tongue around his, kissing him deeply. He whimpers lightly when I grip his hair.

I pull back from the kiss and press my forehead to his, running my hands down his juicy ass. "You're lucky the food will be here soon, little mouse. Those squeaks are gonna get you fucked again."

"I don't know whether I should squeak or not, then," he says through a giggle. "Thanks for ordering food for us." He grabs his backpack and pulls out a pair of gym shorts and a T-shirt.

"Of course, meet me in the living room when you're dressed. I can't stand in here with you anymore. Your body is way hotter than you realize. How often do you work out?"

He shrugs. "A few days a week, but I don't have a regimen or anything. I have a routine that I do, but it's pretty loose." He gestures toward my body. "Nothing like whatever you do, to look like that," he says, grazing my abs through my shirt.

"I've had a really strict diet and exercise plan since high school. It's gotten more intense, but I'm used to it. Prepared meals, exercise—I don't really eat sweets..." I give his ass a squeeze. "I ate something sweet tonight, of course."

"Oh, ass isn't part of your daily meal plan?"

"Nope"—I pump my eyebrows at him, while he slips into his gym shorts—"but maybe it should be."

"I wouldn't complain," he says. His eyes widen while he covers his mouth. "I didn't mean to assume, like, that you meant me, or my ass. I just meant, I would like it if you ate my ass every day." He tilts his head backward. "I didn't mean that—I'm gonna shut up."

I pull him by the hand toward the door. "You're funny. You don't have to get so flustered. I was talking about *your* ass after all."

For some reason, I really like leading him around by the hand. Maybe it's because that's what I did at the bar. We walk into the living room, and he's still clutched on tight.

"Oh, is this where I'm sleeping?" he asks, gesturing to the blankets on the couch.

The scary thing is that I think he was genuinely asking me that. I shake my head at him and release his hand. "No." I drop an eyebrow at him. "You're sleeping in my bed, why would you sleep out here? This is for our sleepover. You said you never had one, so I thought we'd order Chinese and watch movies on the couch. I know *Twilight* is your favorite, but I don't know which one, or I would have rented it already."

"Really? You want to watch *New Moon* with me?" He presses with both hands on the gray leather cushion and looks at me. "Bouncy."

I pull my head back and sit on the couch. He can't have been testing it for sex. But with that look he gave me, I kind of think he was checking to see how good it would be for that.

Edward sits on the opposite end of the couch and covers himself with a cream-colored blanket. It's a large couch, there are probably five cushions in between us. Why is he sitting so far? I pat beside me and pull the recliner out. "Can't find out how bouncy the couch actually is later if you don't come over here."

He's covering his head with the blanket. "Why do I do the stupidest things in front of you?"

I scoot beside him and pull the blanket up, covering my head with it, too. "There, now it's like a little clubhouse where we can both do stupid things."

His hands are cupping my face, as he leans in for a kiss. His soft lips are pressed against mine, and his tongue is moving slowly, almost shyly.

I pull back at the sound of the doorbell coming through my phone. "Food's here," I say, unravelling myself from the blanket and standing up, while adjusting my very obvious situation below. Damn. We just had sex, and I really want to do it again. I exhale and open the door.

The delivery driver passes me the brown paper bag. "Oh, you're, uh—Jacob, right," she says looking at the bag.

"Yep and I'm all set. Thanks!" I start to close the door, and she peeks around me.

"Oh, um—you didn't need anything else?"

"Nope. All set. Have a good night." I close the door before she can say anything else.

I walk back toward the couch and place the bag on the coffee table. "I'm so hungry. Do you want to eat in here, or would you rather eat at the bar, or in the dining room?" I ask.

"It's your house. I'll eat wherever you want. Is it really okay that you eat this? You said your diet is really strict. I feel like I'm making you break it, just because I'm hungry."

I wave him off and open the bag. "I planned to cheat on my diet today, besides, I already ate something sweet about an hour ago, and since it was your ass, you're directly responsible for that. But the Chinese, this was all me." I give him a wink and pass him the container of food, along with a napkin and plastic utensils.

"This smells so good, thank you," Edward says. He opens the lid on his food and scoots closer to me.

I grab the remote and quickly rent the movie. "Let's do it."

Eating with Edward is so much different than eating with the team, and it's far better than eating alone. I'm trying not to stare at him, but he's obviously memorized this whole movie, so every once in a while, his lips move in sync with the dialogue. I can't help but smile when he does it. It's really cute.

I don't know what this feeling is—it's like when you hear a song and the words don't mean anything to you, but for some reason the song entrances you, it pulls you in, it comforts you, it makes you want more of it, over and over—whatever that is, that's what I feel looking at him.

I'm trying to tell myself that it's okay for me to like him, that it's okay for me to want a relationship with him. But I'm a bit worried that he doesn't fully understand what that would be like. I wouldn't want to do anything that could hurt him. But if I make sure that doesn't happen, then I think it's okay for me to want this.

We finish our food, and Edward scoots in close beside me, pulling the blanket over himself. I wrap an arm around him, and he leans against my chest. "This is really nice. Thanks for doing this with me."

"You don't have to thank me. I'm glad we did it." I rub his arm and feel his body completely relax against mine.

Chapter Nine
He Made Soup For Me

EDWARD

The first thing I notice when I wake up is how much my body aches. The second thing I notice is that I'm not in bed. And the third is that Jacob is behind me and has his arm wrapped around me. An alarm has woken me, and by the stirring against my back, it woke him too.

"Sorry," he groans. "I forgot to turn my alarm off."

I yawn. "That's okay. I should get up now anyway and get ready for work."

We had fallen asleep on the couch after our cute boys' sleepover and *New Moon* rewatch. It reminded me of the romance plotline in *College Boys Pillow Fight*. I really need to re-read that.

I'm still in awe of everything that happened—not really the sex, though that was mind-blowing, but more that Jacob continues to *want* to be around me, and he seems to care for me and what I think of him. The guys back home would have just sent me away after they got what they wanted, they wouldn't have gone through the effort of setting up a cute at-home date.

"Alright," he says with a defeated sigh, "we'll get up. I've got some breakfast in the fridge."

I push myself up to a seated position, my ass pressed firm against his, uh, *firm* crotch. I then realize that my aches and pains aren't *just* from falling asleep on the couch…because I have more than just aches and pains. I also have a queasy stomach and a half-stuffed nose. Crap. While it looks and feels like the flu, I'm pretty confident it's just exhaustion catching up with me, what with the move and setting up the store and everything. I've done this to myself a few times, and a good long sleep usually fixes it.

Jacob pushes himself up to sitting as well, and then hugs me from behind, kissing my ear. "I enjoyed last night. Immensely."

"Me too," I say. I can even hear the slight scratchiness in my words.

He hugs me tighter and sighs, letting his body sink into mine. Then he eventually gets up and says, "Come on, let's eat."

I follow him, trying not to let my ill feeling affect my gait or the expression on my face.

"Do you like overnight oats?" Jacob asks. He's already in the kitchen, bent over and looking in the fridge. "It's about all I've got since it fits with my meal plan. But they're really good."

I come into the kitchen, trying my best to hide my discomfort. "I could do oats."

He looks at me. "Are you okay? You don't look so great."

I nod. "Yeah, just a bit tired still is all."

He looks at me like he doesn't quite believe me but doesn't want to push the point too hard. Instead, he reaches into the fridge and pulls out two mason jars with oats. "These have blueberries, almonds, and Greek yogurt mixed in for extra nutrients and protein." He opens both jars and puts a spoon in each, handing one over to me. "I don't have coffee, but would you like some tea?"

I take the oats from him. Admittedly, they look delicious, but with how my stomach is right now, I'm not sure how well I'll handle this. Caffeine, though… "Tea would be great."

I soon have a steaming mug in front of me. Even just the smell of it helps a bit.

I manage to make it through breakfast, despite the nausea I'm feeling. We quickly get showered and dressed and hop into his car, heading to the shop. The movement isn't helping my stomach, and each bump in the road seems to make everything burble inside me.

We make a quick stop by Chad's apartment, and I sneak in quietly. Thankfully, Chad and Lucas seem to both still be asleep. Unfortunately, the parrot is not. "Awrk! Who's a slut?"

I quickly dart into my room and shove a bunch of clothes in a suitcase. I had packed a couple things in an overnight bag last night *just in case*, but with low expectations, since a guy had never asked me to sleep over before, I hadn't thought to pack work clothes. I'm shoving some bookstore-appropriate attire into the suitcase so I can change at the store…and, fuck it, I'll throw in some casual clothes too. What if he asks me to stay over again? I have no idea how this works. I'm weirdly nervous packing all this up. Like, what if for all he says he likes me, he changes his mind and doesn't want me over anymore?

I shove the worries and wonderings aside and zip up my suitcase. More than anything, I want out of this apartment before Chad wakes up and starts interrogating me about last night.

"Bye, Petey," I say on my way out.

"Who's a slut? Awrk!"

I make it back to Jacob's car without Chad or Lucas seeing me. Surely, they must be used to their parrot squawking profanities at all hours of the day and night, so they probably didn't think anything of Petey's outburst.

As I sink into the passenger seat, I feel an ache in my muscles and bones, and it makes me sigh heavily. Thankfully, Jacob either doesn't notice or chooses not to say anything.

If this *wasn't* day two of my store, I would have closed up shop and slept the whole day and be back on my feet tomorrow. But I can't have a grand opening and then follow it up with a day off.

Jacob pulls his car into the lot behind the shop. "I'm excited for today," he says as he shuts off the car. "Yesterday was so busy; I can't wait to see how today goes."

"Let's temper our expectations," I say, "it'll probably be a little quieter."

He leans over and kisses me on the temple. "Have faith in the people of Frosty Bottoms…or at least in their love of dirty books."

He kissed me on the temple…if I didn't feel so sick, I might actually kick my feet and let out a little squeak right now. He's being so sweet to me.

We get out of the car and enter the back of the building. We had taken a little longer than expected to get out of the house, and it's nearly opening time. I figured we'd just wander in and chill out and wait for the inevitable random customer to come in. What I hadn't expected was for there to already be a line waiting. It's only three people, but it's three more than I had expected.

I unlock the door and hold it open for them. "Good morning, people," I say as they pass me to enter the store. "Let's get you inside and warm. What brings you all here today?"

All three answer at once, but I manage to pick out that one is looking for a Christmas gift, and the other two need to stock up on books for the next few weeks.

After directing them to the sections they're looking for, I come around the register and sit on the stool I've got there. Jacob must hear the sigh I let out as I sit down, because he comes up and discreetly whispers, "Are you sure you're okay? I didn't hurt you last night, did I?"

I smile up at him as I remember last night, and also as an attempt to hide my discomfort. I really don't want him worrying about me, especially when I know this is just from overworking and I'll be fine tomorrow morning. "Everything's good, and, no, you didn't hurt me. I enjoyed every moment of it."

"Okay, I just wanted to make sure."

The two customers that needed a stack of books each for the coming weeks both come to the register, and I help them out. The Christmas shopper comes shortly after that with a few gifts for friends and family. With them all out of the shop, I let my façade drop a little bit.

"You're not okay," Jacob says.

"I don't feel great, but I'll be fine," I say. "A good night's sleep tonight will help me get through this."

"If you're sick, you should go home," he says.

"I can't. The store."

"I can watch the store," he says. "I know how to use the register."

"I'll be fine. Besides, I just escaped Chad's place without him noticing me; I don't want to go back there and have to answer a bunch of questions about last night," I say, but then a shiver runs down my spine, and I tremble.

"You can just stay at my place," he says. "It will be fine. I can drive you."

Then I sigh. "Can you really watch the store?"

"Of course. And if there's anything I don't know, I can text or call you," he says. Then he looks me deep in the eye and asks, "Do you trust me?"

I look up at him and see nothing but care for me in his face. "I trust you." Although he likely doesn't realize it, those are lines from *Twilight*. Damn. "Alright," I say. "Take me to your place."

We quickly lock up and head to his car. I shrink into the seat as Jacob drives across town. The only reason I don't feel incredibly embarrassed is because I feel so sick, and I can only focus on that right now. A few minutes later, he pulls into the driveway of his house, next to my car that I'd parked there yesterday.

"Hang on," he says before I can reach for the door handle. He gets out of the car, hurries around, and opens my door for me. He holds out his hand for me, and I take it—not so much because I need support but more because I'll take any excuse to touch him—and then he grabs my little suitcase and leads me up to his front door.

"Come on, we'll take you to bed," he says, leading me by the hand to his bedroom. Sick as I am, my cock springs to life at memories of what happened here last night.

He directs me to sit on the bed and then digs through his drawers. "I'll find you something comfortable to sleep in."

I smile at him, but say, "I'm okay, really. I'll just sleep in this. Or I've got extra clothes in my suitcase."

He stands up and turns to face me, looking like I've offended him. "You need to relax. Besides, I've got the perfect thing here." He turns around again, this time with a pair of gray sweats and a T-shirt in his hands. "This is an old practice shirt; it's *super* comfortable. You'll love it."

He hands them to me. "Thank you," I say.

"Do you need help changing?"

"Um…I think I'm okay."

"I would love to help you change."

Normally I'd be on board with having him help me change, but that boner I got when I walked in here hasn't gone away yet, and I don't want him to see that right now. Since he's in this super supportive nurse mode, I'm struggling to figure out how to distract him.

Then it comes to me. "Do you have any soup or anything? I could eat a bit and it might help settle my stomach."

"I think I might have some prepped. It'd be healthy and perfect for how you're feeling right now. I'll go check." And like a flash of lightning, he's out of the bedroom.

I quickly strip and put on his sweats and shirt. God, this isn't helping my boner problem either. Wearing his clothes and surrounded by his scent? I might come spontaneously soon.

"You're in luck!" he shouts from the kitchen. "Chicken tortilla soup coming up as soon as the microwave is done!"

"Thank you!" I shout back.

I hurry into bed, sitting against the pillows and headboard and draping his thick comforter over my lap and legs. A few moments later, he comes into the bedroom with a steaming bowl. He sits on the edge of the bed and hands the soup to me, putting a couple napkins on the nightstand too.

Before I can take my first spoonful, he puts his hand on my forehead. "You don't feel too hot," he says. "Is it more of a stomach thing?"

I taste the soup before answering. "It's more of an all-over thing. I've done this a few times where I work myself too hard and exhaustion kicks in and I feel like I have the flu but it only lasts a day. I'm pretty sure this is it."

He looks a little crestfallen. "I hope what we did last night didn't add to it. I'd hate to know I made you sick."

"No," I say quickly. "It's definitely not you. And that felt amazing and I wouldn't trade it for anything. Really, it's just the moving to a new city, setting up a store, and not getting much sleep. If I take it easy today, get lots of sleep, and be gentle to myself, I should be back up and running by tomorrow, maybe even by tonight."

"Okay," he says.

"This soup is delicious, by the way. You made this?" I ask.

He's beaming with a smile. "Sure did."

"I'm impressed! I like a man who can cook."

"I don't get to show off my cooking often, so I appreciate that. Thank you," he says. "I'll bring you some water before I head back to your store. If you need anything at all, just text or call me and your wish will be my command."

"Thank you."

He retrieves that promised glass of water, then gives me a kiss on the forehead as he hands it to me. "I'm off now to be the town's bookseller." A few moments later, the front door closes, and I'm alone in his house.

I don't know how I got so lucky here. Any guy back in Twilight Hollow would have just ditched me, but here Jacob is waiting on me hand and foot, eager for me to be as comfortable as possible so I get better. And I really want to get better quickly, especially if it means he'll fuck me again.

I put the empty bowl on the nightstand and slide down under the covers, bringing them up to my neck. His bed is amazingly comfortable. It doesn't take long for my eyes to drift closed and for me to fall into a deep sleep.

Sometime later—it could be twenty minutes or five hours for all I know, it was one of those deep naps where I lose all sense of time—Jacob's doorbell is ringing. I want to ignore it, but whoever it is keeps ringing it like it's an emergency.

Still incredibly groggy, I force myself out of bed and snatch up my phone off the nightstand. The doorbell is still ringing nonstop. I'm stumbling through his house, headed for the front door, if only to shout at whoever it is to stop ringing. God, it better not be Chad pestering me for details, or Kellan here to beg for help.

My phone is suddenly blaring in my hand, ringing loudly and

vibrating. My eyes are bleary, so I can't quite make out the name. It might be Jacob, though. I answer the call as I reach for the doorknob.

"Do not open the door!" Jacob's shouting voice comes through the phone.

But it's too late. The door is open.

Standing on his front step are two women. One is maybe twenty or thirty years older, and the other is quite a bit older and hunched over slightly. They both look kind of like Jacob.

"Jacob?" I say into the phone as I give them an awkward wave. "Who are these people?" I stumble over the words in my still-half-asleep state.

There's a very heavy sigh from the other end of the line. "That's my mom and nonna. Listen, I'm gonna close up your shop for the day since it's almost five and head right over there. Please, just…be patient with them, please."

"Um…okay."

I hear some muffled voices, like he's put his hand over the phone and he's talking to someone who's there. I can make out enough to know it's Chad asking where I am and Jacob telling him I'm here. Then he takes his hand off the phone and says to me, "I'll be there as soon as I can." The line goes dead, and I look up wide-eyed at his mom and nonna.

His mom is carrying a large paper grocery bag, filled with a bunch of things, with half a dozen tomatoes on a vine sticking out the top. She's looking down her nose at me, her gaze trailing down my body and back up. It's only now that I realize I'm wearing her son's clothes, with his number emblazoned across my chest.

His nonna gives me a similar look, then mutters something in Italian.

"Hello?" his mom says to me. "Who are you? Where's my son? Excuse me, please." She comes into the house, squeezing past me before I can step out of the way. Then his nonna comes in too.

His nonna says something in Italian. His mom looks at me and says, "You're dressed awfully casually for a housekeeper." Before I can reply, she hands the paper bag to me. "Put these in the kitchen. I'll be there in a moment to start cooking."

Stunned, I turn around and shamble into the kitchen, putting the bag on the island. My phone is blaring in my pocket again. I pull it out and swipe it open without even looking at it.

"Jacob," I say, "what's going on?"

"That's my question for you," says a voice that's definitely not Jacob.

"Chad?"

"In the flesh. Well, the audio flesh. But that's beside the point and the least important thing right now. *Did Jacob bang you last night, yes or no?*" Chad shouts into the phone.

"I don't have time for this," I angrily whisper. "His mom and nonna are here."

"Holy shit. You're meeting his family *already*? You move fast, brother. At least wait till the second date. Although you did meet his father *before* you got railed, so maybe you're just a premature family-meeter."

"It *wasn't* a date," I say, even though I know it very much was a date.

"You had drinks, you slept over, you likely got bred, you're meeting his family. How is that not a date?" Chad asks.

I groan in frustration. "I'm hanging up now, Chad. Goodbye. Please don't call for at least a few hours." Before he can say anything, I hit the button to end the call.

God, what do I do?

His mom comes into the kitchen. "Where's Jacob's Christmas tree? Surely he has one somewhere."

"Uh…" Do I tell her that his Christmas tree is at my store? Is he out to his mom? I need to play this straight. "I'm not sure."

She sighs. "I'll ask him when he gets here, then. I assume he's on his way?"

I nod.

His nonna walks in and says something very loud in Italian.

"I don't know where the tree is either, Ma!" his mom shouts back. "I don't think this housekeeper knows."

"I'm not a housekeeper," I say. My voice comes out all quivery, though; I find her intimidating.

She looks me up and down again. "You're dressed in sweats and in my son's old practice shirt. And you're in his house alone. Just who are you, exactly?"

Oh God, oh God. I can't tell her I slept with her son. Even if he's out to her, that's not something I would ever say to someone's mom. "Um…I'm just a friend. I wasn't feeling too well today so he told me to take a nap here while he takes care of my bookstore."

She eyes me up and down again. I really hate that look. "My son…lets some strange man stay in his house…while he runs a bookshop? I don't think my son has read a book since college. What's he doing running a bookshop?"

"I'm not some strange man, I'm…I'm a friend."

"What's your name?" his mom asks.

"I'm Edward."

His nonna says something in Italian, to which his mom shouts back, "No, not like *Twilight*, Ma!" Then to me, she says, "If you're sick, go lie down and rest. But if you're not going to do that, you can help make gravy."

"I, uh…" It's only now that I realize I'm feeling much better. That all-day nap cured everything.

She rolls her eyes. "Pull up a seat," she says, pointing at the stool tucked under the island. I do as instructed, and his nonna climbs onto the stool next to me.

"Hi," I say to her.

She says something in Italian to me.

"She can understand English," his mom says to me, "but only speaks Italian."

"Oh…okay…"

His mom starts unpacking the bag, spreading its contents over the island. There's a heck of a lot of tomatoes, garlic, onions, bundles of fresh herbs, and packages of fresh pasta. She sets a cutting board, sharp knife, and a bunch of garlic in front of me. "You can make yourself useful by peeling and mincing these."

"Sure…" I say. I set to work by breaking apart a head of garlic and then peeling the first clove. The skin is sticking to the garlic, and it's a nightmare to get off, even with a knife.

Beside me, his nonna mutters something. When I glance at her, she pulls the cutting board toward her and holds out her hands for the clove and knife I'm holding. I give them to her, and she puts the clove on the board and gives it a little crush with the knife, then peels the skin off in one easy motion. She slides the board and everything back to me.

"Thank you?" I say.

I try to do what she did—crushing a clove under the knife—and it is indeed easier to peel. I don't have the natural quickness she does, but maybe with some practice I can get it going. I proceed onto the next clove, and it goes a little easier. She mutters something that sounds vaguely like approval, and I can't help but smile to myself.

Then I hear the click of the front door being opened.

Chapter Ten
Do You Like Me, Little Mouse?

JACOB

I walk up my driveway and see the rental car that my mom drove here, along with Edward's car parked beside it. I wonder what she's said to him so far. Hopefully nothing completely mortifying. My phone is ringing in my pocket, which means it's either Linley, or my dad—I'm not answering for either person right now.

When I unlock the door and walk inside, I'm smacked in the face with the smell of my mom's gravy, and the sight of Edward at the counter standing next to my nonna. He's wearing the comfy clothes I gave him this morning. My mom rounds the corner with her hands on her hips. "Hello, Mother. Nice of you to tell me you were coming for a visit."

She squishes my cheeks together with both hands, lightly tapping them. "Where is your tree? Your nonna almost had a heart attack when she realized you didn't have one."

I decide to rephrase my question and steal a glance at Edward. I look back at my mother. "Hello, Mother, why didn't you tell me you were coming for a visit. And why are you here?"

She whacks me lightly on the shoulder. "Linley said she mentioned it to you, and so did your father. Does a mother need to tell her son that she's coming to visit? Isn't your house my house?"

"No, Mom, it's not." I chuckle and walk toward my nonna. I want to talk to Edward, and see how he's feeling, but I need to say hi to my nonna first. I lean down and squeeze her tightly.

"Where is your tree? And who is this man?" she asks me in Italian.

I look up at Edward. "She wants to know who you are and where my tree is. Did you guys not do introductions?" I look at my mother. Unbelievable. I hope she hasn't been completely horrible to him.

Edward answers, "We did. I didn't catch your mom's name, and I now know that is your nonna, who also likes *Twilight*." He gives me a nervous smile. He looks better than this morning, he doesn't look as tired. I don't know how that's possible, because being around my mom is exhausting enough on its own.

"We introduced ourselves…didn't we?" my mom asks Edward.

He looks panicked. "Leave him alone, Mom." I turn to my nonna and say in Italian, "This is someone I like, his name is Edward."

My nonna and mother both look at one another then turn their gazes toward Edward. I walk around the counter and pull him by the hand. "I'm gonna go talk to him in my room quickly. I'm not eating whatever you're making, by the way. I had a cheat night last night," I shout over my shoulder.

"Well, Edward helped us make this, so do you really want to make your friend upset? He's never made gravy before, he told me so," my mom says.

I stop and turn toward her before going into my room. "I think you know very well that I'm not going to break my diet for anything."

I lead Edward into my room and close the door once we're both inside, gesturing for him to sit on the bed. "I am so, so sorry. How are you feeling?" I ask him, touching his forehead with the back of my hand.

He smiles up at me. "I'm feeling much better as far as the exhaustion, but I feel like I'm in some kind of a weird world right now. I mean, the past twenty-four hours have been crazy."

I feel so bad right now. I told him he could rest here, and then my mom came and ruined everything. "Did you get to rest? Was my mom horrible to you?"

He's shaking his head and rubbing his hands on my comforter. "No, but I don't speak Italian, so I have no idea what they were saying about me. I just caught the thing about *Twilight* because your mom said it. What did you say to her when she asked you who I was?"

"Oh, I told her I liked you. I didn't say anything else, just that you were someone I like. Sorry they were talking in Italian in front of you. My nonna doesn't speak English. But my mom—I think I told you she can be a bit snobby."

He chuckles. "She kinda pushed past me and I think she may have assumed I was your housekeeper. I was half asleep, but she was nice after a few minutes. Does your mom know that you're gay? I wasn't sure what to tell her when she asked who I was."

"Wait, first off, she does know I'm gay, not really by choice, but it's— she knows. What would you have told her if you had that information beforehand? I'm just curious."

"Well, obviously, I would have said, your son and I first met during a bathroom hookup at the gay bar, but more recently he railed me pretty hard last night and he will in fact break his diet for my ass, he told me so himself. So, I guess I'm someone he likes sleeping with. That would have been fine, right?"

I can't even hold back from laughing. His delivery was perfect, totally deadpan, matter-of-fact-like. "Well, she probably gathered those things from me saying I like you, and you wearing my practice shirt. She likely asked if you were the housekeeper to see if you were gonna say we were sleeping together."

"Oh, well, then I'm glad I didn't say anything. I just told her I was a friend. You saying that you liked me would be enough for her to understand that we are sleeping together, well, slept together? If I said that, I don't think my mom would know that meant I was sleeping with someone."

I lean down and kiss his lips quickly. "I don't like that many people."

His eyes widen, and his look becomes somewhat inquisitive. I ruffle his hair. "Ah. I only *like* you right now. It looked like you were wondering who else I like. But I meant in general, most people annoy me. You would be the exception. So, my mom and my nonna both understood what I meant when I said that."

"You know, you haven't asked if I like you. Do you just assume that I do?"

I nod at him. "Yeah, I do. Same as I assume that you wouldn't oppose to sleeping here with me again tonight. But I can ask if you want me to." I lift his chin and bring my mouth in front of his and whisper, "So, do you like me, little mouse?"

He's nodding at me, while staring deep into my eyes. "I do like you."

He stands from the bed and moves in closer, hanging his arms around my neck, while I pull him in close. "Do you want to stay the night with me again?"

"Mmhmm, I do." He moves his mouth closer to mine. His breath is tickling my lips.

Fuck—being this close to him has got me so hard. I kiss him softly, only allowing my tongue to touch his briefly. "We have to get rid of my mother and my nonna. Then we can hang out. Do you want to rest a little more? I can go back out there with them and you can stay in here. I'm gonna get lectured anyway. Also, you don't have to eat whatever she's making. We'd have to make up some dietary restrictions, though. She and my nonna would take offense to you not eating. But I can get you out of it."

"No, I'm feeling better and I'm excited to eat what she's making. I helped with the garlic. I think I saw your nonna smile at me a few times."

"I'm sure she'll really smile at you, if you talk to her about *Twilight*."

"Oh, about getting rid of them for the night, I feel like I should mention that your mom said—"

My doorbell chimes loudly from my phone. "Now who's here?" I lean my head back at the sight of my father holding what looks like two bouquets of flowers in one hand and some kind of a box in the other. How is this happening right now?

"Let me guess, it's your dad? That's what I was gonna tell you. Your mom said he was coming tonight."

"Holy shit. This is so embarrassing. You don't have to stay. This is a lot, even for me. My parents haven't even been around each other outside of soccer matches in years. I have no idea what this is gonna be like."

He giggles. "I love awkward parental situations. I'm all in on this, but I'm gonna get changed. So, I'll meet you out there in a few?"

I nod at him, while leaving the room. "If you want to escape through the window, just let me know and I'll turn the alarm off."

First guy I've liked in…Oh, I don't know, forever? And he's already met my parents and my nonna. This is not the way I imagined this going. I don't know how something like this even happens.

My mom is locked in an embrace with my dad, standing in the front entrance. Once they break from their extra-long hug, my dad notices me. He's walking toward me with his arms open. "Jacob!"

I take a step backward. "Hello, nice of you to tell me that you were coming over, Father." I turn toward my mom. "And you, nice of you to invite him over here without telling me, Mother."

"Why is he calling me Father?" my dad asks my mom. "Are you always 'Mother' when he talks to you?"

She waves her hand toward me. "He does that when he's upset or annoyed, which is all the time," she cackles. "So many mood swings from our little bambino."

"Okay, stop," I say looking over my shoulder. "I have my own guest that I invited here, I did not invite either of you. Can I just pay for you guys to go eat at a restaurant or something?"

"What guest?" my dad asks looking around me. "A friend from Miami? I thought you were being extra careful—"

My dad's line of questioning or whatever that was turning into, is cut off by Edward walking out of my room. He looks so damn sexy. This guy—he's so innocent, but he's dangerous for me…he's like a cocktail of desire and desperation, and I'm beyond wasted.

What the hell is happening to me? I never feel these things. Any thoughts I had of keeping this man at arm's length are long gone. I swear I like him more every time I see him. Even now with him walking toward me, I'm worried about making sure he's comfortable here. Well, that and I am definitely thinking about the different ways I want to wreck him later.

"Edward," my dad says. "I wasn't expecting to see you here." He whispers loudly to my mother, for everyone to hear. "This is the strange man you were texting me about?"

My mom throws her hands up in frustration. "Well, forgive me. I was not expecting to see him here in Jacob's house. Of course, our son couldn't be bothered to answer his phone, however, he had the time to call Edward, who was asleep, and tell him I was at the front door."

"Stop, stop, stop," I say. "I wasn't expecting any of you to come here. So, I don't know how any of *you* are surprised. Edward is here right now, because I invited him, he was asleep here earlier, because he wasn't feeling well this morning. Now that you're here, I have to change our plans for tonight."

My father looks like he's piecing everything together. He points at me and Edward. "You just met, and he stayed the night last night? Must have really liked the job you did at the bookstore. I may need to get into construction if it's that easy to get laid once you finish a job," he chuckles.

Edward elbows me. "Well, technically we met at the Halloween party, but I didn't reali—"

Oh no, no, no. I drop my head forward and Edward covers his mouth mid-sentence. "Sorry. I didn't mean to say anything I wasn't supposed to."

I don't even want to look up, but I don't want him to think I'm upset. "It's okay," I say.

"You went to Bottoms Up?" my dad asks. "Or a different party?"

My mom crosses her arms. "The gay bar? You said you definitely weren't going. Linley didn't mention that you changed your mind."

I don't even know which of them to reply to first. I exhale and lean my head back in frustration. My nonna shouts over in Italian, "Linley is not his babysitter! She works for him, not the other way around. Leave them alone."

My mother rolls her eyes. "Ma, give me a break, he can't be going to places like that without telling his agent." She points at me. "You told me you weren't going. You changed your mind?"

I nod and place my hand on the small of Edward's back. I don't want him to feel bad about saying anything. I'm gonna have to do something I really wasn't planning on doing. "It doesn't matter how we met, or where we met, or who was doing what to whom while wearing a wolf mask, so that their identity was hidden. Just drop it." My mother looks like she's gonna have some more to say. I point at her and speak in Italian, "You will not make him feel uncomfortable. He's a good guy, don't put me in a bad position here. We've only just started hanging out. He's safe, I promise. Drop it."

My mother nods at me and my nonna gives a little clap of approval.

"You were wearing a wolf mask at the party? That *was* the Bottoms Up party. I saw you, too. I'm glad I didn't go into the bathroom," my dad says.

"The bathroom?" my mom echoes. "He wouldn't have done anything in the bathr—"

I raise my eyebrows at her and shake my head.

"Well," my dad says. "These flowers are for you, Francesca, and these are for you," he says as he passes the second bouquet of flowers to my nonna.

My nonna accepts the flowers and gives him a small insincere sort of smile. I don't actually know how she feels about my dad. She's never really talked about him. My nonna is waving the flowers at my father and walking toward the trash can. She gives him a wide false smile then drops the flowers inside.

"Ma! You can't throw away perfectly good flowers!" My mom rushes toward the trash can and my nonna turns around, ignoring her. She pulls the flowers out of the trash and slips them out of the plastic covering. She's shouting at my nonna in Italian, while my dad is staring over with the stupidest look on his face.

"Does your nonna not like roses?" my dad asks me.

My nonna shouts over in Italian. "No, I don't like *you!*"

"Ma!" my mother shouts, peeking her head up from beneath the counter. "Jacob, where are the vases? You have vases, I know you do."

I drop an eyebrow at her. "I don't think that's a thing that I know, so I don't think you do either. I'm pretty sure I don't have any vases and if I do, I haven't unpacked them yet. Maybe there's one in the garage, but I doubt it."

"I don't speak Italian," my dad says to me. "It seems like your nonna doesn't like me, but why not?"

"Uhhh." I shrug at him. "I've never heard her talk about you. Seeing you around my mom is throwing me off. My nonna hasn't ever said anything about you."

My nonna shouts in Italian, "He asked for salt when I served him spaghetti!"

"Oh, you're ridiculous," my mom says to my nonna. "You can't be mad about something that happened over twenty years ago." She's clipping the stems of the flowers. "These are beautiful, Dick. Is the florist in town?"

My dad smiles at her. "No, it's on the outside of town. What did I do twenty years ago?"

"Let it go," my mom says. "The gravy is almost ready."

My dad lifts the small white box in his hands up. "I also stopped and grabbed some pastries from the Italian bakery outside of town. I know you used to really like cannoli."

My mom takes the box from his hands and carries it into the kitchen. "That was nice of you. Flowers and cannoli—what, do you wanna sleep with me? That's not happening. Once I get off a ride, I'm off, I'm not getting back on, Dick."

Edward and I laugh, while my dad covers his mouth. I don't think she realizes how that sounded.

"Were you ever off?" my dad asks.

My mom's mouth is hanging open. "Of course I was off, that was ages ago! I mean there was that one time during Jacob's—"

"Shhh, don't finish that sentence," my dad says. "I meant—"

"What? What one time during Jacob's what?" I ask.

"Ah you see!" my nonna says.

Edward whispers in my ear, "What's going on? Your nonna hates your dad, but he has no idea why? And what else? I'm having trouble keeping up."

I squeeze his hand and shrug. "I have no idea, but I'm sorry you're seeing all this. I'll have to make it up to you later."

"Can we still watch the next *Twilight* after they leave?" he whispers.

His breath is sending shockwaves to my dick. I can't let him keep whispering like this. Thankfully, my mom and dad have moved over to the kitchen to continue their discussion with my nonna. As much as I want to know what's going on, I'm gonna need to lay a few ground rules here with Edward.

I turn to face him, placing both hands on his shoulders. I whisper in his ear, "I will watch whatever you want, and I will do whatever you want, sexually, but right now, I need you to stop whispering in my ear. I find it very hard to control myself around you, and your breath on my earlobe is more than I can handle right now. So, we'll make a deal, no more whispering and no judging whatever this insanity with my parents is, and I will do *anything* you want for the next twenty-four hours."

His gaze shifts left to right, then meets mine. He takes my hands off his shoulders and says quietly, "Then no touching me, because it's not any easier for me. Before I agree to this, I can have you do anything I want for twenty-four hours as long as I don't whisper while they're here or judge you? That's it? You'll do whatever I want?"

He's so cute. He has no idea how wrapped around his finger I already am. Not that I understand it, so I guess I wouldn't expect him to either. I nod at him. "Yep. That's the deal. Twenty-four hours, I'll be your personal property to do whatever you want with. But I do have to work tomorrow, so maybe we keep this as a before and after work thin—"

He cuts me off, shaking his head. "Nope. You said twenty-four hours; it can't just be outside of work hours. That hardly seems fair."

I back up a step and raise my eyebrows at him. "Wow. Challenging me already." I step closer and place my hands behind my back, bringing my mouth next to his ear. "I love being challenged. Let's see if you can challenge me like this later, when you're on your knees, little mouse."

He places a hand on my chest and looks to the left. My mom, dad, and nonna are all staring over. I'm not sure if I missed something, but my mom has already poured wine for the three of them. There are two empty glasses in front of her, and the bottle is just sitting there open.

I give them all a small smile and walk toward the bar. "Did you finish your discussion? I still need to make my dinner." I glance quickly at Edward. "I'm definitely having dessert tonight, so it's best if I eat now. Don't want to get too hungry." I pick the bottle up and look at Edward. His cheeks are a little flushed. He looks like he's trying not to react to what I said. "Do you want red wine? Or do you have a taste for something else?"

I watch his shoulders rise as he takes a large breath in. "I would really like some red wine, Jacob. I thought you had dessert last night; can you have something that sweet two nights in a row?"

"Jacob ate something sweet?" my mom asks Edward. She opens my fridge and looks inside. "Since when do you break your diet for dessert?"

I slide Edward's glass to him and pour myself a very small amount. I like this game he's playing with me. We're not talking about food at this point, and only the two of us know it. He's really so funny.

"Wait, forget about dessert. You're not gonna eat the pasta?" my dad asks.

"Nope. I cheated last night. I ate so much and I'm really craving what I had again, so just to be safe I need to put something else in my mouth, or I'm gonna be tempted."

My dad shakes his head at me. "I don't know how you do it. I can't stay disciplined when it comes to food. I can swear off a lot of things, but not food. Wait, what about Edward?" He turns toward him. "Do you have a special diet, too? You're in good shape. What are you eating tonight?"

Edward is sipping his wine while staring at me. His gaze flicks to my dad. "I don't have a special diet. I don't know how Jacob does it, either. Although with how much he ate last night—"

"Pftt." I nearly spit my wine out as I cough loudly. He's looking at me like he has no idea what he just said. He's just happily sipping his wine. I grab a napkin and wipe my mouth.

"Are you okay, honey?" my mom asks me.

I hold a hand up to her. "I'm fine. I'm just not used to people making such a big deal about what I eat." I look at Edward. "You liked what I ate last night, too, right? I feel like there was one point that you were almost squeaking about it."

Edward coughs and covers his mouth.

I quirk an eyebrow at him. "Are you okay? I'll have to make sure that you get that again really soon."

"Concede," he whispers. "I concede." He giggles and finishes off his wine.

"Food is ready for everyone that's eating," my mom says.

After everyone has their plates, I sit on the stool beside Edward and rub his thigh under the counter. I'm actually not very hungry anymore. Well, I'm hungry, but not for food.

He looks down at my hand while eating his pasta. "I own you for twenty-four hours," he whispers beside my ear. "And you're not allowed to touch me while your parents are here. Remember?"

He doesn't realize what he just did. I smirk at him. "You just lost your rights to that deal when you whispered in my ear. But I'll overlook it just this once."

"You touched me first, anyway," he says with a chuckle. "But, I have a real question. Is it okay to compliment the food your mom and nonna made? I don't want to say the wrong thing."

"Of course. They'd both like that."

"This is absolutely delicious," Edward says. "Thank you both for letting me make the gravy with you."

My nonna smiles and glances at his plate from the other side of the bar. His food is almost gone, which I'm sure is the reason she's smiling.

"Thank you," my mom says. She looks at my dad, who is eating at a slow, leisurely pace. "Is there anything wrong with the food? Or is this the speed you normally eat? I seem to remember you being a speedy eater."

"Depends on what I'm eating," my dad chuckles. "Some things need to be savored."

My nonna drops an eyebrow at him and mumbles in Italian. She just called him an ungrateful pig. Thankfully, he didn't understand her, so he's just smiling obliviously, while he eats his food.

"What were you two planning to do tonight?" my dad asks me.

"Just hanging out. We watched *Twilight* last night because it's Edward's favorite, and tonight we're going to watch another one. So, the sooner you guys leave, the better."

My nonna smiles and stands up from the counter. She points to the TV and walks into the living room, taking a seat on my couch. "I'm ready!" she says in Italian.

No, no, no. I cannot have them all here watching a movie with us. I need to get Edward naked and in my bed, as soon as possible. How do I get them to leave? I'll try to whisper to my mom, maybe. I stand from my stool and take Edward's empty plate, bringing it around to the sink with me. "Mom," I whisper. "It's nice that you guys are here, and I'm happy-ish to see you, but it's only the second time that Edward and I have really hung out. Are you planning on staying the night here?"

My mom looks over her shoulder at Edward and then glances at my father. "I thought I could leave your nonna here and I'd go home with your father. It's only one night."

I shake my head at her. "Absolutely not."

She lightly whacks me with a dish towel. "Honey, I'm kidding. Your father has extra room, and he invited us to stay there. But are you really sure you know what you're doing? I'm a little worried about you letting someone stay over two nights in a row. People in the town will start talking…"

I nod at her. "I know what I'm doing."

"Alright. I'll be quiet," she says. "But *you* are gonna tell your nonna that you're not watching *Twilight* with her. She's isn't going to be in a rush to get to your dad's place. I had no idea she was harboring a grudge against your father over something so ridiculous. First time she's mentioned that in at least ten years."

My father stands and walks his plate over, leaving Edward sitting at the bar alone. "You want me to take these two out of here, so you and Edward can get a little wedding night action going?" he asks me.

My mom laughs loudly. "Wedding night?"

"Yeah, in one of the movies they get married and have crazy sex."

"Oh, Dick," she says, giggling. "I think they just want to watch a movie. Not every man is as anxious to get into bed as you are."

He moves a bit closer toward my mom. "Well, he is my son, so I'm gonna guess, based on the fact that you said Edward was already here when you arrived, that he was probably recovering from whatever they got into last night. The bigger question is, what are we going to do with your mom so we can get into our own trouble tonight?"

"Oh, disgusting. Please leave," I say to them, and head for Edward.

I'm not allowed to touch him until they leave and everything in me wants to. I sit beside him and smile, folding my hands on the counter. "Sorry, hopefully, they're leaving soon, but we'll wait to start the movie until after they're gone."

He rubs a finger along my forearm. "I'm allowed to touch you, right? I just can't whisper?"

I raise my eyebrows at him. "I don't think you should."

"How sensitive to my touch are you?" he asks, tracing his finger along my tattoo. "Jacob, I really want your parents to leave."

Holy shit, my dick instantly responded to that. I'm so fucked. I can't sit here hard with my parents in the room. I suck my lips in and point at his empty wine glass, then clear my throat. "Do I have the wine to thank for this?"

"Nope. You have your big dick to thank for this."

I bring my mouth beside his ear, being careful not to touch him. "You really wanna tease me when my parents are standing right there? I wouldn't recommend it."

"You can't threaten me. I own you for twenty-four hours."

"Oh, little mouse, I owned you the second you dropped to your knees in that bathroom."

He blows air from his mouth and moves his face from mine. The corner of his mouth curves upward in a sort of smirk. He places his hand on my leg, inching slowly toward my dick.

My eyes widen. "Be careful. Don't do that unless you're prepared to be teased later. You have no idea the level of restraint I have."

"Like handcuffs or ropes?" he asks, just a little too loudly.

My dad's head turns toward us. "Kinky."

I hold a hand up toward my dad, telling him to stop. "No. Not kinky. We were talking about two different things."

My dad walks over to us with the craziest grin on his face. "Do you want me to get them out of here?"

Edward's fingertips are lightly grazing my dick through my pants. This is torture.

I nod emphatically. "Yes. Yes, please. No questions. Just go, I'll do whatever you want."

"No, you won't," Edward says. "I own—"

I cover his mouth with my hand and look at my dad. "Please go, like as soon as possible."

My dad grabs the small box of pastries off the counter. "Why don't we take these back to my place?" he asks my mom. "We can watch a movie there and talk about old times. Jacob gets up early for the gym, he's probably anxious to get to bed."

My mom drops an eyebrow at me. "I might not see you tomorrow before we leave, are you in that much of a rush to get rid of me?"

"Yes. I am." I can't stand because my dick is so hard right now, there's no way for me to adjust it without being completely obvious.

My nonna stands from the couch and walks toward me. Damn it. I exhale and look at Edward then glance down at his hand, that's resting on my cock. "You're gonna pay for this later."

"Are you gonna choke me? I'd like that."

My eyes feel like they might fall out of my head. I want to say no, but I just shake my head, while my mouth hangs open like an idiot.

My nonna hugs me and whispers in my ear. "I think you can trust this one. He seems good."

I smile and hug her back. Then she gives Edward a polite wave, grabs her purse off the bar and walks toward the door.

My dad hangs an arm loosely around my mom's neck and whispers something in her ear. I honestly don't even want to think about whatever it was, based on the way my mom is smiling, but at least she's walking with him toward the door, flowers in hand. I would like to point out that she hasn't even said goodbye to me, but this is pretty typical for her. She says she came here to check on me, but obviously she came to see my dad.

"Bye, Bambino," she finally says over her shoulder as she steps outside. "Oh, and goodbye, Edward. Was nice to meet you."

Now that they've all left, I look down at Edward's hand. "You are in so much trouble."

CHAPTER ELEVEN
CHOKE ME.
JUST A LITTLE.

   JACOB   

"A little bit of trouble sounds okay to me," he says and leans in toward my lips.

As much as I like him, there are things I won't do, just because this, whatever this is, is still a bit too new. I tap my pointer finger against his lips. "How drunk are you? I can't fuck you if you're drunk, despite what my dick is telling your hand right now."

He's shaking his head at me, while my finger rubs against his bottom lip. "I'm not drunk. I had one glass of wine," he says, then starts licking the side of my finger, while rubbing me through my pants.

I'm pretty sure he isn't drunk, but I *need to be* sure. "How much does it typically take to get you drunk?" I ask him. Fuck. The way he's licking my finger…my restraint is really slipping here.

"Oh, I get it. You're trying to make sure I'm not drunk because you're worried about consent? Is that it?" He sucks my finger into his mouth and stares into my eyes.

I nod at him. "Mmhmm. Consent all the way."

He pulls my finger from his mouth and brings his lips close to mine. "Jacob…" he murmurs, making my name sound like a filthy invitation. "Jacob Rizzo…I want to be fucked by you. You have my consent to do anything you want to me. I am not drunk." He kisses my lips softly, sending chills up my spine and a rush of pleasure straight to my dick. "What is it going to take for you to fuck me? I'm begging you to trust me. I'm not drunk. I even asked you to choke me earlier, did you think I was drunk when I said that? I told you I wasn't." He kisses me softly again.

I stand up from the stool and take him by the hand, bringing him toward my couch.

"If you're taking me outside for a sobriety test, that's really not necessary."

I grab his face, pulling him close, and kiss him, then pull back for just a moment. "Shhh. I know you're not drunk now." I press my mouth against his again and slide my tongue inside, kissing him deeper, wildly licking the entirety of his mouth, desperately swallowing the taste of him, while he moans, grabbing at my belt.

I pull his bottom lip between my teeth, staring into his eyes. I want him so badly.

He tugs my pants down and firmly wraps his hand around my cock. My head drops back when he cups my balls and squeezes them lightly, bringing his mouth beside my ear. "Jacob, will you fuck me now?" he whispers.

I grab the back of his head, gripping a fistful of his shaggy hair. "On your knees, little mouse. Show me how bad you want me."

Edward drops to his knees, so fucking obediently. He wastes no time taking my cock deep into his throat. My eyes close instinctively and my cock pulses, already leaking pre-cum into his mouth. His sucking becomes more intense, and he looks up at me, pulling my dick out of his mouth. "Mmm, I've been dying to taste your cum. I want more," he begs, closing his eyes and taking me deep again.

I thread my fingers through the top of his hair, petting him while he sucks my cock like a fiend. "I want you to ride me." I step back lightly, and he grips my cock tighter, jerking and sucking, making the sloppiest noises. He's not backing off, and I'm finding it hard to pull away. If he wants my cum in his mouth, it's only a matter of minutes until he gets it.

He takes me deep into his throat again and whimpers when I push just a bit too far. I grip his hair lightly, and he makes eye contact with me. "Ride me, Edward. I'm not asking."

He nods and pulls my cock from his mouth. "Mmm, gladly," he says, as he stands and strips from the waist down. I reach into the end table and pull out the lube and a condom.

He makes a strange face at me, when I close the drawer. "I don't like that," he mumbles.

I pull his shirt off, sliding it over his head. "You don't like what?"

"Nothing. Never mind," he says, kissing me and pushing my body onto the couch. He straddles me and pulls my shirt over my head.

I lean forward and suck his nipple. I love the way he feels in my arms. I can't find a place for my hands to settle because I just want to touch all of him, to rub all of him—all at once.

"I'm in charge, right?" he asks.

I glance at the time, grazing his nipple with my teeth when I pull back. "You're in charge until 8:37 tomorrow night." I lean in toward his nipple, holding his chest with one hand, and squeezing his ass with the other. He's guiding my hand to his neck.

"Do it. Choke me. Just a little."

My thumb strokes his Adam's apple, and I shake my head softly at him. I won't do it. I can't. I slide my hand around the back of his head, massaging my fingers through his hair, then grab the lube from beside us. I get my fingers and his hole nice and wet and begin massaging him. "You're tight, little mouse."

He looks at me briefly with something like disappointment or confusion. Whatever it is, I refuse to have that look on his face when I'm getting ready to fuck him. I pull him closer, allowing easier access to his ass, and lick his neck, while I finger him.

"Mmm," he moans. He reaches beside me and grabs the condom, tearing it open with his teeth, then covers my dick with it.

I squeeze his waist, my fingers holding tight onto him while he positions himself onto my cock. Once the head finally pushes inside, he relaxes a bit, slowly rising up and down, while I guide him, matching my thrusts with his pace. He turns his face away, wincing every time we fully connect. I turn his face toward mine, rubbing my finger across his bottom lip. "Look at me. I want to see your face while you ride me." I've never wanted someone to look at me so desperately, and with him, fuck—he makes me crave something even deeper. His big brown eyes do something to me. I wrap my arms around him, sliding my hands up his back. His head drops back, while he grinds harder, his hole clenches tighter, squeezing my dick with every thrust. He's riding my cock like it's the sole purpose he was created for. I grip his ass cheeks and reposition myself, lifting him. He lets out a little squeak and I raise my eyebrows. "Ah, there it is." I knew I wasn't hitting his spot. I press into him again using the same angle.

His hands scratch at my chest, and his head drops back again. "Haah—oh fuck—mmm."

"You want more? Do you want to come?"

He nods at me, with his eyes half lidded.

"Look at me. Tell me what you want. Say it, or you don't get it."

"I'm in charge. You're my slave right now," he says.

I stand from the couch and lift him, keeping my cock buried inside. His breath hitches, when I place him down and grind into him. Looking down at him, with his legs wrapped around my body, I ask, "Who's in charge, little mouse?"

"Fuck—Jacob. You—you are."

"That's right." I pound into him, watching his body writhe in pleasure beneath mine. I want to do more than make him come. I want to mark him from the inside. It's primal and fierce this feeling. My cock is ramming into his prostate, and he squeaks out my name, "Ja—cob."

"Say my fucking name. Say it and I'll fill you right now."

"Fuck—Jacob—I'm coming—Jacob—ungh—"

The feeling of his hole tightening on my cock, as his cum shoots in between us, brings forth a wave of pleasure, and I come while buried deep inside of him. "Fuck yes—mmm, that's a good little mouse."

My head drops on the armrest beside his head. "Thanks for helping me break in my new couch," I say and kiss him on the cheek. That's kind of funny, now that I say it out loud. A few minutes ago, I was dreaming of a way to mark him from the inside, and now he's basically marked my couch. I don't think I'll ever be able to sit on it again without picturing him. Fuck. My head is so messed up right now, I don't—all the walls that I've built up are just—they're cracking. He kisses my cheek and rubs his fingers on my back.

"I'm sorry," he says.

I lift my head and look down at him. "What are you talking about? Why would you be sorry?"

"I saw you take the condom and the lube out of the drawer and I just—I got so upset, jealous, angry, I don't even know what to call it. I just, I hated thinking of all the people you'd probably slept with on this couch."

I shake my head and slide out. "Me? What have I done that would make you think that I've fucked a lot of people? What would make you think that I'd had sex with so many people on my couch?" His arm is draped across his forehead, and he's not answering me. I grab my shirt off the floor and wipe the cum off his abs. "Come on," I say, pulling him with me toward the bathroom. I toss the condom into the trash and turn the shower on. "Silly little mouse. I haven't had sex with anyone else in this house…I also haven't had sex with anyone else since I had sex with you at the bar."

"I am so dumb. I'm sorry. I just assumed. I don't know how to be in a relationship, or if this is technically a relationship. I'm feeling things for you that are pretty confusing."

I slide the glass shower door open, and we both step inside. As the water washes down my face, I'm reminded of the conversation that I've had with myself at least twenty times since meeting him. I can't be in a relationship with him. I can't be in a relationship with anyone. It will only hurt him. I don't want to hurt him, but I want to be around him and spend time with him. This shouldn't be so hard. I grab the shampoo and wash my hair. "I'm not sure what to call this, honestly. I just, I can't really be in a relationship because of my job."

"Your job as a contractor?"

"Pftt. No. My actual job as a soccer player. There are so many rules and so many things I have to follow. It would take me so long to explain it all to you."

He takes my hand softly in his. "Tell me. I want to know."

I squeeze his hand and give him a smile, while letting out a sigh. "Thank you for that. I think we should wash off and maybe head to bed, though. It's a bit much to try and explain. You're not familiar with any of it, so it will all sound crazy to you." I grab the bath pouf and squeeze some body wash on it, quickly scrubbing myself down. I notice there's another bath pouf on the opposite side of the shower. I point to it. "When did that get here?"

He picks it up and winces. "Ah, that's mine. I grabbed it out of my suitcase earlier."

I watch as he begins scrubbing his body down. His tattoos are gorgeous, and watching him clean himself is mesmerizing. I'd almost forgotten about the uncomfortable conversation we were having. "So, are you gonna tell me?" he asks.

I rinse my body off and kiss him on the forehead. "Come to bed after you're done and we can talk. I can't focus on anything right now. Between your ass and your tattoos, I'm not really able to think properly. At this point, I just want to eat you out. And I have a client pretty early in the morning, so I should get to bed."

"Okay. I'm just gonna rinse the soap off. I'll meet you in there."

I walk over to my sink and brush my teeth. I'm not sure how much of this to tell him, and since I've never talked about it with anyone who didn't really understand my status, I have no idea what to expect. I've also never had this particular talk with anyone, so I'm a bit nervous.

I walk into my room with my towel around my waist and grab a pair of briefs and sweatpants out of my dresser and quickly put them on.

Once I climb into bed, Edward walks into my room. His towel is slung low and wrapped tightly around his hips. I watch as he opens his suitcase and rummages around, finally pulling out underwear and comfy pants. He drops his towel like it's the most natural thing to do, like being naked around me doesn't bother him at all. Once he's dressed, he slides into bed beside me. "Now, what's all the stuff that I won't understand?"

I tap his nose with my finger and turn toward him. "Where do I even start? I mean, the thing is that being in a relationship has always been something that I've always known would have to come second to soccer. I've never had a problem with that. I focus on my job and at being the best and that's really all I have to do. With a relationship, that means asking someone that I care about to sacrifice our time together on a pretty constant basis. It means that this person has to share me with other people, and I have to do the same. People don't see me as a person, I'm just seen as an athlete, a commodity. My agent has always been pretty overbearing but after the suspension, she's gotten so much worse."

"If she's that bad, can't you get a different one?"

"Well, yes and no. She's under contract, so no, but yeah, I could always break it. I would never do that, though. Linley truly has my best interest at heart. I know this just based on what happened in the last few months. She did so much for me to be here, away from the public right now. I don't know what I'd do if she weren't my agent. I don't keep anything from her. Well, I didn't until you. She doesn't know about you yet."

"Well, what's there to tell? You said earlier you weren't sure what to call this, so why would she need to know?"

"I tell her everything. It's how she knows I won't ever cause trouble. Oh, and that choking thing—I can't do that. Imagine for a moment that you were someone who wanted to take advantage of me."

"I could never."

"Yes, I believe you, I do. But imagine that you were. If I left fingerprints on you, my career would be over in an instant. In the court of public opinion, there's rarely a fair trial. People would see those marks and automatically assume I hurt you. Then there's the whole thing about never having any privacy. We talked a bit about that, but it's so much worse than you're imagining. People will judge you and your looks on a constant basis, they'll judge the way I play as a reflection of your influence on me. So, if I screw up, it will be your fault because they'll imagine some random thing happened. If I play well, then people will say that you had something to do with that. People get jealous of those in relationships with athletes and celebrities. They feel like they have some sort of a weird claim on me. When I got suspended, you should have seen the cards that people sent to me, they feel personally connected to me without knowing me. Sometimes that's nice and sometimes it's pretty terrifying. I can't—I couldn't allow all of those things to happen to you."

"Wow. That is a lot. I mean, is it really...all that bad? I've never experienced anything like that, so I want to understand it, just—"

"It just sounds crazy?"

"Well, not just that, but I mean I'm used to guys making up excuses and this doesn't sound like an excuse not to be with me, but it definitely sounds crazy."

I rub his face softly. I find it hard to believe that anyone would lie to get out of being with him. He's got such an honest face; it's one of the things that draws me closer to him. "That's another one of the reasons I'm hesitating here. I told you I like you, and I do. I just can't pull you into all this without you understanding what you're getting into. And I'm not really offering to pull you into it, because I don't think it's fair, but at the same time, I know that I can't stop thinking about you and part of me just wants to give in to that and say fuck it...but I have so many obligations, there's so much to consider. I need to think, but that's hard when you're lying so close to me."

"I mean, if we're not really in a relationship, then do you even have to tell your agent? I think that's the part I don't understand. Does she kind of judge what's best for you, and you do whatever she says?"

"Pfftt." I laugh and place my hands behind my head turning onto my back. "She wishes. I wouldn't be here right now if I listened to her. I do have to tell her about you, though. To be honest, I should have already done that."

"Why does it matter, though?"

"Well, by the loosest of standards we *are* in a relationship. I mean I've had sex with you a few times now, and you've met my parents. The latter was not really by choice, but it still happened. I've been ignoring her texts and calls for the past two days, which is how the mom stopping by thing bit me in the ass. She would have warned me of that. Either way, you said guys are always lying and making up excuses for not wanting to be in a relationship with you, that's not what's happening here. I'm gonna tell her about you. She's gonna freak out, though. Then she'll run a background check, dive into all your personal history, you name it."

He pulls his head back and his eyes widen. "Are you joking?"

I shake my head. "Not one bit. And if you think her doing those things is bad, you should be really happy we didn't meet in Miami, your face would have been everywhere online by now. I only have the freedom to hang out with you like this because I'm here. So, maybe for now, we just enjoy being together and see where things go. Will that be enough? Before you think that's me saying I want to hang out with other people—it's not. It's me saying I like you and I want to be near you. That's the most I can give you right now." I turn to look at him and he drapes his arm across his forehead, nodding at me.

"It's enough for me," he says softly. He scoots beside me and kisses me, then turns on his side, letting me hold him.

"Good, because I really like having my squeaky little mouse here in bed beside me. You slept over two nights in a row, maybe we can make it three tomorrow."

He giggles a bit. "That sounds nice, but can you really call me *your* squeaky mouse? Feels kind of like a claim on me…"

"It is."

"Then are you *my* Jacob Rizzo?"

"Mmm…using my full name doesn't sound as personal as nickname."

"Well, what should I call you then?"

I squeeze him tighter and kiss the side of his neck. "You'll think of something."

Chapter Twelve
All Bricked Up

 **Edward**

As I step into my shop the next morning, I'm not entirely sure what to expect, despite Jacob repeatedly assuring me that he took good care of the place. I trust him, but running a store isn't in his work history. But when I enter the store and flick the lights on, I'm impressed. This is cleaner than I'd left it on the opening day.

"Wow…" I say.

He comes up behind me and puts his hand on the small of my back. I feel heat and electricity at his touch. "I told you. I did some of the chores throughout the day because I didn't want to stay late—and so when I had to make the emergency departure last night because of my mom, all the chores were already done." He leads me around the register counter to show me the computer there. "I was poking around in the software and found a report of what sold over your first two days. I assume you're going to want to do a restock already, because some shelves are looking a little sparse."

"Thank you," I say. I'm feeling almost overwhelmed at the care he's given to me and my store. Really, it's kind of small, but it feels big. It's the kind of thing that would appear on my BBL. In fact, it might be there; I might've added something like this after reading *Falling for the Intern*.

I do a quick scan of the books on the list; it seems the readers of Frosty

Bottoms lean heavily toward smut-filled MM books. I approve of this obsession.

He looks at the time on his phone. "I really gotta head; I'm supposed to be at my first client in ten minutes. I think she wants me to change a lightbulb."

I shake my head, wondering if I heard him right. "Change a lightbulb?"

"She says she's too scared to go on the ladder and she has a high ceiling, and she's single and lives alone so she has no one else to do it."

I snicker, remembering the eye candy on opening day. "You know it's a ruse to get your ass in the air, right?"

He gives me a scowl but there's lighthearted humor in his eyes. "I'm more than eye candy, you know."

"Oh, I know, but being eye candy is part of your package deal."

He gives me a wink. "I'll swing by at lunch. You didn't pack anything to eat, so I'll take care of it."

"You don't have to."

"Edward...I want to. Besides, I'm your servant today, right?" And with that, Jacob turns and leaves.

I watch that ass as it shimmies out of my store. There's no denying the sexual attraction I have for him, but with it is a growing sense of, like, deeper attraction. I can't kid myself...I find I'm falling for this man...hard.

And that scares me a little bit. Not because of what he was saying last night about people paying attention or whatever or having to tell his agent. I'm kind of scared because I've never had a relationship work out beyond a handful of dates. Guys always make excuses like they're not ready for a relationship or they're not as out as I am or they want to just sleep around— I've heard it all.

But with Jacob...something tells me it could be different. I feel almost foolish believing it could be true, but that's what my heart has settled on.

I try to squash down these feelings for now so I don't get too into them and end up getting hurt. Before I open the door and get the day started, I open my emails and see that Kellan has lined up some guys for the Book Boyfriend Auction. Since he knows the local guys better than I do, he had volunteered to help set it up.

Already feeling a little accomplished for today, I go switch the sign to open and welcome in the two people who were waiting outside.

"Come on in," I say. The first person I don't recognize, but the second one I do. "Welcome back, Leora."

"Those books were so steamy," she says. "I tried reading excerpts to my boyfriend, but I don't think his pacemaker could take it."

"I might have a recommendation for you then…" I lead her to the menage section and put a book in her hands. "This one has high heat but isn't quite as explicit. Should be pacemaker-friendly."

"Perfect! I'll take it! But I think there's also a sequel to *Debriefing the Lawyer*? The ending seemed to indicate there was more to come."

"Ah, yes, and I think I have it." I lead her to the right shelf and pull out the book for her. "*Debriefing the Lawyer 2: Now's It's a Jockstrap*. The plot is a little thin, but we don't exactly read these for the plot, do we?"

She gives me a lecherous wink. "While I do enjoy a good plot, sometimes I just want some banging. I love it when the leads work out their relationship while going at it like animals."

"Oh, agreed," I say. "And if they throw in things like cute pet names for each other, you get that mix of raw sexuality with heartfelt emotion. That always gets me going."

We make our way to the register and I ring her purchase through.

Before she heads out, she says, "I hear you've got a Book Boyfriend Auction coming up. Do you have tickets on sale yet?"

"Oh, *shoot*," I say. "I got some tickets, they're here somewhere…and I need to make a poster."

"How much are tickets?" she asks, pulling out her wallet.

"Five dollars," I say. I finally find the roll of tickets I tucked away in one of the cubbies under the register. "Here, you can be ticket holder 0001. Are you going to bid on a hot guy?"

She tucks the ticket into her wallet. "Oh, no, dear. I don't think my boyfriend would enjoy the competition. I'll just be there for the show."

"Well, I'll see you there!"

She winks as she picks up her books. "And if *Debriefing the Lawyer 2* is as good as I expect it to be, you might see me here tomorrow looking for book three."

I bid her a good day as she walks out and then immediately set to work on putting together the poster for the auction. The plan is to hold it here in the shop, and when I glance back at the email, it looks like Kellan arranged for Chad, Lucas, Tony, and Mayor Dick to participate, and there are a few maybes from other guys who are yet to confirm.

Once I get a colorful poster put together, using some poster board and art supplies I had tucked in my boxes of marketing stuff, I tape it in the front window, right by the door. And as soon as I do that, I get a customer asking about it.

"How much are tickets to attend the auction?" a woman asks.

"Five dollars each," I say, picking up the roll, ready to hand one over to her.

"Is Jacob going to be on auction?"

"Jacob?" I say. "No…unfortunately not."

"Oh," she says. Her expression kind of deflates. Then she says, "Thanks anyway," and leaves without buying a ticket.

After a few more people ask about tickets and also walk out without buying one after hearing Jacob won't be up for auction, Kellan comes in.

"Thank you, Kellan," I tell him, "for lining up guys for the auction."

"Of course, happy to help! I was by yesterday to tell you, but Jacob said you weren't feeling well. All better now?"

I nod. "I just needed a good, long sleep. Fixed everything."

"Awesome," he says. "How are ticket sales going?"

I shrug. "Not great. There's been interest since I put the poster up, but only one person's bought a ticket so far."

"Huh," Kellan says. "I wonder what's holding them back?"

I roll my eyes. "They all want Jacob to be on the auction block."

Kellan's eyes suddenly flare. "And how do *you* feel about that?" he asks.

"What do you mean?"

"Your car hasn't left his driveway in days."

I shrug my shoulders. "So?"

Kellan rolls his eyes. "It's so obvious, even Tony could figure this one out."

I say, deadpan, "I have absolutely no idea what you're talking about."

He lets out a frustrated exhale. "Fine, keep your secrets."

The door opens again, and Kellan's husband Braden comes in. He gives Kellan a kiss on the cheek, then says to him, "Did you get the dirt yet?"

"No," Kellan says, giving me the stink-eye. "He won't tell me anything."

Braden pats Kellan on the shoulder. "Some people don't kiss and tell, you know." Then to me, he says, "Can we get two tickets to the auction?"

"Of course," I say and hand over the tickets as he passes me the cash. "What are you two doing here today anyway? It's Monday, aren't you supposed to be running your shops?"

"Most of the businesses downtown are closed Monday," Braden says, "so we have a little rugby group for pick-up games, though we more often than not just go for lunch—enough that I sometimes wonder if we should just be a lunch club." That explains their get-ups, I guess, with both of them wearing leggings under shorts, and long-sleeve tees under T-shirts. If I didn't know better, I'd think they were going to jazzercise class.

"Well, well, well," a voice booms as the door opens.

"Good grief," I mutter as Chad walks in.

"There's my wayward little brother who hasn't been home for two nights now," he says. Trailing behind him is Lucas. Both of them are wearing ridiculous workout outfits like Kellan and Braden. Lucas's crop top has *Official Team Stress Reliever* emblazoned across it. I almost feel like I need to pop in one of those old exercise DVDs my grandma used to watch.

"Your wayward little brother that *swears* there's nothing going on to talk about," Kellan says.

"And if you pull my other testicle, it plays the tuba," Chad says.

"No one is pulling your testicles," Lucas tells him, "at least, not without me watching from a chair in the corner of the room." Then he turns to me. "You don't have to tell these guys anything."

I shrug my shoulders. "What's there to tell?"

All four of them groan at the same time.

Then the door opens again. Mayor Dick comes in wearing some ridiculous get-up. He has an old Tina Turner sweater with the sleeves cut off halfway and the collar cut out too. On his lower half, he's wearing some tight-fitting pink sweats that make his legs look like toothpicks.

"Are you part of this rugby club too?" I ask him.

He looks at the other four, then down at his own clash of fabrics and colors that make up his outfit. "No, it's laundry day so this is all that's clean. I'm even down to wearing these." He reaches into his sweats and pulls up the lacy waistband of what looks like panties. "Though they're surprisingly comfy."

"That may have been too much information, Dick," Kellan says.

Mayor Dick comes through the guys to approach the counter. "Can I get a ticket for the auction?"

"You don't have to buy a ticket," I tell him, "since you're one of the men on the auction block."

"Ah, but this is about setting an example of supporting our town," he says. "Besides, if I don't have a ticket, I can't bid on one of the other men." With that, he glances over his shoulder at Lucas, who in turn shudders.

"Then I'd be happy to sell you a ticket," I say, handing one over as he gives me a five-dollar bill.

"It was really nice seeing you last night," he says as he tucks his ticket in his wallet. All four men behind him kind of lean forward, like they're eager for gossip. "And for all the bluster Jacob's mother and nonna put on, they enjoyed meeting you too."

My gaze goes to the guys. Kellan and Braden's jaws are almost on the floor, Lucas has a big grin, and Chad has a look on his face like he just won the world's longest game of Monopoly. I had accidentally told him yesterday that I was meeting Jacob's mom, so this is probably just confirmation for him that it was more than a passing greeting even though it was entirely accidental.

"It was lovely to meet them too," I say to him.

The door opens one more time, and in comes Jacob with a paper bag in his hands. "I brought lunch, master!" he says. Heat instantly rises to my neck and warms my face when I lay my eyes on him. Then Jacob sees all who are gathered here in the store. "Oh…"

All five men turn to face him.

"Who's the lunch for?" Chad asks him.

"I'm hungry," Kellan says.

Braden whispers loudly to Kellan, "If you're hungry, I've got something you can suck on."

"Perfect timing," Mayor Dick says, "I'm famished."

"Okay, first of all, what the hell are you wearing, Dad?" Jacob asks. "Second, for everyone else, lunch is only for Edward."

And with that, all five men turn to face me.

"Sounds like you *do* have something to share," Kellan says.

I'm saved from having to answer that when the door opens yet again. "Good god, why are there so many people here?" a woman asks. "Oh, Kellan, just who I'm looking for!"

Kellan turns toward the door. "Rachel, I'm kind of busy with important stuff," he says.

The woman—Rachel—pushes through the crowd of men. "I need you to step up as Snowflake Princess and tell that piece of trash Bethany that she is forbidden from making an *official* Snowflake Festival coffee cocktail because *I* have one and I've *always* had one."

Kellan sighs. "Your *official* coffee cocktail has always been *unofficial* and you know it. The festival doesn't have official anythings. Is this going to be a yearly thing with you? Last year it was a fight over sandwiches, this year it's a drink. Do you just love drama?" he asks.

She harrumphs. "Leora would have stepped up."

"She absolutely would not have and I was there years ago when she told you before that your drink can't be official," he says.

Rachel scoffs. "Just because you have a tiara doesn't mean you're a real Snowflake Princess."

He gasps theatrically and holds his chest, while Braden pats him on the shoulder. "No," he says, "I'm Snowflake Princess because the town Chamber of Commerce voted for me to be so—including you."

"God, get that candy cane out of your ass," she says, then leaves.

"Did you tell her?" Braden whispers to Kellan, loud enough for all of us to hear.

"Tell her what?" Chad asks them.

Braden blushes. "None of your business." Then to Kellan, he says, "Seriously, did you tell her?"

"Of course I didn't tell her. Why would I do that?" Kellan says, not even bothering to whisper. "It's just an expression with a Christmas twist."

"What, exactly, did you two do?" Chad asks.

"None of your business, like I said," Braden says. "But for now, what we *will* do, is go for lunch. Come on, Kellan," he says, grabbing his husband's hand and pulling him out of the store.

"Wait," Chad says, following them out, "I want to hear about the candy cane!" Lucas follows him out the door too, leaving just Jacob and Mayor Dick.

"What the fuck was all that about?" Jacob asks.

"No idea," I say. "What did you bring me for lunch?"

That seems to break the tension that's settled on top of us. He comes forward and places the paper bag on the counter. "I went to Tony's and got one of those twelve-inch subs he's apparently famous for. Though it might be a bit much food for you…"

"Oh, I can eat," I say. I pull the sandwich out of the bag and peel back the wrapper. "Especially when it's Italian meat. I can't get enough of that stuff."

Both Jacob and his dad snicker, and then I realize what I've said.

"I can give you a second serving of Italian meat later tonight," Jacob says.

"And that's my cue to leave," Mayor Dick says. "Always lovely seeing you, Edward. I'll help spread the word about your boyfriend auction."

"Dad…" Jacob says, "you didn't answer me earlier, why are you dressed like that?"

Mayor Dick looks down at himself again and shrugs. "It's laundry day."

"Please don't tell me Mom and Nonna saw you wearing that."

"Your mom has seen me in worse…and in nothing," he says. "Anyway, I should head and move that laundry to the dryer. Later, boys."

When Dick is gone and it's just Jacob and I, I take a bite of my sandwich and then ask him, "How did your morning jobs go? Get that lightbulb changed?"

He rolls his eyes and leans on his elbows on the counter. "I did, but then she had me double check every light fixture in her house. And to make sure I was safe, she held the ladder for me."

"I bet she did," I say. I really want to lean across the counter, pull him close, and shove my tongue down his throat. But there are people walking in, so I'll just keep giving him my *fuck me* eyes.

After a few minutes, one of the customers comes to the register and I ring her purchase through, and shortly after that the second customer does the same, leaving Jacob and me alone in the store again. Now my dick is starting to get hard.

"How's the sandwich?"

"Super good," I say after swallowing a bite. "You want some?"

He holds up his hand. "No. I really do, but I shouldn't."

"I could…make you. You know, being my servant and all."

His eyes go dark and sexy. "There are other things of yours I'd much rather have in my mouth." His gaze flickers to the door. "You wanna lock up for lunch and we can go in your back room?"

I glance at the door and then at the entrance to the back room. We could do it. I could get railed to within an inch of my life and then have a wonderful afternoon. Before I can agree, the bells on the door jingle as someone comes in. "After work, I guess," I say to him.

I nod a polite hello at the customer as he enters and starts wandering around the store.

"I should get back to work anyway. I've got a client in ten minutes," he says. He glances over his shoulder at the customer, then whispers to me, "I really want to kiss you right now."

I give him a grin. "Nothing's stopping you."

He stands up straight and his eyes are still dark with lust. "I've warned you about teasing me, little mouse."

"You'll have to remind me of those warnings…later." I might've teased him, but one thing I love about him is how he responds when I do that.

"Oh, we will definitely be following up on this later." He gives me a wink and then heads out.

While I wait patiently for the customer, I finish the last of the sandwich and toss the wrapper in the wastebasket beneath the counter. Before he can finish up and come to the register, the door jingles again as someone else comes in. The afternoon proceeds like this, with a steady trickle of customers coming in and out. Some buy, some just browse. This is still a whole lot more than what I got back in Twilight Hollow; there, I was lucky to have five customers on any given day. If it wasn't for my few regular customers who went through several books a week, I likely wouldn't have been able to stay open. Here, though, it looks like I won't have to rely on heavy readers like that—not yet, anyway.

Throughout the afternoon, I also had several people ask about the Book Boyfriend Auction…and nearly all of them asked if Jacob was on the auction block. I only sold one additional ticket. At this rate, the event is going to bomb. I try to shove aside my worries about the event; I'm sure it'll all work out fine in the end.

When the end of the day comes, I flip the sign from open to closed, just as I hear the rumble of Jacob's Mustang pulling into the back parking lot. I quickly lock up, set the alarm, and walk out.

"Hey," I say as I settle into the passenger seat.

He glances around, confirming that there's no one in sight, then he leans over and gives me a slow, gentle kiss on the lips. "I've been waiting to taste you all day," he says when our lips part.

I sit back in the seat and melt from that kiss. Then I realize there's a brightly-wrapped box on the back seat. "What's that?"

"One of my clients today gave me some homemade cookies," he says. "I'm sure she was flirting with me."

I can't help but bristle at that. "You don't even eat cookies."

He chuckles. "I know, but you do."

"I am pretty hungry and a cookie sounds good." Taking my mind off the cookies, I tell him, "Take me to your house, servant."

"Yes, sir, absolutely, sir," he says. The car roars as he heads down Main Street and then winds his way through the gated entrance of his neighborhood.

When he pulls into his driveway, he grabs the cookies from the back seat and hurries out of the car and around, opening my door and giving me a deep bow as I step out. He then rushes ahead of me to open the door to the house before I get to it.

"Welcome, my liege," Jacob says with another deep bow.

I pat him on the top of the head. "Thank you, servant."

When he follows me in, I turn around and say to him, "Now we get to have a little fun."

His eyes go dark with lust. "Yeah?"

I turn and walk across the main floor to the bedroom, with Jacob hot on my heels. He leaves the box of cookies on the kitchen island.

"Now, get down on your knees."

He falls to the floor, resting on his knees and bringing his face to just the perfect height. Wordlessly, I unzip my fly and shove my pants and briefs to mid-thigh. I grip the base of my hard cock and hold it in front of his face.

"Beg for it," I say.

"Please let me suck your cock. Use my mouth."

"Open wide."

He opens his mouth perfectly and I angle my cock to slide inside, past those luscious lips and across that velvety tongue. When he closes his lips on my shaft, I feel like I'm in heaven.

"Suck it," I order him.

He starts bobbing his head back and forth, swallowing my cock down to the base and sliding out to the tip and back down again. He raises a hand and cups my balls as he sucks me, using them almost as a handhold.

Then he whimpers and that needy sound is going straight to the sex-crazed part of my brain. I want more of this—more, more, more.

I place my hands on either side of his head and hold him in place, then start fucking his face. He takes it down his throat like a good boy. He slips his hands up my legs and to my ass, grabbing a cheek in each hand. I can almost feel him fighting the urge to pull my cheeks apart and start fingering at the center. But he holds off and focuses on his duty of servicing me.

His mouth is good—so fucking good—and the little whimpers of need and desire he makes are making me hornier for him. I start thrusting harder into his mouth, slipping into the back of his throat.

"Oh, fuck," I mutter. "Fuck, you're amazing."

That just seems to make him tighten his lips around my cock, squeezing even more pleasure out of me. Eventually—finally—I can feel my pleasure rising and can see the oncoming crush of orgasm. I hold his head a little tighter, push my cock a little deeper, and that crush finally hits me and I feel a surge going through my whole body. My muscles go rigid and my body trembles and Jacob works his mouth so amazingly, making this moment feel even more intense.

I gasp and my eyes roll back in my head as I unleash a torrent of cum into Jacob's mouth. I'm lost in bliss as my ongoing orgasm rocks my world and everything I know.

When it eventually subsides and I can see again, I look down at Jacob. My softening cock is still in his mouth and he's looking up at me with both satisfaction and lust in his eyes.

As my cock slips from his mouth, he asks, "My turn?"

I wink at him. "You're the servant, not me," I say. I zip up my pants. "Besides, I thought we'd check out some of the Snowflake Festival stuff tonight."

Jacob laughs incredulously as he stands up. "You're serious? I'm all bricked up here and you want to go out?"

I blow a kiss at him. "Come on." I turn and head to the living room, lying down on the couch and pulling out my phone.

He comes in the room and has his hand down the front of his pants, adjusting himself. "You're gonna pay for this when the twenty-four hours is up, you know."

"Maybe I'm looking forward to the punishment," I say with a smirk. "It looks like there's a Christmas movie on tonight. But because it's been so warm they're going to do it at the park instead of at the theatre. It starts in…forty-five minutes. We should go. What do you think?"

"You're the boss, for a few more hours, at least," he says. "But if I'm this pent up all night, your ass better be ready come 8:37."

"I'll be more than ready," I say.

"Good. Because you'll be begging me to let you come," he says. "But, uh, at the movie, uh…"

"Don't worry," I say. I know what he's on about. "*To me*, this will be a date. But to everyone else, we'll just look like two friends checking out a movie."

He gives me a weak smile. "Thank you. I'm sorry."

"Come here," I say, holding out my arms. He comes to the couch and hugs me, then lays across my body. "I know you need to be discreet and I'm okay with that. As long as I get all of you when we're here in this house, I don't mind if I only get some of you when we're outside of it."

He gives me a kiss. "Thank you, little mouse."

"Of course, um…big mouse."

He laughs. "I'm not a big mouse."

"I still need a nickname for you, though. I don't know what to pick."

He kisses my nose. "You'll think of something."

"Big cat? Cats prey on mice. Maybe that fits?"

He laughs. "Let's go to that movie."

Sticky
Gingerbread Man

Edward

He gets up off the couch and pulls me to my feet, then leads me to the garage where he digs out a couple lawn chairs and outdoor blankets. We carry these to his car and load them into the back seat. Then we get in the car and he pulls out of his driveway.

"How did your work day go?" he asks. "Did you sell a lot of auction tickets?"

"No," I say, looking out the window. When I look back at him, he has a questioning look in his eyes. "At least a dozen people asked me if you were going to be up for auction and when I said no, they decided they didn't want tickets."

"Aw…" he says. "I'm sorry."

"Not your fault you're so damn desirable." After a pause, I add, "But if you were in the auction, we'd probably sell out of tickets."

"And then someone would buy me and, what, I'd have to go on a date with them?"

"Dinner that night, yeah," I say.

He looks at me. "And you'd be okay with that? Me going on a date with someone else, out in public? I haven't even taken *you* out on a date in public."

I hadn't thought of that part. I swallow the jealousy I feel rising and say, "Sure, yeah. It's for charity, right? It wouldn't be a *real* date." I swallow down that jealousy once more.

"I could bid on myself," he says, "and go for dinner by myself."

"Sorry, that's against the rules," I say. "But maybe I could bid on you."

"But you get me for free," he says. "Seems like not the greatest use of your money." Then he sighs. "I probably shouldn't do it anyway. We'd have to make sure no one takes pictures of me and no one tags me on social media and I think it just wouldn't work. I'd have to ask my dad what he thinks. I'd ask Linley but she'd just call it community service or something and make a big deal of it."

"I wonder if you might be overplaying it a bit," I say, almost wincing as I speak. "It's a fun little charity fundraiser, not a big media event, but I don't want you to do anything you're uncomfortable with."

"Thank you," he says, but he sounds disappointed. Somehow, I know he's not disappointed with me, but disappointed more with the shackles the media has on him right now. "Let me think about it, okay? Maybe we can find a way to make this work."

"Okay," I say, placing a reassuring hand on his thigh.

He gives my hand a squeeze, then returns his hand to the steering wheel to navigate us through the park. It's a large place, but we find the field with the movie pretty quickly—there's a little community stage set up in one of the fields, so it made sense that's where the movie would be held.

"Um…are you sure about the start time?" he asks me as he pulls into a parking spot.

I lean forward to look past his body. *Elf* is already playing. "Um…I guess I'm not." I watch the screen to figure out how far into the film it is. "Looks like it's half-in already. Wanna still watch the rest?"

"Sure," he says. "I've seen it before, so I'll catch up quick. Come on."

We get out of the car and grab our stuff from the back seat, then trudge across the semi-frozen grass to the large field. There are maybe a few dozen people here, most sitting in clusters that look like family groups, with a few larger groups that are probably high school kids out for an evening together. Toward the back and along the sides are a handful of couples. I think the two at the front on the far side might be Kellan and Braden.

"How about here?" Jacob whispers to me. It's near the back—no one is behind us—but also a fair distance from the other couples, giving us some privacy and discretion.

"This is perfect," I say.

   JACOB   

I place the chairs down and double check my surroundings. I'm kind of nervous right now. It's a weird state of mind to be completely happy looking at him, and also terrified at the notion that something, anything—could disrupt this amazing thing we have going. I relax into my chair once I see that no one is turning around to look at us. Our chairs are close together, and as much as I want to scoot it even closer toward his, I feel like, just to be safe, I should move it further away.

"Oh, yeah, this is almost over," Edward says, looking at the screen. He covers his lap with the blanket and holds up a side of it toward me.

I pull my beanie down tighter and shake my head at him. "I don't think I should do that, but if it's what you want, I can do it. I—"

Disappointment flickers across his face, but it's quickly replaced with more of an understanding look. He gives me a soft smile. "Two guys who are just friends probably wouldn't share a blanket while sitting close together at an outside movie," he says.

"Probably not, but we're not just friends." Those words should force me to share the blanket with him, but they don't, they somehow have the opposite effect, and I feel even more terrified than before. What am I doing? I'm out in public with a guy I'm sleeping with? I haven't taken him on a date because I know what's at stake—one picture, one phone call from some tourist, or some jealous person and all the privacy that I have with him will be gone in an instant. I can't be here. I can't do this.

He leans forward, and his eyes widen. "Cute! That's a soccer ball he's kicking over there!" He nudges me with his elbow. "See that, I remembered what sport you play this time."

I smile at him, finding it hard to hold myself back from kissing him. When I look at him, every worry melts away, it's crazy. Thirty seconds ago, I was ready to bolt and now I'm not worried at all. I'm not gonna kiss him right now, but at least I feel comfortable again. "Yeah, you remembered the sport, I'm proud of—"

"Rizzo!" a voice shouts.

Oh no. No, no. It sounded like a small voice, but I'm too terrified to look.

Edward is looking over toward the voice and he's smiling. "It's that little kid! He's pretending he's you! Look at him!"

I turn to the left and see the small boy doing the same thing that I do when I miss a goal. It's a pretty good imitation, and it makes me chuckle a bit.

"Why is his shirt in his mouth like that?" Edward asks. "And look at his hands on his hips. Is that what you look like when you play?"

"When I miss, yeah. Or when a teammate misses."

The little boy grabs the ball and tries juggling it on his knees then drops it after a few unsuccessful attempts. He points ahead then lines up his shot. "Rizzo for the win!" he shouts and kicks. "Yeah!" he screams, running around the field. I wanna go kick the ball around with him, but I have no idea if his family are locals or not. I watch as he grabs the ball and runs back. His eyes meet mine briefly, and I see a version of myself in them, a version of me that would have loved to meet my favorite player. I stand up from my chair and walk toward him, while looking for his parents. A man standing nearby notices me and I change course and head for him. I'm looking left to right with my hands in my pockets.

"Holy shit," the man says as he gets closer to me. He's definitely not a local. "You're Jacob Rizzo. What, what are you doing here? My son and I are huge fans. How are you here right now?"

I shrug at him and smile. "Is that your son?" I ask, pointing to the small boy.

"Yeah, his name is Luca. He's gonna be so excited. I'm gonna call him over!"

I put a hand up and wince. "Here's the thing. I'm not supposed to be here. If you're fans, then you know that nobody—"

"Nobody knows where you are. You punched a ref who probably deserved it, then disappeared after you got suspended."

I exhale and pull my beanie down. "Yeah, but I saw your son playing and he was pretending to be me. I wanted to go over and give him a few tips. But I have to ask for your word that you won't take any pictures or tell the media about this. I can send him a jersey and an autograph once my suspension is over, but for now, this needs to stay between us. He's a kid, so I don't expect him to keep it to himself, but it's more important that *you* don't say anything about it. If that's all fine, then I'd love to meet him."

I look over and see Edward watching me. It's only now that I realize I didn't tell him what I was doing. I'm a shitty date. But I saw the kid and moved without thinking. I casually glance at him and smile.

"Oh, of course, and don't worry. Luca isn't going to say anything either."

"I don't feel right asking a kid not to, just as long as no one knows exactly where I am, it's okay. You guys aren't from around here, right?"

"Nope, we're here for the Snowflake Festival. We live a few towns over. Don't worry about your privacy, your secret is safe with us. I'm just so excited to meet you."

I take a deep breath and shake his hand. "Thank you."

Walking toward Luca, I gesture for Edward to come over. Luca notices his father, then his eyes meet mine. He drops his ball and starts running toward me at full speed. Before I can say anything, he's clutched onto my legs, hugging me. "Woah. Hello," I say, ruffling his hair.

"You're him, you're Jacob Rizzo!" he says, looking up at me.

I pat his small back, and squat down to his level. "I am. And your dad told me your name is Luca. It's nice to meet you."

"Can I show you my kick?" he asks. "I can score just like you!"

"Sure, let's see it." I say and stand up.

Edward comes closer to me and smiles as Luca runs toward his ball.

I'm a bit worried that the movie will be ending soon, and people will start to gather once they see me, but with the screen being on the other side of the field, I think this is fine.

He smiles over at me and rests his foot on the ball. "Ready? This is my championship kick." I walk a bit closer to him, watching his foot placement.

"Do it!" I shout.

I watch his small body back away from the ball, then approach it with a kick. "Rizzooooo!" he shouts.

I clap and smile. This is one of the best moments I've had with a fan in a long time. "Wow! That was a great shot! I think you're better than me."

I give him a high-five, and he smiles up at me. "I could be like you one day! We could play on the same team!"

I chuckle a bit. "That would be awesome. I'd like that."

He tilts his head at me. "Why did you punch the ref?"

Oof. One of the best things about kids is that they don't hold back. I smile, trying to look unaffected by his question.

"No, you don't have to answer that," his dad says. He pats his son's head. "Luca, we don't ask things like that."

"It's fine," I say, then squat down to his height. "How old are you?"

"Five!" he says proudly.

"Wow, five is the coolest age there is. Can I tell you a secret that no one else knows?"

He nods and zips his lips.

"I wish I hadn't done that to the ref. Because no matter how angry someone makes you, there's never a reason for that. When I got mad at him, I should have walked away. I didn't have the right to do what I did. And I'm sorry that you had to see that."

He nods at me and unzips his mouth. "My dad says the ref was an idiot that probably wanted the other team to win."

"He might have, but I could have walked away and that's what I should've done. I made the wrong choice. But, now the good thing to come out of all this, was that I got to meet you. And I met him, too." I point up to Edward.

"He's lucky he gets to be your friend."

I chuckle and ruffle his hair. "Well, I think I'm the lucky one, because you know what? He's really nice."

"Can I be your friend, too?" he asks.

"Of course." I bump fists with him. "I told your dad that when I get back with my team, I'll send you a special jersey and some other stuff. How does that sound?"

His face lights up, and he looks at his dad, then back to me. "Really?"

"I promise. Now let me show you something." I show him where his foot should connect and give him a few tips on juggling. He's a fast learner, it's pretty impressive watching a kid his size take it all in.

I look over my shoulder and see the movie has about fifteen minutes left.

"You probably don't want to give me your phone number," his dad says. "So, here is my business card. You can use this address when you get around to sending the jersey, but no rush."

I take the business card and slip it into my pocket. "Thanks. I'll send it. It was nice meeting you both. Thanks for hanging out with me Luca. Keep practicing so we can play on the same team one day."

I give him a high-five, and he squeezes my leg in a hug. "Bye, Rizzo."

Once he lets go, Edward and I walk back to our spot. Edward grabs the blanket, while I quickly fold and pick up the chairs. "Ready?" I ask. Edward nods with a slight smile, and we start our walk toward my car. He hasn't said a word. I don't think he's mad that I did that, but I did leave him just sitting there without an explanation. "Sorry about that," I say.

"What are you apologizing to me for? Did you do something wrong?"

"I don't think so, but you haven't said anything. I didn't tell you what I was doing, so I thought maybe you were upset that I left you sitting there. I just kinda decided to do it and moved before I could really think it through."

He's looking around like he's checking for something. "Too many people around, otherwise I'd show you how I feel."

I chuckle and pop open my trunk. "Can't you just tell me? I don't want you to be upset."

He shakes his head at me and reaches for the passenger door handle. I reach in front of him, opening it before he can. "I *am* still your servant. You shouldn't have to open doors."

He sits inside, and as much as I want to lean in and kiss him, I can't do that right now. Once I close his door, I feel my phone vibrating in my pocket, but I'm not dealing with whatever it is. It's most likely Linley…I really need to call her in the morning. I sit in the driver's seat and start my car, turning on the seat warmers and heat.

"Jacob—I." He reaches for my face, then pulls me in and kisses me. He's kissing me so soft, and sweet, his tongue barely rubbing against mine. It's different than the way he's kissed me before. After a few seconds, he pulls back. "That's how I felt about that. I didn't realize there were even little kids that looked up to you."

I pat his lap and smile, then start driving toward my house. "Yeah, it's one of the best things about being an athlete, except for in my case where I just had to explain that I made a mistake. I felt bad about that."

"He seemed okay with it, his dad did too. I think I finally understand why the team owner wanted you to do the community service."

"Yeah. I guess so. It was stupid for me to punch him; I can admit that. He deserved it, though. I just wouldn't say that to a kid."

Edward pulls his phone out and leans his head back in frustration. "My brother just can't help himself. He wants to know if I'm spending the night, even though we aren't sleeping together."

"Ah, but we *are* sleeping together. Wait, you *didn't* tell him that I agreed to be your servant for the day, or that we're sleeping together?"

He shakes his head at me. "Definitely not. I don't think he's stupid, though. Wait, you wouldn't care if I told him those things?"

"Hmm. I kind've assumed you already did, to be honest. I'm not too bothered if you talk to your brother about us. I mean, I'd prefer the details about our sex be kept between us—but as far as acknowledging that we're sleeping together…it's fine. As much as I don't really enjoy being around

Chad, I don't think he's gonna tell people about us. But just to be sure, maybe ask him not to."

"I'll think about it. I just won't say it in front of the parrot, although, he only seems to repeat the filthiest things."

I pull inside my garage and turn the car off, then quickly disarm the security system from my phone. "That's funny about the parrot. Now. No more funny business. Listen to me carefully. I'm going to fuck you so hard for what you did to me earlier. But I'll give you a twenty-second head start. Whichever room you're in when I get inside, is where I'm gonna fuck you."

His eyes widen, and he hops out of the car while I count down to myself. I have no idea which room he's going to pick, and I honestly don't care. I need to be inside of him.

I give him a few extra seconds, then head inside, sliding my shoes off by the door. He's not on the couch, and he's not in the kitchen. "Which room did you pick?" I call out. I walk inside my bedroom, and he's not in there. I didn't really mean for this to turn into a game of cat and mouse. I pull my beanie off and toss it onto my dresser, along with my coat. "Little mouse? Where are you hiding? Give me a little squeak as a hint if you're not gonna answer me." I giggle at the sound of Edward making tiny squeaking noises. I think they came from upstairs. "Are you in my office?" I don't want to run up there if he's somewhere else, so I'm gonna have to draw him out. I pull my shirt off and toss it beside the stairs, then take my pants off. "Edward—tell me where you are. I'm practically naked. My cock is already so hard from imagining the things I'm going to do to you, it's throbbing in my hand."

"I'm in your office! But before you get up here, don't forget that I'm still in charge."

I left my phone in my pants, so I'll check the time when I get upstairs. I feel like the twenty-four hours is almost up, because the last time I checked he had only ten minutes or so. I make my way up the stairs and see Edward sitting on the small couch in my office, he's holding the box of cookies that my client gave me. I approach him quickly and hold my hand out for the box. "Give me those. Are you hungry?"

"I am."

"I'm starving too, but I'm not sure what I want to eat. I think I'd rather watch you eat first." I take his hand and rub it hard against my dick.

He scoots closer to the edge of the couch and looks up at me, tracing my cock with his fingers. "I'm still in charge, though. So maybe a cookie *and* this?"

Fuck, he makes me think the filthiest things. I glance at the clock and notice the time. He has two minutes left if I really want to play fair. His hand is still rubbing my dick through my underwear. I know he's just as hard as I am. "Tell me what you want me to do, then. Because it's obvious what I want."

He stands from the couch and kisses me softly. I press my tongue inside, trying to take control, and he pulls back. "What should I do with you?" he asks.

I look over my shoulder and see that it's 8:37. I smirk at him and reach for the button on his pants. "Too late. I'm not your slave anymore. And now you're gonna pay for what you did to me earlier."

His eyebrows raise, and he smiles while I unbutton his pants and tug them down. He starts to take his underwear off, and I stop him, firmly placing my hands atop his. "Not yet." I lift his chin and bring my mouth beside his ear. "Kneel for me."

Edward drops to his knees and brings his face in front of my cock. His warm breath seeping through the fabric of my underwear makes my dick even harder. I run my fingers through his soft, thick hair and look down at him. "I'm torn, little mouse. Because with you on your knees, I want nothing more than to stuff my cock in your pretty mouth, but I also really want to try something." I grip his hair tighter, and my cock twitches.

"Do it, whatever it is. I want you so fucking bad."

Squeezing a fistful of his hair, I bring his open mouth closer to my dick, then pull my cock out and trace it across his lips. He rolls his warm, wet tongue around the head, circling it slowly, while pulling my briefs down.

I love watching his tongue lick around like that, but I can't let him do it right now. "No sucking and no licking," I tell him. "Just open your mouth for me." I've never had anyone warm my cock before, and I really want to know how it feels.

Edward nods at me and opens his mouth, while I brush his cheek with the back of my hand. "Good boy." I stick my cock inside slowly, holding the top of his head in place. "Haah… So fucking warm…so good for me. Now, stay still, just like that." I don't know how long I can do this for, but there is something deeply erotic about seeing my cock inside his mouth and watching him submit to my will without question—It's almost enough to make me come. His big brown eyes are looking up at me, seemingly waiting for my next command. "You told me you were hungry…I want you to imagine my hot, thick cum spilling in your mouth." I stroke under his chin with my finger. "Would you like that?"

"Mmhmm," he moans on my cock, and the sensation causes precum to spill out. "Fuuuck," I growl, gripping his hair tighter.

I feel him start to suck and I pull back, taking my cock out of his mouth. "I told you not to suck. Now, get on the couch."

He's licking his lips and giving me the filthiest grin. "I couldn't help myself—I got a taste of your cum and it was so fucking sweet. I wanted more."

While he repositions himself on the cushion, I grab the box of cookies. "You like the way I taste?"

He's nodding at me while rubbing his dick through his tight black briefs. "I do. I wanted a cookie, but now all I can think about is your cum. Let me taste the real thing." His hand slips inside and I watch mesmerized as he pulls his fat cock out and strokes it.

I want to tell him to stop, but my eyes are solely focused on the show he's putting on for me. The way his tattooed hand is working his length up and down, while he bites his lip…it's all too sexy, and he knows it.

I take a gingerbread man out of the box and put the rest on my desk. "You told me the other day that gingerbread was your favorite kind of cookie."

He nods, maintaining a slow but steady pace while he continues jerking himself. "I like all cookies, but those are my favorite. Are we gonna have cookies with sex?" I can tell he's getting close to coming, because his breaths are quickening, despite the way he's pretending to be unfazed.

I hold the cookie beside my cock and tilt my head at him. "You want this cookie, or you want my cum? You asked for both."

He squeezes his eyes shut. "Both—fuck, Jacob. I can't—hold on much longer."

I press my mouth against his and roll my tongue inside, while my cock presses against his hand. I pull back, but keep my face close to his. "Both?"

He nods, pulling my face back in. "Come on that cookie for me. I know you want to…but you're afraid I don't want you to." He grabs my cock with his spit-slicked hand and my eyes close instinctively. "Jacob. I really do. I want you to come on that cookie and feed it to me. Do it."

I reach down and stroke our cocks together, both thick and hot, pressed against one another. "Mmm…mmm," he moans and leans forward to kiss me, shoving his tongue inside, tangling it quickly with mine—it's sloppy, and deep. A tiny squeak breaks through his soft moans. He's so fucking close to coming, and so am I.

I wipe the precum from his tip and lick it off my fingers. His eyes are locked on my mouth, and he slips his tongue back inside, joining mine once again. He places his hand atop mine, jerking us together, panting, looking up at me with eyes that would do anything for me in this moment, eyes that are begging for me to give him what he wants. Looking at him like this, is making me realize that the things I'm feeling for him…they're not just—

Edward squeezes my hand, panting. "Haah—haah—fuck—" A soft squeak escapes him, as his cum spills over, dripping down my hand—bringing me to the brink of my own orgasm. He's still panting, but leans forward, and licks across my mouth.

He pulls the cookie from my grip and holds it beneath the tip of my cock, while I jerk myself harder, until my cum shoots onto it, covering the gingerbread man and his hand. "Holy fuck." I blink hard, dropping my head back. Every time he makes me come it's more intense than the last.

He's holding the cookie looking at me with such a filthy grin. "Does it bother you that I like kinky stuff like this?"

I lick my lips and shake my head. "No. Definitely not. I like dirty things." I raise my chin toward the cookie. "Are you gonna eat that? Or you just wanted me to come on it?"

He holds the cookie up. "Feed it to me."

Holy fuck…this feels much hotter than it probably should, but my cock, which should be completely spent, is starting to tingle at the thought of him eating it. I raise my eyebrows and take the cookie from his hand, and he opens his mouth, sticking his small pink tongue out slightly.

I hold the cookie near his mouth, and he looks up at me, sticking his tongue out further, and licks across the entire top of the gingerbread man.

"Haah," I exhale. Holy shit, that's hot. I didn't realize I was holding my breath, but I must have been. He continues licking the cookie while maintaining eye contact with me—the sight of him doing this makes my heart race, and I can feel my cock thickening again, when he finally bites into the cookie.

"Mmm…Jacob. I'm not even lying, your cum takes better than this cookie. How do you taste so good?" He takes the rest of the cookie in his mouth and finishes it.

I thread my fingers through his thick black hair and cup the side of his face. I want to say something sweet or dirty, but I don't even know what to say—because right now my cock is screaming for me to take him downstairs and fuck him, but my heart—it's screaming for me to hold him close.

I lean down and kiss him softly, while rubbing his cheek, then kiss his forehead. "Let's wash up and I'll make you something to eat."

He smiles and eyes my dick, then looks back up at me. "Doesn't look like you want to wash up—looks like you're ready to go again."

I shake my head and grab my underwear off the floor. My dick is embarrassingly hard right now. "Ignore him, he'll go back to sleep in a minute. You just make him feel too many things. He's all confused."

Edward chuckles. "He doesn't look confused, he looks hard. Are *you* confused?"

"Nope. But I'm gonna rinse off. You can join me if you want." I should have said yes. I should have told him that I've never been so sure that I want to be in a relationship with someone in my entire life, and that fact alone makes me more confused than I've ever been—but I didn't say any of that. I walk toward the bathroom inside my office and Edward follows behind me, grabbing his clothes off the floor. I flip the light on and Edward looks around holding his arms out.

"How do you have two bathrooms this size? When we came by the other day, I assumed this was a smaller bathroom…but it's clearly not. Where do you keep the shower stuff? Like towels?"

I slide the glass door open and turn the water on. "I think it's a normal size bathroom. It's not custom built or anything." I point to the large closet. "There are clean washcloths in there and towels, too."

I step inside the shower and let the warm water wash over me. I think this is only maybe the second time since I moved in, that I've used this shower. Edward steps inside with me and without thinking, I pull him in close, squeezing him tight. He wraps his arms around me and rests his head against my chest. I have no idea why I did that but holding him close like this—it instantly calmed me.

"What are you thinking about?" he asks.

"Hmm. Right now, I'm thinking that I like the way you feel in my arms. I'm also feeling bad because you said you were hungry earlier, and aside from that cookie, you haven't eaten anything." I break from the hug, and he passes me one of the washcloths.

"I'm fine," he chuckles.

I scrub my body down and watch Edward do the same. His tattoos are all so sexy, but then again, maybe it's just that *he's* sexy. I wonder if each one means something special to him. I have to ask him about them later, but not now, because right now my cock is starting to stir while my eyes are locked on him, cleaning his dick with that washcloth. He's got such a firm grip on it, I've never wanted to be a washcloth until now. I shake the thoughts of railing him in the shower away, because, as much as I love the feeling of pushing inside him, the lube is downstairs.

"What are you gonna make me for dinner?" he asks while he squeezes shampoo into his hands.

"My mom left the pasta from last night here, if you want some of that we could heat it up, or I can make you some chicken and vegetables. I have some other stuff, too."

Now that we're showered and dressed in comfy clothes, Edward is standing beside me looking inside my pantry. I don't think I have anything that he likes, which I'll need to fix if he's gonna be staying over as much as he has been.

"You don't eat cereal?" he asks me. "Or pancakes?"

"Not really, but I can get that stuff from the store if you want it. Are you in the mood for breakfast, or are those just things you noticed that I don't have?"

He leans his head against my shoulder, while I wrap my arm around his waist. "I feel like having breakfast, but your pantry is such a grown-up pantry. There's nothing fun in here." He giggles. "No sweets at all and no trace of any junk food. What do you eat when you want a snack?"

"You," I say, patting his ass.

He laughs, elbowing me playfully. "I'm not a snack—I'm a whole meal, thank you."

"That's true. So, when I actually want a snack, it just depends on what time of the day it is. What should I make for you? I can make you eggs and toast, if that sounds good. Other than that, if you want breakfast, it's just the warm oatmeal or overnight oats."

"Oooh, I'll take whichever one is easiest, because they all sound good, but I think I'd like the overnight oats best."

I pass him a mason jar full of oats, and he happily digs into them, while I warm up my chicken. "These are really good. They taste like cookie dough." He looks at the jar, then up at me. "How are these healthy?"

"Healthy enough that I'm allowed to have them. Everything in there serves some purpose. They're supposed to have chia seeds in them, but I never add them."

He takes another spoonful, and his face lights up. "I just realized that you *do* have sweets in this house, because those cookies are still upstairs."

"That's true." I take a bite of my chicken and give him a smile. "I'll grab them for you when I'm done, unless you want them now? Are you one of those people that eats dessert with dinner?"

He shakes his head at me. "Nope. But I did hear it's better for you if you eat it at the same time. And I don't need a cookie right now, nothing is gonna beat the one I just had." He pumps his eyebrows at me, then licks his spoon. "These oats are a lot sweeter than I thought they'd be."

"Maybe it's the honey? I don't know." My phone vibrates on my counter, and I see it's my dad calling. I texted him earlier about Edward's auction, so I should answer it. There's a fifty percent chance he says something dumb, though. I smile at Edward and pick my phone up. "I have to take this, it's my dad."

"Hey, Dad."

"Oh, I wasn't expecting you to answer. I was getting ready to leave a voicemail," he says with a chuckle.

"Should I hang up? I can send you to voicemail. Easier for me that way."

Edward's mouth is wide open. He looks like he can't believe I said that.

"No, no," my dad says. "I'm confused by your text. You want to know if I think it's a good idea for you to do the auction? Or are you asking if I think people will keep quiet about you being in the auction?"

"Both, I guess? I know Edward really wants me to."

Edward pulls his head back and points to himself. "What does Edward want you to do?"

I hold a finger up to him, telling him to wait a minute.

"Are you guys in a relationship or just having fun?" my dad asks. "I didn't get to talk to you about it with Edward there, but before I answer, I'm just curious how serious you guys are."

I sigh looking at Edward across the counter and reach for his hand. He puts his hand in mine, but tilts his head. "What's going on?" he whispers.

I rub his hand with my thumb and smile at him. "I like him," I tell my dad. "But I already told you that. He's here with me now if that helps clear things up."

"Jacob, I think Edward is great, and I'm happy that you found someone you like." He lets out a sigh. "It's not really my place at your age to stick my nose in, but you worked really hard to keep your presence here a secret. This may sound terrible, but if people realize you're ineligible, things could change quickly. I'm not saying they would, but you're very lucky no one has said anything about you living here yet. If you start openly dating someone, there are gonna be people that will take advantage of that information. So, just be careful. There are also a lot more tourists around this time of year. Unless you plan on asking every one of them not to say something, you're gonna need to be as inconspicuous as possible. For those reasons, I think it may be a bad idea to do the auction. But, if you *are* in a relationship with him, as in—more than just having sex, then you should do it because his event is gonna tank without you. Kellan was talking to me about it today, he's a nervous wreck that it's gonna flop."

I pat Edward's hand. "Gimme a sec, I'll be right back," I tell him, then walk out of the kitchen and into my bedroom. "What do you mean it's gonna flop? Is this just Kellan freaking out or is it really gonna be a disaster?"

"Oh, I think it's gonna be a disaster unless he gets you to do it. Everyone in this town has pretty much slept with everyone else once or twice, except for Braden, Tony, Edward, and you, as far as I know."

"What does that have to do with anything? Who's talking about sleeping with anyone? We're talking about a Book Boyfriend Auction. It was just a cute little idea for people to have fun with. Why are you talking about who's banged each other?"

My dad laughs loudly. "Jacob. The evening is meant to end with sex, which is why I was surprised that Edward would want you to do it, especially since he wouldn't be able to afford you, even if you do decide to do it."

"I don't think that's the case. I think that's just what *you* think." I remember our brief discussion about the event and how uncomfortable Edward looked when I asked him if he'd be okay with me going on a date with someone else for the auction. He definitely didn't like it, but was probably conflicted because he knew I could sell tickets, not because he thought I'd sleep with someone.

"Call me old fashioned, but dates end with sex, especially ones that end up costing a lot of money. You'll have to put out for whoever takes you home," he chuckles.

"No. That's out of the question and I really hope you're kidding. But I do want to do the event. So, could we try and close off the venue from anyone who hasn't bought tickets, and just tell Larry at the newspaper not to cover his event? If we do those things, I think it should be fine."

"Jacob…What did your agent say about all this? She was probably happy because it's community service, but she can't be happy about Edward."

"I haven't talked to Linley about him yet. I plan to do that tomorrow, after I deal with my clients. But, Dad, I'm not telling her about this event. I'm doing this for him, not for me."

"Alright. I'll start letting people know. We might need to switch to a bigger venue. Once people find out you're gonna be up for auction, it could get out of control."

"Nah, it'll be fine. But thanks. Talk to you soon."

I sit on the edge of my bed and stare at my phone. I have this nagging feeling that I should call Linley while I'm alone, but I left Edward sitting out there, so I'll just do it tomorrow.

"Everything okay? Do you need me to leave?" Edward asks, standing in my doorway.

I pat the bed, and he sits beside me. "What's with you always thinking I want you to leave? I told you I wanted to be near you. That didn't change just because I had to talk to my dad for a few minutes."

"What did you tell your dad that I wanted you to do? You looked really nervous before you came in here."

"I was just talking to him about your event. He wanted to know if you and I were serious or not. Seems like a crazy question to ask at this point—"

Before I can explain myself, Edward pulls his head back a bit and looks at the floor.

"Hey," I say softly, turning his face toward mine. "Don't get upset before I even finish my sentence. You don't even know what I was gonna say."

His eyes are searching my face so intently, while I stroke his cheek with my thumb. "I'm not upset. I just—I know what you said about the relationship stuff, and I don't want to pressure you, but this *is* a relationship and we're not just fucking, right? I feel stupid even asking, and I know what you said, so I want to believe you and part of me does, but—"

I lean in and kiss him gently, barely sliding my tongue against his, then pull back and look into his eyes. "We're not just fucking," I say softly. "You have no idea what you're doing to me. I've never second guessed my entire way of thinking until you. I like you so much, little mouse."

"But what if I like you more?"

"You don't. It's not a competition, but if it were, I'd win."

"Jacob, I haven't even had a conversation with my brother in days. I'm supposed to be living with him. I only just now realized how rude I've been, because *you* are all I've been thinking about. It *is* a competition, and I win."

I shake my head at him. "First, yeah, you should talk to your bother, because even though I think he's kind of…it doesn't matter. You should talk to him."

"But I win, right? You don't have anything like that going on."

"Listen to me carefully. I like you so much that I'm willing to go on a date with someone else, just to make you happy. I think I win based on that."

"What? I don't want you to go on a date with anyone else." His eyes widen. "Wait, are you saying you're gonna do the auction? Really?"

"Yep. Just talked to my dad about it. He thinks it should be fine. You'll lose the local news coverage of the event, though. But if I can make things better and help you sell tickets, then that's all that matters to me. Not the fact that I'm gonna have to go out somewhere with someone that isn't you and be completely terrified that someone is gonna take advantage of that."

He's smiling so big. "You're gonna do that for me?"

I nod and pat him on the thigh. "Yep. So, tomorrow I can try and help sell tickets to clients if you want."

"Woah. Stop," he says, waving me off. "If you ask a client if they want to buy a ticket to an auction that you're in, I think someone could possibly take that to mean you want them to bid on you. Kind of like an invitation."

"Yeah, maybe you're right. Do you think whoever I'm gonna go out with will expect me to treat it like a real date? No, right? I just have to show up and be polite, there's nothing that says I have to hold hands or have sex or anything."

His eyes look like they're gonna fall out of his head. "Sex?! What?! With you?!"

He's really so adorable. "Calm down. I'm not gonna do it. My dad was just explaining his idea of what he thinks is supposed to happen. I don't really know how to go on a fake date with someone, though, mostly because I've never gone on a real date with *anyone*. I'm gonna be completely lost."

"Oh God," he says as his mouth turns down and he shakes his head. "That's disturbing. Don't make me think about it." He's covering his mouth with his hand like he's gonna puke.

I quickly run through what I just said and quirk an eyebrow at him. "What are you talking about? I said I've never been on a date, how is that disturbing?"

"Not that," he says, shaking his head. "Your dad bought a ticket to the auction. I'm pretty sure he was eyeing up Lucas. So that means he—"

"Don't think about it anymore," I chuckle. "Maybe I need you to show me what I'm supposed to do on a date? We could pretend we're on a date and you can show me what's expected of me. Could be fun."

"Pretending that my Jacob is going on a date with someone else and imagining all the things they might try and do to you? Hmm. I can think of about twenty other things that would be more fun than that…"

I lean in and kiss him quickly, then pull back and look at him. "You just called me *your Jacob*…that was cute."

"I'm so embarrassed," he says, covering his face. "I don't know why I said that." He flops back onto my bed, and I lie beside him. I want to squeeze him and tell him that hearing him say that was the furthest thing from awkward, but he really looks mortified.

I pillow my hands behind my head and look over at him. "I mean it. I need your help. I was kind of on a date with you tonight. I just left you sitting there when I decided to go talk to that kid. Was that okay? Should I not have done that?"

He sits up and tilts his head at me. "You can't be serious, though. You've seen movies of people going on dates, TV shows...even if you haven't done all those things, don't you know what you should be doing?"

Looking up at him, I can tell he thinks I'm kidding, but I'm not. "Honestly, every date that I've seen in movies ends in sex...and if I'm being completely honest—a lot of my friends have sex *before* they go on actual dates... You just told me that wasn't the case. So, I think it's safe to say that you should maybe tell me what I'm supposed to do."

"Okay, sit up," he says. "Let's pretend. I'll show you some things that are not okay. Keeping in mind that I have no idea who is gonna end up with you, and as the person who is *actually* sleeping with you, I'm incredibly uncomfortable thinking about this."

"Makes sense but think about it this way," I whisper in his ear, "right now, my body is your possession, so tell me how you want me to use it."

He blows air from his mouth and rubs my chest with one hand. "Sexy. So sexy. First of all, no one is allowed to touch you. No holding hands and no doing *this*..." He rubs his hand across my pecs for emphasis. "Your chest is so hot. No one else is allowed to touch this, ever."

"Mmhmm." I nod. "No one is allowed to touch my chest or hold my hand. What if we're watching a movie after dinner?"

"After dinner? A movie? This is *just* a dinner. You don't need to go out to a movie with someone. No one would expect that." He's still rubbing my pecs slowly. I don't know what he's thinking, but the air between us is definitely shifting to something a bit more sexual.

"This person that pays for me, might pay a few hundred dollars. I don't know how much they'll end up paying, but if this were happening in Miami, we'd be talking about several thousand. Does that change whether you want me to go to a movie with them? What if it's that older lady, Braden's grandma? Should I take her to a movie?"

"Leora? Definitely not. You have no idea the stuff she reads, and if she finds out you're sleeping with me, she's gonna want a book about it. Doesn't matter how much someone pays for you—you don't need to go to a movie. I don't want that." I nuzzle instinctively against his hand while he holds my cheek. "You shouldn't wear a tight shirt like this either. Do you have anything that doesn't show off your arms and tattoos?" His fingertips graze the tattoos on my forearms, and he stands, placing his body in between my legs. "Now, if you're sitting in a chair and your date stands in between your legs like this—that's a no."

"So. I shouldn't put my hands on their waist like this?" I ask, giving him a little squeeze.

He steps in closer taking my hands off his waist. "No. That would be bad." We're both wearing loose-fitting gym shorts, so it's easy to see that his dick is craving a bit more than a lesson in dating. Mine is pretty strained right now, too. "Your legs... No touching those, like this." His hands are resting on my thighs, and I have to bite my lip from reacting, as he teases the edge of my shorts, sliding his fingers under the thin black fabric. "This is worse than bad—don't let anyone touch here either," he says, eyes locked on mine, gently massaging his way up my legs.

"Your finger just grazed my cock, little mouse. I'm gonna fuck you soon, if you don't stop." I squeeze my eyes shut, unable to hold his gaze, the sensation of his fingers just gently teasing me, while he gropes the inside of my thighs, is too much. "Mmm—fuck," I groan.

My eyes are closed, but I can feel his breath on my ear. He whispers, "Don't. Let. Anyone. Do. This." The warmth of his touch has moved to my waist, as he slides my shirt up and straddles my lap. I lift my arms, allowing him to pull it off. "Jacob Rizzo...your chest is so hot...I wanna lick it."

My hands grip my comforter, while he leans down, bringing his tongue near my nipple. I can't sit here and be teased much longer when he's sitting on me like this. I need to touch him. "Choose your next move carefully... I think I've learned enough for the night."

"How much longer do I have? Before you teach me a lesson?" he whispers.

"Time's up." I grip his ass and switch positions, pinning him to the bed and slide his shirt up. "This comes off, now." He pulls it over his head, while my hands rub all over his chest, stopping on his nipples, teasing them between my fingers, then taking one in my mouth. His breath hitches and his eyes close when I graze my teeth on it. "Are you sensitive, little mouse?"

He nods at me, pulling my face up and lifting his mouth for a kiss. I press our lips together, rubbing my tongue against his, kissing him deeply, eliciting soft sweet moans from him. His cock is rock hard, rubbing against mine through our shorts and I can't fucking take any more. I yank his shorts down and back off the bed, standing near the edge. Quickly, I strip down naked and grab the lube and a condom out of my nightstand. It's a new bottle, so I rip the plastic covering off it and toss it on the bed. "Bend over and lift your ass for me. I'm going to fucking devour you."

Edward does as he's told and climbs to the top of the bed, propping himself on his elbows. I press on his shoulders. "Lie down and let me eat you." His head drops onto the pillow and he spreads his legs wide, arching his back, like a sexy little slut for me. "Mmm, so fucking hot." I lick around his hole, teasing him just a little then dive inside. The sweet taste of his skin turns me into an absolute animal and within moments I'm sucking and lapping at his hole like a sex-obsessed glutton. Edward's moans are low, just like the first time we were together. I slap his ass. "How many times must you be taught the same lesson? If you like what I'm doing, I want to hear you. Don't hold back."

He presses his ass against my face and whimpers when I stick my tongue inside. "Mmm—Jacob—Mmm. Fuck me."

I place a final kiss on his hole, tracing his rim with the tip of my tongue, then pull back. "You taste so good. I could eat you all night… But I need to be inside of you. I want the moans that you give me when I hit your spot… I want your ragged breaths when my cock pounds you, I want to hear every fucking sound you can make when you come, little mouse." I grab the lube and rub some on my finger, greedily taking a few more licks of his hole before lubing him up. "There, nice and wet for me." I work my finger inside, pumping him slowly, before adding a second.

"Nngh—yes—mmm—" he moans, while rocking on my fingers, helping to ease the second one inside. He's so warm and so tight. His legs spread wider, while I finger him, it's so hot. I love looking at him like this, spread open and desperate to be fucked. I lube my dick up, pressing the head against his entrance.

"Tsss—Ahh—Fuck—" he mumbles.

"Louder, Edward." I slap his ass and continue pressing inside.

"Ungh—do it again, please. Spank me."

I slap his ass, making a loud cracking sound that echoes in my room. Then fully slide inside. "You like to be spanked?"

"Yes," he says nodding and hanging his head down. "Choking, spitting and spanking. I like it rough." He presses back against me, and I slap his ass again.

"Dirty little mouse." My hips are moving back and forth, while Edward's hole clenches tightly onto my cock. The sounds of our bodies, wet and hard, slapping together combined with our heavy breaths is enough to bring me close to coming.

"Jacob—yes—harder—haah—haah," he begs.

I thrust harder and faster, over and over, finally hitting his prostate, and bringing with it a squeak when he comes and cries out my name—broken and beautiful, "Ja-cob." That squeak is the sweetest sound I've ever heard, and before I know it, I'm coming—groaning and panting, squeezing the meat of his ass.

Chapter Fourteen
You're In Trouble

   JACOB   

I walk inside my house quietly, unsure if Edward is still asleep. I tried to wake him before I left for the gym this morning, but he said he was too tired to go with me. I can't blame him, it's pretty early. But, if he's gonna be staying over, I have to make sure to stick to my normal workout routine, even if all I really want to do is stay in bed with him. I don't hear him moving around, but I should probably wake him up. Ah, he's still in my bed, right where I left him.

He looks so cute asleep, damn, he makes me feel all kinds of things just by existing. I rub the top of his head lightly, then drag my finger down his arm that's outside of the covers.

"Jacob—please. No gym. No six am. Please. I'm so tired."

I chuckle. "It's 7:30 and I already went to the gym. You should get up and get ready for work. I have a client first thing this morning, so I can drop you off at your shop if you feel like getting in a bit earlier."

He opens his sleepy eyes and stretches. "Yeah, that sounds good," he says, rubbing the mattress and smiling up at me. "Your bed is so comfortable. Did you have a good workout?"

"Yeah," I say, taking my shirt off. My eyes widen at the sound of my doorbell. "Who the hell is here so early? Must be Kellan or your brother." I look at my phone and am greeted with a terrible realization, standing outside my door. "Holy shit, holy shit." I toss my shirt back on and race across the room.

"What? What's wrong?" Edward asks. "Who's at the door?"

"It's Linley. Shit, I don't even know what to do," I say, walking in front of the bed. Damn it, this is my fault. I know better than to ignore her.

"Should you…maybe let her inside?"

"Oh shit, yes. Definitely. You don't need to hide in here, but don't feel like you need to come out. You're not ready for her yet." I quickly make my way to the front of my house. Linley looks pissed when I open the door. But she can be as mad as she wants, I'm not happy either. "What are you doing here, Linley?"

She pulls her oversized black sunglasses down to the tip of her nose and looks at me. "You wanna try that again? We start with good morning, then an apology. Let me inside," she says pushing her way past me.

"Good morning, I'm sorry I wasn't clear. What the hell are you doing here?"

She's walking around looking for something. "Where is the man who belongs to that car in your driveway?"

Shit. "What car in my driveway? Is there a car in my driveway? Wait, how did you get here?" I look outside my front window and see a small sedan parked beside Edward's car.

She walks over, giving me a look that tells me I'm actually in pretty big trouble. "There, see that red car? I drove that here. It belongs to the owner of the car rental place. There's another car right beside it. That's not your car, it's Edward's. So where is *Edward?*"

The hair on my arms stands up straight when she says his name like that. "Who's Edward?" I shrug.

She drops her mouth open and puts a hand on her hip. She's wearing the black suit she usually wears for deal brokering, so I really need to stop screwing around. "Rizzo, listen to me. You are in so much trouble. Don't try to deny it, your mother told me everything. Even if she hadn't, judging by the oil stains under that car, it's been here a few days. Is he asleep?"

"I don't know what you're talking about. I just got back from the gym. I was getting ready to send you my numbers for the morning."

"Cute. You haven't sent me your workout stats in days. You haven't even checked in with me. You knew you had to do that when we got permission for you to come here. You have gotten the both of us in so much trouble. Marco is really pissed off."

"I don't know what to tell you. You came here just to tell me Marco is pissed at me? That's nothing new. I'm really getting tired of this. I—just want to live my life. I can't play soccer right now, so I'm here doing my own thing, why do I have to check in like this? Why do I have to explain everything to you? Why are you here?"

She's tilting her head at me like I'm the stupidest person she's ever seen, as she puts her purse on my couch. "Sometimes I have to remind myself how much money you make me…because I tell you, this is ridiculous. Why do you have to check in? Did you forget about the twenty-five-million-dollar contract that Marco gave you? Did you forget that we're in the midst of negotiations? Did you also forget that you are legally obligated to respect the code of conduct? Jacob, you—where is this guy? I wanna meet him."

I shake my head and sit down on the couch. "That's not happening." Unfortunately, I know that Edward is gonna need to get to work and I told him I'd drive him. I can't have him be late opening his shop just because of this shit with Linley. "You can meet him later, just leave him for now."

"See, when your mom called me in a panic, I told her she had nothing to worry about because I trusted you enough to tell me if you were getting serious with anyone. I also trusted enough that you, for damn sure, wouldn't be letting anyone stay in your house after all the hoops we jumped through to set things up for you. What are you thinking? You know you can't have a relationship with someone. When I agreed to be your agent, I knew you were young and brash, and admittedly back then, your boyish charm won me over—that and the money, of course. But do you remember what you told me when I said I was worried about signing on as your agent?"

"Nothing will ever come before soccer."

"So, you do remember. Now, what changed? You met a guy, fixed up his bookstore, and fell in love?"

I look over my shoulder toward my bedroom door that is still partially opened. "I didn't say love—just, Linley, I'm asking you to try and see it from my shoes. Is it really so bad that I want to have my own life?"

"Yes. Yes, it is. You can't have both."

"This is bullshit. I just want to see where things go with us and not worry about soccer for a bit. I can't play anyway, so why is it such a problem?"

"You have obligations. Have you done any of your community service?"

"Is this why you're actually here, though? To yell about the community service? Or did you come here to meet Edward? I was gonna tell you about him, but, I mean, we just started seeing each other."

"Ha! He's already met your mother and your grandmother. How did that go, by the way? Your grandmother hates your father. How did she handle him being here?"

"How do you know she hates my father? I didn't even know that. You know too much about me. Super-agent…more like super-stalker."

"Very cute," she says with a smirk. "Yes, it is technically my job to stalk you and those around you. It's what I'm paid for, it's how I keep you safe. You don't even have security here with you, Rizzo. You and I both know how much it took to get you settled in this tiny town." She sighs and puts a hand on her hip. "I'm hungry and I haven't eaten, let's go out." She points toward my bedroom. "Bring the book boy along."

"Ha, now you're being cute. I have to work this morning and so does he. I told him I'd drive him, so I can't take you out to breakfast. I only have two clients this morning, and the rest are after lunch, so I could maybe do a brunch, or lunch. I don't know what you're gonna do for the next few hours. Should have told me you were coming," I say, standing from my couch. If I can get her out of here without forcing Edward to meet her, that would be ideal, but I don't think that's gonna happen. I gotta try and change the subject. I walk toward my front door and gesture toward it.

"Why are you driving the owner's car? That's what you said earlier, right? Did you make friends with him when you came here last time?"

She's shaking her head at me with her arms crossed. "There were no rental cars available, so he let me borrow his since I'm leaving tonight. I haven't talked to him until today, but he recognized my name as your agent, so he was more than willing to let me take it. Charged me only the cost of gas for the day. I do admire the small-town charm of this place. He also said his kids would get excited knowing that you were in their car."

I hold my hands out. "I didn't say I was getting in that car, and I'm definitely not."

She waves me off. "I want to meet Edward before I leave today, and I need at least an hour with you before I meet with him, or we meet with him together. So, figure out a way to make that happen and text me." She sighs and pulls the keys out of her purse. "Can't believe I had to come here for this. I'll save the yelling for later, separate from the meeting with Edward, of course."

"I'll text you as soon as I'm done with my clients this morning." A bitter cold wind blows in when I open the door and Linley shivers.

"So damn cold here. I'm gonna go to that cookie place. They should have breakfast stuff, maybe there's Christmas themed pastries. I'll see you in a bit."

I'm so glad she's gone, but now I have to go explain all of this to Edward. This really isn't fair for him, and I don't want to stress him out. I walk into my room and find him sitting on the edge of my bed, looking over at me. "Is the bad lady gone?"

I chuckle at that and take his hands in mine. "Temporarily, but she wants to meet you at some point today. Is that okay?"

He stands and hugs me tightly. "Of course, but I feel like I'm causing all these issues for you. Are you sure this is all worth it?"

"Mmhmm." I kiss the top of his head and squeeze him tight, resisting the urge to rub down his ass. "And you're not causing any issues for me. My job causes issues for me, and will likely cause issues for us, but you will never be the problem. Technically, both our jobs are a problem right now, because we need to leave. Are you okay with oats, or do you want to stop and grab something? I wouldn't suggest Braden's shop, because I think that's where Linley is heading."

He nuzzles his face in my neck, making me tingle. "I'm not really hungry. I think I'm fine not eating breakfast today."

I'm not sure if he's upset, or just genuinely not hungry, and I don't want to push him. Maybe he doesn't always eat breakfast. I wouldn't want to be one of those guys that force whatever they do on the person they're with. "Alright, let me get dressed really fast, then we can head out," I say, reaching into my drawer.

He's smiling at me while leaning against my door, just watching me get dressed. "You look very sexy for work. I asked you last night if you had anything that didn't show off all of you, and I guess the answer is no."

"Pftt. I don't know what you're talking about, these are just regular work clothes. Besides, I don't care who's looking at me, I'm pretty used to it. As for me, I only want to look at you."

It's moments like these when I'm really glad I met him here instead of Miami. I don't know how he'd react to seeing crowds of people chanting my name, or people constantly asking for pics when I go out places. I don't need to worry about any of that right now, though. Right now, I think it's kind of cute that he seems to be a little worried about people looking at me.

I run a brush quickly through my hair, then grab my keys, walking toward him. "I was just thinking that lunch will probably work out for the three of us, unless you'd prefer later than that? I can text you when I'm done with my morning clients. I have to actually install a few things today."

"That sounds good," he says moving to the side, so I can open the door. "What are you installing today? Batteries in smoke detectors?"

I chuckle and hold his hand leading him to the garage. "Ah, there's a new client this morning, he needs me to install a few wine racks for him. I think his boyfriend is coming for a visit and he wants to impress him. The other job is fixing a few kitchen cabinets." I press the garage door opener and walk toward the driver's side while Edward stands completely still pointing to the driveway. Great, Linley is still here. She's sitting in the driver's seat, kind of looking like she isn't paying attention, but she definitely is. "Hey, what are you doing?" I shout at her. "Move the car, we need to go." Edward is frozen in place, standing by the passenger door, looking quite helpless. "You can just get inside or maybe wave to her, then she'll probably leave. I'm sure she's just being extra nosy and wants to see you before meeting later."

He gives her an uncomfortable wave, and Linley gets out of the car. "Oh no," he mumbles. "You said I wasn't ready."

I have to save him; he's not gonna move. Walking toward the back of my car, I shout at her, "Hey, we're gonna be late! We don't have time for introductions. He already waved at you. I need you to move, please. Can't believe you've been sitting out here all this time."

Linley rolls her eyes at me and waves to Edward, it's easy to see that she's sizing him up. I really hate seeing that uncomfortable look on his face. "Shoo," I tell Linley. "I'll call you after my morning clients." I quickly make my way around my car, and open the door for him, encouraging him to sit. "I'm sorry," I whisper, once he's inside.

"He's much cuter in person!" Linley shouts over. "Don't even think of avoiding me today. Text me as soon as you're done playing contractor this morning."

I give her a salute and open my door, dropping my head on the steering wheel once I sit inside. I really didn't want her to meet Edward yet. It's fine, it would've happened eventually anyway, but Linley is an uncomfortable reminder of the life I have in Miami, a reminder that things won't always be as easy as they are now.

The feeling of Edward's fingers tracing along my back snaps me back to reality, and it instantly soothes me. I don't care about Linley being here, I care about *him*, and I don't need to worry about what's going to happen, I just need to be here, in this moment with him. I lean over and kiss him on the cheek. "I'm really sorry."

"Don't be sorry. It's okay. She said I was cuter in person, so that was kind of a compliment. Besides, I should be the one apologizing. Twice I've met people that are important to you, when you didn't even mean for it to happen. It's almost like life is forcing me into these situations, kind of against your will."

I drop an eyebrow at him. "How do you figure that to be true?" I ask, while reversing out of my driveway. "I don't do things against my will. It's one of the pros of having a stubborn personality. I do things the way I want to. Besides, every time you met someone in my family, did I seem embarrassed for them to meet you, or worried about you being comfortable?"

He smiles and rubs my thigh. "You were worried about me. I haven't seen your stubborn side yet," he chuckles, "so I'm not convinced you have one."

"Ha. You could ask anyone that knows me. I'm definitely stubborn, set in my ways, but these days there seems to be an exception."

"What would that be?" he asks looking out the window.

We're hitting all green lights, it feels almost like a sign. "A tiny little mouse would be the exception. I just can't seem to get him out of my head, or my bed."

His hand is gently squeezing my thigh, almost teasingly so. "I don't know, I think I heard that mice are pretty territorial. You may want to rethink this whole thing. Even if you wanted to get rid of him, I'm not so sure he'd be willing to give up," he says, inching his fingers toward the inside of my leg.

His touch drives me crazy. Just the feeling of his hand on my thigh is enough to make me feel things. The lot behind the building is empty, as I park behind Edward's shop. I look down at his hand. "I'm not looking to get rid of my little mouse. In fact"—I look around—"I kinda wish I could take him here in this parking lot before work." Glancing at the clock on my dashboard, I can see that we definitely don't have enough time for that, though.

He leans his head against my shoulder. The air between us feels different suddenly. I'm not used to worrying about people's feelings, so I might not be very good at it, but he seems almost bothered. "You okay?"

"Yeah, kind of," he says meekly. "There's not really anything wrong. I just feel like..." He sighs, shaking his head. "What are you going to do if Linley says that we're a bad idea? Will you just walk away? I don't know much about your career, and I want to, but with the way she talked to you, it seemed like, I don't know, she could tell you what to do and you'd have to listen."

"Please don't say that in front of her," I chuckle. "She wishes I listened to her, and if I did, I wouldn't be here right now. She never thought me going off the grid would work, but she did it anyway. She's really not here to try and get in between us, she's just here to make sure things are okay. We had an agreement that I'd check in and I didn't do that. I mean, she was probably freaking out like my mom because you'd obviously slept over, and who knows what my mom told her. It doesn't really matter, though."

People are starting to pull into the parking spots behind the building, he really needs to get inside. His store opens in fifteen minutes, and I need to get to my client, but I want to make him feel better. I turn in my seat and hold his face in my hands. "I need you to trust me when I say that you don't need to worry about Linley. I'll protect you from the bad lady. All I need you to do is meet her at lunch, then after work, I'll pick you up and we can finish what your hand on my thigh started a few minutes ago."

He smiles at me and presses his lips against mine, slipping his tongue inside softly. His mouth tastes minty and sweet, and I want more. I pull his face in closer, kissing him deeper. I want him to know how much I want him, how much I feel for him, even if I can't explain it. Our heads are moving side to side, and I'm not even sure how long we've been kissing for, and, honestly, I don't even care. This connection—this kiss—I can feel him putting his trust in me, even though no words have been spoken. "Mmm, Jacob," he murmurs, in between breaths. "I don't want to go to work."

It's taking everything in me not to tell him to skip work, because I just want to kiss him all day. But he's worked so hard to get his store open, and it would be selfish of me to do that. Fuck—if only his mouth didn't taste like heaven. I pull back just a bit and look him in the eyes while rubbing his bottom lip softly with my thumb. "I really like kissing you," I say, fighting the urge to dive back into his mouth.

"I like being kissed by you," he says. "Text me when you have a time for lunch." He reaches for the doorhandle and sighs. "I really don't want to go, but duty calls, I gotta go sell tickets, so that other people can throw themselves at you."

Chapter Fifteen
Anxious Hamster

Edward

I'm almost, like, nervous as I lock up my shop for a lunch break. I'm meeting Jacob and—shudder—Linley at the café at the corner in town square. Sticky Bunz or something like that.

I'd been feeling dread ever since I received the text from Jacob with the time and place for our lunch meeting with his agent.

I walk down the street toward town square and find myself waving and nodding at people as I pass them. This town is so friendly and welcoming. I've been here less than a week and already people are getting to know me and making me feel like I've been here forever.

When I reach Sticky Bunz, I see Jacob standing outside waiting for me like he said he would. I give him a smile when our eyes meet and when he smiles back it makes something flutter in my stomach. My dick also rises when I remember how we left things in the car before I started work; he must be as pent up as me.

Past him, through the window, I see the distinct figure of Linley seated at a table, thankfully with her back to us. That's an instant boner-killer.

"Hey," he says. I can tell he wants to hug me, but this is too public of a place to do that.

"Hey," I say back.

"How's your day been?"

I roll my eyes. "Exhausting. Your dad must have done a good job about letting people know about the auction, because as soon as I opened, I had swarms of people coming in to buy tickets. I'm almost sold out."

"That's good," he says. He has a sparkle in his eye that I see when he's happy for me and it makes me kind of giddy. But then I glance past him again and see Linley still sitting at the table and my smile falters.

He glances over his shoulder too, seeing what I'm looking at. "Thank you," he says when he turns back to me, "for everything. But especially for agreeing to this."

"Of course," I say. "I'd do anything for you, including having lunch with people who intimidate me."

"You can get through it," he says. "Although…"

"Although what?"

He sighs. "If you thought she was too much this morning, you should have heard her over the past two hours. I have no idea what she'll say to you. Lunch might be hideous."

I take a deep, steadying breath, then say, "Okay, let's do this."

Jacob leads us into the restaurant, and the man at the podium inside says, "Welcome to Sticky Bunz. How many in your party?" Then he looks up and sees Jacob and his eyes go wide. "Jacob! My hostess said she saw you come in earlier! What brings you to my café?"

He gives his winningest smile to the man. "We're having lunch with a friend of mine. She's over there."

"Well, anything you order will be on the house, of course." Then in a lower voice, the man adds, "And on your way out, could I ask for a couple autographs for my kids? They're huge fans—we're all huge fans at our house!"

"Of course," Jacob says. "I'd love to do so. I'll find you before I head out. But I can pay for our lunch."

"Thank you so much for choosing Sticky Bunz for your lunchtime treat!" the man says, holding his arm out toward Linley's table and giving a slight bow.

"Thank you so much," he says as we walk past.

"That was interesting," I mumble.

"What was interesting?"

"Nothing," I say, deciding to keep my thoughts to myself. The idol worship of Jacob is going to take a little getting used to, although it is cute when it's him giving tips to a young soccer player like last night.

When we reach the table, Linley gives me a polite nod. It's a square table, and Jacob and Linley are on opposite sides, so I take one of the other sides, putting me between them. I pick up the menu and glance at it, but Jacob just puts his aside. I realize then that he probably isn't going to eat anything, since it doesn't fit in his meal plan. When the server comes, I order a small salad and Linley orders a Reuben and fries. Jacob just orders a peppermint tea.

"It's nice to meet you, Edward. As in, formally meet you, not in passing as you're running away with your tail between your legs," Linley says as the server leaves. My heartbeat kicks up a notch at becoming her focus; the words she'd said this morning still ring in my ears. "Ninety percent of my job is looking to protect Jacob's interests and with how long I've been in the business, I've seen a lot of red flags pop up when players start"—she glances around, then lowers her voice to a whisper—"dating regular people."

Jacob opens his mouth, but Linley holds up her hand. "Stop, I know what you're going to say. You're not *dating*, and while that's true, I still need to do my due diligence."

My eyes go wide again, and I look at Jacob. He's giving her a stern look as he whispers, "If you want to so indiscreetly talk about *that*, we should have had lunch at my place."

"Oh, hush," she says, "I know how to be discreet. I've slept my way through half a women's soccer team and not a soul knows."

"Well, *we* know now," Jacob says.

She rolls her eyes. "You know nothing, Jacob. You don't know which team, you don't know who, and you don't know when. Discretion. I have it."

Jacob just crosses his arms and looks away.

"Anyway," Linley says, "Edward, I ran a background check on you."

My eyes go wide. Though Jacob had tried to prepare me for this and had told me she would indeed run a background check, it still feels surprising and a little bit invasive to know that it's actually happened. "Oh…"

She continues on, seemingly oblivious to my discomfort. "I had to make sure you didn't have any skeletons in the closet. Other than your poor grades in college, you're clean as a whistle."

My voice feels weak as I say, "I would have told you anything you needed to know."

"People lie, my dear," she replies. "So if I want to protect Jacob, then I need to go that extra mile." She cuts off the conversation as our food arrives, and Linley and I put our napkins in our laps. When the server disappears again, she continues. "I've examined you inside, outside, upside down, back, and forth, and you're squeaky clean. With that being said, I don't approve of where this is going."

"Linley!" Jacob says. When he realizes how loud he was, he glances around, then whispers, "You can't talk to him like that."

"Pish-posh," she says. "Look at him. He's quivering like an anxious hamster. You think he'd survive the media attention?"

Jacob glares at her.

She waves her hand dismissively. "Let's just drop it for the time being. It's not like you listen to me anyway. Now, we've been talking all morning and we still haven't come up with a plan for your community service. I'm not leaving town without a plan in place. Your community service is important; it's how you repair your public image, and how you return to professional soccer."

While I feel a little relieved that the focus is no longer on me—and maybe it's because I'm indeed an anxious hamster, and I'm no longer in the spotlight—I can't help but feel like my hackles are still up with Jacob being her new target. Yes, they've known each other for years and they have a supposedly good working relationship, but I don't really like how she talks to him. It often sounds like a schoolmarm disciplining a wayward student.

"I'll get to it," he mutters.

"You'll get to it?" She looks at me. "He'll get to it, he says." She turns back to Jacob. "What's there to get to? You've been here for over two months now and you're telling me you haven't done one single thing for the community? You haven't expended one iota of energy on someone other than yourself?"

"Nothing worth reporting anyway."

She grunts in frustration. "What about Edward's store? You renovated it, didn't you?"

His eyes flash to me and there's an unmistakable heat in them, but also clear protectiveness. "That wasn't community service. That was a paid job."

"A paid job can still play good for your public image," she says. "*Jacob Rizzo, International Soccer Sensation, Renovates an Independent Bookstore to Help It Open.* There's a certain charm to that. You'd at least win back the female demographic. It might even bring business to Edward's store."

If there's one thing Jacob's *not* lacking, it's the female demographic. But, of course, I don't have the guts to say that out loud.

"No," he says. He glances around again, then lowers his voice. "Edward stays out of this for now. One hundred percent out."

She rolls her eyes. "Whatever." After a bite of her sandwich, she says, "Regardless, you need to work on repairing your image. Surely, there's *something* you're doing here that can play well with the press."

He glances at me for a moment, then says, "I'm enjoying not being a puppet for the media for once. I know I can't have a normal life, but this is at least normal-ish, and making a media blitz out of what I'm doing now would just blow things up unnecessarily."

"But if you don't do that, then the media will continue to see you as a wildcard who can bring a bad name to the team at any time. You're volatile, uncaring, self-centered."

"That's not fair. He's none of those things," I blurt out. Then my eyes go wide and my cheeks burn with a blush, and I just look down at my salad.

"It doesn't matter what he actually *is*," Linley says. "What matters is what people *think* he is. When it comes to the media and public perception, fairness means little."

Jacob sighs. "I'll do something soon."

"So you've done *nothing* here?" she asks. "All you've done is work? Come on, Jacob, the media might think you're a bit of an asshole but I know you're not. I know that behind the bluster, you're the kind of guy to put others first and you care for whatever community you're a part of, so don't give me this bullshit that you've done zero community service."

His jaw clenches, but then he forces his face to relax. "I've been a little busy. If I do something, I'll let you know."

She rolls her eyes. "You're impossible, you know that?"

"But I make you the most money." He gives her a wicked grin.

"And that's why you're my favorite client."

We soon finish up our lunch, and I leave them to head back to my store. The weather is still unusually warm with no snow on the ground. The Christmas tree in town square almost looks out of place without snow all around it.

I make it back to my store just a few moments later and find several people already waiting outside for me. I greet them as I unlock the door and let them in. The afternoon proceeds fairly briskly with people coming and going—not all of them buy books, but most of them buy auction tickets.

About midway through the afternoon when there's a quiet spell with no one here, the bells on the door jingle as it opens. I look up to greet the person but the words die in my throat. Linley.

She gives me a smile and then glances around the store. "Nice place," she says.

"Th-thanks," I say. Damn my anxious hamster persona.

"The Sapphic books?" she asks.

I point directly across the room. I'd put a little lesbian flag on the shelf next to the section to help shoppers find what they want. She heads over there and starts flipping through some of the books. I try to ignore her and focus on my work—I have to do a refill order soon with how much people are buying. I make sure to stock up on the entire *Debriefing the Lawyer* series for Leora. But in all that, I don't fully remove my attention from Linley.

Eventually, she crosses the store, her heels clicking on the floor. She puts a stack of three books on the counter, but eyes me up.

"It's a shame about Jacob," she says.

"Um…what's a shame?"

"Oh, I shouldn't have said." Then she looks at me again and leans forward almost conspiratorially. "All he has to do is a few simple things to repair his image—an act for charity, maybe offer a coaching session to a kid's team, reading books at the hospital…not much is asked of him, but he does *nothing*."

I keep my mouth shut, but I want to tell her the truth, about how amazing and generous he is. It almost hurts to hear her talk about how she sees Jacob as so selfish and self-centered.

"I know he's a good guy," she says, continuing on, "but I expected more from him, you know? He's just out here stupidly doing whatever he wants and not thinking about his career or the people affected by his foolish behavior."

I grind my teeth, trying to hold back from a remark about how she's got him all wrong. "These three books?" I ask, trying to redirect our focus.

"Yes," she says, pushing them toward me.

I ring them through the register. "That'll be $42.37," I say.

She holds out her credit card, and I pass her the machine so she can tap it. When she puts her credit card away, she pulls out a business card and passes it to me. "Jacob is getting himself deeper and deeper into this mess. Here's my card. Keep an eye on him for me, will you? I just want what's best for him." She lets out a heavy sigh. For all the bluster and abrasiveness, I can see that she really does care about him.

I take the card from her and look at her name and number written in shiny black ink.

Before I can decide if I can trust her or not, she says, "Well, I best be off then."

As she heads out the door and it jingles as it closes, I find I'm conflicted. Jacob should be able to live his life how he wants to live it, and he doesn't need needling from her over this community service thing. But on the other hand, if he'd listen to her, it sounds like he'd be back in the good graces of soccer and prepped to return to the team next season, and not here doing carpentry—though I'm even conflicted about that since being here doing carpentry means he's here with me.

I shove the business card in my pocket and sit on the stool behind the register, ruminating on it all. When the door jingles and a new customer comes in, I do my best to ignore my wandering thoughts and give this person a smile and offer to point them in any direction they might need. As the afternoon rolls on, with a somewhat steady stream of customers, I find the issue of Linley and Jacob sits at the back of my mind.

As the end of the day slowly approaches, I decide that I want to have a beer with Chad before heading to Jacob's. I need to tell him how this day went, because I can't really vent to Jacob about it. I pull out my phone and text Jacob: *Hey, I'm gonna have a beer at Chad's bar and have some brother-brother time. I might get dinner too if you're okay with that. Can you pick me up around 6:00?*

A few moments later, my phone dings with a text from Jacob: *Of course! It looks like this job is going to run a little late anyway. Have a great time!*

When five o'clock rolls around, I turn the sign to closed and then hurry across the street. The day seems to have turned a little colder, so I cross my arms over my chest to bundle myself together for warmth.

I push open the door to Bottoms Up and find Chad at the bar with Lucas out on the floor wiping tables. There are a few customers here, scattered about, but it's before the evening rush. Chad looks up and catches my eye, giving me a beaming smile as I cross the room and climb onto a stool at the end of the bar.

"What can I get you, little brother?"

"Something cheap," I say.

"Sorry, Lucas isn't on the menu," he jokes, but then he pulls a weak beer out from under the counter, and pops the cap off for me.

"And maybe a sandwich and fries?" I add.

Chad flags Lucas down from across the bar. When he arrives and says hi to me, Chad asks him to make my meal. When he disappears into the kitchen, Chad says, "Now, will you tell me honestly what's been going on?"

I eye him as I take a swig of beer. "What do *you* think is going on?"

"I think my little brother has fallen for"—when I give him a stern glare to indicate he be careful what he says since we're in public, he lowers his voice considerably—"a certain someone…and since you've spent the night at that certain someone's house three nights in a row, I'd say those feelings are reciprocated." He crosses his arms and leans his ass against the counter behind him. "Am I right?"

I nod. "I'd say so." His eyes light up like he's about to shout something obscene. I quickly hold up a finger, silencing him, even if just for a moment. "*But*…I only have permission to confirm that for you on the condition that you don't breathe a word to anyone, especially not to that loudmouth parrot of yours."

He gives me a wicked grin and thankfully doesn't ask me how big Jacob's dick is. Instead, he says, "Well, if I can't start a parade through town celebrating the dick my little brother is getting, then the least I can do is tell you I'm happy for you. A little jealous, yes, but happy."

"Thank you," I say.

"So does this mean you're never coming back to the room you've got at my place? I've been dying to go through your stuff and if you're not coming back…"

"Don't touch my stuff!" I blurt out, maybe a little too loudly.

"You brought your dildo collection with you, didn't you? You don't want me to see how much of a skilled bottom you are, right?"

A slight blush hits my cheeks. "There may be a toy or two," I admit. "I'll be there soon. I can't stay at his place forever. Besides, we need some more formal brother hangout time that isn't just me sitting at your bar."

"Agreed on the brother time. But I can't promise I won't go through your stuff," he says.

Then Lucas comes out and places a plate with a loaded and toasted sandwich and piping hot fries in front of me. "Good to see you, Edward," he says. "Petey misses you."

I pick up an extra-hot fry and shove it in my mouth. "You can tell Petey I miss him too, though I think he'd just reply with something offensively sexual."

Lucas glances at Chad. "Well, like father like son, I guess." Then he grabs his cloth and heads back out to wipe down more tables.

"Have you and, uh, him figured out what's going to happen when he, uh," Chad glances around and lowers his voice once more, "eventually goes back to work at his regular job out of town?"

My smile falters. I hadn't really thought of that yet. I give him a shrug. "We'll figure something out," I say.

"You can make it work if you want to," he says. "I know of a couple that spends most of the year apart—one guy lives here and the other lives in Los Angeles. They fly back and forth regularly, and they're a solid couple despite the distance between them."

I take another swig of beer, then put it down on the little cardboard coaster with a sketch of a beer bottle wedged between a pair of butt cheeks. "So, about his work—"

"One sec," he says, interrupting me. He hurries down the bar and quickly makes a customer a cocktail. While he's gone. I manage to finish off my sandwich and start picking at the pile of fries that still remains. When he returns, he says, "Sorry, about his work..."

"Well..." I start picking at the beer's label with my thumbnail. "I met his agent today. She's...a unique individual. Very loud and opinionated, but seems to care deeply for Jacob and his well-being."

"And...?"

"She was on his back about the community service thing. He told her he hasn't done a single thing yet and I know that's not true—he helped fix the sleigh for the Snowflake Festival, and she even said the work he did on my store could count. So, she's left thinking he's doing nothing and just, I don't know..." I can feel myself getting worked up about this already. My pulse has definitely picked up speed.

He pulls out another beer from under the counter and it's then that I realize I've drained the first one he gave me.

"Do you care what she thinks of him?" he asks me.

I finish off the fries and take a swig of the new beer. "I don't know if I do, but I think he does, even if he doesn't act like it. But the thing is, he's doing all these things and no one knows about it. Like, yesterday we were at the movie in the park and he saw a little kid kicking around a soccer ball. He went up to the kid and taught him a few things and helped him hone his skills."

"So…" Chad says, "do you feel like you should have spoken up and defended him? Lucas and I let people talk a lot of gossip about us, but if we ever feel someone is unfairly criticizing us, we speak up. We set people straight." I can almost feel the weight of Linley's business card as he says that, but I try to ignore it. Then he says, "Especially since it sounds like she's unnecessarily hard on him."

I shrug my shoulders, pushing aside the thought of speaking up and instead focusing on Linley. "I don't know if *unnecessarily* is the right word. It's clear she cares for him, like, in more than just a 'he's my client' sense and if he won't help himself, then she needs to give him a poke now and then." I sigh. "She's worried about him. Deeply."

Now Linley's card feels like it's burning a hole in my pocket. I could… No, I shouldn't. But if he won't…

"Edward," Chad says, bringing my attention back to him, "are you okay? You're really not yourself today. When's the last time you got railed? Maybe you just need a good pounding."

I drain the last of my beer. "I'm okay, really. I'm okay. I just got a little worked up about this, I guess." I put the empty bottle on the coaster. "We should hang out soon, just you and I. I've been so wrapped up in my time with Jacob that I've kind of been ignoring you."

He gives me a big smile. "I'd love that. And we definitely want to see both of you on Christmas, so mark that in your calendar."

My phone buzzes in my pocket, and I pull it out…along with Linley's card. I look at it for a long moment before turning my focus to my phone. *Done with my client. Ready to go if I pick you up in ten?*

I text Jacob back: *Definitely. Meet you out front!*

To Chad, I say, "I'll text you, okay? We can sort something out?"

"Of course, Edward." He tips my empty toward me in salute. "Have a good time, alright?"

I wave one last goodbye to him and Lucas, then divert to the men's room before heading out. I'm suddenly rock-fucking-hard when I enter because this is where it all began. That's the stall right there. I quickly do my business, as difficult as it is when I'm this incredibly hard, and wash my hands.

Chapter Sixteen
A Beautiful Mess

When I step out of the bar and into the street—my still-hard bulge leading the way—I find Jacob pulling up to the curb at that exact moment. I hop into the passenger seat. The two beers in me make me really want to lean across and kiss him on the lips and shove my tongue in his mouth. But the responsible part of me that isn't too drunk yet knows we're in public, so a light squeeze of his hand will have to do until we get to his place.

He squeezes my hand back, but seems slightly off. When we pull away from the curb, he says, "I'm sorry for today. I know Linley can be a bit much sometimes."

"Hey, you don't need to apologize," I say.

He glances at me. "Are you sure?"

"I'm sure. Her job is to take care of your best interests and that includes checking out people like me," I say. Was I feeling intimidated? Yes, but I'm not about to say that to him. And I feel like my privacy was invaded a little bit too.

He gives me a smile. "I was worried all day and even more so after lunch. I didn't have any time to visit you and I was worried that you were mad about the whole thing."

"Honestly, don't worry about it." I don't want him to dwell on this, so I change the topic. "How were your clients today?"

He laughs. "Lots of getting up on ladders for single women. One of them offered me lemonade and said that if I wanted my dusty clothes washed, she'd happily run them through her laundry machine. She, of course, confessed she had nothing for me to wear while my clothes would be in the laundry."

I giggle. "And what were you doing for her that got you so dusty?" I look at what he's wearing. "You certainly look perfectly clean. You didn't take her up on that offer, did you?"

"I did *not* drop my pants for her," he says. "But you don't really get dusty doing a site visit to provide a quote."

"So you didn't actually do *any* work at her place and she offered to do your laundry? I wish I had the balls for that kind of thing."

"I'd drop my pants for you with just a hot glance. No flimsy excuse needed." He turns into his neighborhood, navigating the curved streets and eventually pulling into his driveway, parking next to my rust bucket.

"I'm sorry about my car," I say. When I look down the street, there are only gleaming, newer cars in the driveways.

He narrows his eyebrows at me. "What are you talking about?"

"My car," I say, pointing at it. "I heard what Linley said this morning, about how it stands out and anyone would know it's not yours and that we're not being discreet."

"Ah…you heard that."

I nod. "I can park it at Chad's, if you want. Or behind the store. It seems like a nice enough town that it'll be safe there."

"No, your car belongs here," Jacob says. He points at his garage. "We can park it in there. Then we'll keep Linley happy."

"Are you sure?" I ask. "I don't want to be an imposition."

"Edward, you could never be an imposition."

Before settling in the house, we grab my car keys and move my car into the garage. It seems even more out of place here with its pristine cement floor and neatly stacked boxes, but he seems extra happy to have my car there—not because it's out of sight from the street, but because it's *inside his garage* and that seems more special somehow to him.

"What do you want to do tonight?" I ask as we go from the garage to the house.

"Well…" he says as he wiggles his eyebrows at me.

"I mean other than that, because we can't do that all night."

"I can go all night," he says, "and I know you can too."

I come around the island and wrap my arms around his shoulders. "We can test your hypothesis if you'd like."

He kisses me slowly, then says, "I'd like that. We can get some Red Bulls and granola bars so we can keep our energy levels up."

I roll my eyes. "Or we can just fuck and see if we want to fuck a second time right away."

"Where's the challenge in that? I'm an athlete, after all."

"Well, mister athlete, I'm going to shower since I feel all sweaty from work. You wanna hit the showers team-style?"

He chuckles. "I think you have the wrong idea of what happens in the showers after a game."

"Oh?" I say innocently. "No one hooks up in the showers?"

"I can't say it's come up," he says. "But we can start our own tradition tonight."

"I like that," I say, drawing a finger down his nose to the tip. "This tradition is just for us."

He pulls me even closer and slips his hand down the back of my pants, grabbing an ass cheek in each hand and giving them a squeeze. I give him a grunt of pleasure and buck my hips toward him.

He pulls his hands from out of my pants and then rests his fingers on my waist. A moment later he shoves my pants down, along with my underwear, leaving me bottomless in his kitchen. Before I can protest or grab for his pants, he pulls my shirt over my head. Now I'm completely naked and he's fully clothed.

I feel shy for some reason, and my hands move to my crotch to cover my dick.

"No," he says, brushing my hands aside. "Don't hide anything. You're gorgeous, Edward."

I try to project some confidence and sexiness.

"You have me at a disadvantage, Jacob."

"Let me rectify that," he says, then quickly pulls his clothes off.

Even though I've seen his glorious naked body many times, I can't help but trace his tattoos with my gaze, getting caught on the taut muscle and that huge, hard cock. He steps closer to me again, his cock poking against my lower abdomen. He puts his hands on my shoulders and leans in to kiss me.

Then he slides his hands down my body, rounding over my ass cheeks. And then—with a grunt from him and a gasp from me—he picks me up with my legs on either side of his body and my chest pressed hard against his. I wrap my arms around his neck and kiss him. Beneath me, his rock hard monster of a cock is pointing straight up and teasing at my hole, making me long to be filled with him again.

"Take me to the shower," I say.

"Yes, sir, little mouse." Carrying me with ease and with a sheer strength I didn't know he had, he takes us across the house to the master bedroom and the en suite bathroom. He sits my bare ass down on his vanity counter as he turns to start the shower and get it steamy. His back is all muscle and his ass is firm and round. There isn't a trace of body hair on him.

I lean back a little bit and grasp my hard cock, slowly stroking it up and down as I watch this perfection of masculinity fiddle with the shower. When he finally adjusts it to his liking and turns around, his eyes go wide with surprise and then narrow with lust when he sees I'm stroking.

He comes close and takes my hands, making me release my cock. Then he puts my hands on the counter with his hands over mine, holding them in place. He gets down on his knees in front of my crotch and brings his face to my cock and opens his mouth…but doesn't take me in. He doesn't suck me. Instead, he exhales his hot breath over the sensitive skin of my tight shaft. Then he puckers his lips, concentrating the strength of his breath and turning it cooler as he blows the sensitive head.

"God, Jacob…" I moan. "Please…"

Before I can beg some more, he stands and releases my hands. "Come on," he says, "let's get in the shower."

I groan with denied need and hop off the counter, then step into the shower. He comes in behind me and presses me against the wall. Soon, his hands find mine again and he pins them against the wall above my head. He slides his free hand down my back, following the trails of water as they trace my spine and slip into the crack of my ass. His fingers soon find the tight knot of flesh at the center of my cheeks.

"Jacob…" I whisper.

"Edward…" he growls. Then he's kissing the back of my neck as his arms snake around me and he hugs me from behind. He presses his body against me, forcing me to smush my body against the shower wall. His fat cock is nestled against my ass crack, sliding up and down as he thrusts his hips back and forth.

"Fuck me…" I moan.

"Beg for it," he commands.

"Fuck me…please, Jacob…fuck me hard…" I whine.

"Suck it first," he says authoritatively.

He releases his hold on me enough to let me turn around and slide down to sit on my heels in front of him. The hot shower water cascades over my head. He towers over me. I look up at him and just see planes of muscle—and that heavy cock dangling in front of my face.

"Open wide, little mouse," he says.

I do as commanded, and he slides his cock into me, filling my mouth. He slides all the way in until his cockhead hits the back of my throat. I close my lips around his shaft and we both moan. He sinks forward, bracing his arms against the wall, and I wrap my hands around his thighs.

He puts a hand on my head. "Are you ready, little mouse?"

I mumble a yes, and then he starts fucking my face—nice and slow at first, but soon picking up speed and force. Eventually, he brings his second hand to my head, holding each side of my face.

"Oh…fuck, Edward…" he groans. "Fuck, I want to fuck your ass so bad."

I try to moan an "I want it too," but it comes out as mumbled gibberish.

He keeps thrusting harder and harder into my mouth, until I'm sure he's going to come, but then he suddenly pulls his cock from my mouth.

I look up at him, and he looks down at me with a face red with exertion and his chest heaving with gasping breaths.

"Are you going to finish?" I ask. I want his cum in me. So badly.

"Not here," he says, his words breathy. "In the bed. I want to hold you while I fuck you, have you look into my eyes as I claim your body as mine."

I stand up, and we kiss urgently, passionately, hungrily. While we kiss I grab his thick, hard cock and he reaches around me and grabs my ass, groping and squeezing.

"I need you," I moan into his mouth. "I need you inside me."

He growls in response, squeezing my ass harder. "Let's move to the bedroom. Now." He slams his hand against the shower handle and shuts it off, never taking his hot and hungry eyes from me.

When we step out of the shower, he finally tears his gaze from me so he can grab towels and we quickly dry each other off. When I crouch down to dry his legs, I get him to turn around.

"What are you doing, little mouse?" he asks.

"Something I've wanted to do ever since I first saw this ass of yours. Can I take a small bite?"

He looks down at me with a grin on his face. "It's all yours," he says.

I lean forward and bite his right cheek, eliciting a gasp from him, and then bite his left a little harder, earning a yelp. It's so juicy and hard and perfect. It's, like, muscular and somehow soft at the same time.

When I stand up again, he takes me by the arm and leads me into the bedroom, tossing me onto the bed. I bounce a bit until I settle, just watching him staring down, ready to devour me. He's given me a lot of scorching looks since we got together, but this is a new level.

He comes around to the other side of the bed and hooks his hands under my armpits, pulling me close to him, to where my head is hanging off the side of the bed. His hard cock is dangling against my lips.

"Open up," he says.

I do and he pushes his cock inside. And he pushes *deep*. But with the angle I'm at, I can accommodate his length into my throat. I'm driven by lust, and I'm eager to swallow him.

He groans and falls forward onto my body, shoving his cock deep again. I love it. I love every fucking second of it. Then he buries his face between my legs, licking at my taint. With a tug of his hands against my legs, I lift my ass and his mouth finds my hole. He's licking and digging in and driving me wild. If I didn't have his cock shoved down my throat I'd be screaming in pleasure already. He lights up every nerve ending in my body and rocks my world in a way I didn't think was even humanly possible.

I slide my hands over his back, coming down to cup his ass. Even though he's deep in me, I pull his ass hard, trying to get him deeper. It makes him moan, which vibrates against my hole, which in turn makes me moan and vibrate against his cock. God, he's phenomenal at sex. My mind is blown and soon my load will be too.

He's got a hand on each of my ass cheeks, and he's spreading them, pulling them apart, stretching my hole, loosening it so he can dig in deeper with his tongue. God, I'm so fucking wet from him, and my neglected cock is so achingly hard it's leaking pools of precum everywhere. I don't dare touch it—I want this to last forever. The way he makes me feel…it's indescribable, and I never want it to end.

Then he sticks a finger in my spit-slicked hole. I gasp and moan and writhe under the touch. He digs the finger in deeper, easily reaching my prostate and sending a jolt of pleasure through me—a jolt that almost makes my straining cock explode with orgasm.

I finally wrench my head to the side, and his fat cock slides out of my mouth and rests along my face. "Just fuck me already," I beg. I'm breathless and lightheaded.

In response, he digs his finger in deeper, flicking forcefully against my prostate. My hands fly to my sides, and I grip the comforter, fisting it hard. I let out a guttural sound of pleasure as he continues to dig for gold in my ass.

"You're going to make me come," I warn him through gritted teeth. "Like, really fucking fast."

"We can't have that," he says, with a flick across my prostate. "That would end this all too soon." Flick. "I need to draw this out a little longer, and make your orgasm one you'll never forget." Flick. I clench my jaw and do everything I can to hold back from coming.

Then he mercifully pulls his finger from my ass. He stands up, looking down at me. My head is dangling between his thighs.

"Look at you," he says. "You're a mess." He caresses my face. "A beautiful mess."

I try to say something, but all that comes out is a whimper.

"Good boy," Jacob says. "Now turn around so I can fuck you. I want to look deep into your eyes when I'm coming inside you."

I try to casually spin around, to present him my ass instead of my mouth, but he's already wrecked me and all my movements are clumsy and uncoordinated. When I'm finally laying on my back with my ass to him and my legs slightly raised, he looks at me with hunger and approval in his eyes. "Good little mouse."

He reaches into the nightstand, pulls out a condom and puts it on, then pulls out a bottle of lube, squirting some into his hand and then slicking up his thick shaft. He then takes a finger and applies some lube to my already wet and loosened hole.

"Are you ready for me?" he asks, his voice low and gravelly.

I hook my hands behind my knees and pull my legs tight to my chest. He looks down at me with sexual hunger. "Fuck me hard," I beg. After a pause, I add, "And choke me a bit." There's a flicker of uncertainty in his eyes, but he doesn't say no. Given what he said before, though, I'm not too hopeful about the choking thing. For now, I'll just have to be satisfied with his giant cock rearranging my insides.

He angles that cock of his toward my knotted flesh, pressing firmly against it. Even though his fingers and tongue had just been in there, I'm tight, and I let out a little gasp when his head breaches my entrance.

"Breathe…" he tells me.

He takes my legs from me, letting them rest against his chest. I let my hands fall to my chest and focus on breathing and trying to relax my body. Slowly, I feel myself loosening up and he slides into me, bringing his pelvis firmly against my ass. When he's fully inside me, he stops and holds his place, looking down at me with eyes almost glazed with pleasure. I'm sure I'm looking up at him with the same, because, holy fuck, he fills me so perfectly.

He leans forward, pressing my legs against my chest, and I stretch my neck up to meet him halfway, kissing him deep and hard. And mid-kiss, he starts moving his hips, dragging that fat cock out of me and then slowly shoving it back in. Every inch of friction has my body lighting up with fireworks.

I wrap my arms around his neck, keeping his lips pressed against mine. I push forward with my tongue, parting his mouth and slipping inside. His tongue meets mine, wrestling, caressing.

His hips start moving faster as he pounds into my ass. His cock goes from full depth to just the tip and back in just a fraction of a second. He's fucking me with every ounce of energy he has, and I'm taking it like the good bottom I am. I love what this man does to me and how he makes me feel. My cock is still untouched and still incredibly hard between our stomachs and steadily leaking precum—and it's dangerously close to careening off that cliff of orgasm. That point of no return is mere moments away, especially with his cockhead dragging over my prostate with each thrust into me.

"Jacob," I murmur into his mouth, then I let out a whimper as he hits my prostate again.

"Edward," he murmurs back.

"I'm close…"

He grunts as he thrusts particularly hard into me. "I'm close too, little mouse."

I bite his lower lip, then say, "Fill me. Come deep inside me."

He growls, then nips along my jaw and down to my neck, then he trails kisses up my throat and over my Adam's apple, returning to my lips. "I don't want this to end," he says.

"Me too, but—unh—I'm so close to coming, Jacob. So fucking close. Do it," I beg.

"Yeah? You want my cum?" he says.

"I want your cum. Fill me, Jacob, fill me. Empty those balls into me."

He starts fucking me even harder. "I'm gonna come in that hot little ass of yours," he groans out.

I kiss him hard, shoving my whole tongue in his mouth. When I do, he slams into me harder than ever before. I yelp with the collision of our bodies, but it's a yelp of pleasure. And this time, he doesn't drag his cock out of me to pound me again. No, he stays there, our bodies pressed painfully hard together, him buried deep in me. He's shuddering and gasping, and I swear I can feel his cock throbbing and pulsing as he rides through a powerful orgasm and fills my ass with his hot cum.

He collapses on top of me, panting and gasping. My legs slide down his body, until I hook them around his legs. When he regains his breath, he starts kissing my ear and the side of my face. He raises his head a bit, kissing me on the lips, driving his tongue into my mouth.

"You need to come," he murmurs into my mouth.

I chuckle and pull my mouth from his. "I, uh…I think I already did."

He rolls half to the side, and we both look down our bodies. Our stomachs are covered in my load. I had lost it in those last few moments when he was driving himself deeper. He rolls the rest of the way over onto his back and tugs me along so I'm rolling on top of him.

We make out a bit more, and when our make-out session slows and dies off, I find we're still gazing into each other's eyes with heat and affection. We decide to take a shower, and Jacob leads me into the bathroom; I stare at his hot, muscled ass the whole way. He gets the shower nice and steamy, and we step in and wash each other off. When we're good and clean and my fingers start getting a little wrinkly from all the water, we step out and dry off.

What I feel for this man…

We get ourselves ready for bed—basically by brushing our teeth and just pulling on some underwear—and then we climb under the covers. We snuggle close and I roll over so he spoons me against him. God, his body fits so perfectly against mine.

It doesn't take long for him to fall into a slumber. He falls asleep before me, and I can feel his soft breath against the back of my neck. This is a moment of pure bliss, pure heaven. Jacob is an amazing man and so wonderful to me; I can't believe I could be so lucky to find a man of his caliber that is into me.

If only Linley saw him the way I do. I don't mean, like, fully naked and balls deep in me, but nice and gentle and kind and generous. When she came into my shop, I could tell she was worried about him not doing community service—or at least *she thought* he wasn't doing community service. She'd worry less about him if she knew he was doing stuff, like the Book Boyfriend Auction.

Almost as if he's sensing me think about him, Jacob stirs. He mumbles something in his sleep about sports and then rolls onto his back, his arm falling from my body and onto his chest. I glance at him over my shoulder and can't help but smile with how cute he looks when he's asleep.

I'm still torn about this Linley thing, like it's eating at me. Maybe if she knew she didn't have to worry about him, she'd be a little gentler with him or not press so hard.

I glance back at Jacob one more time; he's fully and deeply asleep.

That conversation with Chad had really crystalized my thoughts. I should have said something to Linley. Maybe if I told her, she'd ease up on him.

I bite my lip as I consider my options. But before I can think too hard, I'm reaching for my pants on the floor and digging through the pockets, looking for my phone and Linley's card. I quickly type and send her a text message.

This is Edward. I wanted to tell you that you don't have to worry about Jacob. He's doing good things here in Frosty Bottoms and even if he's not claiming community service, he's helping the community. In fact, he's participating in my Book Boyfriend Auction that's helping raise money for charity on Friday. He cares about his community and the people around him.

My heart was weirdly thudding as I typed that out, but I'm smiling as I hit send. As I turn off my phone and shove it back in my pants pocket, it buzzes. I pull it back out and see a reply from Linley.

Thank you for telling me. I'm glad to hear that.

I smile again and shove my phone back into my pants, letting it all fall in a crumpled heap on the floor. Rolling onto my back, I stare up at the ceiling, feeling good. I did the right thing. He'll get recognition from Linley for doing community service and get back in the good books of whoever it is that owns the team.

Jacob rolls toward me again and buries his face in the crook of my neck and his hand comes to rest on my belly. I am so contented and so at peace and so happy. Everything is going right for once. I close my eyes and I soon fall asleep.

Chapter Seventeen
The Boy Toy

   **Jacob**   

"Ugh," I groan, reaching to turn my alarm off. I'm so tired. I don't feel like doing anything today. Finding the will to exercise while Edward is lying beside me, is almost impossible. But after my reaming from Linley yesterday, I know I need to get up. I rub his face softly, he wanted to go to the gym with me this morning, at least he said he did. "Hey," I whisper. "You wanna work out?"

Edward nuzzles against my hand. "Nooo," he whines. "Can you just set an alarm for another ten minutes? Just a few more minutes in bed together and after that, I can do it."

"You're gonna get me in trouble one of these days. Ten more minutes," I say, grabbing my phone. What the fuck? I wipe my eyes awake and sit up. What the actual fuck am I looking at? No, no, no. My heart is beating so fast at the sight of over two hundred text messages and a completely full voicemail. No. Please. I can't think straight—the media—everyone—they know. They know where I am. How could this happen? I must be dreaming, only I'm not, because I'm vaguely aware of Edward's hand on my back.

"What's wrong, Jacob? What is it? Why are you breathing so fast?"

I stand up from my bed and run to my window looking outside.

There's no one out there, they haven't figured out where I live yet. Fuck. How? What am I gonna do? What am I gonna tell Edward?

"Jacob, look at me," he says, standing beside me.

I'm so out of it that I didn't even notice him there. I can't fucking think. What do I do? I swallow and shake my head slowly looking at my phone. Interview requests, messages from Marco, messages from Linley, messages from my mom, my dad—everyone.

"Edward, I have to call Linley. She has—this emergency plan for if the media figured out where I was and I—I guess I have to use it because everyone knows where I am." I hold my phone facing him, showing him the texts. I have to resist the urge to just turn it off and run away. "I don't know how this happened. Maybe Linley—"

Edward looks panicked, his hands are covering his mouth.

"It's okay," I tell him, rubbing his arm, somehow able to comfort him, when I can't even comfort myself right now. "We can figure—"

"This is my fault," he says. "I—I'm sorry." Tears fall from his eyes, and I wipe them away.

"This is not your fault. Someone probably just saw us together and got upset, who knows. It's not your—"

"Jacob, it *is* my fault. I...I texted Linley last night when you were asleep."

All the blood in my body is rushing to my head, and I'm finding it hard to stand. I sit on the edge of my bed and take in what he just said to me.

He sits beside me, fighting back tears. "I just—I wanted to tell her that you had been doing your community service and that you were even doing the auction. You've been doing so much here, and she talked so meanly to you yesterday. I just wanted to stick up for you. I wanted her to know that you were doing stuff, that you weren't—" he sniffles. "I couldn't stand that she thought you were being selfish, when you're not. I didn't think—I didn't think she'd tell everyone."

I cover my hand with my mouth to stop myself from saying anything I might regret. I don't want to yell, but I am so fucking upset. I can't even talk to him right now, because he truly has no idea what he's done. But Linley knew, she knew exactly what would happen.

I press Linley's name in my contacts and walk into my bathroom, slamming the door behind me.

"How fucking dare you!" I shout before she says a word. "How could you do this to me? You knew what would happen, you knew exactly what would happen and you—how did he even get your phone number? Did you give him a card? Tell him to keep an eye on me? What the fuck am I supposed to do now?!"

Linley is silent, and I'm not in the mood to try and play nice. "I pay you so much fucking money and this is how you repay me? By telling everyone in the world where I am and what I've been doing? Couldn't you just trust that I was going to do the damn service? I just wanted to be fucking normal for once in my life! I've been playing soccer since I was eighteen, for fuck's sake, I was just a kid when I signed my first contract! I can't believe you would do this to me."

"Are you done?" Linley asks calmly, seemingly unfazed by my shouting, which only pisses me off more.

"No. I'm not, but I'd love to hear an explanation from you."

"Rizzo, listen, I gave you your way, you broke our arrangement, you failed to do the community service that you said you were going to do, I had Marco breathing down my neck, every single one of your sponsors has been asking for you, begging for you to issue a public apology. This isn't a game. You play a game, but the decisions you make are very real and they impact millions of people. I'm sorry that you're pissed off, but I stand by what I did. Giovanni will be there shortly to provide detail for you. I don't care if he has to sleep in his car, you will keep him near you until the press from this dies down. I'd recommend not going anywhere publicly with Edward unless you want to deal with that shitstorm, too, and if that's what you want, at least give me a heads up, so I can plan for that."

"Ha. You can't be fucking serious. I should give you a heads up? No. You can just deal with whatever I do, that's what you get paid for."

"You forget your place. I may work for you, but I don't need you. Cancel my contract and you'll still be paying me. I did this for your own good. You may not realize it now, but someday, you will. Now, you can use this to your advantage if you shut up for a minute and let me explain."

"I'm not gonna shut up, because I have questions, and based on your answer I'm gonna need you to do something before we can continue working together." Since she hasn't interrupted me, I'm just gonna press on. "Now, I know damn well he didn't text you with the intention of outing my location to the press. Did you explain to him what you planned to do when he told you about the community service?"

"No, I didn't because I was under no obligation to do so. He's honest. I'll give him that. Stupid, but—"

"Apologize," I say, firmly.

"To you? No. I'm not gonna apologize to you, because I did what any good agent would do."

"Not to me, to him. Apologize to Edward within the next thirty minutes for betraying his trust, or we're done. After you've done that, text me what the plan is that I need to follow. If you don't do that, I'll have my attorney contact you." I toss my phone on the counter and lean over my sink. I can barely catch my breath, there's so much adrenaline coursing through my body right now. Did I just threaten to fire Linley? Fuck, and Edward is just sitting in my room, all alone. I need to comfort him, but I don't even know what to say.

When I leave the bathroom, Edward is still sitting in the same place I left him. His gaze meets mine in an almost pathetic way, as if he's too afraid to look at me. I don't want to tell him that Linley is going to call him, because if she doesn't, he'll feel even worse. I walk past him over to my nightstand and open the top drawer. My teammates will undoubtedly have heard what happened. I probably could just turn the TV on and see how bad the news has exploded, but I don't want to scare Edward. I turn my other cellphone on, it's been off since I moved in, leaving it off was the only way to fully disconnect from everyone. My teammates don't have my business phone number, I really only used it for Linley, my parents, Edward, and any clients… Fuck. If the media gets ahold of the fact that I'm running a contracting business—what the fuck am I saying? There is no contractor business anymore, there's…there's nothing. What am I gonna do?

"I'm sorry. I really didn't mean for this to happen. If—if I could take it back, I would," Edward says. He's avoiding looking at me, he's just looking at the floor, while holding his phone.

I can't find anything comforting to say, but I don't want him to feel like I'm mad at him. I walk around the front of my bed and sit beside him, while holding both phones. My personal phone is going to probably overheat at the rate that the old messages are pouring in.

"You have two phones?" he asks me. "Is that a work thing?"

"Yeah. I have one that I haven't used since I moved here. It was the only way to cut myself off from everyone. But I need to see what's on it now that everyone knows."

Edward looks at his phone then looks down again. "I should probably go. I can't imagine you want me here after what I did. I just—I really don't want to leave."

"You can't leave by yourself; I need to take you to work. I don't know what's gonna be waiting for you at your store."

He looks down at his phone again. "Linley is calling me. Why? Is she calling to break up with me for you? I've seen celebrities that have people dump people for them. You didn't need to have her do that."

I tilt my head at him. I hate seeing his face all sad like this. "That's not the situation. Just answer the phone and see what she has to say."

"Hello?" he says.

Linley is so damn loud that I can hear her. "Edward, I owe you an apology. I know that you were just trying to be sure Jacob wouldn't get in trouble and I took advantage of your naivety. I have my reasons for doing what I did, but I shouldn't have dragged you into it."

"Um," he mumbles while looking at me. "I, um, I'm still not sure what any of this really means, so I'm just gonna hang up now."

I'm suppressing a laugh, because I'm sure Linley is too shocked by his response to say anything back to him. Good thing she called him, even though I would have fired her if she didn't, I'd definitely have been screwed.

He ends the call and puts his hand on the bed between us. "Did you tell her to call me?"

I exhale loudly, I'm still not really sure how to deal with all of this. I'm still mad at Linley, but now that this door to the other part of my life has been opened, I have to decide if I pull him in with me, or not. It's not even a matter of whether I want to be with him, it's more that I need him to understand that there are things that he can't do—things like calling my agent. But do I even have the right to expect anything from him, when I don't even know how this is gonna work out? First and foremost, I need to make sure he's safe today, and to do that I'm gonna need to talk to him. "I may have told her that if she didn't call you, I was going to fire her."

My old phone still hasn't caught up with itself, and now my work phone is going crazy with texts from Linley. I put them on the bed beside his hand and stand. Looking in my mirror, I can see him behind me, just staring over. The silence between us is deafening, and I hate it. I've never felt so conflicted in my whole damn life. How am I so pissed about something he did and yet, I'm not mad at him?

"You told her you'd fire her? For me? Why? It was my fault. I wouldn't have expected you to do that," he says meekly. "Couldn't you have gotten in trouble?"

I turn around and lean against my dresser, facing him. His face is full of worry, and I just want to make it better. Everything in me wants to just kiss him, but I have to take care of this. I let out a long breath and shake my head. "I can get in trouble for a lot and yet I can't really get in trouble for anything. This part of my life is weird, I'm not sure how to explain it to you. I have enough money to make all my problems go away, and yet all the money in the world can't fix some things. This problem right now— money can't fix. I'm gonna have to do it. It's gonna involve a ton of press conferences, interviews, apologies, appearances… Oh, and my security guard will be here soon. It's Linley's job to fix it, well, because it's her fault, but also as my agent it's her job, but as for the stuff that has to be done, that's on me."

"None of this makes any sense to me, but I want it to. I want to help fix things, especially because it's my fault—which you seem to keep not mentioning." He looks down at his hands, then glances at my phones. "I hadn't considered that you were so busy that you'd need two phones, or have all of these things that you'd need to do—"

I interrupt him, "You didn't know, and you didn't consider—which is the problem, a problem that doesn't fall on you. It falls on me for not really explaining things to you, and it falls on Linley for taking advantage of you. So, while you lit the match, the fire is not your fault."

He looks like he's really thinking what I've said over. "I don't know which part to focus on because I've been so—naïve, like Linley said, but what do I need to do? You said you have security coming here, is that really necessary?" He's holding his forehead and his face is starting to look a little flushed.

I honestly don't think he's watched any of my games, or looked up anything about me—but how much of a dick would I sound like if I ask him if he has? Do I show him magazines, show him stuff online? How do you make someone understand something like this? "It's definitely necessary. Sports weren't big back in Twilight Hollow, huh?"

He's shaking his head at me. "Nope. I've never been interested in sports until I met you and, even now, I don't really understand. The kid at the park, all that stuff with the whole town kind of keeping this secret for you, a security guard—it all doesn't feel real somehow."

"Sometimes I wish it weren't. Why don't you pick up one of my phones and tell me how many messages are on either one. The one on the right is the personal one that's been off since I moved in, it's probably gonna explode. I'd guess there are more than a thousand messages and missed calls. Speaking of, take a peek, then pass me the work phone, because we really have to get you to your store, but I need to see what Linley has worked out before we leave."

Even though the community is gated, I feel the need to look out the window again. Luckily, there's still no one out there.

Edward picks up my work phone, which is an interesting choice, he's not interested in who's texting me, but interested in the business side…for some reason that makes me happy. "Jacob," he says, firmly, "there are more than two-hundred texts here. Your email"—he points to the screen—"has three hundred new emails, three hundred and one now, what the hell? Why does everyone need to reach you so badly?"

"Hmm. Good question," I say as he passes my phone to me. "Looks like Linley has already scheduled a bunch of interviews, so most of these are wardrobe questions, location questions, security questions…fucking apology questions," I say, tossing my phone onto the bed again. "I gotta get dressed. I have a conference call with Linley and Marco in an hour, and I really need to call my dad back. I can do the conference call from the back room in your store. I'm not asking your permission by the way. I'm not gonna leave you alone until I know you're safe."

"Jacob, listen to me," he says tugging on my hand, as he stands from my bed. "I'm really happy that you're not mad at me," his statement sounding more like a question than a declaration. "But, what are you keeping me safe from, exactly? No one even knows who I am. It's not like anyone knows we're together."

"I didn't say I wasn't mad. I'm mad, I just don't know how to process it with you, because I like you too fucking much. No…"—I say pulling him close—"mad isn't the right word." I wrap my arms around him, and he sinks into my embrace. "It doesn't matter. I need to keep you safe from stalkers, fans, people who want money, people who hate me, really just people in general. And, yeah, no one knows we're together, but one reporter, one bribe, one picture can change all of that. Everyone here has been really nice, but money can make people say and do crazy things. Also, I think you're forgetting what drew them here. Linley spread the word about the Book Boyfriend Auction, so where will people need to buy tickets from? If they'd just found out where I was, you wouldn't really be in any immediate danger, and, yeah, not to sound like an asshole, but there are gonna be a lot of people calling and stopping by to get tickets. Could get messy. Not a chance I'm willing to take…not with you."

"Thank you, and I'm sorry," he says and kisses me on the cheek. "Before you tell me to stop saying sorry, don't. Until this is fixed, I'm gonna feel bad. So, tell me what to do. How do I fix it?"

I chuckle and pull back from him. "Get dressed for work, and do whatever else you need to, and I'll get dressed, go over Linley's texts and call my dad. Fair warning, though, I'm only gonna get madder as the day goes on, not at you, but just at everything else. I'm already frustrated, and the day hasn't even started. I feel like you should know that. So, if I'm pissed today, or seem on edge, it's not because of you, just keep telling yourself that. I'll try to tell you, too, but I don't know where I'll be or what I'll be doing." I rub his arms and tilt my head at him. "Okay?" I ask him, as softly as I can.

His eyes meet mine, but he looks down at the floor when he answers me. "Yeah, okay. I'll try to remember that," he says meekly.

I pull his face in and kiss him softly. "Remember this," I say, pressing my forehead against his, "no matter what happens today, I like you and I want to be near you."

"That's all I needed to hear," he says with a smile, then walks toward his suitcase. "I'm gonna get ready in the bathroom. I'll just be a few minutes."

Damn it, there are so many messages on my phones, but I have to get ready first. I look down at my work phone and my stylist, Danny, has sent me a bunch of requests. This is too much. I'll text him back in a few minutes. For now, I can wear something casual, but not too casual, at least that's what Danny said. It was nice not thinking about this stuff for the past few months. I grab a long sleeve black and pink team shirt from my closet, along with a pair of black pants, and knock on the bathroom door. "Hey, can you just pass me my deodorant?" I ask with a chuckle.

"Sorry! Why didn't I think about that?" Edward asks, and passes it to me. "Do you need anything else?" he asks with the door open.

The sight of his naked chest draws me in for a second, but something in me knows I can't screw around right now. I pull my gaze from him and quickly turn away. "No, thanks. All good."

Once I'm dressed, I take a deep breath and sit on the edge of my bed. Okay, the plan that Linley has mapped out sucks. I'm gonna try and do most of this stuff from the bookstore. I'm not gonna leave him alone, but I need to call my dad to see how bad the downtown area actually is. My text from him says everything is on fire, and I have to assume he didn't mean that literally.

"Hey, Dad, how bad is it?" I ask, while scrolling through the messages on my other phone.

"What in the hell happened? You just decided to tell everyone where you are? Without talking to me? I gotta be honest here, kid, this is a nightmare. What would make you do this?"

"Woah… Stop. I did nothing. Linley decided to tell everyone, and I'm still considering firing her for it. We'll see how I feel later, I guess."

The sound of horns honking and people shouting in the background make my father's voice sound muffled when he finally replies, "Well, I was not expecting that to happen. Why would she do that?"

"No clue, but what's done is done for now. What am I dealing with? How many people?"

"How many people where? The whole town? I have no idea," he says, sounding more aggravated than I've ever heard him. "Edward's store— there's a line down the street that wraps all the way down to the community square. The streets are a mess, we have Snowflake Festival crowds already taking up the extra space and now this—between news vans and fans, there's no parking anywhere. What about security for you? And don't give me any macho shit, you didn't need security before, but, at this point, you for damn sure do."

"Thanks, Dad. I'm aware. Gio is on his way, he should be here within an hour or two, I guess, depending on traffic? He was taking a private flight this morning." I lean my head back, groaning in frustration. "I have an interview this morning with Marco and Linley that I'm gonna do from Edward's shop. Can you block off the entrance to the back of the building? I mean, can Robby do it? I have to be able to get inside unnoticed, then I can just stay in the back room, and make sure Edward is safe while I get all this stuff done."

"Edward is gonna be less safe with you there. You know that, right? I understand wanting to be where he is, but this seems exceptionally stupid."

"How do you figure that? I'll be there and Gio will be there. If I'm not there, he'll be all alone. I'm gonna have him ask Chad to stay with him in the morning before Gio gets here. I have to stay hidden, so I'm not gonna make anything worse for him by being there. But I assume all those people are lined up for tickets, because otherwise they wouldn't be there."

"Right, well, they're also there because you now have a connection with the store since Linley told everyone that you fixed it up. Some people are probably gonna have questions about that. Jacob, I can't really stay on the phone much longer, but you need to remember a few things, first you absolutely do not let it slip that I'm your father, second, don't let your feelings for Edward force you into doing anything stupid, and lastly, tell Edward that he can only sell seven hundred tickets total, and we're moving the event to the community center. Oh, and he needs to up the price, it's for charity, so tell him to raise it to $20 a ticket. There are more than seven hundred people here already, so he should sell out fast. I can block the side entrance to the back lot off, and ask Robby to help, too. He's wrangling women in the front of the store right now, so I'm sure he'd be happy to move down the street."

Edward walks out of the bathroom with a half-smile on his face. He really is the cutest man I've ever seen. I stand up from my bed and grab my wallet and keys.

"I like that shirt," he says walking closer to me. "Are the team colors black and pink? The shirt you let me wear the other day was a blue and pink one. Can teams have three colors?"

"Oh, yeah, black and pink are our colors, the blue is just for special games. I have a bunch of these shirts, you can have one if you like it that much." I hold my hand out toward him. "We should go, I'll fill you in on the way, do you want to grab something to eat?"

He smiles and holds my hand, looking up at me. "Oats are good. Most people can't eat when they're nervous, but I'm the opposite. On a normal day, I don't usually need breakfast, but today, I'll probably eat whatever I can shove in my mouth."

Now is not the time for dirty jokes, I tell myself. "Here you go, this is the same kind you had the other night." I pass him the jar and take one out for myself, along with a spoon for each.

He thanks me for the oats and we head to my car. I'm trying to figure out what I'm gonna say to Marco, or anyone else that I'm gonna have to meet with today. I don't want to deal with any of it, but I really don't have a choice. "Can you do me a favor and call your brother?" I ask, opening the passenger door for him. He's clearly confused by my question. "I know you said earlier he was texting you, but I have a favor I really need from him. I can talk to him if you don't want to."

"Uhhh, you need a favor from Chad? I can't have heard that right," he says with a smirk.

"I'm surprised, too." I shut the door and quickly jog around the front of my car and sit inside. "I forgot your car was in here beside mine. It's a good thing we moved it yesterday. About your brother, can you do it? Will you call him for me?"

"Yeah, but you're already driving and it's illegal to talk on the phone while driving, right? I wouldn't want you to get a ticket."

"Just put him on speaker. I don't have a lot of time." I'm driving a bit slower than normal as we leave the neighborhood.

Chad answers the phone after one ring. "Hey, holy shit, what happened? Is your boy toy freaking out? Everyone knows where he is and also the line on the street is fucking crazy right now. Where are you?"

"Hey, it's the, uh, *boy toy*," I say through gritted teeth. I'm really not a fan of his, but he's Edward's brother so I have to press on. "I need a favor."

"Oh, shit. Hi, Jacob. Sorry, I thought you were—"

"Yeah, it's fine. You're on speaker, and I don't have a lot of time. I need you to come hang out with Edward this morning at his shop... To keep him safe. My bodyguard will be there within a few hours and then I won't have to worry as much, but for now, I really need someone to help him with the store."

Edward's mouth is hanging open. "Wait, I don't need him to do that."

"Yes, you do," Chad and I say in unison.

"I think that's the first time you've ever agreed with me," Chad says. "Yeah, I can do that. I'm already at the bar anyway. Tony is here hanging out, too. Your dad posted in the local business owners group early this morning with a status update, so we were kind of ready to help if need be. I don't have to open the bar until later, and Lucas can likely help if you need him to. Tony, uh, I don't think opens until around lunch time. But, Jacob, why did you tell everyone—"

Edward interrupts him, "He didn't, it's my fault. He's just trying to fix everything, probably before he dumps me later."

"No," I say, shaking my head.

"I don't think so. If he wanted to dump you, I'm looking at about five hundred people outside your shop that would gladly help him with that. Also, you're not really *together*, *together*, so he wouldn't really have to dump you."

"Thank you for that," Edward says to Chad.

"Okay, bye, Chad, we'll be there soon. Thanks." I nod at Edward and he ends the call.

"Holy shit," I say at the sight of the immense traffic jam. The streets are so narrow here that there's not even any way for me to get around. This is nothing compared to the streets back home, but for this tiny town, it's way too many people. Edward's eyes are wide looking around, as we stop in the middle of an intersection. A few of the local cops are standing in the middle of the road directing traffic. We're just a few streets away from Edward's store. I can get to it, if we can just make one more turn, but that turn lane is the one that's backed up the most. Shit. I drop my head against my seat. I didn't even call any of my clients for today. I assume they've seen all this but still. "Can you do me a quick favor?" I ask, reaching into my pocket. "My password is 0404," I say, passing him my phone. "Can you look at my calendar, please, and just send texts to the three people that say client next to their names. Just tell them I have to cancel their service and I'm sorry. I can't reschedule anything, so there's no need to say anything else."

"Of course," he says.

"Thanks, sorry to have to ask. I just don't want people waiting for me, because I'm not gonna show up. At this rate, I'll be late for the call with Linley and Marco. I'm gonna be in so much trouble."

"Your phone is going crazy over here," Edward says. "Every time I try to hit send I get interrupted with a new notification. Looks like you have a suit fitting tomorrow. Do you have to wear suits for things normally?"

"Sometimes, yeah. Does it say why? That would be from my stylist or Linley, which one sent that?" The traffic still isn't moving, and we're about twenty car lengths away from being able to turn. At this rate, we'd be better off walking, but obviously we can't do that.

Edward passes my phone back to me. "I can't tell. I don't know what I'm looking at." He leans to the right looking down the line of cars. "So many of these cars have your team stickers on them. What do you think they're all here for? Just to see you, or to buy tickets?"

"Probably a mix of both of those things, plus reporters. I really can't wait any longer, though. I have to get inside your store, and so do you."

I call my dad quickly. "Hey, I'm stuck at the intersection of sixtieth and ninth. I have to get out of this mess, I can probably ride the shoulder, but can you call one of the officers and let them know I'm back here? If it's okay with them, I'd like to try and get around everyone. Sorry to even ask, I'd hop out myself, but I don't think that will go well."

There's a pause accompanied by the sound of car horns, and my father's heavy breathing. Sounds like he's—yep, he's jogging over. I see him making his way into the intersection. "I'm here," he says, looking down the line of cars. "Hey, Dan," I hear him say to the officer beside him. "Jacob is back there, he wants to use the shoulder to get around." I watch as the officer assesses the shoulder and traffic around him.

This is actually really dangerous; what if there were an emergency? Everyone is just deadlocked here because the streets are too small, and there's no room for everyone.

"We can get him out of there, no one is headed south, so he can come over into this lane," Dan says. The officer is talking into the radio attached to his uniform. I can't hear what he's saying, but my dad is making his way over toward my car. "Did you catch that?" my dad asks me.

Well, this is completely inconspicuous—surely, no one will know that the person who is being escorted into the other lane is the person they're all here to see. "Yeah, I heard him, but—"

"Uhh," Edward interrupts, obviously still a bit in shock at the sheer chaos around us. "We're gonna go into that lane? That doesn't seem safe, what if someone comes the other way?"

As soon as Edward finishes his question, another cop blocks the way from oncoming traffic with his car. My dad shoves his phone in his pocket and points my car out to the new officer. The cop waves me over and I carefully pull out of the line into the other lane, as the officer urges me with his hands to move around quickly. Cars are honking around me, but my windows are too dark to see through, so they can assume it's me in this car, but they can't know for sure.

"This is the craziest thing I've ever seen. It feels so weird driving on this side of the road," Edward says, sinking down in his seat. "What would these people do if they knew it was you in this car? Like, ask for autographs?"

"No idea," I say, pulling back into the right lane now that I've gotten around all the cars. There are so many horns honking all at once, and after being here for the past few months I'd almost forgotten what they sounded like.

The lot behind the store is blocked off, but Robby, the officer, notices my car and quickly moves the barricade allowing us to pass. Damn it, I see so many news crews here already. Since we're behind the building, I have no idea how many people are out front, but the traffic in the streets leading to it are enough of an indicator that shit is definitely crazy out there right now. Once I pull into a spot behind Edward's shop, I look left to right to be sure no one is watching. It's empty back here, except for the same few cars that belong to business owners on this street.

I hug my steering wheel and exhale. "I really wish this wasn't happening… I don't know what today is gonna be like, but if you need me, just come get me from the back room," I say, glancing over at Edward.

"Well, just—do whatever you have to do, and if I can help, then tell me. I'm sure I'll be fine, but I'm starting to get worried about you. You've been calling people worrying about me, but should I actually be worried about *your* safety?"

"Hmm, if I was going out there all alone right now, maybe? But I'll stay in the back where no one can see me. If a big, tall guy, dressed in black that looks like he could take thirty guys out at a time comes in, that's Giovanni. You'll know him when you see him. Just picture any bodyguard you've ever seen in a movie, he fits that description. But he'll probably call me first. I'm sure he'll flash his badge as soon as he walks in. Oh, and people from the crowd that are really familiar with me will recognize him, so if you do see him, get him to the back near me as soon as possible. The less people that know he's here, the better."

Edward's knees are lightly bouncing in his seat. "Hey," I say, placing my hand on his thigh. "It will be okay. If you're too nervous, I can just pay you whatever you would lose from staying closed today. I don't want you to be forced to do something you don't want to do."

"Nope, but that's sweet. I'm ready to go sell tickets to a bunch of people who drove here immediately after finding out where you were, just for the chance to possibly pay money to spend time with you. Doesn't make me uncomfortable at all," he says, looking at me.

I pull his face near mine, touching our foreheads together. "Don't forget what I told you to remember today," I say, then kiss him softly.

He's smiling nervously at me. "I'll try."

CHAPTER EIGHTEEN
NO BREEDING, SLAPPING, OR CHOKING

   JACOB   

I grab my bag out of my backseat, and we quickly make our way into the back entrance of Edward's store. The back room is blocked off, so I still can't see how many people are out there, but I can definitely hear them. I flip the lights on inside Edward's office and set my laptop up. I only have about ten minutes before I'm supposed to meet with Linley and Marco. I have to hurry.

Edward wanders out of the room, while I stay in the back. "Oh my God. What is this nightmare? This is too many people. Jacob, I don't think you realize how many people are out here," he says.

"Do you see your brother? Or Tony?" I call out while turning my laptop on.

"Mmhmm, they're both right next to the door, but as soon as I let them in, it's gonna be like a scene from a movie. They might get trampled... Do I just sell all these people tickets? That's all they want, right?"

"Yeah, that or to see me, or to ask you questions about me. Some could be here to buy books, too. Maybe try to let just your brother and Tony in first. Just shout that you're opening in another five minutes or something. I have to start this meeting now. I'll check in as soon as it's over. You good?"

"It's fine, good luck," he says.

I quickly close and lock the office door, then sit at Edward's desk. Doing this meeting here was a bad idea. How am I supposed to focus when I know what's going on out there? I take a deep breath and join the meeting. Linley and Marco are already on camera. *Smile, Jacob, smile,* I tell myself.

"Good morning, Linley, Marco," I say.

"Oh, it's good to see your handsome face again," Marco says. "Now, let's get down to it. How much of the community service have you done?"

"I've done a few things here and there, but the auction should count as more than enough, right? This should bring in a ton of money for charity. The other stuff I did isn't important. I was trying to keep a low profile, like we explained when I came here. I didn't want to do too much and draw attention to myself."

Marco laughs in a way that makes me uncomfortable. He values me as a player, but he definitely feels ownership over me as a person, too. "Always entertaining me with your ideas, Rizzo. We'll need a bit more than just this one act of charity, I'm afraid. What about the apology? You scheduled that for this afternoon, correct?" he asks looking at papers in his hands.

"I need to go over that with Jacob first," Linley says.

"What's there to go over?" Marco asks. "Go over it now. It's two words, followed by an explanation. Looks to me like it's scheduled for three o'clock. Are you ready to tell me why you punched Doug, or are you gonna continue to look like the asshole, here?"

Instantly, I'm pulled back into a memory, a memory of my fist connecting with Doug's face. I'm not apologizing. I don't care what happens.

"Why is your camera shaking?" Linley asks me.

"Sorry, I was bouncing my leg, I guess. Didn't realize it was moving the table."

"Ah, asshole it is," Marco says. "Why do you do this to me? Don't I treat you well? I gave you the biggest contract ever awarded to a player, and you, you spit in my face when I ask you to apologize. What's so hard about it?"

"I can apologize for my actions, and apologize to the league and the fans, but I won't apologize to Doug." I shrug my shoulders and hear the doorknob rattling. I can't get up to see who it is, shit—it could be Edward. "Just a minute," I say to Linley and Marco. Quickly I make my way over to the door. "Who is it?"

"Rizz, it's me," a deep voice says. I'd know that voice anywhere, it's Gio. I unlock the door and shake his hand. "Sorry about this, thanks for coming," I say.

He holds both palms up to me. "No worrying. I have everything under control. I met the owner of the store, he's a nice guy. Seems to be fighting off a lot of questions about you out there. How long do you want to stay here for?"

"I'm in a meeting now," I say pointing at the computer. "Then I have another one immediately after, and a few other things."

He holds his phone up to me. "I have the schedule. I asked how long you *wanted* to stay here for, not how long you are supposed to stay here for." He pumps his eyebrows mischievously at me.

I laugh and we bump our fists together. "I don't know. I have so much to tell you, but for now I have to get back over there, and you should probably stand outside the door."

He's shaking his head at me. "I don't need you to tell me how to do my job. Do I tell you how to kick a ball?" He grabs the handle and looks back at me. "I haven't seen the new place. Is there a bed for me, or am I sleeping in my car?"

"You can sleep in your car, it's not my job to make sure you're comfortable," I say with a smirk.

He lets out a laugh. He's been my bodyguard since I was eighteen. He knows I wouldn't make him sleep in his car. "Oh, I missed you. If you need me to get you out of any of these meetings just let me know. It's kind of rough out there by the way. How much do you want me to step in? You want me to just stay by the door, or should I be helping with crowd control, too?"

"Keep an eye on Edward and let me know if he looks uncomfortable, and if anyone gets too pushy with him, I want to know."

He's shaking his head at me. "That sounds a bit personal. We can dive into that later. I'll keep an eye out and let you know," he says and finally leaves the room.

Well, that's one thing I guess Linley didn't tell him about. He wouldn't pretend not to know about us if he did. I quickly sit back down at the table and Marco and Linley are locked in an argument.

"Thanks for joining us," Marco says. "Are we interrupting some sort of pretend contractor job? I had no idea that was happening. That ends now. You are this club's greatest asset, you absolutely cannot run a contracting business in Cold Butts, Vermont."

I sigh and correct him. "Frosty Bottoms. The business didn't hurt anything. I'm licensed, so what does it matter?"

"This kid..." Marco says massaging his temples. "You seem to have no idea who you are right now. Rizz, you've always done what you wanted, but this little life you have down there, it's a placeholder until your suspension is over. Don't forget that. You have a contract—"

Linley cuts in, "Marco, his life is his life. He hasn't broken any terms of his contract, we cleared everything with you. You want to sign a new contract as soon as possible, right? Telling him you own him isn't a good look right now."

While I'm glad that Linley is sticking up for me here, she's also probably afraid I'm going to fire her. So, it's really just a show, she's just trying to show me that she's valuable to me.

"Is that so?" Marco asks. "The three of us know he's not going anywhere. So, let me be clear. I want that apology done today. No more contractor business, and I want to see you in Miami within the next week or so."

"No," Linley says. "He doesn't have to go to Miami. He's been suspended by the league. And before you say the meeting is discretionary, and start rattling off a bunch of bullshit, he's not doing it. So, the wording of the apology, we will discuss, the contractor business, we will discuss, but the meeting in Miami is not happening. Anything else?"

"There most certainly is more!" Marco shouts, as his face reddens in anger. "I want to know what happened. Tell me what Doug said that pissed you off so badly that you had to punch him in the face? It's hard to defend your actions when you haven't even told anyone what happened."

I'm generally good at maintaining my composure, but not right now. "There is nothing in my contra—"

I can hear Tony shouting, but he doesn't sound close to the door. Shit, I lost my train of thought. What the hell is happening out there?

Marco is waving in front of the screen. "Hello? Is there something more interesting going on over there?"

I have to focus. Edward is fine, Gio is just outside the door if things get too crazy for Tony to handle. I turn my attention back to my laptop. "Yeah, no, well, yeah. I'm just a little distracted, there's a lot of noise outside the room I'm in. I'll make the apology this afternoon, but I—" Shit. I can't do this. There's too much noise out there, and I can hear Edward's voice. "I'm sorry, I have to go. We can pick this up later if you're unhappy with the apology I give. Thanks for your time," I say, pulling my earbuds out and closing my laptop.

I know going out there is stupid, but I can't help myself, this is my mess and it's not fair for Edward to be dragged into this. I open the door and hear shouting and arguing, it sounds like Tony...

Gio's large body is blocking the entry to the hallway that leads to Edward's office. He turns toward me, eyes wide, shaking his head. "Get back in there, don't be an idiot. Everything is under control."

I gesture for him to come in the back room with me and he quickly follows. "What is happening? Why is Tony yelling? Is Edward okay?"

"They sold out of tickets and people are pissed. Now, stay." He looks past me and holds his arms wide. "You have another meeting right after the first one. Why is your laptop closed? Are we leaving?"

"Help me out," I say.

Gio raises his chin at me. "With what?"

"I need to go out there. I have an idea." The arguing is getting louder. I step toward Gio, and he blocks my path.

"No. You can't."

"Help me out," I say again, giving him my best smile, the one he constantly threatens to slap off my face.

"No." He snaps his fingers at me pointing inside the back room. "Get back in there. If you want to leave, we can do that."

"Help. Me. Out. You owe me for Cancun." I raise my eyebrows at him. "I need five minutes, walk out there with me, and keep people back. I'll sign a few things really quick and tell people my plan. Come on, I wouldn't ask if it weren't important to me."

Gio groans loud and long. "Can't believe you would bring up Cancun. Okay, fine. Give me thirty seconds to clear a path. Then you go out, you stay close to me, and you speak quickly. And no signing anything— definitely no to that. I can't take that chance with you. Also, do that thing where you ruffle your hair up. It's kind of a mess. Danny is gonna kill me if he sees footage of you like this."

Quickly, I run my fingers through my hair and follow Gio toward the crowd. He holds a hand backward, telling me to wait. The sound he makes when he whistles, pierces through the small room, immediately stopping the shouting and movement inside the store. "I need all of you to back away from this area," he says, gesturing wildly toward the bookshelf on the closest wall. "Hey, can you hear me?" he says to someone. "Yeah, you, I said back up." Gio turns and looks at me shaking his head.

"What are you doing?" I hear Edward's voice call out. I assume he's talking to Gio.

Once I step closer to the crowd, I'm met with screams, and phones, and shouting, all the things I haven't missed since I was here. Gio's body is on my right and he's keeping people back, while I make my way quickly toward Edward's register. There's nowhere to walk inside the store aside from the path Gio is making. It's packed with way more people than I imagined. If it weren't for Gio, I definitely wouldn't be safe. Technically, no one *in here* is safe.

Edward was obviously not expecting to see me. Our eyes meet for a split second before more people crowd around. I can hear his voice. "What are you doing out here? It's not safe."

Gio is blocking a few people from getting too close, so I quickly move behind the counter beside Edward. "Don't worry about me. I just have to hurry. Did you sell out of tickets?" I ask him, then smile up at the massive crowd.

Edward looks completely exhausted already. He points to the small trash can, showing me the ticket roll is empty. "I, I did, and people are just asking so many questions. Barely anyone is here for a book. Chad is lost somewhere in all these people and Tony has just been letting people in and out, so no one gets trampled."

I want to hug him, or just pull him out of here with me, but I can't do either. "Okay, I'm gonna do something, then I have to get the hell out of here," I tell him.

"Hi, everyone!" I shout above the cheers and voices. "I know you're all upset that the tickets are sold out, so the owner of the store and I have decided that we'll hold a separate raffle for a ticket to the auction."

"Will you breed me? I want to have your babies!" a voice shouts over.

"What the fuck?" Edward mumbles.

"Me too!" a deep voice shouts.

Gio whistles loudly, silencing the crowd momentarily. "He's not breeding anyone. Next person to yell about breeding doesn't get to buy a raffle ticket."

"What about choking?" a voice asks. "Or slapping? I'll pay for either."

Edward giggles and says quietly, "Not worried about that one, you won't even choke *me*."

"Uhh, no to all of that," I say loudly. "One drawing, entry fee is $20, money goes to the same charity that the auction is benefiting. You can buy as many tickets as you want, but the winner is just getting admission to the auction, it's not a guarantee that you're gonna be the winner of the date."

"And," Edward says loudly, "it's just a dinner!"

"He can eat me for dessert!" someone shouts from the crowd.

I look at Edward seriously. "If anyone gets disrespectful with you—"

"Like they just did with you?" he asks with a smile.

"Yeah, pretty much. Just call me. I'm gonna head out in a few. I have to get ready for this apology and I have a meeting with my stylist and three other things, I think." I smile at him. "I lost count. Hard to focus knowing that you're out here."

"Rizz," Gio says. "We gotta go. You said in and out." He whistles loudly and holds his arm toward the crowd, making a path for me.

Damn, I want to hug Edward before I go. Why do I feel so bad leaving him here? "I'll see you later. Don't forget what I told you in the car this morning."

"I won't forget and thanks for your help with the raffle, Mr. Rizzo," he says loudly.

Gio guides me toward the back, while attempting to block me from the crowd. So many phones are pointed at me, and so many voices are calling my name. But the only voice that matters to me is Edward's, and it's getting further and further away.

Once we reach the back hallway, Gio playfully shoves me. "You like him?"

"Who?" I walk inside Edward's office and flip my laptop open, ignoring Gio's question. He does need to know that Edward will be sleeping over, but he can figure out the rest on his own. "Ahhh, the next meeting already started. Should I go late or just skip it?"

"Whatever you want," he says standing in the doorway. "You shouldn't skip, but you could postpone if you need to. Tomorrow is gonna be crazy, too. I think the most important meetings are the one you just had and the apology… Which you *are* doing, right?"

"Shh," I say, holding my hand out. "Edward sounds upset. Should I just go back out there?"

"No, and he doesn't sound upset, he sounds like people are asking him questions about you. Since he doesn't know you that well, he's probably just having a hard time answering them. Can't expect that the local bookseller has inside information on international soccer star, Jacob Rizzo, can they?"

Well, never mind, I guess he's already figured out there's something going on between us. "Fine. I won't go out there. Let me make a quick call. We need to get you the number of the local officers, right?"

He holds his arms out wide. "Are you shitting me right now? I have the numbers. Linley set me up with everything. Grab your stuff and let's go. I need to do a quick perimeter check before we head out, but I can't leave you now that everyone knows you're in here."

Quickly, I close my laptop and call my dad. "Hi, Jacob," my dad says. "How are things going?"

Gio already knows that my dad is the mayor, but you never know who else is listening. "Good. But, uh…Mayor Dick, is there still security behind Edward's building? We need to get out of here."

"The back lot is still blocked off. You should be able to get out of there easily. You need to be careful, though. Giovanni messaged a while ago and let me know he'd made it to Edward's shop. He doesn't have a car, though, so are you just using yours?"

"Yeah, I guess." I can feel my blood pressure rising. Stress doesn't usually affect me like this, but today it seems to be washing over me in waves. So much is happening all at once.

My dad groans into the phone. "This agent of yours, I really hope she knows what she's doing. This was not part of the plan when you came here. The hotels were already at max capacity. Gonna be a lot of people sleeping in their cars, unless they plan on driving back to wherever they came from. Anyway, if you need anything, just let me know."

"Alright, thanks for your help."

Gio finishes texting someone and puts his phone in his pocket, raising his chin toward the back door. "They said there's an officer at the end of the lot that will let us out. Let's go, superstar."

"Don't fucking call me that," I say, shoving him. "You know I hate it."

"Fine, move your ass, average guy. And stay close to me."

Shit, it's freezing outside. Luckily, there's no one in the lot behind the store. Looks like the same cars that are usually parked back here. My car alarm chirps as I disarm it.

Gio whistles. "Nice, gimme the keys," he says, holding his hand out.

"Gah…I don't want you to drive. I've been so happy driving here. You can ride shotgun." I really wasn't ready to give up the little things like this. Driving is so relaxing for me, and having Edward with me has only made driving that much better. There's something about his hand on my leg that makes me feel safer than this giant two-hundred-pound man standing in front of me. I look over toward the back door, remembering that Edward is in there. Maybe I should go back inside.

"Keys," Gio demands. "And don't get all dreamy eyed looking at the back of a building. What's with you? You're acting so weird."

"Here," I say, pressing the key into his palm. "Yeah, I feel a little weird. Then again, being awoken by the news that the quiet little life I built for myself has all come crashing down, was probably not the best way to start my day."

Gio opens the passenger door for me, and I sit inside. I feel like a kid. "You want to buckle me in, too?"

"Got a mouth on you today," he says, shutting the door.

Once he gets inside, I see him reach for the seat controls. "Don't adjust my seat, come on. Do you know how hard that is to get right?"

He's all hunched over, trying to get comfortable. Gio is one of those people that drives with the seat way back, but he quickly shrugs it off and starts the car. The officer at the end of the street lifts the barricade and lets us pass with a wave. The traffic is still unbelievable. "Alright, out with it, what did you punch Doug for? There are only two reasons you would do that, so which was it?"

"Only two reasons? Interesting. What are they?" I ask.

"Technically, I think I just met reason number three, but he wasn't a factor back then..."

"Why are there cookies on your desk up here?" Gio asks, shaking the box at me. "You'd never catch a box of cookies left out in Florida, ants would be everywhere." He taps the top of the box. "But you don't usually eat cookies. Is this a Christmas thing, or an Eddie thing?"

Visions of Edward eating that cookie the other night are flooding my brain. His wet little tongue was just licking across the top... "*So hot,*" I mumble.

Gio is nodding at me. "So, it *is* an Eddie thing, or you've developed a cookie fetish?"

"What? Eddie? You know, did you meet Tony today at the store? He calls Edward, Eddie, too. His name is Edward."

Gio lets out a loud chuckle. "And your name is Fucked. You know that, right?" he says playfully. "Take these away. I don't wanna know what happened with them… Actually, I do, but you're not gonna tell me." He holds the box toward me and pulls it back as I grip it. "I'm not gonna lecture you, just—you need to get ready for the apology, so go meet with Danny, and get ready. You're really sure this is what you want to do, right?"

At this point, I don't know if he's talking about Edward, or the apology. Either way the answer is the same. "Yeah. I mean, you heard the conversation with Linley in the car. It's fine." I take the box of cookies and make my way toward the stairs. My phone has been vibrating in my pocket non-stop, which sucks for a bunch of reasons, but the worst one is because Edward was really the only one texting me and now, I never know what I'm gonna see.

"Alright, but before you go, I'm gonna do you a solid. I may have heard from someone that Scott and the guys were gonna try and make their way here to surprise you."

"Noooo. No, no. Definitely no." I tap the box of cookies against the banister. "Gio. Do not let them come here. Tell them I left, tell them there's no hotels, tell them I'm dead, tell them whatever." I run my hand down my face. "Just—fuck. I really don't want them here."

"You really are acting weird. These are your teammates, your brothers in cleats, what's the problem? I thought you'd be happy. I only told you because I know you hate surprises."

I start walking downstairs. "Guys couldn't win a single playoff game without me, and you think I should be happy to see them? I hope they aren't actually coming here. There aren't any hotels anywhere, what are they planning to do?" At this point, I'm just talking to myself, because I'm already in my bedroom. I really didn't want Edward to meet these guys yet. Maybe they aren't actually coming and they were just talking about it. My other phone is still plugged into the charger where I left it this morning.

There are way too many messages to deal with—and now my work phone is ringing. Shit, it's my stylist. "Hey, Danny, gimme a sec, I can hop on camera." I flip my camera on and smile at him.

"Jacob, what are these pictures of you that I'm looking at? I said you could go casual. Your hair is a mess, when was the last time you had it cut? You need to get to the barber tomorrow. I'll schedule it and text you the location. I also scheduled a fitting for you at a tailor. You need a new suit."

"I don't want to do any of that. Why do I need a new suit?"

"Someone is going to pay a lot of money for a dream date with you. Do you think it would be right for you to show up in your uniform?"

"Pftt, a dream date? It's just a Book Boyfriend Auction. It's just a dinner. I don't need to try and make it feel like a real date."

Danny groans loudly. "You are aware of the effect you have on people, right? People want to be close to you, they want to touch you, to know you, to talk to you. Some person is going to pay a lot of money just for the chance to spend a few hours with you. The very least you can do is look like a book boyfriend—wait, do you even know what that is?"

"Yeah, I think so." I'll need to ask Edward later, just be sure.

"A book boyfriend is a hot guy that fulfills every reader's fantasy, and is perfect in every single way. He says the right things, he does the right things, he anticipates his partner's needs, and he's great in bed. Completely unachievable for most mere mortals, but you are no mere mortal."

"Well, *this* book boyfriend is going out to dinner and that's it. But I'll get the suit and the haircut. Is there anything else? I need to get ready for the apology and I have another call with Linley to go over some stuff before that."

"Perfect. As for the apology, I want you in a nice jacket and tie. I don't know what you have with you, but no patterns, just the navy one with a..."

I can't even focus on what Danny is saying right now because a text is coming in from Linley, and it looks like everything is being pushed back by a few hours. I need to call Edward and tell him that I won't be able to pick him up. Damn it, I really don't want to disappoint him.

Chapter Nineteen
We're Just Friends

 EDWARD

What the hell is wrong with all these people?

There's been a constant flow of Jacob's fans coming and going all day. There's been no fewer than a hundred people in here at any given time. Sure, some are here for books, but most are here for tickets to the auction, and a lot are here just digging for information.

And all this craziness is happening with Tony acting as the bouncer at the door. I shudder to imagine what this day would be like without Tony's help. People would be packed in here tighter than sardines in a tin can. Despite nearly selling out of tickets, this day is a total disaster.

In the midst of a frazzled and tiring day, I finally see a friendly face who isn't here to harass me about tickets to the auction or private information about Jacob.

"Busy in here today," Leora says as she finally makes her way to the register. She has another stack of books in her hand.

I wave thanks to a handful of people heading out the door after spending more than an hour perusing shelves, though it was likely just them hoping to catch a glimpse of Jacob.

"Yeah, it's been nuts," I say to Leora. "But I've got help." I nod my head over my shoulder toward where Lucas is standing. "I had Chad earlier but he had to take care of the bar, so Lucas took over."

"Hi, Lucas," Leora says, blowing him a kiss.

He pretends to catch it and then sends one back. "Does your boyfriend know you're flirting with other men? Taken men, for that matter?"

"Oh, you're the flirt," she says.

"You're the one that blew a kiss," he points out.

She giggles and blushes, then she says to me, "Is there more in the *Debriefing the Lawyer* series? I didn't see them on the shelves."

I run her books through the register and the bells on the door jingle as more people come in. "I don't have any on hand but I've ordered the rest of the series. There are two more books; part three, *Drop Them Drawers and Those Charges*, and part four, *Is That An Indictment In Your Pants Or Are You Just Happy To See Me?* I should have them on the shelves shortly after Christmas."

"Don't even put them on the shelves," she says, "just put them aside for me. It'll be a Christmas gift to myself."

"I'd be happy to," I say. We process the payment for the books she's purchasing today. "And I'll see you at the auction."

"Of course," she says. "I've got my eye on some of the merchandise." She blows another kiss to Lucas.

"You don't need to buy me to have a dinner date with me," he says.

"Say the word and I'm there, dear," she replies.

"Do, uh…" I say, "do you two need a moment alone?"

Leora laughs all the way out the door. When I give Lucas a questioning look, he says, "She's a sweetheart."

After she leaves, a customer comes to the register with a pile of books. I cheerfully process her sale for her and we thankfully talk about things other than Jacob. After I finish, Lucas offers to walk around the store and tidy up a bit. I look out at my store and the place is a mess. The shelves are disorganized, someone has moved around the furniture, and the floors need mopping.

"Thank you," I say before he disappears into the crowd.

Before I can think too long on the state of my store, two women come up to ask about tickets to the auction. They're bummed when I tell them we're sold out, but their spirits raise a bit when they find out about the raffle for the last ticket.

While I'm telling them about the raffle, my phone starts buzzing with a call from my mom. I silence it; I don't have time now.

The afternoon continues on with the absolute madhouse of a crowd. Thankfully, I don't get any more arguments or angry people over the lack of tickets, but I definitely get disappointed people.

Most of the news crews had left when Jacob left, but there are still some hanging around. There's Larry who I recognize from the local paper, *Inside the Bottoms*, and the hunky field reporter from the regional TV news. Both ask to interview me but I decline on both counts. I don't want to draw more attention to Jacob, though that's still going to happen anyway. Once this hits the news cycle, there might even be more people coming out in search of him. They interview a few of the people in my store and I can tell they're lingering, hoping Jacob will come back.

Now that I can see this insanity in front of me, I finally understand what Jacob was trying to tell me, even if he couldn't quite put it into these words. It seems people want access to him—whether it's for a photo or a handshake or a kiss or an interview—people want him and they want to use him. So, I can also understand why he was upset that his break from all of this had come to an end.

I feel awful about it, even though he's told me several times now that he's not mad at me and that this would have happened soon anyway.

My phone rings again with a call from my mom, but I again send it to voicemail. Here and now is not the best time to take a call from my mom and answer her invasive questions.

A moment later, a voicemail and a text pops up from her: *Call me soon?*

I lock my phone and shove it in my pocket as a customer comes up to the counter.

Toward the end of the afternoon, the store mercifully clears out for a bit and it's just Lucas and I. The place is even more of a mess than last time I'd had an opportunity to look around.

"Hey," Lucas says, interrupting my spiraling thoughts about the state of my store, "I just want to say that I get it."

I turn to face him. He's leaning casually against the wall. "Get what?"

He shrugs one shoulder. "Dating a celebrity."

My gaze travels from Lucas to my shop window where I can see Bottoms Up across the street. I try to hide my absolute confusion before my gaze returns to Lucas and I'm not sure how well I manage it. "Chad's not a celebrity."

"The owner of the town's only gay bar, the central figure in the county's queer scene, and a hot piece of ass to boot? He's a celebrity."

I look again at the absolute state of disaster my store has been left in by crowds hoping for even the briefest glimpse of Jacob. Then I look across the street—the front of Bottoms Up has a big window and I can see the place is almost entirely empty.

"I'm not sure we're talking on the same scale here," I say.

He waves his hand dismissively. "The scale is different, of course. I was here with you in this madhouse, so I saw. But the core issue is the same—our men are sex symbols that everyone wants to be with. The level of attention they get can be uncomfortable, but we just have to be okay with it."

I start to catch on to what he's saying. "I trust Jacob," I say. "We haven't really said we're in a…uh…relationship yet, but we've said we're exclusive to each other."

Lucas gives me a smile. "That's really sweet. I can tell he really likes you."

"Thanks," I say. "Yeah, we're figuring things out. I kinda messed up our opportunity to grow closer by telling his agent about this Book Boyfriend Auction thing. Jacob was trying to tell me that this media frenzy would come eventually, but he was hoping it wouldn't be until much later. I feel awful about all this, even though he's said he's not mad at me."

"You can ride through any complication as long as you two trust each other and you like each other, and it sounds like both are true in this case." He laughs for a moment. "And if you have a jealous streak like me, just stake your claim when you need to."

We're interrupted by three people coming in. They come straight for the register and ask about tickets, and when I tell them about the raffle for the final ticket, they enter. Before they head out, they decide to check out the store. A little while later, they come back to the register, each with a few books in their hands.

A little before closing, Kellan comes walking in. He and Lucas exchange glances that I can't quite read. It's almost like glances that acknowledge a mutual respect for battles won. I really don't get it. It must be from a previous adventure before I moved here.

"A visit from the Snowflake Princess," I say. "I'm honored."

He does a royal wave. "Continue to show proper respect for the crown and you'll get on my good side," he says.

I give him a little bow. "I will do my best, Princess."

He chuckles and then takes a look around my shop. "It looks like a pack of Santa's elves got hyped on sugar and candy canes in here."

I puff out my cheeks with an exhale. "It's been a bit busy here today. I don't know if you've heard, but Jacob's kind of a well-known athlete."

"Oh, that's where I recognize him from," Kellan says, with a giggle.

"People have been in and out all day, desperate for a chance to see him." Even as I say that, someone cups their face against my shop window, clearly looking to see if Jacob is inside. We all watch the guy until he notices us and speed walks away, trying to hide his embarrassment.

"Yes," Kellan says, "it is rather *interesting* that nowadays if people want to find Jacob, they need to just find you, Edward."

I look him dead in the eye and say, "Yeah. Funny coincidence, that."

"I noticed your car isn't in his driveway anymore," Kellan says.

I shrug.

"It's in the garage," Lucas says. I shoot him a dirty look.

Kellan's eyes flare wide open. "That seems like a big move."

"Not that big of a deal," I say.

"Yeah, doesn't seem like a big deal," Lucas says, "you just turn on the car and drive forward."

Kellan pauses like he's deciding on a different approach. "Are you and Jacob dating?"

Thank God this place is empty or else I would've smacked him. "Jacob and I are friends," I say. "Nothing more."

My phone, which is sitting on the counter face-up, chooses that moment to ring, displaying Jacob's name in big bold font. Kellan gives me an amused look as I pick it up and answer.

Kellan stage-whispers to Lucas, "It's his *friend*."

I half turn away from Kellan and shakily say into the phone, "Hi…"

"Hey…"

There's a little bit of silence for a moment, like neither of us is sure of what to say. Me mostly because I have Kellan and Lucas standing just a few feet away from me.

"How is the media stuff going?" I ask, finally filling that silence.

"Eh, it's okay. Since I haven't done this in a while, I'm completely exhausted," he says. "How have things been at the store?"

"Some reporters were here for a bit, but I didn't tell them anything. It was nothing like what you saw this morning." After another little silence, I say, "I'm looking forward to being with you tonight."

"Me too," he says, "but about that… My schedule is completely blown up. I've got three interviews over the next ninety minutes, and then a few more meetings with Linley and other people. So…"

He probably doesn't want me to come over because he's going to be too busy, but he doesn't want to disappoint me. I can offer first. "I can sleep at Chad's tonight, if you'd rath—"

"No, thank you. I'd much rather you come to my place after work, if you're feeling up for it."

"Okay," I say quietly. That makes me feel a whole lot better.

"It's just that I won't be able to pick you up," he says, "but I could send an Uber for you since your car is here."

"You don't need to get me an Uber, I can maybe ask my brother or Lucas, since he's still here," I say.

Kellan clears his throat, grabbing my attention. "Do you need a ride to your *friend's* place? I can help you out."

"Is that Kellan?" Jacob says.

"It is," I tell him. "He just offered to drive me to your place."

I can sense a happier energy from him, like he's glad to hear that I have a safe way out from the store. "Get a ride with him. If you can. My stuff ends around eight, or at least I'm calling it quits then, so we can hang out after."

"I'd like that," I say with a smile.

"Alright, I have to get going, I've got that interview in a few minutes. The code on the door lock is 0404. Let yourself in. I can't wait to see you."

"Me too."

When I end the call, I turn around to find Kellan and Lucas still standing by the register, but clearly staring at me and making no attempt to hide that they were eavesdropping. "Can't a guy have a phone call with a friend in private?"

"Of course," Kellan says. "I like a little privacy when I'm on the phone with a buddy and whispering sweet nothings to him and being all lovey-dovey."

I roll my eyes. "Maybe I can still get that Uber to his place."

Kellan waves his hand dismissively. "Braden and I close when you do and we're headed straight home, and we live right next door to your *friend's* place."

"Thank you," I say. "And, uh, any chance I can hang out a bit? He's doing interviews till eight. I'd like to give him some privacy."

"Yeah, no problem," he says. "Plus, it'll be nice to get to know you a bit better."

Kellan heads on back to his shop—why he even stopped in here, I still don't know.

Lucas and I set to organizing some of the shelves. He doesn't know where all the books go, but he at least helps me get them all standing upright. Once all this nonsense is over, I'll do a thorough sort of my store, ensuring books go where they're supposed to. But before we can get too deep in organizing shelves, more people come in and the place just gets messy again.

When it finally hits five o'clock, Lucas leaves, and I thank him for staying with me today. I lock the door and do a few other quick shut-down things, like counting out the register and locking some money in the safe in the back room for a deposit later in the week.

Shortly after I finish up my nightly chores, I hear a rapping on my door. Kellan and Braden are standing out there. I quickly let them in and then lock the door again.

"Thanks for the offer of a ride," I say.

"Of course," Braden says. "It's nuts out there, we don't want you going on your own."

"Nuts, but good for business," Kellan says.

"We're parked behind your building," Braden says. "Can we use your back door?"

"I'm pretty sure someone else is using his back door already," Kellan says.

"We're just friends," I say. After shutting off all the lights and double checking the door is fully locked, we head through the store to the back room and the exit to the back lot. It's mercifully quiet here, though I can still hear the echoes of people from the street.

"This is us," Braden says, leading us to a very masculine looking truck.

"How very straight of you," I murmur under my breath. Kellan catches what I say and laughs, but neither of us let Braden in on the joke. I get in the back seat behind Kellan and buckle up.

He starts his truck and pulls out of the spot. When he pulls into traffic, he says, "How are you liking Frosty Bottoms?"

"It's nice," I say. I watch out the window as we drive down the main street and all the Christmas displays slide past me. "It's scary moving to a new town but the people here have been super welcoming."

"I know someone who's been extra welcoming," Kellan mutters.

"Kellan…" Braden says. "You promised."

"But he's telling us Jacob is *just a friend* when we both know what's clearly not true," Kellan says.

Braden briefly makes eye contact with me in the rear view mirror. "Still, we let him tell us when he wants to tell us. There might be special circumstances with Jacob's job."

I can almost hear Kellan rolling his eyes, but he says, "Alright, fine. Edward and Jacob are friends."

"My friend's hands are really soft," I say, if only to rile up Kellan a little more. I think it's kind of funny when he gets worked up.

Kellan throws up his hands. "I give up. Whatever. They're friends and nothing more."

Braden eyes me again in the rear view mirror. "I'm changing topics," he announces. "What's your favorite Christmas tradition? I'll go first. For me it's unwrapping a gift with our cats, Mister Fluffykins and Senator Tunacan. We don't actually get them anything, we just stuff a box with tissue paper, wrap it up with some paper and tons of ribbons, and they go nuts for it and spend a solid two weeks just hanging out in the box."

When I'm silent and don't answer, Kellan fills the void. "I love the boys…but that's your favorite Christmas tradition and it's not us getting engaged at the Snowflake Festival two years ago?"

Braden sighs. "That's a *memory*, not a tradition, because it only happened once. But I can propose again to turn it into a tradition, if you'd like."

"Would that mean a second honeymoon?" Kellan asks.

I try my best to hide my snicker, but I think Braden catches it because he looks at me in the mirror again. "We didn't do much for Christmas back home," I say. "As much as this is a Christmas town, where I'm from is a Halloween town. I'm looking forward to making new traditions this year."

"With Jacob?" Kellan asks, probing again.

"With Jacob and all my other good friends, yes."

"He's impossible," Kellan says to Braden.

Thankfully, he pulls into Sticky Pines shortly after. He turns past the guardhouse and into the community, driving down the winding streets. As we near their place, I catch sight of Jacob's. It looks pretty dark, but there's a light on in the living room and another on the second floor. Part of me wants to jump out, barge in Jacob's house, and sweep him into my arms. But the mature part of me knows I should stay out till eight so I'm not distracting him during his interviews and media calls.

"Here we are," Braden says. He pulls into the neighboring driveway.

The house looks very similar in style, but it's somehow not as welcoming as Jacob's. "Kellan said you were going to hang out for a bit before heading next door. If you're okay with leftovers, I have some lasagne in the fridge I could warm up for us to eat."

"That'd be wonderful," I say. We get out of the truck, and my feet almost automatically take me over to Jacob's, but I manage to right myself and follow Braden and Kellan to their front door.

When they open the door, we're met by the meows of two very fluffy orange cats.

"Boys," Kellan says, "say hello to Edward. He's your new part-time neighbor."

I take my shoes off and then squat down. Both cats rub their cheeks against my knees and then one of them flops to the floor and starts purring loudly. "They're adorable."

"That's Mister Fluffykins on the floor," Braden says. "And Senator Tunacan is the one giving you the look like he's disappointed in us for being late with his dinner."

"Cats have really mastered that disappointed look," I say. "I had a cat growing up and it would always stare at me like it had expected more of me and was disappointed with my life choices."

"I sometimes get that look from my mother," Kellan says. "I know it well."

I give Mister Fluffykins a scritch behind the ears. That's when I notice he's wearing little Christmas bells on a bright red collar around his neck. Senator Tunacan is wearing a similar one but in a coordinating dark green color.

I glance past the cats and see that their house is decorated like a high-end Christmas store. It's really nice. There's even a real tree in the corner of the living room.

"You have a beautiful place," I tell them. "It's very Christmassy."

"When you're the Snowflake Princess, you have to keep up appearances," Kellan says. "Christmas traditions are very important around here." Then he steps into the entryway to the living room and pauses, looking at his husband. "Speaking of…"

"Ah," Braden says, "mistletoe."

I look above Kellan's head and see mistletoe dangling from the ceiling. Braden steps closer and gives his husband a deep kiss.

"Come on," Braden says after breaking from the kiss, "let's get everyone some dinner." He heads to the kitchen and all four of us follow him, with Fluffykins and Tunacan meowing loudly. After Braden puts dishes of tuna on the floor, he sets to warming some lasagne up in the toaster oven.

The Christmas décor continues into here too; there's a row of little Christmas trees on the windowsill, I realize the cats' dishes have little Santa-cat figures painted on them, and there's a beautiful wreath sitting on the island with a giant candle in the middle of it. A moment later I realize that Kellan likely made that candle himself.

"Ah," Kellan says, looking at his phone. When we both look at him, he says, "The Jacob stuff has been all over the major news networks. My socials are flooded with articles about him." He turns his phone for us to see, and the feed is flooded with photos of Jacob.

"Is that the big punch?" I ask.

Kellan glances briefly at Braden before asking me, "You don't know about it?"

I shrug a shoulder. "I know the ref said something to him and Jacob responded with a fist to the face. Because of that, he's suspended for the rest of the season and that's why he's here."

"Has he told you why he punched the ref?" Kellan asks.

"He hasn't," I say. "Does it matter? Aren't sports generally violent?"

"Not like this," Kellan says, "and certainly not when it comes to soccer. He hasn't explained to anyone what that was about. It looks like he released his apology today." He stares at his screen as he scrolls through a post. "However, it looks like he doesn't give any details...nor does he actually apologize to the ref."

"He lost his temper and punched the guy, which he shouldn't have done, but we all get angry sometimes."

Braden leans his ass against the counter behind him and crosses his arms over his chest. "If this were pretty much any other sport, I'd probably agree with you, but in soccer the players are seen almost as role models for younger players. They bring kids out on the field with them at the start of every game; it's a big thing in this sport. So for Jacob to do something so unsportsmanlike is a big deal. He set a poor example for the younger fans."

I think back to the young boy at the movie night in the park and how Jacob went out of his way to set a good example for him.

Kellan continues scrolling through his social feeds. Suddenly, he stops the scrolling and smirks. "It looks like Jacob's *friend* is in a few of these photos," he says, turning his phone to Brayden.

When he turns it for me to see, I'm looking at a pic of Jacob's appearance mid-day where he came out of the back room. Standing just behind him is me.

"What?" I say. "How am I on this? Why? What right do they have to do that?"

Kellan smirks. "You're hosting a Book Boyfriend Auction with *the most eligible bachelor* in the world of soccer and you think people aren't going to notice you now and then?"

"But they can't, like, just print a photo of me. Can they?"

"The media can do what they want," Kellan says.

This is so unfair for Jacob; these are the things he was trying to tell me about.

The timer on the toaster oven dings and Braden pulls out the tray of lasagne leftovers, quickly dishing it out onto three plates. "Grab one and let's head to the dining room," he says.

I pick up the plate with the smallest portion and carry it through. Before I even sit down, Braden pops open a bottle of wine and fills three glasses.

When he hands one to me, I say, "We need to toast something."

"To *friends*," Kellan says. "I toast friends who are *just friends* and nothing more than friends."

I clink my glass against his. "I'll drink to that." Then I take a swig of the wine.

We chat about random stuff as we enjoy our dinner. I find out more about their story—from childhood best friends to lovers and all the zany stuff that happened when they got together.

When we move to the couches in the living room and split the rest of the wine, both Mister Fluffykins and Senator Tunacan come and sit on my lap. I chug the rest of my wine so both hands are free to pet them at the same time. Soon, they're both purring up a storm. From there, we talk about Frosty Bottoms, Twilight Hollow, and the Snowflake Festival.

Eventually, eight o'clock rolls around. "I should head next door," I say.

Almost as if understanding, both cats choose that moment to stand up, stretch, and saunter off somewhere else. "Thank you so much for having me," I say. "It was great to get to know you both a little better."

"You're welcome here anytime," Braden says as we all stand up. "And maybe next time you can bring Jacob."

"That would be great," I say.

A few moments later, I'm heading out into the chilly night and crossing over to Jacob's driveway. When I walk up to his door, I raise my hand to knock, but freeze before my knuckles hit the wood. *He gave me the code,* I remind myself. It feels strange letting myself into his house, but he wants me to do so.

I haven't had much experience with electronic locks, but when I tap it, it lights up. "What was that code again?" I ask myself. Then the memory comes back that it's 0404. I punch the numbers in, but nothing happens. "Maybe I hit this?" I mumble as I tap the number sign.

The deadbolt whirs, and then a mechanical voice says, "Unlocked."

I cautiously grasp the handle and let myself in. The place is dark with just a few lights on in other rooms. I turn around to lock the door and when I turn back, a six-foot-tall man is standing right in front of me.

"Oh my god!" I exclaim, clutching my chest. "Giovanni…you almost gave me a heart attack."

"Just doing my job, keeping my boy safe." He shines a flashlight in my face. "You're not here to rob the joint, are you?"

"No. God, no," I say. "I'm here to, uh…something." I lose my words, realizing I've walked right into a trap of my own making. I either say I'm visiting my friend and hope he doesn't ask why I sleep in the same bed, or I say I'm here for a late-night date and out Jacob to Giovanni if he doesn't already know. Instead of making that impossible decision, I just close my mouth and don't finish my sentence.

"Oh, you're here to *something*, alright," he says. He still has that flashlight shining in my face.

"Uhh..." I say. How do I tell him that I'm invited? Surely, he must know. The fact that he hasn't kicked me out yet should mean he knows.

Suddenly, he lowers the flashlight and points it up, lighting his face like he's telling a ghost story over a campfire. "I'm just fucking with you a bit. Jacob told me you were coming." He glances over his shoulder toward the bedroom, then looks back at me. "You're welcome to join him. But if I ever find out that you're here to hurt him or take advantage of him, you'll have to deal with me. Understand?"

I nod, a little shakily. "I understand, sir."

"And last thing," he says, "cut that 'sir' bullshit. It's Giovanni."

"Thank you, Gio..."—he gives me a look—"vanni?"

He squints at me. "Are you always like a high-strung chinchilla?"

"Why does everyone keep comparing me to rodents?" I ask. "Though I like when Jacob calls me his little mouse." I slap my hands over my mouth. How the eff did I let that slip out?

Giovanni just smirks at me. "I'll be upstairs in the office if you need me. And, heads up, your boy's asleep," he says. Before I can say anything back to him, he turns and heads up the stairs to Jacob's office.

I stay standing there for a long moment, ensuring Giovanni fully retreats upstairs. When he does and it doesn't seem like he's going to come back down, I slip off my shoes and quietly head into the bedroom. When I enter, I see that he is indeed asleep. He'd likely crashed on the bed and fallen asleep unexpectedly since he's fully dressed and the light is still on.

I quietly walk closer to the bed and—oh, my...Jacob has a pair of glasses half down the bridge of his nose. They look kind of...can glasses be slutty? Or is it the man that makes the glasses look slutty? Either way, things are stirring in my pants as I watch him softly breathe.

I finally tear my gaze from those slutty spectacles and take in the rest of his body. His shirt has tugged up a bit, exposing his abs, and whatever he's dreaming right now has gotten him rock hard. It's taking everything in me not to slip my hand into his pants and have fun with his dick.

When I reach for him, I don't let my hands stray south and focus instead on slipping those glasses from his face. I fold them up and place them on his nightstand.

Turning off the lamp, I walk through the dark to the en suite bathroom and flick on the nightlight under the mirror. I have a quick shower in the near-darkness, and I can't help but give my dick a few tugs thinking about Jacob. I don't go all the way though, because if I'm going to come, I want him to be personally involved. When I towel off, I brush my teeth, slip on some underwear, then head back into the bedroom. Even though it's still kind of early, the day exhausted me, plus I need to do a bunch of cleaning in the shop before we open tomorrow.

I had really hoped to talk with Jacob this evening. It had been a hectic day, and even though he said he's not mad at me, I can't help but be a little mad with myself for not seeing right through Linley's ploy. From the little snippet of Jacob's day I had seen, it was exhausting, and I can't imagine a whole day of that. Hell, *I'm* exhausted from everything and I wasn't even the focus of everyone's adoration.

I'll talk to him tomorrow. By then, he'll be fully rested and I will too, meaning we'll be awake enough to have a good conversation. I come around to my side of the bed, gently lift the covers, and slip inside. I move slowly and cautiously so as to not wake him up.

Even though he's asleep, he must sense that I'm here because he mumbles something incoherent and rests an arm across my chest. I slowly roll onto my side to face him, his hand now sliding down to my waist.

The faint moonlight filtering through the curtains gives his face an angelic glow. He's so cute when he's asleep. He's so at ease, so relaxed, so peaceful.

I stretch forward and give him the gentlest of kisses on his forehead. Thankfully, he doesn't wake up, though he does mumble something incoherent again.

And a few minutes later, I'm asleep too.

   # JACOB   

It's dark inside my room. I must have fallen asleep, shit. I told Edward I'd—wait, what the hell happened? Edward is asleep beside me. How did I not feel him get into my bed? I turn and look at my phone, it's 2:00 am. I shouldn't wake him, but I need to get out of these clothes and brush my teeth. Carefully, using the light from my phone, I head toward my bathroom, grabbing a pair of shorts from my dresser on the way.

I ruined everything by falling asleep. I didn't even get to talk to him. I wonder what time he got here? I'll have to make it up to him tonight. Maybe we can go look at Christmas lights after he gets done with work, yeah, we could probably do that. I think it would be safe as long as we stay inside my car. We had so much fun when we picked out our Christmas ornaments, and he's pointed out a few houses with Christmas lights, I bet he'd like to look at some of the displays set up around town. I just want to do stuff together with him.

Quietly, I slide back into bed beside him, tucking my body next to his. He scoots closer to me and lets out a sigh that sounds like contentment. I really like holding him like this, he seems to fit perfectly in my arms. This day… Everything pulled me away from him. I hated it.

His cheek is warm against my lips as I kiss it. "I'm sorry," I whisper, then close my eyes.

"Sorry?" he asks in a sleepy voice and turns toward me. "What are you sorry for?"

He makes me smile so effortlessly. Just looking at him makes me happy. "Hi," I say, kissing him on the forehead. "I'm sorry that I fell asleep. I wanted to spend time with you."

"Nothing to be sorry about," he says, rubbing my arm. "I'm exhausted, too. Thanks for letting me stay the night."

"You don't have to thank me for that. How was the store the rest of the day? What about Braden and Kellan? Did you have fun with them?"

He blinks hard, rubbing his eyes. "What time is it? Is it morning?"

"Technically, yes. It's just a little after two. I didn't mean to wake you." I wrap my arm around his waist and pull him back toward me, sliding back into a spooning position. "We can talk in the morning."

He brings my hand to his mouth and kisses it. "If we have time to talk now, I want to talk. Giovanni told me I should let you sleep, though. I was trying so hard to be quiet when I got here. The day was insane. It was just—really crazy seeing the way that people talk about you, and know so much about you. There were people there that knew way more about you than I do. One lady has been watching you play soccer since your high school days. I didn't know that you getting signed at eighteen was such a big deal. She knew all your stats, and facts about random things, I just listened to her and a few other people talking about their favorite moments in your career. Another family drove two hours, so the dad could possibly win the date with you—not for the date in the traditional sense, he just wants to ask soccer advice for his kids. Then there were the people asking about your personal life, whether you had a girlfriend, where you live, what kind of car you drive. It was just—I had no idea everything that went with your job."

"Yeah. Fans are intense sometimes. I'm sorry that you even had to deal with all of that. I will say, that was such a small amount of people compared to an actual signing event or a game. So, it's probably better that it happened here, versus you seeing all that happen in Miami. I hadn't considered that people would use the date to try and get advice out of me. That wouldn't be so bad if that happens. What else did Gio say to you? Nothing bad, right? He rarely talks to people when he's on the job, so he must like you if he said more than a few words."

Edward chuckles. "Maybe he's still deciding. He didn't say too much. How was the apology? I know you didn't really want to do that. Well, I know you didn't really want any of this."

"Lots of questions from people that I refused to answer. I apologized for my actions, to the fans, apologized to my sponsors, to the league, and to my teammates, but I didn't apologize to Doug. Marco seems satisfied for now, kind of. He wanted me to come to Miami to meet in person, but Linley got me out of that. We're in the off-season now anyway, so there's no reason for it." I squeeze him tight and kiss his cheek. "Don't worry about that stuff. It was all okay. It's my job, and I would've had to eventually do it anyway. Just would have been much easier if I was in Miami. How about Braden and Kellan? Their place is so full of Christmas, right?"

"Mmmhmm. Their cats are so cute, too. It was fine. I like being around them, they're so in love, it's nice to see. They remind me of a few couples in some of my favorite books."

"Which one would be the book boyfriend out of the two of them?" I ask. This is a good opportunity for me to figure out if I really do understand what a book boyfriend is.

"Book boyfriend? Out of those two?" he asks looking over his shoulder at me. "Neither... They seem to both take care of each other, so I can't say one seems more like the perfect man over the other. Not that I think either are perfect, at least not for me... Don't listen to me," he giggles, "I'm half asleep. Damn it, my mom..." he mumbles.

"Your mom? What does your mom have to do with anything?"

He sighs against the pillow. "She's been calling since I got here, and I haven't had the time to talk to her. Today she left me a long voicemail, I meant to call her back and I didn't get around to it."

I can tell he feels bad about that. I wasn't really sure what his relationship with his parents was like, it makes sense that he's just been too busy to talk to her. I didn't even get to talk to my mom today either. I did text her, though. The skin on his hands is so soft, I can't help but to rub it. "I'm sure she's anxious to know how things are going with the store and the move. I'm sorry that everything that happened today got in the way of you talking to her."

"How do you do it?" he asks me. "How do you—have time? For anything?"

"In the off-season I have time, but during the season it's pretty crazy. Truthfully, I've never tried to make time for anyone or anything outside of soccer. I started playing so young, so the regimen was in place before I went to college. I studied when I had to, and outside of studying, it was all soccer."

"Didn't you ever—want to go out with anyone or be in a relationship? Ever?"

I shake my head and kiss his cheek. "Not really. My mom made sure to tell me every day how lucky I was to be given a contract at my age, so I just stayed focused. I've never let anyone get close to me." His hand is trembling a bit, so I intertwine my fingers with his. "Until you."

"So, when you said you'd never been on a date, you really meant that? It's just so hard to believe," he says through a giggle. "Especially now that I see the way people throw themselves at you." I'm pretty sure a few people asked you to get them pregnant. The best one today was a girl who brought an Omegaverse book up, she said that the thought of you being an Alpha was the hottest thing she could think of. She had a whole fantasy worked out, where your teammates were just a bunch of omegas…"

"I don't, uh…know what that means. I'm not sure I want to, either. I'm sorry that people made you feel uncomfortable. That's the last thing I want. I thought about you so many times today and I just couldn't wait to spend time with you tonight. I hated not being able to be around you."

Edward nods. "Me too. It was okay, definitely rough, but, hey, there was a picture of us on one of the websites. Kellan showed it to me."

"Of us?" A million thoughts are racing through my head right now. But since no one asked me anything about him during my conferences, it couldn't have been anything sexy.

"Yeah, I guess one of the reporters took a picture when you came out to announce that there would be no breeding or choking for anyone. I didn't know people could do that. Just take pictures for articles without permission. Doesn't that bother you?"

"I never look online unless I have to. I could probably get it taken down if you want, I'd just need to let Linley know. I am kind of curious what our first picture looks like together, though. We made a good team today." Team, shit. I should probably tell him what Gio said. "This probably won't happen, but Gio told me that some of my teammates were going to come here and surprise me tomorrow. I already have a haircut and a suit fitting… I don't have time to deal with those clowns."

Edward yawns, tucking in even tighter. "You *did* say that you hate clowns."

"Well, I do, but these guys are an extension of my family, so I don't hate them, but they definitely get on my nerves. I don't want them to come visit, that's why I disconnected from them once I came here. But, if they end up coming, I—I want you to meet them."

I wait a few seconds for a reply, but Edward hasn't said anything. Maybe that was too much to ask of him? No, I think he just fell asleep. I need to go back to sleep, too. Tomorrow is gonna be another long day.

Chapter Twenty
A Haircut, A Suit, and A Corset

   Jacob   

My alarm wakes me at six, and I quickly turn it off. I'm not going to the gym right now. I don't feel like dragging Gio there, and I definitely don't want to be away from Edward unless I have to.

"Do you want me to go to the gym with you?" Edward asks through sleepy eyes.

"Sorry, that's the second time I woke you up on accident. But, no, thanks. I'm gonna soak up these few minutes with you before all the crazy starts today."

He smiles at me and closes his eyes. "Okay. But when was the first time you woke me up?"

Does he not remember our conversation last night? Maybe he had a few drinks before he came over? "Last night, well, this morning at two, we had a long conversation… Do you remember?"

"Of course I remember," he says, playfully tapping the tip of my nose. "I thought you meant after that. I don't know when I fell asleep, though. Do you think the day will be like it was yesterday for you?"

Part of me thinks this day will be *worse* than yesterday, but I'm not gonna say that to him. Shit, the guys might really be coming today. I need to check my other phone. "I don't know. I have a few meetings this morning, then the barber and the suit fitting. I wish you didn't have to work. It would be fun if you went with me."

"I'd like that, but I'd hate for people to stop by for a book and see the shop closed." He pulls his mouth to the side. "Then again, I sold barely any books yesterday, and I don't have any more tickets to sell, so I'll just be disappointing people all day. What time are your appointments for the fitting and haircut?"

I reach around and grab my phone from my nightstand and quickly check my calendar. Son of a b...there's a text from Gio. Seems like the guys *are* coming. Ugh. "Haircut is 12:15 and the suit fitting is after that. The tailor isn't in Frosty Bottoms, but I think it's still close by. Are you thinking about skipping out of work to come with me?"

"I'm thinking about it. I'll see how the morning goes."

"Okay, well, if you want to, let me know and I can pick you up. Were you awake last night when I said that some of my teammates were coming to surprise me?"

"Hmm...I don't think I remember you saying that. But that's fun, right? Are you excited?"

"No. First of all, I hate surprises, and they all know that. Second, there is nowhere in this town for them to sleep, so what do they plan on doing? Most of all, I don't want to see them right now because they're gonna ask why I punched the ref. I really don't want to get into it with them. It was just so much easier for me to leave until things quieted down, it also removed me from...situations. And not to mention that they sucked in the playoffs, couldn't win a single game. So, no, I'm not happy they're coming."

I feel like that was a lot to dump on him, but in reality, I'm holding back about thirty other reasons why I don't want to see them. I also have no idea who's coming or how they're getting here, or when they're getting here.

"You didn't tell your teammates why you punched him?"

"Nope. Turned my phone off and ran away from my problems like an adult. Figured I'd deal with it once I went back to Miami, or if I ended up signing with another team, I wouldn't have to deal with it at all."

"Could that happen? Could you sign with another team?"

I pillow my hands behind my head. "Yeah, it could, but Marco won't let that happen. If I'd stayed there and things blew up, then maybe, but—" I close my eyes and sigh. "I don't want to deal with this right now. But about today, the sooner you let me know if you want to go with me, the better. With all the shit going on, a solid plan is the best defense at this point."

I turn on my side and stare at him. He looks like he's deep in thought. His cheeks are so soft, I can't help but rub them. He's nuzzling against my hand, and it may be the cutest thing I've ever seen. His smile is everything. "I want to take you to look at Christmas lights tonight. Would you like that?"

He looks shocked and I can't tell if it's a good shocked. There we go, there's the smile. "Christmas lights? I love Christmas lights. Could we really do it?"

"Yeah, unless something crazy happens, then we'll do it. We'll need to bring Gio, though."

"Ah," he says, giving me a pout. "No blowjobs in the car, then?"

"Pftt, no, not with Gio in the car. Thinking about that already?" He's not the only one, my dick is already hard just looking at his mouth.

"Been thinking about it since around eight last night, actually. I had no idea you had sexy glasses, I wanted to jump on you so bad. I hadn't even imagined you with glasses, so seeing it last night was very difficult for me. So hot."

I slide my hand down my gym shorts. "Why didn't you jump on me then?"

"You were asleep. I couldn't do that. I didn't want to wake you and ask if it would be okay, so I just hopped in the shower, touched my dick a little and then came to bed."

I exhale and squeeze my dick—it's throbbing, begging to be inside of Edward. The thought of him touching his cock in my shower is so fucking sexy. "Look at me," I say, raising my eyebrows at him. "You have permission to do anything you want to me while I'm asleep, because I'll eventually wake up and be very happy about it. Just can't leave any marks."

Edward is leaning over toward me, he's got a mischievous look in his eyes as he leans in close to my ear. "You have my permission to do anything you want to me while I'm asleep, and I don't care if you leave marks." He's kissing my neck softly, while I stroke my cock. I have to fuck him before we head out in a bit.

"Rizz!" Gio says through the door, while knocking. "You're late for the gym. Get up!"

Edward drops his head on my shoulder. "No fun for us this morning. After Christmas lights we can pick this back up," he says and kisses my cheek.

I look down at my dick and shake my head. "He's gonna be upset all day." Edward kisses my shaft through the thin fabric of my shorts and gives my dick a pat. The brief feeling of his warm breath on me drives me crazy. "Don't do that, not right now," I tell him, while I roll out of bed and open my bedroom door. Gio is already fully dressed, I should have texted to tell him I wasn't gonna go. "I'm not going to the gym, but I'm gonna drop Edward off for work in a few minutes. You can stay here."

Gio looks around me and I squeeze the door closed a little more. "You're not going anywhere without me. What are you doing skipping the gym? You never skip the gym. This is a no bullshit day, so tell me what happened."

What am I supposed to say to that? I don't want Edward to feel bad, but the truth is that I skipped because I want to be near him before the day starts. I shrug my shoulders at Gio. "Just didn't feel like going. We're leaving in a few minutes, so we can go over our plan for the day on the way to drop Edward off."

"Gio, what the hell are you doing?!" I shout from the back seat. "You're gonna break my rims. You said you had a plan!" Gio pulls my car onto the shoulder and speeds past the rest of the cars. He apparently isn't waiting in any traffic today—oh, that's right, he told me it's a *no bullshit day*, which means someone pissed him off last night, or this morning.

"I have a plan. Do you want Edward to be late for work?" he asks me.

"Your da—Mayor Dick cleared the shoulder riding with the officers over there. Just relax, superstar."

"Okay, who pissed you off this morning?" I ask Gio. "I know you aren't this pissy just because I didn't go to the gym."

"Superstar," Edward whispers. "Can that be my nickname for you?"

I shake my head at him. "Absolutely not," I say quietly, before raising my voice. " I *hate* when Gio calls me that, but since he's being a dick this morning, he called me it on purpose."

"Of course I'm pissed off, I had to fucking deal with Doritos this morning. And not at six am, buddy, I've been getting updates from him all night long."

"Is he saying he has an upset stomach from Doritos?" Edward asks me.

"No," I say with a chuckle and lean toward the front seat. "Wait, why is Doritos texting you?"

"He's driving the van with everyone, well they're all in the van, taking turns driving. It's a twenty-four-hour drive and they've been on the road since yesterday morning. I'm not in the mood for him. I thought it was gonna be the two of us, easiest thing in the world to protect you, but this schmuck comes around and always screws something up."

I drop my head against my seat. That means my teammates will be here soon. Shit. I can't believe this is really happening. I turn toward Edward. "Doritos is one of the team security guards. He's who they call in for small trips, or if there are only a few people. He and Gio have opposite styles—to say the least."

"But why do you guys call him Doritos?" Edward asks.

"He was eating Doritos when he was supposed to be on watch at the hotel," Gio explains. "Kid had cheesy fingers and crumbs on his mouth. How's he gonna protect anyone with his hand in a Dorito bag?"

I pat Edward's thigh. "His name is actually Dominic, you can call him Dominic Doritos if you want. He's really nice. Wait, Gio, who is in the van? I know Scott is there, that's a given."

"Yep, your shadow is in the van, he probably organized the whole thing," Gio says.

Before Edward asks, I start to explain. "Scott, is the friend I told you about that loves *Twilight*. His nickname is Shadow because he follows me everywhere, usually doesn't leave my side if he can help it."

Gio jumps into the conversation. "He also copies everything Jacob does. I don't think he even questions something if Jacob does it first, he just does it. He's a shadow on and off the field. Alejo and Tim are coming, they're together now from what Doritos tells me. And Brian and Gabriella are with them, too. Edward, I'll tell you everything you need to know."

"No, no that's not necessary," I say to Gio. "Besides, since when are you so talkative to someone else when you're on duty?"

Gio narrows his eyes at me in the rearview mirror. "Since when do you allow some guy to start sleeping over and park his car in your garage? No offense, Edward, I like you, I think."

"None taken," Edward says with a smile. "I'm happy that I'm the first. I am interested to hear about all the players, though, but only if Jacob is okay with it."

I lean my head against the small window. "Go ahead," I tell Gio.

"Alright, Edward, so there are only a few players coming. Scott is the shadow, like I said. He's basically a Jacob clone, without the talent Rizz has. Brian is the goalie, he's nice, but he can come off like a prick when you first meet him. Gabriella is the team nutritionist, and Marco's daughter…she's not really *with* anyone. Just always hanging around. Tim is an asshole, he's loud and rude, and Alejo is a sweet kid. Not sure how those two are together. Maybe Doritos said the wrong names…"

When we finally pull in behind the bookstore, I squeeze Edward's leg. I'm not gonna kiss him in front of Gio, even though he knows what's going on. I smile at him, while Gio walks around the car quickly opening the passenger door. "Send me a text and let me know about this afternoon. I'm sorry I can't stay here with you today. Once people know that you don't have tickets, maybe they'll just leave, so hopefully it won't be as crazy as it was yesterday."

Edward smiles at me, I can tell he wants to kiss me and as much as I want him to, I can't do it with Gio here. "Okay, yeah, if it's bad, I can always call my brother. Kellan also offered to help if I needed it. I don't know how he's always leaving his store."

"I don't think rules apply to Kellan. But if people start getting pushy, just know that you don't need to stay open. I can pay you to close the store for the day, I'll cover whatever you want me to. You could even overestimate how much you need to recoup. I'd be okay with that. Technically, you could do that at any time though."

"Thanks," he says, keeping his eyes locked on mine.

His big brown eyes are pulling me in. I shift my gaze to Gio and pat Edward's leg. "Alright, text me in a bit. If I don't respond right away it's because I'm in meetings."

"Alright, I'll text you in a little while," he says, and gets out of the car.

I drop my head against my seat. I probably messed that up. Gio lifts the front seat for me, and I climb out of the car, then get into the passenger seat.

"This is no good, boss," Gio says.

"What's no good?"

"I don't want to lecture you, but you've always put soccer first, you know? And today, I watched you skip the gym for the first time ever. This is what Linley was worried about. She's not worried about Edward, she's worried about what a relationship would do to you."

I hate when people say they don't want to lecture you and then they do it anyway. It's so frustrating. "That's why I'm not calling it a relationship yet, because everyone has got me so damn afraid of what will happen. I'm just trying to figure things out, but no one needs to worry about the effect Edward has on me."

Gio looks over at me while stopped at a red light. "You don't have to call it a relationship for it to be one. You're in a relationship with him, whether you call it one or not. So, I think you need to take some time and ask yourself if a relationship is what you really want."

Mercifully, Gio's phone rings interrupting our conversation. He answers it on speaker, "Doritos, what is it now?"

"Stop calling me Doritos! It was one bag, one time. I'll never live it down," Dominic says with a chuckle. "Just updating you. It's looking like we'll be there around six or seven. Is there room for everyone at Rizzo's place? Or is everyone sleeping in the van?"

"You're all sleeping in the van," I say. "I didn't ask *any* of you to come here. My spare rooms are full of boxes and Gio is already using the office."

"Oh, hey Rizzo!" Dominic says. "How ya been? This is a great surprise, right?"

"It's an ill-advised surprise," I say. "But I guess if there's nowhere for you guys to go, you can sleep at my place. Didn't you look up hotels before you decided to drive for twenty-four hours? Or everyone just assumed they could stay with me?"

"Is that Rizz?" Scott says in the background. "I love you! I'm only mildly hurt that you turned your phone off for months and abandoned me!"

The sigh that escapes me feels like it drains half of my life. I look over at Gio and shake my head.

There are other voices coming from inside the van, but Gio drowns them out. "Yeah, yeah, alright Doritos, just let us know when you get closer. Don't need to update me every hour."

He ends the call, and I lean my head against the window. How am I supposed to tell Scott what happened? How am I supposed to explain it to all of them?

"He *is* your closest friend, you know," Gio says. "I understand why you did what you did, but you're gonna have some explaining to do. And, not to pile on, but if you bring Edward around them, those guys— especially Scott—are gonna know you're in a halflationship as soon as they see you together."

"What did you just say?"

"I said you're gonna have some explaining to do. You had to know they're probably pissed at you too, right?"

It's too warm in this car right now. I turn the heater off and switch my side to cool air and lean my head back against the window. "Not that, I'm talking about what you said about Edward."

"Oh, the halflationship. It's when you're in a relationship with someone but not doing all the couple stuff. I don't know, you said you didn't want to call it a relationship. Halflationship seems accurate, especially as far as Eddie is concerned. He's not gonna get any hand holding, or sitting close to each other, hugs in public, you can't do any of that, so yeah, it's a halflationship. But if you don't really have him around the guys or go out too much with just the two of you, then it should be fine."

"Thank you for that. I hated everything you just said."

Gio smiles as he pulls into my garage, after what feels like an hour. I glance down at my phone. "I'm late. I gotta get inside. Can you try and find out from Dominic how long they're planning on staying here for? I don't have food here for all these people. So, I should do a grocery delivery or something."

Gio laughs out loud. "Oh my God, you sound like your mother! That was one hundred percent your mom that just came out of your mouth. Are you okay?" he asks through laughter.

"Very funny." I shake my head at him while I make my way toward the door, tapping the hood of Edward's car when I walk by. I need to order some stuff that Edward would like, too. I hope everything is okay at the store. "Just let me know how long they'll be here for. I'll be on this call for a while."

Quickly, I make my way into my room and grab my laptop. I see my glasses on the nightstand and can't help but think how cute it was that Edward took them off my face while I was sleeping. Still, I wish he would have jumped on me, getting woken up by sex would be pretty hot.

I take a deep breath and join the meeting with Linley. "Good morning, sorry I'm late."

Linley looks aggravated; she's tilting her head at me while rubbing her temple with two fingers. "Tell me that you did not skip the gym today. Tell me that Giovanni was wrong, and you just forgot to send me your workout stats." She leans back in her chair and folds her arms. "I'll wait."

"I did not skip the gym today. Gio was wrong and I just forgot to send you my stats," I say with a smile—one that she clearly isn't amused by.

"Are you kidding me right now? You just met with Marco yesterday. We are about to enter renegotiations, and you think this is a good time to skip the gym? What's going on inside your head right now?"

"Ah jeez, I don't know, see everything was going great until some person decided to tell everyone where I was, throwing everything into chaos. On top of that, I just found out that some of my teammates are on their way here to surprise me, on a day that I promised to take Edward to look at Christmas lights." Why did I say that? Why didn't I stop before including Edward? She's gonna eat me alive.

"Jacob Rizzo! Can you hear yourself right now? Twenty-five million dollars is what your existing contract is worth, let that sink in. The next contract will be worth more, so what should your priority be right now? Let me answer for you—soccer. Soccer is the only answer." She holds a hand on her head. "I cannot believe you brought up looking at Christmas lights. You also said tonight, so is the whole team going to look at lights with you? You left to protect them and yourself, you can't just have a relationship with Edward out in the open. Jacob—you know this, we've been over it."

"Halflationship," I say.

She's really not in the mood to play. "I don't even want to know what that means. What I want to make clear is that you have responsibilities and commitments that you have to take care of. You cannot put Edward before contractual obligations, and your health *is* a contractual obligation. I don't want to hear of you skipping the gym again. Damn it, I wouldn't even have to babysit you this closely if you were back in Miami. Can this end now? Since everyone knows where you are, do you want to sell the house there and just move back?"

I had hoped today would be slower in the store. But the drive in should have shown me not to put too much into that hope. The traffic was just as bad as yesterday, and the sidewalks were just as packed with pedestrians.

After Jacob drops me off and I slip in the back entrance, I set about cleaning up the place…in front of an audience of people who have their faces pressed against my shop window. Clearly, they're looking for Jacob, but what they're getting instead is a bookseller whose patience is wearing thin, sorting books and mopping floors.

When I open the doors, I'm instantly inundated with crowds, nearly all of whom come to line up at the desk and ask for tickets for tomorrow's auction. Thankfully, no one gets upset today about the lack of tickets and most enter the raffle for the final ticket.

There are a few customers actually here for books, and I process their sales.

But when a news crew comes in, I just about lose it. Thankfully, I bite back what I want to say to them and instead give them a smile as the newscaster comes up to me.

"Are you Edward, the owner of this shop?" the newscaster asks. She's confident and forthright and clearly takes no BS.

"I am," I say. "Welcome to Hot for Plot."

She glances around like it's the first time she's noticed I sell books. "Is Jacob Rizzo here? We'd love to do an interview."

"I'm sorry, he's not. I'm not sure where he is today."

She looks briefly disappointed, then she says, "May we interview you? You could tell us about the auction and how you managed to get Jacob to participate."

I politely decline, and she tries to sweeten the deal by giving me coverage of my event, but I decline again. Thankfully, she doesn't push further, but when I look out the shop window no more than ten minutes later, I see her talking to the camera in front of my store, likely telling the story anyway.

When I have a moment with no customers or media at the desk, I pull out my phone to check my messages. There's another text from my mom, so I send her a quick reply. *I'll call you later today.* And then there's a text from Jacob asking if I'd decided yet on joining him for the suit fitting.

I glance out the window again at the newscaster, then look around my half-full shop at all the people not buying books but who are instead lingering in the hopes that Jacob will appear. Deciding to just go with it, I text him back: *Let's do it! Where do I meet you and when? I can close the shop for an extended lunch.*

Jacob immediately texts me back with the details—it's a haircut in town and a tailor outside of town, and he'll be here in about ten minutes to pick me up. I put my phone back in my pocket and shout to the crowd, "We're closing for lunch in five minutes! If you're here to make a purchase, please come to the register!"

"Where's Jacob?" someone shouts.

"We want Jacob!" another shouts.

"Is Jacob here? Oh my God, he's here, isn't he?"

Suddenly they're all screaming that he's here and there's a chaotic rush, but they're all rushing in different directions because Jacob is, in fact, not here at all.

"Everybody out of the store!" a *very loud* voice shouts. I look toward the door and see Tony standing there. He looks frazzled and exhausted. "If you're not here to buy a book, please leave. We're closing for lunch in five minutes."

There's an audible groan that ripples through the crowd, but thankfully some people start to head toward the door, and the place slowly empties.

When the store is empty, Tony comes to the register. "Have you had much trouble this morning?" he asks.

"Other than that mass panic just now, no. It's been super busy with just a few sales, but no one's been causing trouble. How's your place been?"

He gives me a smile, and there's a little sparkle in his eyes. "Business is booming. With hundreds of people camping out by your store with no food and my restaurant being right next door? I'm making a killing." He pauses, then says, "I think in the summer there's a film fest a few towns over. I don't suppose you know any hot movie stars that could be photographed here and make this whole thing happen again."

"I don't," I say, "I just know soccer players. Well, *one* soccer player."

"Cool, cool," he says. He seems distracted by the books on the counter in front of him. "There's a lot of shirtless men on these book covers. This one has three shirtless men. Is it like a sports adventure or something?"

I glance at the cover of *Double Overtime for the Team*. "There's sports in it, I think," I say. "Did you want to buy it and discover that yourself?"

He puts the book down, but doesn't tear his gaze from it. "Not today, but maybe soon." Then he picks the book up. "Okay, let's get it today."

When he leaves to head back to his restaurant, I say goodbye to him and lock the store up. After doing one last check that everything is good to go, I head through the store to the back door and find Jacob's car waiting.

I hop into the front seat and almost lean over to kiss Jacob, then I realize Giovanni is in the driver's seat, not Jacob. "No kisses till you call me Gio," he says, "and no calling me Gio until you at least take me out to dinner."

"I'm back here," Jacob says. I turn and see him sitting in the back seat.

"Oh, like this morning."

"Yeah, Gio insisted on driving again, so here I am." He pats the seat beside him. "You could sit here."

"Sorry, Giovanni," I say, "I got a better offer."

He chuckles. "You're not my type anyway."

I get out of the car, push the seat forward, and re-enter and sit beside Jacob. A moment later, Giovanni pulls out of the parking space and takes us out of the lot. I look over at Jacob; I want to slip my hand into his, but he's barely looking at me. I know what it's about—he's most likely uncomfortable, since Giovanni is in the car with us. Eventually, he looks over at me and gives me a soft smile.

Jacob relaxes into the seat a little and I relax into mine, though we still keep firm distance between us. I give him a recounting of my morning and he tells me about his and all the running around he's had to do.

Eventually, we're interrupted by the sound of Giovanni clearing his throat. "We're here, boss."

Jacob straightens his clothing. "How do I look?" he asks.

"Like you're the hottest fucking man alive," I say.

Before we open the car doors, Giovanni says, "Please tell me you're getting 'Rizzo' shaved into the back of your head."

"Only if you get 'Giovanni' shaved into yours," Jacob says back.

They both chuckle, then we all get out of the car and head into the barbershop—The Well-Trimmed Bush. Inside is cozy, clean, and very modern looking. A sound system is piping in ska versions of Christmas carols. Thankfully, this place is free of Jacob's fans.

Giovanni is all business now. He does a quick walk around the perimeter, even poking his head past the curtain into the back room. When he's satisfied, he positions himself near the main entrance, standing sideways so he can keep one eye on the passing crowds and the other on his charge.

"Jacob," the barber says. He's a younger man about our age with a handlebar moustache and a well-coiffed head of hair. "It's a pleasure to meet you. I'm so glad your stylist set up this appointment. My name is Harrison."

"Good to meet you," Jacob says. He seems a little closed off now, a little stiffer. This is his public persona that doesn't let people get too close. After seeing the crowds yesterday and today, I get it. "Yeah, I've got a thing tomorrow, so I should be extra-presentable."

"Oh, that's right, I heard about the auction," he says. Then he looks at me and extends his hand, which I take in mine. "You must be Edward, the bookstore owner." He looks at my hair. "You're here for a haircut too, I assume?"

"Um…no…" I say. And I had felt so confident about my looks and hair today. "I'm…I'm good. I'm just tagging along here."

"Hmm," Harrison says, "okay." Then he turns to Jacob. "Sit down. What are we looking for today?"

When Jacob sits, Harrison puts one of those capes on him. He spins the chair so Jacob is looking into a mirror lined with Christmas garland. "Just a cleanup."

"We can manage something like that," Harrison says, grabbing his scissors and doing a few practice snips in the air.

They soon fall into the same old barber banter, with Harrison asking Jacob about his job as if he's an accountant or something. I can tell Jacob wishes this haircut would be in silence, but he's too professional to be *that rude* about it, so he keeps his answers short and leaves little room for follow-up questions, though Harrison is too practiced at this to be stymied by a non-communicative client.

Twenty minutes later after what felt like very little work, Harrison is done. But when he holds up a mirror for Jacob, I catch a reflection myself and see what that "very little work" has done—he is hot. Like, holy fuck. Cleaned up Jacob can do what he wants with me. I don't say any of this out loud, of course, though I do feel my cheeks warm a little bit, and my cock goes stiff.

"Before you go," Harrison says, "may I take a photo of you for my wall?" He waves his hand toward the wall behind me in the waiting area. It's lined with framed photos of dozens of celebrities who have come here for haircuts.

"Is that..." I said, pointing at one of the photos.

"Yes," Harrison says, "we've had more than a few celebrities in here over the years, including a few actors. I almost convinced a certain vampire to dye his hair blue, but his publicist stepped in moments before I started mixing the dye."

I look at the photos again. It feels kind of weird that Jacob's photo would be on this same wall with politicians, movie stars, and music icons.

"I'm cool with a photo," Jacob says.

After the photo, Jacob pays an astonishing amount of money for the haircut, and we get back in the car.

"You look good," I tell him as we pull away from the curb.

He looks at me and gives me a little smile. "Thank you."

Giovanni taps the navigation console. "We should be at the tailor's in fifteen minutes. It's in the next town over, a place called Butte Crack."

When Giovanni takes us out of the city limits for Frosty Bottoms and we're in the countryside between towns, Jacob seems to relax a little more, likely because there are no people around. When we cross city limits, he starts tensing up again.

Giovanni pulls into a parking spot in front of the tailor shop, and immediately does a slow three-sixty look around us.

"I doubt anyone would think to look for us here," Jacob says.

"I'm not Doritos, boss, I do my job all the time." When Giovanni seems satisfied, at least for the moment, he gets out of the car and then pushes the seat forward to allow Jacob to climb out. I scoot across the bench seat and get out too. Giovanni leads us to the door, opens it, and then ushers us inside. Like with the barbershop, he does a circuit around the place as the staff person comes up to us.

The store looks classy and clean with mannequins all along one wall showing off suit designs. Each one is wearing a Santa hat atop its head. A black and white fake Christmas tree stands in the far corner.

"Mister Rizzo," the employee says. He's maybe a little older than us but classier, with a suit that looks like it was custom made for him—and come to think of it, it probably was—and graying hair styled even more perfectly than Harrison's. "It's a pleasure to meet you. My name is Chester."

"Hi, Chester," Jacob says. "Thank you for meeting with me today. That's my bodyguard, Gio, at the door, and this, uh, this is Edward."

Chester and I exchange polite greeting nods, but after that, he pretty much ignores me. I go and sit in a chair that looks spectacular but is really rather uncomfortable.

"Up here, sir," he says to Jacob.

He steps up onto a little platform, and Chester starts taking some measurements of his arms and neck and chest. Then he goes further south, doing Jacob's waist and inseam. As he slides the measuring tape up Jacob's inner leg, I see Jacob's eyes flare momentarily when it looks like Chester's hand accidentally makes contact with his balls.

A few moments later, Chester disappears into a back room and Jacob comes up beside me. "He's getting some samples for me to try on for colors and fit and style and stuff," he says.

"Is that a corset?" I ask, pointing toward the mannequin at the end. We walk over to it. It is, indeed, a corset designed for men, with mostly black material and metallic piping up the sides.

"Looks uncomfortable," Jacob says, as he runs his fingers up the piping.

I smirk. "I bet this would look hot on you," I whisper.

His eyes go wide, but then they take on a hungry look. "Even better on you. I'd love to see you in this when I have you sprawled out on my bed."

Just then there's a clattering behind us as Chester sets up a little rack with some sample pieces. Jacob returns to where Chester is, and I watch as he tries on different pieces and he and Chester discuss the materials and fit. He looks incredibly sexy in a suit, and this one isn't even customized to fit him yet—when it fits him like a glove, then he'll be even more irresistible than he already is.

"What do you think?" Jacob asks me when he and Chester have picked all the pieces out. "The cuffs have to be sewn, the waist taken in, and the pants hemmed, but this is what we're looking at."

I really hope my boner isn't bulging right now. "It looks really good," I say.

Jacob changes back into his regular clothes and processes the payment. While he does that, I step outside for some fresh air and to hopefully calm my raging hard-on. When Jacob comes out, closely followed by Giovanni, he's carrying a bag.

"I thought you were coming back tomorrow to pick it up," I say. "All the adjustments and stuff."

He holds up the bag, and he has a devilish grin on his face. "This isn't the suit. Get in the car."

Giovanni holds the seat forward and I go in first, scooting to the far side, and then Jacob gets in after me.

"Where to, boss?" Giovanni asks when he starts up the car.

"Back to the shop, I assume?" Jacob says, looking at me.

"Yeah, I need to run the store for a couple more hours," I say.

"Back to the shop it is," Giovanni says.

When we're on the way, Jacob slides the bag across the seat between us. I take it from him and open it and look inside.

It's the corset.

I turn to him, about to say something sexually inappropriate, but then I catch him glance at Giovanni, reminding me that we're not alone. So instead of saying something that would make both Jacob and Giovanni uncomfortable, I instead slide the bag back to Jacob, giving him the hottest eyes I can manage.

A good twenty minutes later, Giovanni pulls up behind my shop, and I take the back entrance. When I go through to the front of the store, I find people again waiting outside.

Once I'm ready, I let them in, and I'm instantly fielding questions about Jacob and the Book Boyfriend Auction. People are disappointed and frustrated that they've missed out on tickets, but ultimately, they're understanding. And amongst all the Jacob fans, I do get a few people genuinely in search of books, all of whom purchase at least a couple items before heading out.

When I get a bit of a calm moment in the afternoon, I text Jacob: *I'm looking forward to Christmas lights tonight!*

A few moments later, Jacob replies: *Can I call you?*

Chapter Twenty-One
Dates End With Sex

 Edward

When I give him an affirmative answer, my phone then rings in my hand. "Hey," I say, my voice sounding almost breathless to my ears.

"Hey, remember Gio was talking about the other guys on the team?"

"Yeah," I say, "they're driving up here or something, right?"

"Yeah, and, well…they want to go for a big dinner."

I feel my mood crash down, but I try to hide it from him. "Oh, so no lights?"

"We can do lights," he replies quickly. "We'll just be a little late because we'll have dinner first."

"We?" I say.

"Yeah…you wanna come?"

"Sure, I can be up for that. It'd be nice to meet them." I'm feeling kind of nervous about this. Maybe it's because these people are important to him and I want to make the right first impression, and sports people aren't usually the type of people I blend well with—Jacob being the first notable exception. "When and where is it?"

"We're aiming for 6:30 at Tony's place. He's going to give us several tables in a special reserved section."

"That should be fun," I say. "I'm thinking maybe when I get off at five, I should head over to Chad's and have a shower there. I've got some clothes at his place still, so I could find something to wear for tonight. And, well, if I come separately, then we're not walking in together."

There's a little bit of relief in his voice when he says, "That sounds great. I'm stuck in meetings till six or so. I could send Gio to pick you up but he gets antsy being sent away from me, like he's not doing his job properly."

I chuckle at Giovanni's dogged determination to do his job right. "I look forward to tonight. It'll be fun."

"It will," he says. "Before I let you go, what's your favorite cereal?"

"Definitely Fruity Pebbles, no question, no doubt, no hesitation."

"Um. Okay. Well…I should let you go. I don't want to, but I've got a call with Linley in about two minutes."

"Linley," I say, some darkness tinging my voice, but I shake it off. "I'll text you when I get to Chad's and maybe I'll text you some of the shirt options."

"I can't wait," he says. "And if you happen to *accidentally* text me a shirtless pic, or a…you know…that would make this day a whole lot better for me."

I laugh and then say, "I'll see you at 6:30."

After we end the call, I text Chad to let him know I'll be stopping by his place. Both him and Lucas will be at the bar, but I don't want them to come home and feel like someone had been there.

A couple hours and a whole lot of disappointed Jacob fans later, it's five and I'm closing up shop. I give things a quick cursory tidy and give the floor a quick mop. Despite the high foot traffic, the place isn't as big a disaster as yesterday. I'm feeling good about everything—Jacob, the dinner with his friends, the bookstore, the new life I'm making for myself here in Frosty Bottoms.

As I walk down the street, a biting wind comes rushing into my face. The weather has definitely taken a turn toward wintery. I zip my coat up a little higher and hunch my shoulders as I hurry down the street and then eventually turn off and walk into the suburbs. From here, it's not much further to Chad and Lucas's place, and soon I'm letting myself into their apartment.

"Drop your pants!" Petey shouts at me. "Drop your pants!"

"Hey, Petey," I say. "Are you being a good boy?"

"Good boy! Awrk! Good boy! Awrk!"

"Wow, good thing I didn't call you a bad bo—uh…never mind. I didn't say anything." Before he can pick up on what I *almost* said, I hurry into what was my bedroom for, like, one night and is now just a place where I store some of my things.

I quickly text Jacob with an update, and then turn to my bed. Before I can dig through the random pile of clothes sitting there, my phone rings. I answer it without looking at the screen, "Hey, Jacob."

"Now that's interesting," a voice says that is definitely not Jacob.

"Umm…hi, Mom." I grab some of my hair in a fist, mentally kicking myself for that mistake. "Uh…how are you?"

"The real question," she says, "is how are you?" She pauses like she's waiting for me to jump in. When I don't, she continues, "You moved to a new town, opened a new store…and now I'm seeing you all over the media in the background for all these Jacob Rizzo stories. It's even made the nightly news here in…God, where am I again?"

"I think you're in Uruguay," I offer. "Right?"

My mom is a travel writer, and she'd always hoped I'd follow in her footsteps of writing non-fiction books. While she loves that books are such a major part of my life, she's a little less than enthused that I'm obsessed with books where the main characters fall in love and have a ton of sex. She's not sure it contributes to the world of literature, but when I'm curled up in bed at two in the morning I want to read about dudes rutting in the dark, not how the local politics in Uruguay have influenced food culture, or whatever it was her assignment is about.

"Uruguay!" I can hear her snap her fingers. "That's it! Thank you. Last week was Paraguay and I keep getting them mixed up." She again leaves a little bit of silence between us, likely hoping that I jump in with all the answers to her questions before she can even ask them, but I don't. With Mom having travelled so much when I was growing up, we were never super close. She's tried a few times to build those bridges now that I've gotten older, but they've always felt a little awkward. When she gives up on waiting for me, she says, "Tell me everything—the move, the store, staying with Chad...whatever your friendship with Jacob is about..."

I decide I need to meet her halfway, so I give her a recap of the move and the bookstore opening, while leaving out some details like mashing my face into Jacob's balls. I steer well clear of talking about what's happening between me and Jacob, more so out of respect for Jacob than anything else. When I realize I'm starting to babble about the insanity of the past few days, I clam up.

"I'm so glad to hear it all went so well, and your new store sounds cute. You'll have to send me photos," Mom says. "Now...do you realize how many times you said Jacob's name in all of that?"

"Umm..."

I can tell Mom is slipping into her travel writer mode, looking for the story. "Tell me about Jacob."

"Uh, what's there to tell? He's a soccer player that was, for a time, running a contracting business, and he helped me set up my store. But then the media got wind of the whole thing and it all blew up and now he's not a contractor anymore and this town is overflowing with people in search of him. I don't know, it's complicated."

"Mmhmm, I know who Jacob Rizzo is," she says slowly, as if she's writing something down. "So, what's the deal with you guys?"

"We're sort of together," I say, "but not, because of his job, and I think he's just trying to figure out how I fit into everything. I don't know, I can't explain it."

"And how do you feel about that?"

"I think I feel fine with it. It's new-ish, kind of."

"Honey, it's okay to say how you feel. You've always been this way, people don't know that you don't like something unless you tell them, so if you don't like something then you need to tell him."

"I didn't say that I didn't like something—it's new, and I'm really happy, it's just that a lot of stuff has happened over the past few days, so I'm still trying to figure out if I'm gonna wake up in the hospital and find out I have amnesia or if this is one of those transported into a book scenarios. Just all seems unreal at times."

"I see. He's not any better than you just because he's an athlete. And with the way I saw him look at you, he doesn't think so either. I'll stop because I don't want you to clam up on me, but just take a moment to enjoy what you have, you moved to a new town, you opened a brand-new store that looks really successful already, and you have a guy who seems to really like you. Not that you are unlikeable, of course, the problem in these situations is that every once in a while we find someone that we just don't feel good enough for, and I think it's because our hearts know the tremendous burden we're about to place on them, our heart knows that caring for this person is going to mean pushing so much of ourselves aside to make room for someone else. And it's not that the heart is selfish, it's that the heart doesn't realize how much it has room for, and this person seems so great, that our hearts, the little things that they are, have no idea what they're capable of. So, the heart immediately thinks it's too hard, or this person is too great, and it tries to protect itself by closing off. That's you—you close yourself off to people, you've done it your whole life. Open up to him, tell him how you feel. If he's the right one, he won't run away."

"I'm happy. I should have said that. You're catching me at a bad time because I'm getting ready to go out to dinner and meet some of his teammates, so I'm just nervous. I don't know anything about soccer."

"So what? Does mister dreamy eyes care about that? I bet he doesn't. Just be you. Oh, and I think your father has been trying to get ahold of you, too. I don't even know which state he's in right now," she says with a giggle. "But try and call him next time you're free."

"Drop your pants!" Petey calls from the living room.

"Pardon me?" Mom says, shocked.

"Oh, that's, uh…that's Petey. It's Chad's parrot," I say. "It seems to only know sexy stuff. It's a little crude."

She chuckles as she says, "As is Chad, from what I hear from your father."

"Petey definitely learned it from someone."

"And how is that going? You and Chad? You barely knew him before moving in with him."

I sigh. "It's been nice. I haven't been here all that much, though. I've been over at Jacob's for, like, day two and onward since I moved here. I'm just back at his place now to grab a shirt that I left here."

"So, you're good, Edward?" Mom asks. "Everything is going right in your world?"

I feel a bit of warmth in my chest at her asking that, at her seeking the confirmation of my happiness. "I'm very good, Mom, thank you."

We talk for a few more minutes about her trip and some of the interesting things she's seen and done, but eventually static enters the line, and we decide to end the call with a promise to catch up again in a few days.

When I end the call and just soak in the good feelings I've got going on right now, Petey screeches from the living room, "Good boy!"

I laugh and push myself to my feet. I open the closet and dig through it until I find the turtleneck I'd come in search of. It's perfectly black and in tiny white print across the chest it says *I'll be your nightmare before Christmas*. I only bring this out for special occasions in December.

"Right, shower first," I tell myself. I put the shirt on the bed and head to the bathroom. As I let the shower warm up, the bathroom gets steamy and I strip off my clothes. I take a few naked selfies, with the mirror fog obscuring my dick, and then send them over to Jacob. He responds a moment later with sweating emojis and eggplants.

After showering and getting dressed, I get my shoes and coat back on and say goodbye to Petey.

And with that I head out into the evening. The sun had long set—it had gone down when my shop closed—and so it's dark outside, lit by streetlamps. A few flakes of snow are starting to fall. I know this town prides itself on its winter, and with the unseasonable warmth of the last week, the population is probably antsy for snow. With luck, this will be the start of making Frosty Bottoms a winter wonderland.

It doesn't take me long to walk to Tony's place. Rather than go straight to it, I walk slowly on the other side of the street, passing Chad's bar and Braden's cookie shop. From here, my bookshop looks darn good. It's cozy and cute, just the way I wanted it.

When I turn my attention to Tony's restaurant, I can barely see the shop windows because of the line-up to get in and the crowds pressed against the glass. Word has absolutely gotten out about Jacob and his team being here. I grimace a bit as I cross the street—not at the fact that Jacob draws these kinds of crowds, but at the fact that these crowds can be unruly when they get worked up. I'll be glad when the novelty of Jacob being here wears off and people start going home.

I head straight for the door and a tall, skinny man I don't recognize is standing there like a bouncer. He's wearing dark shades despite it being fully nighttime. He also looks a little cold. For some reason, I know exactly who this is.

"Are you Dominic?" I ask.

He smiles and points a finger at me. "Edward?"

"The one and only," I say.

He angles his head over his shoulder. "Head on in," he says.

"My name is Edward too!" a man shouts. "Can I go in?"

"And my name is Esmerelda, which starts with E like Edward!" a woman shouts. "Let me in!"

"Ain't nobody getting in!" Dominic shouts. "Except for you," he says to me, "now move your ass before they riot."

"Thank you," I say as I pass by him.

Tony spots me from the kitchen and waves, so I wave back. Then I approach the table. Jacob has his back to me but I recognize him instantly and he's who takes my attention immediately. He's wearing a backwards hat. Fuck. I want to bottom for him right here and now, but Tony would get in trouble with the health inspector. Oh, and the fans in the restaurant and outside would freak. *Keep it together,* I tell myself. *Be a mature adult for dinner and then he can rail me afterward.*

I force myself to raise my gaze and take in the other people as I approach. I don't yet know who is who, but there are four other guys seated with them and a woman too. I think Giovanni had mentioned something about the owner's daughter tagging along, so that must be her. And then there's Giovanni standing near the tables and keeping a watchful eye on the room. When we make eye contact, he doesn't smile—he's in full professional mode—but there's a flicker of what looks like welcoming in his eyes. He unhooks the ribbon divider to let me through.

"Thanks, Gio," I say. When he gives me a glare, I clarify, "Giovanni. I meant Giovanni."

"Edward," Jacob says as he turns around. "You made it."

"Of course," I say. I stand behind the empty chair right next to Jacob and look around the table of people—and they've all stopped, and they're looking up at me. "Hi," I say to them, "I'm Edward."

They all just continue staring at me, looking like goldfish at the pet store.

Finally, Jacob says to the group, "This is my-my friend, Edward. He owns the bookstore next door and he's running the Book Boyfriend Auction tomorrow that I'm participating in."

Thankfully, everyone's gaze turns to Jacob as he talks. It's clear Jacob is someone everyone looks up to. If he gives the okay, then it's okay.

I pull the chair out and sit next to Jacob. I can feel the body heat radiating off him, and it's soaking into my skin and warming me.

"This is Scott," Jacob says, introducing the guy sitting next to him. Scott seems to be the most eager when looking at Jacob, like he idolizes him. Then he goes around the table introducing everyone else. "That's Brian, and they're Alejo and Tim, and that's Gabriella." The guys give me that tight smile nod that guys give each other, and Gabriella gives me a warm and welcoming smile.

"Good to meet you all," I say.

The group soon resumes their talking as if I'm not there, which suits me just fine. I'm weirdly nervous right now, but I don't think it's so much because I'm sitting at a table full of people I don't know.

I glance over my shoulder and see that almost everyone's eyes are on us. And it looks like a bunch of people are discreetly trying to take photos of the group. My gut clenches a little bit. It's photos and videos like those that reached my mom down in Uruguay, and so many other parts of the globe. I get that Jacob and the guys are likely used to it, but it'll take me a little while I think.

"Hey," Jacob whispers to me, "are you okay?"

I turn to face him. "The cameras. They don't bother you?"

He briefly glances over his shoulder at them. "They do, but I just kind of filter them out. We don't have to stay if you don't want to."

"No, it's okay," I say. "It's fine. I promise."

Gabriella then leans forward and says, "Jacob, I'd really love to talk to you in private before the night is over."

I wonder what she wants with him. I've seen that kind of look before from certain guys who wanted to sleep with me.

Jacob kind of waves his hand dismissively at her but doesn't give her a real answer.

"So, Edward," Scott says, leaning forward to see me past Jacob's chest, "tell me about yourself."

"Um…" I try to focus on Scott and his question. "I, uh, I moved here about a week ago to open a romance bookstore. Not much to say beyond that, I mean, I'm just kind of finding my feet here in Frosty Bottoms and finding my place in the community."

"That's so cool," Brian says. "What draws you to romance books?"

"I think it's the happy endings that draw me in," I say. "I read for fun, so I want to have a good time, and for me that means a book has low drama, fun characters, a whole lot of love, and a happy ending that has you smiling when you close the book."

My gaze flickers briefly to Jacob, and I see him kind of looking a little proud that his friends seem to like me so far.

I happen to then glance at Gabriella, and she's watching Jacob with a frustrated look on her face. She wants something from him, and his dismissing her request earlier to talk hasn't satisfied her, nor does she look ready to drop it.

"I read romances sometimes," she says. "I love it when they're *extra dirty*. The more sex the better, if you ask me." When she says that last part, she's staring straight at Jacob again.

"I like the sex too," I say. "It isn't a romance if they don't bang in chapter one, as I often say."

The guys chuckle at that.

"So, what's this auction our boy is participating in?" Alejo asks.

"Yeah," Tim chimes in, "that's what helped us finally find out where he is, and why we're here now."

"Well," I say, "this town has a big Christmas event called the Snowflake Festival and all the businesses set something up. I'm doing a sort-of auction for dates with local guys, with the money raised going to charity."

"That's sweet," Alejo says.

"Wait," Scott says, slapping Jacob on the chest with the back of his hand. "You're going to put out for some random person that buys you?"

"What?" Jacob says. "I'm not having sex. Who says I'm having sex?"

"Dates end with sex," Scott says.

Jacob scoffs. "Maybe in your perverted world. This is just a charity thing, a dinner with someone that wants to talk to me or something."

"…and bone you," Scott says.

"You're being ridiculous."

"I'm right about this," Scott says. He turns to the rest of the table. "Right? Date means sex, right?"

There's a round of nods and a chorus of "yeah" from the guys.

Scott leans forward to look at me past Jacob's chest. "You might not know this, but our boy Rizz has no experience dating. He just doesn't know these things yet."

I just look at Jacob, and he's staring into the middle distance, gone as still as a statue. I can tell he's uncomfortable. I gently knock my knee against his, and he breaks out of his trance to glance at me. There's a silent look of apology in his eyes, but when he turns back to the guys, he's brooding again.

"Anyway," Scott says, "first round of drinks is on me! Server!" When a server comes over, Scott orders a round of the Dark and Snowy, a Christmas twist on the Dark and Stormy, for the table.

Tim and Alejo burst into laughter at some shared joke between them. Then Gabriella leans across the table again and says, "Jacob, can we please talk later?"

"Appetizers are here!" the server announces as he comes to the table with a tray full of platters of food. Behind him is another server with a tray.

The guys and Gabriella dig into the food, pulling portions onto their plates—except for Jacob. He just sips his water. He's got that brooding look down pat. And that look turns me on. I want to drop my pants, straddle his lap, and ride him here and now.

"And drinks are ready too," another server says as he places them on the table.

I take a sip of my Dark and Snowy and sink into the experience of hanging out with Jacob and his friends. I notice several times that when Scott makes a joke or a snarky comment, the first person he looks at is Jacob, like he wants to see if he's made him crack a smile.

When the appetizers are half done and the drinks have all been drained—except for the one in front of Jacob, Scott orders another round of drinks. While we wait for it, with a silent questioning look to Jacob and a tiny nod in return, I switch my empty glass with his Dark and Snowy, and quickly drink that down before the new drinks get here.

"Sugarplum White Russians for the table," a server announces as he starts setting drinks down in front of us.

I load up my plate with more appetizers to help counter the alcohol. It seems the plan is to make dinner out of appetizers since they order a few more shareable plates and no one orders an actual meal. Jacob still doesn't take any food, which doesn't surprise me too much, given how strict he is on his meal plan, but he's also not drinking anything. And while he's engaging in conversation, it's really limited and restrained.

"Hey," I whisper as I lean closer to him, "you okay?"

He looks at me like he's surprised I'd ask the question. "Yeah, I'm fine, why?"

"You haven't touched this drink either. Plus, you're not exactly smiling tonight."

At that he gives me a little smile, and it seems genuine. "I don't usually drink when I'm out with the guys. But don't let that stop you from enjoying a couple drinks. Do you want this one too?" He holds out his Sugarplum White Russian for me.

I glance at it, but don't take it yet. "Once I finish this one, that's three drinks. Three firmly makes me tipsy. A fourth will make me slu—" I cut myself off before finishing that thought and then drain the last of my drink.

Jacob gives me a mischievous smile and nudges his drink toward me.

I pick it up and take a sip as we turn back to the table. The conversation had long moved on to things I don't know and people I've never met, often veering into recounting games I've never watched. Jacob starts livening up a bit, especially when they talk about the games and relive certain thrilling moments. It's fun watching him get excited about it, to be passionate about what he does.

Scott orders another round of appetizers now that the large plates in the middle of the table are empty. Then he turns to Jacob. "How big is your house here?" He glances at me. "How many people are going to share a room?"

Tim and Alejo giggle, and Brian just rolls his eyes. Under the table, Jacob's knee just barely grazes against mine. It sends a jolt of electricity through me, and that brief touch combined with my fourth drink has got me thinking of all the ways I want him to bend me in half when we get some time alone.

Chapter Twenty-Two
The Mouse Is Tipsy

   JACOB   

Keeping my hands to myself is getting harder by the second, inside my pockets is the safest place for them. Edward looks so sexy, and I'm pretty close to just grabbing him by the waist and putting him on my lap. That will keep Scott at bay. But I can't do that. Almost as if he senses what I'm thinking, Gio turns toward me from beside the door and gives me a stern look.

Our server drops off another round of appetizers, and I'm still not gonna eat any of that. These guys, they don't care about their regimen as much as I do.

"Come on, Rizz, don't you want one?" Tim asks, waving a chicken finger across the table at me.

Gabriella giggles, watching Brian and Tim grab at the mozzarella sticks. "You guys are gonna pay for that tomorrow. Mozzarella sticks are the worst thing on this whole menu," she says.

I'm glad she's stopped trying to talk to me for the time being. It's not like she doesn't know what she did wrong—she and Doug are close, he definitely told her what he said before I punched him.

"A round of Santa coladas for the table, add extra pineapple juice in all of them," Scott says to the server. I had forgotten that Tony said he was changing all the drinks to Christmas names for the Snowflake Festival.

Scott leans forward trying to see Edward beside me. "You know what they say happens if you drink pineapple juice, right?"

Edward looks innocently at me, then shakes his head at Scott. "No, I don't think I've heard about anything with pineapple juice. Is it a healthy thing?"

"It makes your cum taste like pineapple," Gabriella says. "Scott is always trying to get everyone to drink it because he never knows who he's gonna end up sleeping with."

I turn my head toward Scott, hoping to interfere with any type of flirtation that he might send Edward's way. He's already been a bit more friendly than I'm comfortable with. Then again, I'm not fucking comfortable with any of this.

"Is tonight gonna be the night?" Scott asks me.

"Never," I say to him. The rest of the team laughs.

"Did you ask him if he would sleep with you?" Edward says leaning forward to look at Scott.

"Of course I did," Scott says. "Look at him. But Rizz is untouchable, unfuckable, despite being so very perfect." He finishes off his drink. "Yep, that's my best friend, no one is good enough for him."

"He means it, too," Gabriella says. She's leaning across the table toward Edward. "Everyone here has slept with everyone else, except for Jacob. Which makes poor little Shadow upset."

"I have not slept with everyone here," Alejo announces.

"Same goes for me," Brian says.

I can't believe they're having this conversation so very loudly inside this restaurant. It's quickly turned into a round of who's slept with who, and I just want to be anywhere else but here. I lean back in my seat, looking around the place, while Gio now looms behind me. My eyes meet Edward's for a moment, and he gives me a smile that I can't quite read.

"Woah, woah," Gio says, moving to the side of the table. "Where you going, big guy?" he asks looking down.

I lean back a bit and see a small boy, and a voice follows quickly. "Sorry! That's my son. He just wanted to say hi to Mr. Rizzo."

"Rizzo is my friend," a small voice says.

Ah, I see, it's the boy from the park the other night. Gio looks over his shoulder at me, and I motion for him to let him over. "What do you know, kiddo? Mr. Rizzo says you can go over. But his other friends at the table are pretty excited to see him too, so I can only let you stay for just a minute or two, deal?"

Gio looks at the boy's father, then over at me. I'm gonna hear about this later. I give him a nod telling him it's okay. Luca ducks under the ribbon divider around the table, and his dad waits until Gio makes an opening for him.

"Rizzo!" he says, coming at me full speed, arms open.

"Hi, Luca!"

He squeezes me tightly, giggling. "I saw you on the news! My dad was worried."

"Oh yeah?" I look up at his father, while the rest of the table has gone silent watching our interaction.

"I'm sorry," his father says. He turns to the table looking a bit starstruck. "I, I wasn't expecting to see all of you here. My son and I are big fans, he, uh, met Mr. Rizzo the other nigh—" he cuts himself off. "We're just really big fans."

Luca looks at my teammates. "We met Rizzo the other night when we were watching *Elf*. He was with his other friend," he says, pointing at Edward. "I showed them my kicks."

Don't react, don't react, I tell myself. Scott makes a noise behind me, while Edward takes a sip of the drink that the server just dropped off. All eyes are on Edward right now, and he's just happily sipping his drink. He's already better at downplaying this than I am.

His dad looks mortified. "Ah, Luca, you just wanted to say hi, so let's just say hi, and let the team have their dinner. I'm sorry, again, kids just say whatever comes to mind."

Luca is standing between me and Edward smiling. I pat him on the back and look up at his dad. "Nothing to apologize for. I'm glad I got to see you guys again."

Gio gives me a nod and holds the barricade open. I notice a few people getting up to talk to him, but he's shaking his head at them. When people came inside, they were told that they couldn't come over here, I assume some people are just asking if the rules apply to them.

"You did a good job with your apology," Luca says. "Even though my dad said you didn't apologize to the ref."

My teammates all react to that with a mixture of laughter and whispers. It's gonna be a long night. "Thanks, buddy," I say, bumping fists with him, and he turns to Edward. "I'm glad I got to see you, too, Rizzo's friend."

Edward chokes lightly on his drink and bumps fists with him. "I'm happy I got to see you, too, Luca."

His dad shakes my hand and they head out of the restaurant. Luca must have been waiting the whole time to come over here. Gio closes the barricade and gives me a look while walking toward me. "You know better than to let people break the rules," he whispers in my ear. "Now, look, all these other people…they think they're one sob story away from coming over here. Don't forget why I'm here."

I'm not going to argue with him over the fact that it was a kid, because I know that he's right, and since we're in public, it's not the place for me to get into it with him. He pats me on the shoulder and stands behind me keeping watch over the restaurant crowd.

"So, now that the kid is gone," Scott says leaning forward, "you guys are friends who go watch movies together? How many times have I asked you to come over and watch movies? You always say no. And *Elf*? A Christmas movie?"

"What will make you feel better right now?" I ask him. "I love *Elf*, what's wrong with that?"

"Jacob, Eddie!" Tony's voice says behind me. "Sorry, I couldn't come sooner. Things were all stopped up, but now everything is flowing smoothly, so I'm good." He looks at the table, locking in on Gabriella. "Oh, you're the owner's daughter. You're even prettier in person."

Tony is staring at my teammates, and I assume they can tell he's the owner, but I should just introduce him. "Everyone, this is Tony, the owner of the restaurant."

"And close personal friend," Tony adds.

"Oh my God!" Scott says loudly. "Another one?"

"Oh, that's rough for you, Shadow. Look at all this competition," Brian says, while sipping his drink.

Tony makes his way around the table shaking hands with everyone, then stares at me and Edward, placing a hand on each of our shoulders. "Oh, guys, which *Twilight* was it that you watched, I heard you telling your brother about it the other day, Eddie."

"Okay, come on!" Scott says. "*Twilight*? *Twilight*, Jacob? *Twilight* is my thing. You watched *Twilight*?"

Almost the entire restaurant looks over at his outburst. I tap his arm. "Scott, seriously, you're being so damn loud." I look up at Tony, while Edward is just looking innocently at me. "We watched *New Moon*," I tell Tony.

"Oh, okay." Tony turns to Scott. "What's, uh…what's the big deal with Jacob watching that movie?"

"The big deal is that Jacob is *my* best friend and he's been gone for months. I assumed"—he gestures to the table—"no, we all assumed he was off meditating or doing some kind of wellness shit, not here in this town just building a life without all of us, while the rest of us couldn't even get ahold of him. Now we're here and he's just been what, watching movies and fucking knitting Christmas sweaters? Playing soccer in the park, and just—I don't know, that's the big deal." He pulls his straw out and finishes his Santa Colada straight from the glass, while staring at me.

"None of that sounded like a big deal…" Tony says.

Edward is kind of giggling, shaking his head. It's a silent kind of laugh that makes me think he's kind of annoyed. I don't want him to feel uncomfortable.

"Just to be clear," Tim says. "Alejo and I were not concerned with what Jacob was doing, we were pissed that he left, but the rest of that is just Shadow's shit. Don't lump us together with all that."

"Same," Brian adds. "Don't care who he's watching movies with, just want an explanation for abandoning all of us."

"Alright, we're not having this discussion here," I say, standing up. "All of you are coming to my house after, we can just talk about it there."

"Where you going?" Gio asks.

I raise my chin toward the back of the restaurant. "Bathroom."

"You gotta take a piss? You gotta wait." He points at the people staring over. "You boys have given them enough to stare at tonight. Don't need to add your dick to the mix." He walks toward the bathroom and goes inside. He must be so mad at me. I've forgotten everything I'm supposed to do when I'm out. I make eye contact with Edward, while pulling my phone out and text him.

Follow me inside. Just don't react to anything anyone says.

Is he drunk? He's looking at the text like he can barely read it.

"I'm gonna get back there. It was nice meeting all of you," Tony says. "Oh, but about *Twilight*. Was I supposed to watch *New Moon* before *Eclipse* or did I do it wrong? Is Bella just really unsure which one she wants?" he asks Edward. "Because she seems confused."

"Me too," Edward says, while slurping the rest of his drink through his straw. "She's not really confused, she's always wanted Edward, there's just a lot going on. You should just read the books."

Gio motions for me to come over, and Edward stands and follows me toward the bathroom. I hear him tell Tony he'll see him later, but don't hear anything from the rest of the table. Gio is just giving me the same look he gives Doritos when he does something stupid. Once I'm in front of him, he looks behind me at Edward. "All clear. Doesn't take two people to take a piss."

"Cancun," I say, patting his chest, then walk inside the bathroom with Edward following behind.

I lean against the long row of three sinks looking in the mirror.

"You have a backwards hat on, and you brought me in the bathroom," Edward says. "I'm either about to get the best blowjob of my life or you're about to really disappoint me."

Oh, he's drunk. I laugh at that and pull him in by his waist, quickly kissing him. I missed the taste of him all day. His hands are all over me, rubbing my dick through my pants, and his tongue is just going crazy inside my mouth, fuck.

"Mmm, Jacob..." he moans, while sticking his hand down my pants.

I'm kissing the side of his neck, while pressing him against the wall, breathlessly sucking the skin sticking out of his sweater. I want him so bad.

"Sorry, bathroom is occupied," I hear Gio say.

"One more," I say, planting a firm bite on the side of Edward's neck, before pulling back.

He's just panting, looking at me. "Your friends are kind of weirddd," he says. "And you look sexy with that hat, but you didn't want to show off your haircut?" He's holding onto my forearms, lightly rubbing them through my sleeves.

"Are you drunk?" I ask him. "I mean, how drunk are you would probably be the better question."

"I'm not drunk. I'm in the sweet spot. Shouldn't drive but not so drunk that you can't choke me later if you want to," he says with a giggle. "Before I forget, can I sign something that says no matter how much I drink, you can do whatever you want to me? I told you already, but in case you need it for something."

I lift his chin and kiss him softly. "No. I don't need you to do that. I just wanted to check on you. I was worried with everything going on out there that you might be uncomfortable."

"Not really," he says unconvincingly. "Maybe a little, I don't know. The girl, she's kind of into you, right?"

I shrug. "I think with her it's more about what she can't have, so yeah, she's into me, but no more than anyone else out there. She's just trying to apologize for what she did, and I'm not interested in hearing it." I can't get into this with him here even though I want to explain everything. "Are you sleeping over tonight?"

"How can I? All those people are sleeping over. How can I do that? I can't do that without people knowing the unfuckable Jacob Rizzo is actually very fuckable."

I laugh and kiss him again. "We'll make it work. Plus, we still have to look at Christmas lights after this."

"We can still do it?" he asks, while wrapping his arms snugly around my waist.

It feels so good holding him like this. I just want to keep him here with me. "Of course. I told you we would. I'm not looking to disappoint you twice in one night."

"When was the first time?" he asks, tilting his head at me.

I give his waist a squeeze and smile. "When we came in here you said something about being disappointed if this didn't end in a blow job."

These *fuck-me eyes* he's giving me are really testing my restraint. He drags his finger down the zipper of my pants and looks up at me. "I have a request. Drink one Santa colada for me… I want to taste it later," he says, grabbing my dick through the fabric.

Fuck. I am so fucked. I can't say no to him, especially not now. I'm already fighting my dick, I can't take on his big brown eyes, too. What is this power he has over me?

His finger is tracing the outline of my cock through my pants. "Jacob…will you do it?" he whispers.

"Hurry it up," Gio says, knocking on the door.

I place a kiss on his lips and adjust myself. This is gonna be really uncomfortable for a few minutes. "Come on, little mouse, we don't have to stay much longer."

We walk out of the bathroom, and Gio places a hand on my chest. "You're lucky people can't see back here from the restaurant. I don't know how long the guys are gonna want to stay but let's try to wrap up soon, since they're all going back to your place anyway." He tilts his head looking at me. "Your face is all flushed. You want me to knee you in the balls to calm stuff down?"

"I hate you. Move," I say, walking around him, with Edward following behind.

"Oh, hello," Scott says. "We made a decision while you were off doing whatever the hell you were doing."

"Wait." I point at the fresh drink in front of Edward. "Why is there another one of those pineapple drinks in front of him? You ordered another round for the table, or just for him?"

Edward lifts the drink and pulls the cherry out, and I try not to stare while he sucks the cherry off its stem.

Scott smiles at me and shrugs. "Ordered a round for everyone else who wanted one. He wasn't here and his drink was empty, so I assumed he'd want another."

I reach over and take the drink from Edward's hand, quickly draining the most pineapple-y drink I've ever had in my life. I'm sucking it quickly through the straw while looking at Scott.

"Oh, it's on tonight, huh?" Scott says. "How are you not throwing up right now? You don't drink sugary drinks," he says while I continue sipping. I finish it off and have to fight the urge to scream from the crushing brain freeze.

Edward gives me a smile and leans back, looking at Scott. "Thanks for the drink," he says.

"Wait, is this really happening?" Gabriella asks. "Are you finally gonna let Shadow have his way with you?"

I can't even shake my head because my brain feels like it's going to explode.

"That's not what it looked like from over here," Tim says.

Edward is flagging the server over. "Can I have another Santa colada?" he asks. "Someone drank mine. Oh, and can you add extra pineapple juice?"

I think he's had five drinks already. I have no idea how high his tolerance is, but based on the way he was in the bathroom, he was only a drink or two away from being completely drunk. Damn. My mouth tastes like pure sugar. I don't doubt that this makes your cum tastes like pineapple. "That was so fucking sweet," I say.

"I can't believe you just drank that," Scott says. "I've seen you have sugar maybe ten times in all the years I've known you." He looks around the table. "Am I wrong? Anyone else ever seen him do that?"

"Are we counting Cancun?" Tim asks. "Because then yeah, but outside of that, no. I don't know, Shadow, it seemed like maybe he just did that for a certain reason."

Scott pumps his eyebrows at me. "Yeah, I think so, too."

He's oblivious, but that's fine. Just want to keep his eyes off Edward.

"Before whatever you're thinking of doing, I assume to make up for abandoning me, we're all watching *Twilight* when we get back to your place," Scott says.

"I love *Twilight*," Edward says, leaning forward to talk to Scott. "So, earlier when you were mad that we watched *Twilight*, it was because you like it, too?"

"He was mad because you're hanging out with his best friend," Brian says. "And, yeah, Shadow loves *Twilight*, we had a party at Derek's place for him this year. It was fun, we all dressed up as vampires and werewolves."

Alejo, who has remained mostly quiet until this point adds, "Well, Tim dressed up as Bella's dad. It was hot. I didn't think Charlie was hot until I got older." He smiles, looking at Tim. "I should've told you I liked you back then."

Tim looks around the restaurant and holds a menu up blocking the people facing us from seeing them, and kisses Alejo on the cheek.

Wow, I've never seen Tim look at anyone like that. Watching him have to hide behind the menu just to kiss his boyfriend sucks, even still, seeing the two of them together, just makes me want to squeeze Edward in beside me. I turn toward him, his eyes are a bit glassy. I need to get him home with me. "Since they decided we're watching *Twilight*, do you want to come back to my place with all of us and watch, too?" I ask him.

"What?" Scott asks. "Come on, you already watched it with him. What's next? You wanna invite the guy that owns this place, too? This isn't fair. Come on, Rizz."

"Oh, come on, Shadow, don't be jealous," Gabriella says. "Edward just said he loves *Twilight*, too. His face kinda lights up every time anyone says it. Is *Twilight* your favorite?" she asks him.

He gives her a shrug in reply. "I mean, yeah, it's my favorite…and Jacob's couch is really…comfortable."

I need to get him out of here before someone asks him something, and he slips up. "Alright, guys, we can do that, but we need to head back. Since it's dark out now, you guys can just have Dom follow us. I'll take care of the bill if you guys want to start loading into your van."

"Who is us?" Brian asks. "Is Edward riding with you, or does he have his own car? Because I'm tired of riding in the van with all of them. It was a long drive, man."

Shit, I can't have him ride in my car. I want to sit in the back with Edward.

Scott stands and places a hand on my shoulder. "Yeah, I'll just ride with you, Rizz. What are you driving?"

"No," Gio says, stepping toward us. "I'm not taking any extra passengers aside from Edward. You guys are here on Dominic's watch. You ride with him."

None of them dare to argue with Gio. I stand to pay the bill, and Edward stands beside me. "Come on," I say to him, resisting the urge to touch him. He follows me, slowly walking toward the counter. He's a bit wobbly, and I'm afraid that if I don't put a hand on him, he might just tip over. But everyone in the restaurant is looking over, including my teammates. "You okay?" I ask him.

Edward leans in toward the large Christmas tree that Tony has set up near the register. "I want a real tree. A really real one…like this one." He sniffs the branch, and I step backward toward him.

"Charge all of that to my card," I tell the employee at the register, while keeping my eyes locked on Edward. "You want a real tree? For the shop?"

His nose is pressed near a branch and he's nodding at me. "Yeah, no, yeah. I want a tree for Christmas. Like this one. Do you like it?"

The cashier passes my card back, and once I sign, I check over my shoulder to see how many people are still watching, and the answer is everyone, everyone is looking over, just staring at me. I step just a bit closer. "Yeah, I like it. A real tree would be nice. Are you ready to go?" I see Scott and the guys watching, but they're out of earshot. "Do you want to go look at Christmas lights now?" I whisper. "Or do you want to stay here with the tree?"

Edward is smiling at me but shaking his head. "No, I want to go wherever you are. So, if you're staying with the tree, then I'm staying with the tree." He's rubbing a branch with his finger. "I do want a tree, but not this one. I want a tree with you and me."

"Oh, okay. We can get a tree. Not tonight, but we could get one. Is that what you mean?"

He hasn't taken his eyes off the tree. "I can't touch you," he mumbles. "Can we leave so I can touch you?" he asks me, looking around the restaurant.

This sucks. I want to hold his hand. I stick my hands in my pockets and nod toward the exit. "Come on." A few people shout things over as I make my way to the door with Edward beside me. I give them a nod and smile, then we head outside.

It's dark outside in the back parking lot, and it's freezing. Everyone except for Scott and Brian have already piled inside the van. Gio is holding the passenger door of my car open, while Dominic stands beside the van in conversation with Scott. "How far is your place?" Brian shouts over. I look around to see if there are any reporters or fans looming and hold my arms out. What the hell is he thinking? Like I can just yell it across the parking lot.

"He doesn't live around here," Gio answers. "Just follow behind us, we have something to do first."

"What do we have to do?" Edward asks loudly. "I'm going with you, right? I thought…wait what did I think? I think I…"

"Come on, we're gonna see Christmas lights," I tell him quietly. He gives me a salute and gets into the backseat.

Before I can get in with him, Gio pushes the passenger seat back into its proper position. "They're all watching you. Sit in the front seat. Don't be stupid. We'll go do what you want, then you're gonna need to find a way to get Edward back home. He can't stay at your place." He can obviously read the frustration on my face, because before I can bite back at him, he holds a hand up to me. "You're not thinking clearly. Trust me. Sit in the front seat."

Just to avoid making a scene, I do as he says. Once Gio closes the door, Edward sighs loud and long.

"I'm sorry," I say, turning in my seat to face him. "I'm coming back there as soon as we pull out of here."

"Whyyy are people so fixated on you?" he groans. "It's so weirddd,

Jacob. You're just my Jacob, why do they all care? And why do they all call you by your last nameee?" He leans his head against the small window and closes his eyes.

I think it's really cute when he calls me *his* Jacob. He's done it a few times now, and each time it does something to me. It's as if he's punching down the wall around my heart without even trying. Like he just belongs there—like he just belongs with *me*. I'm starting to think the wall I've built was meant to keep everyone out but him.

"You and I are gonna have a talk," Gio says to me, when he gets inside. "We can do that later after Edward goes back to his place."

"Edward is not going back to his brother's place. He's staying with me tonight," I say and start to climb into the backseat.

"What the hell are you? Dah! Shit, Rizz, you're gonna kick the stick, or my face, sit down! Don't climb back there!"

Edward lifts his head to look at me.

"Hello," I say with a smile.

"Jacob Anthony Rizzo!" Gio shouts. "Have you lost your mind?! I cannot believe—"

I hold a hand up to him from the backseat, and he stops talking. "Christmas lights, please. Just go to the neighborhood we talked about."

Edward leans his head against my shoulder and closes his eyes. What am I supposed to do? I can't pull away from him, he's drunk and I don't— I don't want to pull away. Gio is shaking his head at me in the front seat.

"I know I'm not supposed to touch you," he whispers, "but you smell good, and my head feels too heavy for the window." His eyes are still closed but he's smiling.

"What do you mean your head is too heavy for the window? Don't you want to look at lights? You have to pick your head up if you want to look at lights. You can't see them if your eyes are closed."

"If you smell me when we get there, I can do it," he says.

"What? How would me smelling you help?" I ask with a chuckle.

"No, I'm smelling you. Just the smell is good. Even if I can't have it for me. I'll just have it for now."

"He had six drinks, sounds about right," Gio says. "You want me to go for the lights or head to your place? I can swing him back by his brother's place first if you want."

"No," Edward says, lifting his head. "I'm gonna go where Jacob is. I won't touch him," he says firmly, before dropping his head on my shoulder.

"You won't touch me?" I ask, looking down at him. "You're touching me right now. Smelling me, too."

"Doesn't count. No one can see me and it's just my head. Look," he says, lifting his hands and nearly poking me in the eye. "Not touching you with my hands and not with…" he lifts his head and looks at me through half-lidded eyes. "You still have your hat on backwards. Oh, fuck, so hot," he mumbles. "I should get a point for not touching you with that hat on, especially after the bathroom." He drops his head against my shoulder again.

"Ahem," Gio says. "The houses you want to see are only two minutes away, so you might wanna pick your head up back there."

"My head is up," he mumbles. "I'm not touching him, Giovanni…and he's not touching…"

Gio glances at me in the rearview mirror. It's the same look he's been giving me all night.

Am I really doing something wrong? I slide my arm around Edward's waist and lightly rub his side through his coat. "Look, we're at the neighborhood," I whisper. "Aren't the lights amazing?"

"Pretty…" Edward says, lifting his head.

"This is something," Gio says. "Every single house is decorated. Their electric bills must be huge. And look at the people just sitting in their driveways."

Edward is just staring out the window. "They're all so pretty."

"Yeah, I've never seen anything like it," I say, giving his side the lightest squeeze. "I didn't realize how many lights were on each of the houses. So many different kinds, too. I still think I like the old-fashioned kind best. My nonna used to have them, they were big lights. Like those," I say pointing to a house decorated with that style.

"I like big ones, too," Edward says.

"Maybe we can try to come back and walk around next week. There's a hot cocoa stand at the end of the street, which I have a feeling you'd like, and I'm pretty sure they have music on the weekends, too."

Edward nods and leans his head back against my shoulder.

"Now this guy is calling me," Gio grumbles. "I'm gonna answer this, Rizz. I don't want to interrupt, but Eddie seems—"

"Who is Eddie?" Edward asks loudly. "I can't call him Gio, but he can call me Eddie. Nothing is fair here." He shakes his head and nuzzles against my shoulder. "And Jacob is touching me, too."

"Did you tell him he couldn't call you Gio?" I ask, while holding in a laugh.

"Nobody calls me that except you." He's just shaking his head at me. "Let me answer this," he says, holding his phone up. "What's up, Doritos?"

Damn, Dom's voice is so loud, I can hear him back here. "What are you driving so slow through this street for? The guys are anxious to get out of the van. What did you need to do on the way to Rizzo's? You didn't explain."

"I don't have to explain. Just follow me. We're only a few blocks away. Tell the guys to look at the lights. I told you not to call me unless it was an emergency. Goodbye."

I feel bad that Edward is kind of missing this because he's half passed out, but hopefully it made him happy. Maybe we can try and find a Christmas tree like he wanted, and then I can bring him here when he's actually able to enjoy it.

Chapter Twenty-Three
Pineapple and You

   **JACOB**   

A few minutes later, we're finally pulling into my driveway. I just want to take Edward into my room and hold him. I've barely gotten to touch him, aside from the bathroom. Why do they all have to be here right now? Couldn't I just wrap my arm around him and pretend I'm keeping him from falling?

As always, Gio seems to have some kind of a sixth sense about what I'm thinking, based on the look he's giving me now that he's parked. "You already know what I'm gonna say, and for once I'm gonna trust that I don't actually need to say it," he says, then gets out of the car.

Edward lifts his head as soon as the engine shuts off and smiles at me. "Oh, we're here already. Where is everyone?"

Gio pulls the seat forward and gestures for him to get out. "Come on, hurry up before they see that he was in the backseat with you."

Edward gets out of the car, and I climb into the front seat and let myself out of the passenger side. It's better that I do this even though it feels so stupid.

Scott is howling loudly while walking up the driveway. "*Twilight* time! I'm thinking *Eclipse*, what do you think?" he asks Edward, while hooking an arm around his neck.

I don't like Scott touching him… I don't want anyone else to touch him. I stick my hands in my pockets and make my way around my car, walking over. "You just touch whoever you want? I don't think Edward is really into people touching him."

Scott looks at him, then at me. "Oh, I'm sorry," he says to Edward. "You don't know this, but tonight Rizz is gonna let me finally take a shot at him. I know this because he drank that Santa colada...plus he needs to make up for being such a dick."

Edward looks unsteady. "That's not why he drank it," he says. "He drank it because—because—shit," he says, holding his forehead. "I forgot what I was saying."

Scott giggles and pats him on the shoulder, while the rest of the team make their way up the driveway.

Edward stays close to me, and the group follows behind while I open the door. Gio and Dom are still standing beside the van, and I can't make out what they're talking about, but Gio looks annoyed. I hold a hand up to the group, before I let anyone inside. "This is not a hotel and none of you were invited, so don't start calling out rooms and shit as soon as we walk inside. We'll figure out sleeping arrangements later, unless anyone is skipping the movie, then we can figure it out now. I'm not doing a full tour with you guys. This house is not that big."

"Bossy tonight," Brian says, once he walks inside. "Technically, you said we could sleep here, so we were kinda invited."

Everyone else is piling in, kicking their shoes off at my door, while Edward is heading straight for the couch. I need to sit beside him before anyone else does. Tim and Alejo flop on the opposite side and close their eyes leaning their head against each other. "Feels good to stretch out," Tim groans. "I don't want to get back in that van for at least a week."

"It wasn't that bad," Alejo says. "But I really want a shower."

"You all need showers, should we skip the movie?" I ask, while I sit beside Edward. The gray blanket is the one that Edward likes to use. I grab it before anyone else can claim it and pass it to him, bringing a smile to his face.

Scott and Gabriella are both headed for the spot next to me while Brian is kind of lurking, seemingly waiting to see where he should sit.

Scott sits beside me and pats me on the leg. "We're not skipping the movie, and Gabs, you're not sitting by Rizz, you can talk to him later. If you sit by him now, I won't be able to hear the movie."

I'm not talking to her later, so she can pout all she wants. The only thing I'm doing later, is having sex with Edward. Quietly.

"I think I'm cool for a shower now," Brian says from the corner. "Where is the bathroom?"

"That's fine," I say, standing from the couch. "Don't take my spot," I warn Scott before leaving the living room. Edward makes eye contact with me, and I can tell he's still pretty drunk.

"I need to use the bathroom," he says, walking past us.

Is he? Yep, he's walking right into my bedroom instead of using one of the other bathrooms. Just gonna hope no one noticed that. "There are three bathrooms," I explain to Brian. "One upstairs in my office where Gio is staying, one in my room, and the other is over here." I open the door to the smaller bathroom down the hall from the spare room. "This is the bathroom you guys can use. There are towels and washcloths in here, and I got some bathroom stuff in there, just use whatever. I wasn't sure what you brought."

Brian looks at me inquisitively, folding his arms. "He's using the bathroom in…your room then?"

"Why do you care? He obviously heard you say you need to take a shower. Would you rather he rushed past you to take the bathroom before you?" Don't overexplain, I remind myself. Overexplaining makes it look like I'm hiding something. "Just take your shower, then you can decide if you want the room across from it, or the one over there, or there's another spare down the hall, but that one is full of boxes. I wouldn't suggest that one."

He nods at me and looks side to side. "Hey, can you do me a favor?"

I already know what he's gonna ask. "No, I won't talk to Gabriella, and no, I don't care if that pisses you off. I'm already letting you guys stay here, that seems like enough of a favor."

He pats me on the shoulder. "If people only knew what an asshole you really were."

"Yeah, it takes one to know one," I say with a smirk. "Have a nice shower." I turn toward my bedroom and see Edward passed out on my bed. Shit. I close the door behind me and lean in next to his face, kissing his cheek. "Are you asleep?" I whisper beside his ear.

"No. Just tired and confused. I need to brush my teeth, but I want to watch the movie." He opens his eyes and looks at me. "I didn't mean to lay down… I just did. I'll get up," he says with a sigh.

"What are you confused about?" I ask, while rubbing his cheek.

"Where am I gonna sleep?"

"I just have to tell people in a little bit that you're leaving. We can pretend there's an Uber outside ready to take you home. Then I can just walk you outside and I'll sneak you back inside through my window. We can pull that off."

"How am I supposed to do that? I can barely think," he says, holding his forehead.

I kiss him softly, then whisper in his ear, "I drank that stupid Santa drink like you asked, and if you're a good little mouse and play along, we can both have more pineapple later. I take his earlobe into my mouth, lightly grazing my teeth on it.

"Fuck me," he moans. "That feels…so good. This isn't fair. I love *Twilight* and I want you, why are these people here? Can we make them leave?"

"I wish," I say with a chuckle and pull him into a sitting position. "We don't have to watch the whole movie. When you're ready for bed, just text me, or look down at your phone and say your Uber is here, then I'll walk you outside."

He stands unsteadily with a groan. "You made me all hard and now we have to wait."

"You can choose how long we wait," I say over my shoulder, while walking toward my window. We need to get back out there, or this is really gonna look obvious, although none of them would ever suspect we're sleeping together. So, it's probably fine, but I need to text Gio.

Opening my bedroom window to test it real quick. Don't freak out.

Gio replies quickly: *You're gonna have him come back in through the window?*

Yeah.

What if he gets hurt? He could barely stand.

I'm not gonna let him fall.

The window makes a chirp when I open it. Shit, it's freezing outside.

Edward shivers walking toward me. "It's cold out there," he says, looking out the window. "I'm getting choked later, right?"

I give him a soft kiss, tasting the alcohol on his breath. I don't like the taste of liquor, but the taste of it on his tongue is driving me crazy. Before I know it, our kiss has turned ravenous, I'm sucking his tongue, deep inside his mouth while he grips my hair. I want him. I need him.

My phone is vibrating in my pocket, and I quickly pull back, realizing that I have a house full of my teammates here, who are all waiting for me. Shit… I hug him tight. "We have to go back out there. You should go out first. Just text me when you're ready. So, in five minutes preferably," I say, pinching his chin.

Edward is nodding at me. "Five seconds sounds…good." He lets out a sigh and leaves my room. I wait just a few moments and head back out to the couch.

"About time!" Scott complains with his hands up. "Don't you watch any porn? Ever? Your watch history is so boring, Rizz." He looks at me while Edward and I sit down on the couch. "We decided on *Eclipse*. Also, we heard you in there."

Oh shit, oh shit, oh shit. "Heard what?" I ask, taking the controller from his hand.

"You said there were five bedrooms when you were talking to Brian in the hall. Such a small house for you. But we got our sleeping situations all figured out. Except for Dom, he's gonna just have to take the couch, unless he wants to sleep in the van."

Edward is giggling beside me. He's drunk, but even he must have thought Scott meant that he heard us. "*Eclipse* it is," he says, tucking the blanket around himself.

I have no idea how I'm going to get him back in through my window.

Hopefully, whoever takes the bedroom beside mine won't be looking outside. It will be fine, what the hell would they be looking out of the window for at night? Thank God, this neighborhood is gated, otherwise the reporters would already have figured out where I live, especially with that damn rental van in the driveway.

"Are you cold?" Edward asks, lifting a side of the blanket up.

"Uhhh—" I shake my head. "I don't think so. Are you cold?"

Scott leans forward. "You gonna share that blanket with him if he's cold? I'm cold, you could share it with me, stretch it across all three of us." He's reaching across the front of me for the blanket and Edward looks like a deer in headlights, a drunk deer in headlights.

That's not happening. I push Scott's hand away playfully. "There are blankets in the closet over there, if you need one. You don't need to share a blanket with him, and I'm definitely not gonna be in the middle of whatever is going on in your mind right now."

"I didn't say I would share with him," Edward mumbles while readjusting himself on the couch.

I feel Scott's elbow digging into me, he's nothing if not subtle. I just want Edward to give me the signal, then I can get him in my room. *After* I pretend to take him outside, come back inside, open the window, and sneak him back in, then hope he doesn't wander back out of my room somehow. This is gonna be a trainwreck. Scott nudges me again, a little harder this time. "Bro, what? Why do you keep elbowing me?"

"I sent you five texts, would you check your damn phone?" he says.

"No. It's in my room and it's off, so I don't know why you're texting it. I'm sitting right here. What do you need?"

"Your phone is off?!" Gabriella shouts leaning forward to see me.

"That explains it," Tim says. "No wonder he didn't reply to any of us."

"That phone has been off since I came here. I turned it on the other day when Linley lit the seventh circle of hell that brought all of you to my house. I haven't even gone through all the messages on it."

Scott is patting my leg. "Ya know, you're my best friend, but you suck."

"Rarely. Only on special occasions," I say, smirking at him.

Edward giggles beside me. "I'm getting an Uber, since they said all the rooms are taken. I'll just go wait outside."

"Oh, wait," Scott says. "You can share a room wi—"

I snap my head to the left looking at him. "Don't. Finish. That. Sentence." My teammates eyes are wide looking at me, and Edward is just grinning looking at his phone. I hope he's not really calling an Uber. Could he have gotten confused? He looks like he's actually doing something on his phone.

"Oh my God," Gabriella says. "Shadow, he really is gonna let you sleep with him tonight. Wow. I'm in shock."

"I need a shower," my idiot of a best friend says. "I want to finish watching this movie, though, is that cool?"

"I don't care *what* you do. I'm going to sleep in probably ten minutes. Just walking Edward out. Come on," I say, pressing the side of Edward's shoulder.

"Bye, Edward, nice meeting you!" Gabriella shouts.

He gives her a smile and waves to the rest of the guys, while I open the door for him. Once I step outside I walk face first into Gio.

Edward laughs loudly at the sight of my face directly pressed against Gio's large chest. "I was not expecting that," he says, hunched over laughing.

That was like walking into a wall. My face hurts from that. "Holy shit, what are you doing just lurking outside the door?"

"Lurking?" Gio looks me up and down, while rubbing his chest. "Are you drunk, too? My job is to protect you, even when you've come up with a very stupid idea. Come on, before Doritos wakes up. He's asleep in the van," he says pointing over his shoulder. "Your window is out of his eyeline, unless he starts wandering around. Which is also his job."

"Thank you, Giovanni," Edward says while clapping his hands. "I, too, think this is a stupid idea…"

"In about ten minutes you won't think it's so stupid," I tell him.

"Well, if I'm being chok—"

I cover his mouth with my hand, shaking my head at him. "No," I whisper harshly. "But you want to be warm, right? It's warm inside my bed."

"Don't want to be warm as much as I want to be chok—" Edward cuts himself off. "Never mind. I'm cold," he says with a pout.

Gio is just shaking his head while we make our way toward my window. "You're gonna get caught. May want to think about telling him he can't drink when you're with other people, or this halflationship is gonna be a problem."

"What?" Edward looks at Gio. "What the hell does a halfling have to do with anything?"

"Just ignore him," I say while Gio lifts my window open.

"Alright," Gio points to Edward, "let's get you in first. Can you hoist yourself up, or you need a boost?"

"I can't believe I'm doing this," he mumbles while walking in front of my window. I place my hands on his waist from behind and count. "Ready? One, two, three, up." Edward climbs in through my window, and I don't hear a thud, but I also haven't seen him stand back up yet. I gotta get in there. I grab the ledge and look at Gio. "Not gonna ask if I need a boost?"

"No. You should be able to do a pullup. You can get up there. Come on, before someone wanders outside.

I can hear Edward mumbling inside my room, and it forces me to pull myself up quicker. Unfortunately, it's not the most graceful of entries, and I more or less almost fall in through the opening. Once inside, I see Edward lying on the floor. I stand quickly to close the window.

"Thanks, Gio," I say with a salute. Before I close the window, he grips the bottom of it. "I can't stress this enough to you—be quiet, please. The last thing you need are the guys to hear everything you two are doing. In the morning, be careful getting him out. I assume he's gonna go before the gym, just give me a heads up, so I know when the alarm is being deactivated."

I nod at him and close my window, then reach down to pull Edward up. "What are you doing down there?" I whisper.

"Tired, so, so tired. Need to brush my teeth…and I'm cold. Your floor is hard, too."

"Yeah, I'm sorry the floor is hard." I squat down beside him, kissing his forehead. "I'm gonna go say goodnight to everyone real fast, and make sure they have everything they need, so we aren't bothered. Are you good? Or do I need to stay in here with you for a few minutes?"

"I'll brush my teeth and get in bed. I can do those. I'm barely drunk at this point—mostly sleepish…sleepy…sleepyish."

He's so cute. I rub my fingers through his hair looking down at him. "I'll be right back, then we can finally be alone. I can finally touch you."

"You can always touch me, I'm the one that can't touch you."

"Well, I'm about to do a whole lot of touching when I get back. Unless your sleepishness wins and you fall asleep first."

I pull him up to a standing position and he sits on my bed. "Jacobbbb…" he whines. "You can do me when I'm asleep…your dick will wake me up. Or whatever part of you will wake me up…probably your smell will."

"Okay, well, I'll try to get back before you fall asleep and I'll keep an eye behind me and make sure that no one walks this way." I kiss him on the cheek one more time before leaving and slide my hand on the outside of his pants. "Try to stay awake."

When I walk back outside of my room, everyone is right where I left them. "Alright, I'm headed—"

"Where the hell did you come from?" Scott asks, pointing toward the door. "I was watching the movie extra close because it was the hot guy part, but how the hell are you standing behind me? Door is over there."

Shit. I am so stupid. Why didn't I remember to come back in through the front door? "Garage. I came in through the garage. Would you have noticed if I walked right past you, though?"

"Yeah, and I'm pretty sure everyone else would have, we're all facing this way. I didn't even hear a door open. Wait, what were you saying?"

"Oh, right. I'm going to bed. You're all set, right? I'm hitting the gym at the normal time, are you guys coming with?" The group seems to be in agreement that everyone is gonna join me, which is to be expected. "Just grab whatever you need from the kitchen. I already told Brian, but there's bathroom stuff in there for whoever needs it, and there are extra towels in the closet outside of the bathroom. Does anyone need anything else?" The group just shakes their heads at me, half are watching the movie, half falling asleep already. And since no one seems to need anything, I should just go straight to my room. I feel a little bad, though, they drove all this way, and whether I asked them to or not, they're still here. "It's weird seeing you guys here, but it's also nice, kind of. Everyone who's going to the gym needs to be ready at five. See you in the morning." I feel like I should give them a tour, but they did say they already picked out their rooms, besides, my place in Miami is way bigger than this. I don't think anyone's gonna get lost in here, but I'm gonna lock my door just in case.

When I get inside my room, I can see Edward's silhouette in my bed. He's already tucked under the covers. Once I lock the door, I lean in close to see if he's asleep. He smells so damn good. The fact that I'm starving is not helping me right now, because at this moment all I can think about doing is flipping him over and drowning myself in his ass. He's completely passed out. I'm not gonna wake him up yet. I'll just brush my teeth first.

My teammates are being so loud in the hallway, I can hear them all the way in my bathroom. But it's not like I can ask them to be quiet because Edward is asleep, besides, I don't think he'll wake up from their voices. Brushing my teeth is normally a good wind down at the end of the day, but listening to all of them out there is making me anything but relaxed. I need to get into bed with Edward, I think I'm just on edge from the whole day, or the past two days, really…and the thought of tomorrow. I'm not sure what the auction is gonna look like, and I really don't want to do it. The last thing I want to do is go out on a date with someone that's not Edward. How stupid is it that I'm gonna be in the same place as him, and have to leave with someone else? I don't even know who I'm gonna end up going out with. Hopefully, it's just someone asking for soccer advice, or money, I'd take either of those over someone that's actually trying to sleep with me.

Edward doesn't move an inch when I slide into bed with him. He's shirtless and wearing loose fitting gym shorts. I think I've memorized every curve of his body at this point, so even though it's dark in here, I know exactly where I'm kissing. "Mmm, Edward," I whisper while making my way up his neck with my tongue. "Are you asleep?" His skin tastes sweet, the same as it normally does, it's a taste I've come to need, and one thing I've learned about him, is he gets sweeter the further down I go. "Little mouse, I want to play. Wake up." His chest is so firm and I'm honestly not sure how he's asleep with all the licking I'm doing. I know his nipples are sensitive, maybe that will wake him. I trace one with my tongue and rub the other softly.

"Mmm—Jacob, my Jacob…" he murmurs.

"Your Jacob wants you to wake up. I've been waiting to taste you all day." I grip the sides of his shorts and lick along the top of his waistband. Even the hair under his navel that leads down his shorts is sexy. I tease the line with my tongue, sucking the skin, and nudging his shorts down with my chin, while I palm his dick through his shorts. He's so hard, I don't know how he's asleep. I reposition myself between his legs and kiss his stomach a few more times, before pulling his shorts down. Fuuuck, I grunt at the feeling of his hot, hard cock in my hand. "Edward, I'm doing what you asked me to…" I lick around the tip and play with his head before taking more of him in my mouth. His cock is so warm and smooth, it's my second favorite thing to have in my mouth.

"Mmm—fuck," a breathy moan escapes him, as he shoves my face down further onto his dick, forcing more of it inside. I reach up, placing my hand atop his and squeeze. His grip tightens in my hair for just a second before he loosens it. "Yessss—this isn't a dream," he says while threading his fingers through my hair. "I can't get a good grip on your hair now that it's cut. But I like your mouth down there."

"Yeah?" I ask, allowing his cock to slip from my mouth. "I want to taste that pineapple." I take him back into my mouth again, and suck harder, alternating between long slow sucks and fast licks along the sides.

"You drank that drink for me," he says, rubbing my hair. "I want to taste you too, slide around. Put your dick in my mouth."

"No. I want you to come for me. You can taste me after." I spit in my palm and Edward's dick jumps. "I forgot you said you like spitting, too." I jerk his dick hard and fast, while licking his crown, teasing his slit, and moaning. He's close. "Come for me, little mouse." His cock is slippery and so slick from my mouth, I'm easily taking him deep in my throat.

A tiny squeak breaks the sounds of my sucking, and my mouth is quickly filled with the sweet taste of his cum and… "Mmm…" I swallow. "Your cum tastes like pineapple."

He's panting with his forearm against his mouth. He must have put it there to stop from squeaking too loud. "Jacob, your mouth, holy shit."

I'm still licking my lips. I'm so hungry and the taste of pineapple didn't help matters. I want to fuck him, but there's no way he can be quiet enough, and I don't want to ask him to hold back. He's hot and panting beside me when I reposition myself next to him on my pillow. I should've brought some water in here. Why didn't I think of that earlier?

"You woke me up with my dick in your mouth. That was…the best way…to be woken up…hah," he says smiling at me, while rubbing my cheek.

"Hmm. I don't know. Since you've been sleeping over, I've been pretty happy waking up every day. So, for me the best way to wake up is with you beside me." His big brown eyes are just staring at me in silence, while his breaths start to even out. There's a stillness between us that feels warm, I can't explain it, but it's so comforting.

Edward scoots in closer toward me, rubbing my abs. "I thought that was a dream. The only way I knew it was real is because you weren't choking me," he says teasingly, while slowly sliding his hand down the front of my shorts. When he finally reaches my semi hard cock, I bite my lip, closing my eyes, as he grips it. He kisses me softly, gently rubbing his tongue against mine, quickly making my cock harden inside his warm hand. "Mmm…I can taste the pineapple," he whispers against my lips, before moving down between my legs. "You made me so happy drinking that tonight," he says while pulling my shorts down. "But, I don't like—" he shakes his head at himself and kisses the head of my cock. "Never mind."

As much as I want to ram my cock inside his mouth, I can't. "What were you saying? You don't like what?"

He shakes his head and lays his face beside my dick. "It's nothing. I'm used to people flirting, but Scott, he just seems overly flirty, and I really don't—" He kisses the side of my dick softly. "I don't know, I just didn't like it."

"Hey, he's an idiot," I say, running my fingers through his hair. "He wishes I would, but he's just really like that with any—"

Two light knocks on my door make me freeze.

"Jacob, are you awake?" Gabriella's voice whispers.

Edward pushes himself up on his palms, mouth open.

Oh my God. How is this happening? I don't know whether to answer her, or not. I just want her to go away. Shit, if I reply, she might not leave until I agree to talk to her. Or she'll just sit out there talking. I rub Edward's cheek and hold a finger in front of my mouth shaking my head. I need to tell him what happened with Doug, so he knows why I don't want to talk to her.

"Jacob, come on," she pleads. "I just want to know what happened. Are you really asleep?"

Edward lies back down beside my dick which has definitely gone down, and he's just lightly petting me down there. I want to scream and tell her to go away, but I know that not answering is the quickest way to end this.

After a few moments, I hear her footsteps leave my doorway and head down the hall.

"That, I don't like that," he says nuzzling against my dick, kissing the side of it.

"I don't either. But I like the soft kisses you're giving me, and I think he's hoping you'll give him a few more," I say, gripping my dick and stroking it beside his mouth.

He lifts his head and moves back down, taking my hand off my dick and replacing it with his. "I can do that."

His tongue is softly circling my head—fuck that feels good. I tighten my grip on his hair, and he continues circling but with more pressure. "Fuuuck," I groan. I sink back into my pillow and exhale once he takes most of me into his mouth.

"Rizz, open up," Scott's voice says outside my door, along with two knocks.

"Are you fucking kidding me?" I shout.

Edward takes my cock out of his mouth and looks up at me. I'm sure it's a shock that I just screamed, well, that and the fact that we're being interrupted again.

"No, but you must be kidding yourself if you think we're not talking tonight. Open up," Scott says whispering.

"Bro, go to sleep," I say. "Tomorrow is the auction, and I have so much shit going on. I'm not letting you in here."

"Are you serious? I didn't think you were really flirting with me, but you know if you're stressed, I can help you out."

Edward's mouth drops open, and he holds his hand out, gesturing toward the door.

"Scott. Go. To. Bed. Come on, man. I'm not staying up talking, and I'm not letting you in here for any other reason. I'm pretty sure you know that."

"Fine. Can I have Edward's number? Would it be weird if I texted him?"

"What?!" I shout. "No, why would you?"

I rub Edward's face softly with my thumb. The same feeling from earlier is coursing through my body. I don't want Scott to text him, but am I supposed to say that?

"Is he in a relationship? Otherwise, I don't see why not. He's hot."

"Yeah, he is hot. But you can't text him. The guy he's seeing wouldn't like that." I lean down and place a quick kiss on Edward's lips.

"But the guy he's seeing doesn't mind him hanging out with you?"

"Mmm. He's okay with it. Go to bed. I'm tired. We can talk tomorrow."

"Fine. He didn't seem into me anyway. See you in a few hours for the gym. Also, it's freezing here, can you turn the heater on?"

I reach beside my bed and turn the heat up on my phone app; it was already on, but I forgot these guys aren't used to the cold. "Done, goodnight."

"Alright, goodnight," he finally says.

Edward tilts his head at me, then scoots up beside me. "That was… interesting."

"Ahhh," I groan, while pulling my shorts up.

"Woah, woah," he says, reaching down. "What are you doing? I'm going back down there. I just need a second to process what just happened. Keep them off." He leans in close beside me, laying his head against my chest. "I just need a minute."

I kick my shorts back off, but pull the blanket up. "I'm sorry that both of those things happened. But now you can see that he really doesn't want to fuck me, he wants to fuck anyone. It's just the way he is. He had a few bad relationships and ever since then, he's just kind of decided to not get serious with anyone. But he's really sensitive, so it doesn't usually work out the way he wants. He'll say he isn't getting serious, then end up getting hurt anyway."

"Yeah, but," Edward says. "How have *you* made it this long without any heartbreak? How hasn't someone hurt you? Actually, never mind—I guess they wouldn't have been able to since you haven't been in a relationship."

"I've been hurt before…my parents hurt me, my friends hurt me—my whole life everyone has just used me. They don't care about me, or what I want, or how I feel… They care about the version of me that serves them best. It's how people have always treated me. It's why I've never let anyone else in."

"It's not the same," he says, while rubbing my chest with his fingertips. "It's similar but it's different. You've never been used and thrown away the way that I've been. People have used you, but they still *want* that version of you, but for me, getting used behind a Burger King, and never being talked to again, that's my reality. And there's nothing I can do about it. Even with my parents, they were always traveling for work, so they'd come into town and spend an hour with me, then be back on their way. I'd always get so excited when they'd come home, because I knew I'd get an hour of their time. I'd laugh and be really happy with whatever they wanted to do, then they'd leave almost like they were on a timer, like they could only stand to be around me for so long—"

His voice cracks and I rub his arm softly. "I'm sure that wasn't it."

"It doesn't matter how they meant it. I just—it's always been this way."

"Hey," I say softly, squeezing his shoulder in close. "I've told you a few things over and over, one of them is that I like you, and the other is that I want to be near you. That's not going to change. I like you right now, more than I did before, and I want to be around you, more than ever. I don't know how many times you were used behind a Burger King, which you've brought up a shocking number of times now, but I can tell you right now that I only see you. And you are the first person to see me for me. You're also the first person that I want to take care of. I'm constantly thinking about you and how things affect you. I was going crazy at the restaurant worried about you being uncomfortable. I hated not being able to touch you."

I lift his chin from my chest and kiss him softly. His lips open against mine, and I breathe him in, while holding his face in my hands. He has no idea how much he means to me, what he's done to me. "I like you so much," I whisper.

He presses his lips against mine, slowly moving his tongue inside my mouth. "I like you, too," he murmurs, while slightly pulling back. His fingers are tracing my abs under the covers, while he begins kissing his way down my chest. "Do you want me to do this?" he asks, licking below my navel.

"Fuck, yes…please." My cock hardens quickly, responding almost instantly to Edward's tongue and fingers. So fucking sexy.

"Jacob…" he whispers my name almost like a question, while he massages my balls, and kisses around the base of my dick. "You didn't forget what I taught you a few nights ago, right?"

My cock begins to leak, and I grip his hair. "I remember."

He swipes the pre-cum from my tip, using his finger, and I watch entranced, mouth open, while he drags his tongue slowly up his palm before sticking his finger in his mouth, sucking it.

My eyes almost roll in the back of my head at the sight of him. I've never been so fucking turned on in my life. "Mmm..." He grips me just right, and I'm so pent up from being interrupted twice. "Fuck, I want you so bad, little mouse." He's sucking harder, diving deep, and I'm finding it hard not to ram my cock into his throat. My hips shift upward, craving more, and he pulls off my cock, stroking it.

"I want to taste the pineapple." He's flicking the head of my cock rapidly with his tongue, making me squirm in anticipation. "I want you to come deep in my throat." He jerks me harder, faster, squeezing my cock up and down, while alternating between licking and sucking. It's loud and wet and so fucking hot. "Mmm, please, Jacob, come in my mouth."

I hold the back of his head with both hands and start fucking his face, panting with each thrust. He takes me deep, over and over, softly moaning but keeping pace with me.

"Fffuck..." I grip his hair tight with both hands, and he dives deep, moaning while I come.

"Mmm, mmm," he whimpers, milking every last drop of cum out, slurping on my head like a cum-obsessed glutton. "Pineapple...and my Jacob," he whispers, licking his lips wickedly.

"Come here," I say, hauling him up under his arms. I want to kiss him, but for some reason I freeze. All I can do is stare at him, when it hits me... This, I want this. I want this with him, every night. Him and me in my bed, no cameras, no people, just us. I kiss him softly. "You're so good at that," I say, rubbing his cheek with my thumb.

"I think you did most of the work there at the end." He kisses my cheek then lays his head against my chest. "I didn't think you could taste any better. We'll have to thank Scott for the pineapple tip someday."

Chapter Twenty-Four
Slutty Gym Socks

 **Edward**

"Edward..." a voice in my dreams says. I feel my body gently rocking. "Edward..."

My eyes snap open; that voice is Jacob, and the rocking is him shaking me. "I'm awake," I say. Then I groan at how tired I am and at the slight hangover headache at the back of my skull. "But I'd rather not be. God, what time is it?" I pull the comforter over my head and groan.

"It's early," he says. Then he ducks under the covers with me, pulling me close. "We need to go to the gym."

"*We?*" I ask. "Why we? Me wants to sleep."

He kisses my cheek. "Because I really want you to come along. But..."

I sigh as I struggle to accept the fact that this is my new wake-up time. "But what?"

"You snuck in here, remember? No one knows you're in the house."

I let that information sit in my brain for a long moment as the gears struggle to turn and make sense of things. I snuck in here, so...

"Oh, crap. No," I say. "I'm not climbing out the window."

"It's just a little jump," he says.

"I don't want to," I whine.

He pulls me even closer and kisses me behind the ear, making me melt. "I'll go with you, we can hold hands."

"What? Why would you go with me?" I ask. "Everyone knows you're in here, so why would you have to sneak around?"

"Call it moral support," he says. "Besides, I really want you to go to the gym with me, and if this makes you say yes, I'll do it."

I flop my arms out, pushing the blanket off my face and down to my chest. "Alright. If we're going to do this, let's just do this."

We get out of bed, and I start getting dressed, pulling some clothes out of my suitcase. Because I'd climbed in the window, my winter coat is on the chair, so I slip that on. Jacob's coat isn't in here though.

"Are you sure about going out with me?" I ask.

"Of course," he says, without even the slightest hesitation. "Where you go, I go. Ready?"

I look at the window. It's pitch black out there, and there's frost at the edges of the glass. "I guess," I say.

The room immediately floods with cold air when Jacob opens the window, making me instantly regret living in a state where winter exists. I grimace as I look at him, but he just looks back at me with puppy dog eyes.

I think I'd do anything for those puppy dog eyes, but when I look outside, it actually looks kind of high off the ground. I can't believe drunk me was able to get inside.

"Don't be nervous," Jacob says. He sits on the windowsill and hooks a leg over so it's dangling outside, then holds his hand out for mine. "Come on."

"Okay, but if I fall, you have to catch me."

"I'll always catch you."

I take his hand and sit on the window ledge with him, hooking a leg over like he did. I look out at the ground below, and it looks so far down. Really, we're not that high, since we're in a windowsill on the main floor, but when it's pitch black outside, it's freezing cold, and I'm half asleep, it looks like I'm jumping off a cliff.

With a little coaxing, I copy Jacob, and we both put our second leg out and over the edge.

"Do you want me to jump first?" he asks. "Or do you want to jump together?"

I tighten my grip on his hand. "Together."

"Three…" he counts down, "two…one…"

Together, we jump. And half a second later, we're on the ground without even so much as a jolt to my knees or ankles. When we stand upright, the windowsill is at forehead height.

"You okay?" he asks. He holds my arms like he's investigating me for damage. When he finds none, he brushes imaginary snowflakes off my coat.

"What now?" I ask. "Because don't your friends think you're in there?"

He glances up at the window. "We'll figure that out when we get to it."

We turn around and both stop in our footsteps when we see we're not alone out here.

"Well, howdy, neighbors," Kellan says. He and Braden are standing in their driveway.

"How long have you been there?" Jacob asks.

"Long enough to see your Bonnie and Clyde getaway," Kellan says.

"Why on earth," Braden asks, "would you need to escape from your own house?"

"We're going to the gym," Jacob says.

Kellan gestures toward the front of the house. "And you don't want to use…the door?"

"I don't question your workouts."

"Kel," Braden says, "let's go. I have to start rolling out dough anyway." When Kellan rolls his eyes and walks toward their car, Braden gives us a little wave and a smile. "Always a pleasure to see you two."

When they're gone, we head to the front door. The chilly weather has woken me up, and I feel almost invigorated hurrying behind him, like we're on an adventure together.

"So, how are we playing this?" I ask. The logic of this whole thing suddenly feels shaky to me. "Am I coming in like I come here eager for gym workouts? Is this, like, normal? I come across town to your place and then we head to the gym that's within walking distance of Chad's?"

"They don't know where you live," he says, like that explains everything. Then he adds, "Yeah, you come here to go with me. Maybe you live a few doors down or something."

Jacob types his code into the electronic door lock—but it beeps angrily at him, and a red light flashes. He tries again with the same result.

"Um...did you forget your code?" I ask. "It's 0404."

"I know it's 0404," he says, and tries again. This time, I see him going extra slow with typing in the numbers, making sure he doesn't accidentally button-mash the next number over. It beeps and flashes red again.

Then the door opens—Scott is on the other side.

"What's all this noise?" he asks. He sort of freezes there for a moment, looking at us, and we freeze too, looking at him. Then he looks us up and down. "Why are you outside? What is Edward doing here?"

"Edward goes to the gym with me," Jacob says, sounding cool and confident and not at all like the stuttering mess I would be, "so we carpool."

Before Scott can counter with more questions, Jacob pushes past him, entering the house. As he walks through the living room and toward the kitchen, Scott shouts after him, "You still haven't said why you were outside! You didn't even have a coat. And are you wearing slippers?" Scott turns to face me. "That's kinda strange. How'd he get outside?"

"I don't see anything strange about it," I say, doing my best to match Jacob's confidence and not quite measuring up. However, it's enough to prevent further questions as I kick off my shoes and walk through the house, following after Jacob.

Behind me, I hear Scott mutter, "There must be something in the water here in Vermont."

"Rizzo!" I hear a few of the guys shout as Jacob walks into the kitchen. When I make it there too, I see everyone is awake and ready for the gym—Tim, Alejo, and Brian. The only person missing is Gabriella, but maybe the gym isn't her thing. She's not a professional athlete like these men, after all.

"Are we making protein shakes?" Tim asks. He has Jacob's cupboards open and is rummaging through them. "I think I saw some protein powder back here somewhere."

"Are you rooting through my stuff?" Jacob asks. He picks up his hat off the table from where he'd left it yesterday and puts it on backwards again. God, everything this man does turns me on.

"What the hell is this?" Tim asks. He steps back and has a brightly colored box in his hands. "Fruity Pebbles? Since when do you eat Fruity Pebbles?"

My heart warms at that—he bought me my favorite cereal. He's said a few times that he wants his place to feel welcoming to me, and this is proof he really means it and it's not just words.

"I love Fruity Pebbles," Jacob says. He's playing it confident again and hasn't even so much as glanced in my direction.

"Since when?" Tim asks.

"Since always." He grabs the box from Tim and rips it open. He shoves a hand inside and pulls out a small pile of pebbles and tosses them in his mouth, chewing and awkwardly swallowing them down. It almost looks like it's painful for him to swallow them, and if he wasn't surrounded by his buddies and trying to prove something, he'd be spitting them out.

"You sure look like you love them," Scott says, absolutely deadpan.

"You should be their spokesperson," Tim says, "and on the commercials you swallow the cereal just like that with the same expression on your face and everything."

When Jacob finally swallows the last of it, he stares at the box in his hands, like he's trying to figure them out. "People eat this for breakfast?" he whispers under his breath.

"Oh, Edward," Brian says, like he's noticing me for the first time now. "What are you doing here?"

"He joins Jacob for the gym...or something," Scott says. He looks at me skeptically. All the guys are looking at me now, and I feel a little like an insect under a microscope.

"So, let's go," Jacob says. I can tell he's ushering us along to avoid questions or discussion about me and why I'm here.

"We have to wait for Gabby," Brian says.

"I'm here," she announces as she enters the room. She's dressed in what looks like the trendiest gym clothes, whereas the guys are all in shorts and T-shirts.

"Found the protein powder!" Tim announces.

Jacob just sighs. I wish I could hold him and tell him everything will be alright. Instead, all I can do is give him a sympathetic look when he glances my way.

Alejo helps Tim set up the blender and gets glasses for everyone. As they start putting the protein shakes together, Brian says, "This reminds me of our away games and heading to the hotel gym together." Then he asks Jacob, "Any news about a new contract?"

Oh, right, the contract. The thing that will take Jacob back to Miami. The thing we never seem to talk about. Maybe it's because I can't bear to think about it. The thought of not having him here with me… I've lost a lot of things, but I can't stand the thought of losing him.

"Linley and Marco are working on it," he says.

I manage to keep a smile on my face, but I have to admit it's a bit of a struggle when confronted with this reminder that Frosty Bottoms isn't Jacob's permanent home.

"Shakes are ready!" Tim announces as he and Alejo hand out glasses to everyone.

We all throw our heads back to gulp them down. These things always taste so chalky and chemically, and nothing can ever disguise the taste. But…weird…am I tasting…?

Jacob puts his empty glass on the table. "Did that taste like pineapple to anyone else?"

I almost snort laugh into my protein shake. That's it. That's the thing I'm tasting. I put my glass down next to his. "Definitely pineapple."

Tim puts down his empty glass. "I didn't taste any pineapple." He picks up the protein powder container as his eyebrows pinch. "Pineapple would be a weird ingredient in this. I don't see it on the list."

Gabriella puts her glass down. "I taste pineapple." Then she gives Brian a look and a smile.

"How are you three still tasting Santa Coladas?" Scott asks as he finishes his shake and puts his glass down. "Rizz, you had like three glasses of water after that, there's no way you're still tasting the pineapple."

"I guess the taste is just still lingering," Jacob says. He gives me the briefest of looks.

"So weird that you'd still taste it today," Scott says. "Edward I could understand given how he was pounding back the drinks last night."

"Well, time to go to the gym," Jacob says, urging people to grab their stuff and head toward the door. When we get there, we find Giovanni and Dominic already waiting for us. "Edward and I will ride with Gio, the rest of you can go with Dominic."

"So bossy and in charge today," Scott says. "I like it, of course." He gives Jacob a wink that Jacob rolls his eyes at. I feel a little better about Scott after Jacob and I talked last night.

With very little protest from the guys, we get into our respective vehicles, with me in the back and Jacob in the front.

"Do you know where the gym is?" Jacob asks Giovanni. "Pump 'n' Go, it's near Edward's store."

"I know the place, boss," he says.

Because it's so early, the sky is still pitch black, and the streets are quiet. We pass by the community center, and I'm instantly feeling a little anxiety about tonight. Even though I'm excited to see Jacob in his new suit, I'm really not looking forward to the thought of auctioning him off.

There are a few lights here and there, like when we pass Braden's cookie shop. A little further down, Giovanni pulls to a stop in front of the gym. It's brightly lit with big windows. Inside looks pretty quiet with just a staff person at the front desk. I think I've met him already; his name is Geoff, if I'm remembering right.

"Alright," Jacob says, looking over his shoulder at me, "let's get our pump on!"

We hurry inside with Giovanni close behind, and then the guys and Gabriella quickly pile out of their van and follow us into the gym.

"Welcome back, Jacob!" Geoff says. He gives him a big grin. Then he sees the crowd Jacob's brought with him, with his gaze settling on me first. "Edward, good to finally see you here. Are we setting you up with a membership today?"

Behind us, I can hear the guys whispering. One voice clearly says, "I thought he went to the gym with Jacob all the time."

"Yeah, that'd be good," I say. My cheeks are burning with embarrassment, but the guys don't seem to be questioning it much further. Geoff hands me a clipboard to set up my membership. I step to the side and start filling it out. When the first blank space is for me to put in my address, I already stumble. I don't remember Chad's address, and I've spent way more time at Jacob's than Chad's. In the end, I put the store's address.

"Can we get day passes for my friends?" Jacob asks.

"I recognize you all," Geoff says. He sounds like he's welcoming his childhood idols to the gym. "Your teammates are welcome to join you anytime, Jacob. No day passes necessary. I followed your team through the season and I'm honored to have you all here."

"Guys, you go on ahead, I'll catch up when Edward is done."

I glance up and watch Gabriella and the guys head out into the gym area, quickly finding their way to machines and free weights. Jacob comes around beside me and watches me fill in the form. Once completed, I hand it over to Geoff, and he finishes up my registration, handing me a key fob with a barcode on it.

"Ready?" Jacob asks me.

I take a deep breath as I look out toward all his friends. They're all so athletic and strong. I hold my own, sure, but I'm nothing compared to them. I glance at him awkwardly, then say, "Ready as I'll ever be."

Jacob quickly glances side to side, then leans in and whispers, "You look so cute in your workout clothes. I wish I could take you in the back room right now." Then he turns and heads to his friends.

I'm feeling a little flustered but also a little better about myself. Jacob has a way of doing that to me. He seems to be the only one that knows when I'm uncomfortable, without me having to even say anything.

I watch his ass as he walks away—more specifically, how the gym shorts drape over the curve of it. And my gaze goes lower still to those slutty socks he put on when we were getting dressed. They ride halfway up his calves and hug every muscular line of his legs.

Thank God I'm wearing a longer T-shirt that drapes over my dick, or else everyone would see how much of a boner I have right now.

He helps me get set up on a machine to start my workout, but before he can settle on the machine next to me, his friends pull him over to the barbell area and take turns spotting each other as they do bench presses.

After doing three sets of reps on the leg press, I swap over to the seated chest press, which is right next to where the guys are taking turns on the bench. Gabriella is standing with them, chatting and laughing and frequently touching Brian's shoulder—but she doesn't seem to be taking a turn doing chest presses. Maybe she's just watching them. Which is also what I'm doing, I realize. I haven't done a single chest press since sitting down.

"Rizz, your turn," Scott says.

Jacob gets down on the bench and sets himself up. From where I'm positioned, he's lying away from me...if I slide down just a bit in this seat, maybe I can see up his shorts a bit. Just a little further...a little more...I just need a little peek.

Ah, damn, he's wearing compression shorts under his gym shorts. Such a cockblocking move. Though later I'd love to see him in *only* those compression shorts. I make a little mental note to bring it up with him later. Maybe I'll make him a deal—I'll wear the corset and he'll wear the compression shorts.

Scott comes close to Jacob's head and holds his hands under the barbell, saying "I'll spot you."

"God, Scott," Jacob says, turning his head to the side, "most people wear underwear to the gym. I can see right up your shorts when you spot me."

"It's motivation for you," he says, giving his hips a wiggle. "Eye candy while you push your hardest."

"I'll push harder if you take half a step back so I can't see your junk."

Scott takes that half step back, and then Jacob pushes the weight up. Holy fuck, he's strong.

"Go, Jacob!" Tim shouts. Alejo claps along encouragingly.

I bet Jacob could bench press me easily. Maybe even with one hand.

When Jacob racks the weight again, Scott says, "Man, I miss our regular workouts back home. You're gonna move back to Miami soon, right? The gym isn't the same without you."

"I'm not sure," Jacob says. His words sound hollow in my ears, like I'm in a cave or something. That's like the third time he's said something like that in the last twelve hours. He's not giving a date or a firm answer, but the sentiment is clear—I know Jacob *will* go back to Miami, it's just a question of when.

I give up on my attempts at the chest press and move to the stationary bikes a little further away. Jacob watches me as I cross the gym, making eye contact with me. I try to keep my expression unreadable, so he doesn't know I overheard the talk about Miami.

I turn on the bike's computer and set a short fifteen-minute workout to go through, then grip the handles, lean forward, and start pedaling. I try to push what he said aside, choosing instead to focus on the here and now and watch Jacob. I'm entranced as he lifts weights, his muscles glistening with sweat. I can feel the heat rise from me—not just heat from the workout, but heat from how damn hot he's making me. Those slutty socks, that compression underwear, the way the sleeves of his T-shirt hug his biceps. I can't tear my gaze away.

Suddenly, all resistance on the bike gives way, and the pedals are spinning madly under my feet. I realize then that I'd been staring at Jacob for the full fifteen minutes and my spin workout is done. I hop off and give the machine a wipe-down.

"Hey," Jacob says, coming up behind me. I turn around and see him giving me a heated look, one that tells me he would bend me over here and now if we weren't in public with his friends twenty feet behind him. "We're just about done."

I want to lick the sweat off his temples.

"Cool, I think I'm done too," I say. I glance over his shoulder to ensure his friends are still out of earshot. "That was so fucking hot. I had no idea you were *that strong*."

He gives me a devilish grin. "Maybe I can show off for you a bit later, what do you think?"

"Only if you're wearing those compression shorts and slutty socks and nothing else."

He looks down at his feet. "Slutty socks?"

"Oh, come on," I say with a laugh, "don't pretend you didn't know what you were doing when you put them on."

"Do you have any other clothing fetishes I should know about?" he asks. "Because I'm looking to improve my wardrobe."

"Keep dressing like sex on legs is all I'm asking for."

The guys' voices get louder as they start walking this way.

"Ready to go?" When I nod, he turns to the guys and says, "Let's head out. See you guys back at my place."

Jacob and I find Giovanni and get back into Jacob's Mustang, and everyone else piles into Dominic's van. I sit in the back seat, directly behind Giovanni, so I can see the side of Jacob's face.

"Where to, boss?" Giovanni says. "Home?"

Jacob looks back at me. "Coming back to my place?"

I do a quick run-through in my head of the day ahead of me. "Maybe take me to Chad's? I should try to get to my shop early so I can make sure everything is ready for the auction tonight. Plus, I really need to shower and I think your friends would find it weird if I shower there."

Jacob rolls his eyes as he says, "God, they need to go home so I can just be with you." Then he gives me a smile. "Alright, Chad's place, but on one condition…"

"Anything you want," I say.

"Take me inside so I can see your room." His eyes are dark with lust as he says that.

I help Giovanni navigate through the neighborhood to Chad's place and Dominic follows behind us in the van. When he parks in front of Chad's building, Jacob and I get out of the car. Giovanni gets out too, unfortunately.

"You can wait here," Jacob says to Giovanni.

"The hell I will," he says. "Respectfully."

"Hey!" We turn to see Scott's rolled down the passenger window of the van, which is parked behind the Mustang. "What the hell are we here for?"

"Sit tight," Jacob says. "I'm just running inside Edward's place for a minute."

"How the hell did he get to your place this morning if he lives all the way out here and apparently doesn't have a car?"

"Roll up your window," Jacob orders him. "The big kids are talking."

Scott grumbles but does as he's told. Jacob and I turn to the building and go to the front door. Thankfully, I'd remembered to grab my keys this morning.

I slide the key into the lock, but before opening it, I say, "I told you about Petey, right?"

"Yeah, the parrot?"

"Yeah, he's...uh...a little crude."

Jacob chuckles. "I'm not going to judge you based on your brother's pet," he tells me. Then to Giovanni, he says, "You're staying out here. It's only his brother and his brother's husband in there and they're probably asleep given they run the bar."

Giovanni sighs heavily. "If you get murdered, I'm not taking the rap for it."

"I'll get my ghost to sign papers agreeing," he says.

Giovanni looks like he's debating it, but then nods his head to the side, giving Jacob permission.

I open the door and let us in. The place is quiet and Petey's cage is covered with a sheet.

"Is that the bird?" Jacob asks.

I nod. "Thankfully, he's asleep, otherwise he'd harass you or something."

"Is it weird that I'm disappointed? I kind of wanted to hear what he'd say."

Petey must obviously not be asleep under there, because he suddenly squawks, "Fuck me! Fuck me! Awrk!"

Jacob grins. "Perfect."

I take him to the first door to our left, which is my bedroom. When we go inside, he closes the door behind us.

Half a second later, he has me pushed up against the wall, and his lips are crushed against mine. He grinds his hips into me, his hard cock mashing against mine. I moan and whimper under him, sagging against the wall, which only invites him to press his body harder against me.

He wraps his arms around me, his hands sliding under the waistband of my shorts and cupping an ass cheek in each hand. "God, I need you," he mumbles into my mouth, just before biting my lower lip.

"Fuck me, Jacob. Please, I'm begging you, fuck me." I'm so pent up with lust, it's like the whole universe has fallen away, and it's just me and Jacob and nothing else matters. I slip my hands under the hem of his shirt and run my fingertips over those amazing abs of his.

He moans, then says, "When they go, I'm fucking you so hard and long you won't be able to walk for a week." Then he finally breaks our kiss and pushes himself back a bit, propping himself on the wall with his elbows on either side of my head. "I should go back outside," he says.

I whimper, but I know he's right. "I'll see you later?"

"Of course." He kisses me again, this time a little more gently. "I'll text you throughout the day. I hope I get to see you before the auction."

A few moments later, I'm walking Jacob to the door. When we open it, Giovanni is standing there.

"Why are you scowling?" Jacob asks. "I'm alive."

"You make my life difficult, you know that?"

"By difficult, I know you mean fun," Jacob says.

Once they're outside, I quickly jump in the shower to wash up, get dressed, and then walk back downtown to the store. I use the back entrance because I want a few moments of peace and quiet before the crowds start arriving.

When I walk through the back room and into the main part of the store, I falter in my steps when I see the size of the crowd already gathered, waiting for my store to open. Some are even pressing their faces against the glass, presumably in search of Jacob.

I sigh at the dedication of his fans, as I start straightening the shelves.

I can't help but think of all that's changed since the news broke about Jacob being here. Until that point, we had a quiet, private little thing going, and now we're inundated with his fans, his friends are staying at his house, and everyone wants to know when he's going back to Miami. Our little bubble of comfort doesn't exist anymore.

When the straightening is done, I'm left feeling a little down. I throw on the lights and open the doors. The first six customers are all looking for Jacob and all leave disappointed that I don't know where he is. Then I finally start getting some book-buying customers.

The morning moves pretty slowly in terms of actual business, but people in search of Jacob continue to come and go at a quick pace. At noon, I shut the place down for the day and put a sign in the door inviting people to come back tomorrow. This afternoon will be taken up with setting up for the auction. It's turned into this giant thing—the original plan was a fun and informal event here in the store with maybe a couple dozen people at most. But now it's at the community center with seven hundred guests, and I have no doubt the place will be swarmed by people who don't have tickets; they may not come in, but they'll be camped out in front of the building.

I text Jacob: *Heading to set up for the auction now.*

A moment later he replies: *If you come by the park, we're playing soccer. Do you have time to stop by?*

See you running around and getting sweaty? I'm in!

Several minutes later, I'm walking along the edge of the park. When I see crowds ahead, I know I've found them. Lots of people have gathered around, some sitting on the snow-dusted grass, some standing, some looking cold, but all of them are keeping their distance. I pick up the pace a little bit and then slow when I near. There's a bench facing them that surprisingly no one is sitting on, so I sit down on it and watch Jacob and his friends kicking the ball around.

Despite the frosty weather, they've all taken off their coats and are running around in T-shirts. Steam is rising off their bodies. Gabriella is in a lawn chair on the other side of the field, cheering them on. We catch each other's gaze and she gives me a wave hello and I wave back. When

Jacob shoots a goal through two little pylons they've set up, I whoop in celebration. Jacob catches sight of me and waves, and then the guys see me too and also wave.

I stay and watch them for a few more minutes. They're all incredibly skilled at soccer—they handle the ball far better than I could ever hope to do—but Jacob is clearly a class above them. He's running circles around them, constantly stealing the ball and taking control.

But what has me more entranced is the broad grin on his face. There's a sheer happiness there that I see when I'm with him in private but rarely see out of that context, and certainly not since his friends have come to visit. When none of them are looking, I take out my phone and snap a photo of Jacob running with the ball. Somehow, it's the most magical picture I've ever taken, so I set it as my phone background.

When there's a break in their scrimmage, Jacob comes running over to me. There's a murmur that ripples among the crowd, sounding almost like awe that one of their idols is going to talk with a commoner.

"It looks like you're having fun," I tell him when he sits down on the bench with me, keeping a respectable distance between us.

He laughs, and people start taking photos of the two of us, or at least of him and I'm just part of the set decoration. "I love it. It feels so good to be running around with them again." He breathes deep, catching his breath, then he says, "Heading to the community center?"

"Yeah, I have to start setting up for the auction. It's gonna be a full house tonight." I gesture toward the crowd. "All these people want to pay just to spend time with you."

Chapter Twenty-Five
You're Pissing Me Off

   JACOB   

I chuckle, looking around at the crowd that Gio and Dom are keeping in check. "Yeah, but there's only one person here that *I'd* pay to spend time with. Speaking of, it's not too late, I could say I'm sick, or fake an injury, and just make a big donation to the charity…then I can spend the night with you."

"No. I couldn't let you do that. I want to, because I don't really like the way some people, you know, want you to breed them, or imagine you as an Alpha…" He sighs, "So many things have been said to me."

I want to touch him, but I can't. The crowd is a good twenty feet away, but there are cameras everywhere. I don't trust myself being this close to him right now. I slide my hands in my pockets and lean back against the bench, looking up at the sky. "I think my dad said he was heading over this afternoon to help set up. Do you want me to ditch these guys, so I can help, too?"

"No, because you helping means all these people will just follow you and then I'll be more stressed out. Plus, you're having fun, you haven't played in a while. You should hang out with them before they leave. Wait, they are leaving at some point, right?"

"Strangely enough, no one has said when they're leaving. I imagine it will be soon. Tomorrow night is your brother's party, and I know Scott really wants to check that out, so maybe the next day? I'll try to find out."

"Rizz! Let's go!" Scott calls out while jogging toward us. "What's up, Edward?"

"When are you guys leaving?" I ask, standing up from the bench.

"When I can convince you to come back home. So, maybe tomorrow? Oh, wait, the costume party thing is tomorrow, right?"

Edward stands beside me, and I can see he's uncomfortable, more than he was just a few seconds ago. "It's a masquerade party, not really a costume party. They did have a costume party at Halloween, this is supposed to be a little different, though."

Scott quirks an eyebrow at him in reply. "How is a masquerade different? Are we just wearing suits and masks? Rizz, that's not what you told me!"

"How should I know? I've never been to the masquerade party. But I was told it's full costume, was I wrong?" I ask, turning toward Edward.

Edward shrugs. "I don't know, maybe ask my brother? Pretty sure he said everyone wears a mask, but some people come in full costume."

"Why would your brother know?" Scott asks. "Is your brother a member of the rainbow community?"

"He and his husband own the bar," Edward answers. "It's their place."

"Two questions," Scott says. "Does your brother look like you, and is his husband cool with sharing?"

"You're a moron," I say looking at Scott. "I'll find out later, don't worry about it," I tell Edward.

"I should go," he says looking around. "I really need to head over to the community center."

I want to hug him, or touch him, or walk with him. This—this is stupid. Before I fall too deep into my own self-pity, I catch a glimpse of Alejo and Tim, who have spent all morning pretending they aren't a couple. How do they do it? Edward has only been here for a few minutes and it's already driving me crazy not being able to touch him. I turn toward Edward with a smile. "Alright, I'll see you there in a few hours."

"Yeah," he says looking around. "See you there. Bye, Scott."

When Edward walks away, I can feel myself staring, and no matter how hard I try, I can't pull my eyes from him. If only all these people weren't around. I take a deep breath and remind myself that tonight, I'll get to see him in that corset. I just have to get through the next few hours. Wait, nooo, nooo. I can't fuck him with everyone in the house. It's taken him so long to be loud during sex, if I tell him to be quiet, I'm afraid of how that will make him feel. I shake my head at myself and look over to see Scott just a few inches from my face. "What the hell are you doing?" I ask, shoving him back playfully.

"What am *I* doing? More like what are *you* doing? Why the hell are you staring at him like that?"

I shove him again. "Shut up. I'm not. Just thinking."

"Do you like his boyfriend?"

"His boyfriend? What? What the hell kind of question is that?"

"I'm asking if you like his boyfriend, because if his boyfriend sees the way you're looking at him, I'm pretty sure he's not gonna like you anymore."

"I'm not staring at anyone. Come on," I say, pulling the ball from him.

"Wait," Scott says. "All morning, you've been dodging every one of us that tries to pull you aside. You're not gonna do it with me again. I'm pissed at you, man. How could you just leave like that? How could you just come here and start a new life?"

This is gonna be bad for me if I don't move this conversation off the field or get him to calm down. There are too many people around. I look to the left and see Gio; we quickly exchange a gesture that he understands.

"Why are you rubbing your nose? You feel sick?" Scott asks me. "Don't just ignore me, because we're either gonna talk about this now, or I'm gonna sit outside of your room all night."

Gio quickly makes his way over, and places a hand on my shoulder. "Let's go, playtime is over. I need you to ride with Dom, Scott. He's got a call with Linley he needs to make in the car."

Before Scott can even think about arguing, I turn away from him. "I'll catch you guys back at the house," I shout over my shoulder, then wave to the crowd and the rest of my teammates.

Gio and I head toward my car, which is luckily parked close by. He's shaking his head at me as he opens the passenger door. "Get in, superstar."

"Don't call me that," I say, getting inside. What's he pissed at me for?

He's still shaking his head while he walks around the front of the car. "What did you give me the sign for?" he asks once inside. "You were talking to Scott. Did he find out about Edward? I told you this was gonna happen. You never listen to me. He is the worst person to find out about you two. Everyone is gonna know now." He starts the car and looks around before pulling out of the parking lot.

"He didn't find out about Edward, and what the hell do you mean I never listen to you? He was asking me shit about leaving and I didn't want to argue with him in front of that big ass crowd. I didn't do anything wrong."

My phone starts to ring in my hand and unfortunately, it's not Edward.

"Ah, guarantee that's Linley," Gio says.

He's not wrong. Begrudgingly, I answer the phone. "What's up?"

"Why am I looking at pictures of you on a bench with Edward? Where is Giovanni? I thought this was being kept a secret."

I lean my head back against my seat, quickly running through my actions. I didn't touch him. I know I didn't because I shoved my hands in my pockets. "So, you're looking at a picture of me on a bench? And what, a federal case has been opened?"

"Cut the crap, okay? Are you taking it public with him or not? Because I gotta be honest, these pictures, the way you're looking at him…it's gonna be hard to say there's nothing going on."

I have no idea what she's talking about. I barely made eye contact with him. Damn it, I can't think straight with all this freaking traffic around, and these people that keep walking in front of my car. "I don't know," I say weakly.

"That's all I needed to know. I'm just gonna tell people you were excited about the auction and were discussing making a bigger donation to the charity, on top of whatever someone pays for you. And this should go without saying, but don't have sex with whoever wins you tonight. Don't even touch them. Just open the door to the restaurant, pay for the meal, nice conversation, and smile for the cameras. That's it... Shit. Marco is calling me. I'll call you back," she says before hanging up.

"Is it weird that I want to see the pictures?" I ask Gio. "I don't have any pictures of us. Would be nice to have one."

He gives me his signature fake smile while keeping his eyes on the road. "Oh, sure. Check online, just search, 'Jacob Rizzo is completely screwed'. I'm sure you'll find it."

"Very funny." The window is cold against my head, but it feels good because all this talk about Edward is making me a little heated. He's not used to the attention, and I hate thinking that there are pictures of him being posted online without his permission. He didn't agree to any of this—it's really not fair to him. How the hell do other people do this? At least with Tim and Alejo, they play on the same team, so even though they have to hide their relationship, they're probably still together a lot. But with me and Edward, if I do this with him, how does he fit into everything? Can I really ask him to travel with me? I have no doubts that Marco is gonna offer me a new contract, he likely only hasn't because I haven't gone there in person yet. But what do I do when that happens? "This sucks," I groan.

"What sucks? Be more specific," Gio says.

"All of it. I feel like shit. I feel like all I'm doing is stressing everyone out. I'm not used to it."

Gio takes a deep breath in and lets it out slowly. "You have been stressing me out since the day I shook your hand back on the pier in South Beach. Linley is constantly screaming about the gray hair you're giving her. And your teammates? Well, they've been playing with you for a while, so I'm sure they're used to it, too. Now, if all those people are used to your shit, then who are you worried about right now?"

"I think you know the answer. Just doesn't seem fair to him. He doesn't like big crowds and people in his space, and that's kind of been his life lately. I don't know, man, maybe I'm doing something wrong. But how can it be wrong when I—just forget it. I don't want to talk about it anymore."

My phone is vibrating in my hand, and once again, I look down and find myself disappointed at the sight of Linley's name. "What's up?" I answer.

"I need you on a call with Marco in fifteen minutes. I'll send the link. Just do whatever he says. Whatever he asks for, just say yes. We can deal with everything once we get this done."

"What? I'm not gonna say yes to whatever he asks. Are you crazy?"

"Thirty million dollars, an additional five million if you behave, and ten percent equity in the club," she says, then hangs up on me.

I can't even process what she just said. "Did you hear that?" I ask, looking at Gio as he pulls into my garage.

"I heard. Now, you're gonna go in there like a good boy and let that old man do whatever he wants to you for ten percent stake in his company, which I'm fairly certain is worth upward of two hundred million dollars. It's unheard of. Just do what Linley told you. You won't forgive yourself if you screw this up."

I won't forgive myself if I screw things up with Edward is more like it. Once I get out of the car, I send him a quick text:

Hey, I know you're busy setting up. Can't wait to see you tonight.

My teammates are making their way up my driveway, and Scott is as loud as ever.

"Hey, I'm starving!" he shouts. "Can we order food?"

"Whatever you want. I have a Zoom call with Linley and Marco in a few minutes, and I have no idea how long it's gonna take, so you don't need to wait for me. There are a few restaurants downtown. You guys should check those out, some of the businesses have stuff going on at their shops for the festival, too." I hold the door open behind me for Scott and everyone else.

"Still think it's weird that Edward's car is in your garage," Scott mutters, walking past me. "You don't even like working on cars. Are you even allowed to? Feels like something Marco would have said you couldn't do in your contract."

He isn't exactly wrong. There are a bunch of things I'm not allowed to do, but I don't think working on cars is one of them.

Gabriella smiles walking past me. "My dad knows better than to tell Jacob he can't do things he really wants to. Otherwise, he wouldn't be here right now. Trust me, he wants to keep him happy."

The rest of the guys head inside past me, and I quickly make my way into the kitchen before I have to hop on my call. "Just take whatever you guys need. If you're ordering delivery, just have Dom answer the door, and if you guys are heading out, don't forget the auction starts at five, so if you're all coming, you should be there a little earlier. Gonna be crazy. I think my da—damn brain is gonna explode thinking about it. Pretty sure Edward sold seven hundred tickets or something close to it." Almost just slipped up and started talking about my dad. I can't believe he's also gonna be in the auction. I can only hope he's not wearing some elaborate costume. More than that, I hope he doesn't accidentally call me his son or do something really embarrassing.

My phone is vibrating in my pocket, and I realize that I'm gonna be late for my call. "I'll see you guys after I finish my meeting."

Gio follows behind while I walk into my bedroom. I pull my shirt off and look down at my phone, and this time, it's a text that makes me smile.

Can't wait to see you, too.

"Smiling like an idiot in love," Gio says to me. "Hurry up and put a shirt on. I don't know what you're gonna do about all this, but don't be smiling like that with Marco."

"What are you talking about?" I pull a team shirt off a hanger, waiting for an answer from him, but he just gives me a shrug. I feel nasty putting a clean shirt on without taking a shower, but I'll take one after the call ends. I don't think this is a formal negotiation meeting, since I wasn't given notice or really any speaking notes, so I think it's fine that I'm not in my office. I grab my lap desk from underneath my bed and quickly get set up, then sign into the meeting.

"I'm gonna head upstairs," Gio says. "Actually, let me see what everyone out there has decided. I'll either be upstairs or outside your door. Upstairs if they're leaving, outside of your door if they aren't. I don't want Scott rushing in here during your meeting acting like an idiot. Although Marco is probably used to him by now. But you, be smart. Don't do anything you wouldn't do if I was standing right here. Best advice I can give you."

"Thanks," I say, giving him a salute.

Marco and Linley appear on screen, both smiling at me, which should be a good thing. "There's my favorite guy!" Marco says with an exaggerated smile. "How are things going up there? Gabby tells me the auction is in a few hours."

I have to be careful here. Marco does like me, but obviously his daughter comes first, he never misses an opportunity to remind me that Gabriella is his pride and joy. Hence the reason I had to get the hell out of there when everything happened with Doug. "Yeah, almost time. Everything is good here. Expecting around seven hundred people for the auction. Should be a good time."

"I hope Gabby is having a good time there. She tells me you two haven't spoken that much. Why is that?"

Don't react. Don't react.

Luckily, Linley jumps in. "Oh, come on, he's busy with all the press down there. You saw the boys out there playing this morning, we just talked about that. Gabby looked happy to me in that video clip. What do you expect him to do? Should he have been sitting on the side of the field with her?" she asks with a playful smile.

Marco is staring down at his phone, and I really hate the look on his face. "No, I don't expect that. What I *do* expect is that my daughter isn't being ignored when she's a guest in someone's home. I also don't really like the look of all of you playing on a field in the middle of winter." I assume he's looking at some clips from this morning at the park based on the way he's studying whatever is on his phone. Marco's vibe is always cocky, but when you've got as much money and power as he does, I think that's to be expected. "Cleats are barely sticking in the grass and with the temperatures up there, I can't say I approve of you guys screwing around like this. This was stupid, but boys will be boys, I suppose." He's shaking his head disapprovingly. "Right here, when you cut around, I can see there's no flex here when you did that." He looks up, giving me a broad smile. "But I do like seeing you play again. No one moves like you, so much control and precision, even on frozen grass. Absolutely beautiful."

"Thanks. It felt good to be playing with the guys again. We had fun."

"I'm glad. Of course, it's your fault that you weren't playing for the last few months. Also, your fault that we were knocked out of the playoffs, and your fault that the club lost millions of dollars…" He sighs, placing his phone down and rubbing his chin. "I know that you know I want to make a deal with you. Right?"

"I'm glad to hear that," I say, forcing a smile. I should have talked to Linley first, because I really have no idea what stage we're at. Telling me to agree to whatever he says isn't gonna work for me, because there are some things I won't do.

Marco is mumbling something, and the captions aren't really picking up on it. He's just kind of grumbling to himself at this point.

"I believe you had a few things you needed from Jacob, aside from the community service, based on our conversations over the past week," Linley says. "As much as I want to stay in here all day with the two of you, Jacob has that auction he'll need to get to. What do you need before we can move to contract?"

A few things? Like what?

"Oh, we're not there, yet," Marco replies. "First of all, I still need to know what happened between you and Doug. A simple explanation. You didn't apologize to him, and I let that slide because the media seems happy with it, the league is happy with it, and from what Linley tells me, your sponsors are happy with it. But, that's not enough for me. You and I both know what you're worth Rizzo, but this—I won't move on this."

Before I reply, I take a deep breath. I have to stay calm, despite how absolutely stupid this is. "I'm sorry, you're saying you won't offer me a contract if I don't tell you what Doug said to me?" I look at Linley. "Did you know this was part of the deal? Why should I have to do that? Has nothing to do with my skill or what I bring to the team."

"Why are you being so obstinate?" Marco demands, smacking his hand on his desk. "It has everything to do with what you bring to the team. I need to know that you are not going to do that again. I need to know that next year someone isn't going to say something that pisses you off so badly that you throw away the season for the rest of the team, that you selfishly decide that it's worth it to punch a referee, or a player, or someone else, just because you didn't like what they said. How can I know that if you won't tell me what happened?"

"Jacob," Linley says. "You are making this so much bigger of a deal than it needs to be."

"Am I?" I want to close my laptop and just walk away from this, but I know that I can't.

"What about Gabriella?" Marco asks. "What am I to think of all of this? Doug is her closest friend, he won't talk to her, you won't talk to her. As a father, not the owner of the team, you have to understand the position this puts me in. Family is the most important thing to me. I told you that when I signed you. I'm willing to give you stake in the club, and welcome you into my family, but not until I know that I can trust you. And right now, I can't. Just tell me what happened. Come to Miami, I'll send the jet for you tonight. We'll talk this out in person. You can bring Gabby and the boys, so they don't have to ride back in that van with Dominic. How about that?"

"No."

"No?" he says with a scoff.

"Jacob, think about what you're saying," Linley warns.

Marco scoffs at me. "There is no thinking. He comes here in person, and we talk this out, or we put negotiations on hold until he does. Simple as that."

"So, what's the plan?" Gio asks, while we head toward the community center.

I'd successfully avoided being pulled into a discussion with Gio or anyone else thanks to my conference call, until now. The team went out for a late lunch and shopping, by the time they got back, everyone got dressed, and now we're all on the way to the auction. I know I need to deal with this, but it's gonna cause so many problems, and part of me just wants to keep that from happening. Right now, I'm just trying not to focus on the fact that I'm gonna be having dinner with someone who could be absolutely crazy. "The plan for what? Edward, the auction, the conversation with everyone, or the contract?"

"Whichever one you want to talk about," Gio says. "They're all important. Let's start with the most important one—which one is that?"

"Edward," I answer without hesitation. "I don't know what to do. I'm not ready to go back to Miami, and I don't know if I really even want to. I just know that I—"

"You what?"

"I want to be near him. I want him to be wherever I am."

"Selfish. What if that's not what's best for him? What if you're not what's best for him?"

"How am I selfish? Do you think I haven't questioned that? I can't think about anything but him. He's all I ever think about. I've never felt like this before—you know that. When I'm with him, I'm happy, not just soccer happy, or hanging out with the guys happy, it's different. He's the first person to get to know me, and see me as more than just a soccer player, or someone with a lot of money. I couldn't even focus in that meeting with Marco because I need to talk to him. I need to know what he wants."

"What if he doesn't want you? What if it's all too much for him—the career, the spotlight, the attention?" He shakes his head while stopped at a red light. "What then?"

"I don't want to imagine that." Fuck, why did the thought of that make me so upset? Why am I feeling so emotional all of a sudden? "I don't—I—couldn't do it. I'd do whatever I had to do to make him happy."

"I think you need to go to Miami and clear your head. I think you should go and get the contract stuff straightened out with Marco. Tell Marco what Doug said, then come back here when that's finished. I don't want you making a mistake that you can't take back."

"No. Edward is more important than that."

Gio drops an eyebrow at me but continues driving. "Edward is more important than a new contract? You've lost your mind. Come on, you don't mean that. He could find another boyfriend real fast, someone who isn't gonna have to hide their relationship, someone who won't have to travel and leave him alone, someone who—"

"Gio, respectfully, shut the fuck up. You're pissing me off. Why would you even say any of that? He feels the same way. I know he does… He's my person. He belongs with me."

He pats my leg and grabs his phone out of the cup holder, keeping one hand on the steering wheel. "I downloaded those pictures, well, a few of them that people posted from the park. I want you to zoom in on your faces and tell me what you see."

I have no idea where this is gonna go, but I take his phone from him and look at the first picture. The feelings of anger and frustration that I just felt are gone—because all I can see is him. He's standing across from me, and he's smiling. My smile is a bit more restrained than his in this picture, but when I scroll to the next picture, I zoom in and smile even bigger than before.

"He definitely wouldn't replace you," Gio says. "You can see it in his eyes. And you look like a lovesick puppy. That guy has you whipped already. Look at you. I can see hearts coming off that second one, little birds flying around." He chuckles softly. "You're a different person around him. Anyone who was there today could see that. So as much as you thought you were keeping things under wraps, you weren't. If you want to be with him, which I can see that you do—then do it right. Because I agree with you, as stupid as it sounds. If you screw this up with him, you'll never forgive yourself. Also, full disclosure, there was one where he looked really freaked out by the crowd, but I deleted that one. Still don't know if he can deal with the media and fans, but I think most important was to just do what we did."

"What exactly do you feel like you contributed by doing what you did?"

"I helped you realize that you care about him more than soccer. You're welcome."

"No, you didn't. I already knew that. All you did was piss me off by trying to push me away from him. How was that helping?"

"I just wanted to see what you'd do. And now you know what you'd do and what you need to do. You're welcome."

"You did not help at all. But I'm sending these pictures to myself. So, thank you for those."

Chapter Twenty-Six
You Said You Hate It

There's still an hour to go before the auction, and I feel like I'm woefully unprepared.

I'm not unprepared, I remind myself. I pause to take stock of things. I have a list of speaking notes for the night to help guide me through; I have experience hosting events like this from when I did similar auctions during the Halloween Haunts back home; and I have a line-up of guys for people to bid on. Plus, the room is pretty well set up; when I got here, all the chairs were in place and a microphone was on a stand on the stage.

Even with all that in place, I still feel unprepared. Well, maybe that's not the right word. Maybe unsettled is better?

"What else ya got?" Mayor Dick says, making me jump at his words. He'd come up quietly behind me and taken me by surprise.

He's been puttering around the place since I got here, seemingly desperate for something to do to help. I'd sent him on a chore I'd hoped would take longer, ensuring the sidewalks and stairs weren't slippery from the turn in weather, but he's back already.

I put down the index cards I'd been writing notes on and turn around to take in the space. The community center has several small programming rooms and three gyms, with this one being the largest. Everything looks perfect as it is. In just a little while, this room will be full to the brim with people, and given Jacob's presence, there will likely be dozens and dozens more gathered outside, hoping for a glimpse of him.

"I think we have pretty much everything ready," I tell him.

He folds his arms over his chest and chews on the corner of his thumb.

"Are you nervous?" I ask him.

He looks at his thumb and then tucks his hands away in his pockets. The suit he's chosen to wear for the auction is tight in many areas and obscenely so in one particular area. I refuse to lower my gaze from his eyes, for fear of catching sight of something I don't want to see.

"What makes you think I'm nervous?" he asks.

"The thumb chewing, the being antsy, the running around like you're fueled by coffee…there are signs." I give him a sympathetic smile. "Are you worried about being on the auction block?"

He shakes his head. "It's not me I'm worried for, I can handle myself. It's Jacob I'm worried about."

I get a feeling of discomfort in my gut at that thought of Jacob tonight too. "I'm sure he can handle himself," I say.

"He can," Mayor Dick says, "I know he can. I'm more worried about this crowd getting out of control or the media forcing a story from an unflattering point of view. Even though I know this is good for him and his career, I'm worried about things going wrong."

"Well, if Jacob gets into any trouble, he knows you're here and he knows I'm here. Plus, he'll have Giovanni with him, so things shouldn't get too out of hand."

"I'm also, well, a little concerned about how you're feeling in all of this, you know?"

Before we can spiral down into further hopefully-unfounded worries about Jacob and how the night will go, the door at the far end opens. A few of the guys up for auction come walking in—Chad, Lucas, and Tony, as well Frank and Andrew, two of our local firefighters.

"Little brother!" Chad shouts when he's halfway through the room. "Your prizes are here!"

Chad has put on a dressier shirt and some nice pants, giving him a very masculine but approachable look. Lucas seems to be going for full-on twink, with tight jeans and a bright pink shirt that says *Naughty Boy* in a very feminine font, with flowers and lumps of coal adorning the design. Tony is wearing a dark suit that fits him like a glove, paired with a white button-up underneath. Frank and Andrew are both in suits too.

As soon as they reach the front of the room where Mayor Dick and I are standing, the door clatters open once more, and my heart nearly stops when Jacob comes through. He's wearing that perfectly tailored suit we picked out yesterday, and he's put some product in his hair to have it perfectly coiffed. He looks powerful, athletic, and downright sexy.

His friends, along with both Giovanni and Dominic, come in behind him and he indicates for them to wait at the back of the room. He's likely pulled them in so they're safe from the crowds.

But I don't focus on them. I can only focus on Jacob. I feel my cheeks warming as he approaches us, with his eyes locked on mine from the moment he finds me. It's like the whole world falls away and it's just us. I want to fall into his arms and let him sweep me away like some cheesy nineties romance book cover.

When he reaches us at the front, the guys stop talking.

"Holy shit," Lucas murmurs reverently.

"Yes, Daddy," Chad says.

Jacob scowls and says, "What did I say about calling me Daddy?"

"You said you hate it," Lucas says. Then to Chad he says, "So only call him Daddy when he can't hear you."

I clear my throat, since I know if I don't, the very first words I speak will come out as a squeak. I open my mouth…and out comes a squeak.

Jacob tilts his head sideways at me. There's a slight smirk pulling at the corner of his lips. "A bit early for that, don't you think?"

"Bro," Chad says, "did you just squeak like a mouse?"

"He is a mouse, remember?" Lucas says. "He was the mouse at Halloween."

Jacob keeps his heated gaze on me, but says to Lucas, "Don't call him a mouse."

My cheeks burn hot, but I keep my gaze on Jacob so that my back is to Chad and the guys, and they can't see how I look or how I'm looking at him.

"Oh," Chad says, "so it's not so much a problem with me calling you Daddy, it's that you have a problem with all nicknames, right? He squeaked like a mouse so I'm going to call him a mouse. Sometimes when I'm getting railed I squeal like—"

"Chad," Lucas says, cutting him off. "Jacob, you look very nice."

I clear my throat again, then manage to say, "Yeah, you, uh, you look…" I glance over my shoulder at Lucas. If it was just him and Chad here, I'd say what I want to say, but it's the other guys here that don't know, and so I can't say the things I need to say. "You look…you look nice."

Chad hits my arm. "Don't I look nice too?"

Jacob is giving me a very heated look, and I can't tear my eyes from his. Without looking at Chad, I say, "You look adequate."

"Adequate?" he says.

"Shush," Lucas says, "you look hella sexy."

I'm all too aware that the moment has gone on too long, and the eye gazing needs to end sometime soon, so I regretfully tear myself away from it and turn to face the group. "Thank you all for agreeing to participate, especially since you had to be away from the bar to be here tonight."

"Almost the whole town's going to be here," Chad says, "so that jock we hired a couple weeks ago can keep the place running. I hired him for his biceps, but it turns out he has a brain too."

I take them through the plan one more time even though they should all know it. They'll be auctioned off one by one for dates, with all money raised going to animal charities, and the dates will begin immediately after the auction. For the dates, we've arranged for dinner at Tony's restaurant.

"And if we want to take our dates home?" Mayor Dick asks.

I sigh, then say, "I would advise not, but you do you, I guess." I hear voices coming from the hallway outside of the gym. "Crap, are people already here? It doesn't start for another twenty minutes."

"People want front row seats for the hot guy parade," Chad says. "Especially since Jacob is up for auction. I'm surprised it's not already full."

I realize there's sense in what he says. After all, my store has been full of people for days hoping for the off chance they might get to see Jacob. This is an actual confirmed place and time he's scheduled to be, so people would definitely want to be here early for the best seats. Thank God Braden and Kellan volunteered to be the ushers. They'd stop people from trying to sneak in without a ticket.

"Let's get you all backstage." I lead them to the little green room area I'd set up just down a hallway off stage, in one of the gym's equipment rooms. I'd set up a ring of plastic chairs with a table in the middle loaded with canned drinks and packages of Skittles that I bought from the vending machines in the hallway. Behind the chairs are hockey sticks, basketballs, soccer balls, and more. Giovanni had followed us here, and he assesses the place, nodding briefly at Jacob before retreating to the hallway.

"Swanky place," Chad says.

"Ooo, Skittles!" Mayor Dick says. He rips open one of the packages with half the Skittles spilling onto the floor. "Red is my favorite."

I glance at Jacob and he rolls his eyes at his dad. I know he wants to say more but holds off since his parentage is not common knowledge. Chad and Lucas know for sure, and Tony does too, but I don't know about the two firefighters.

I look up at Jacob and say, "All ready to be sold?"

"As ready as I'll ever be, I guess," he says. "And I'm definitely not going home with whoever buys me."

"Speak for yourself! He said it's *discouraged*, so that means we can if we want," Mayor Dick says as he picks Skittles up off the floor. He brushes one against the sleeve of his shirt and then pops it in his mouth.

"You can just open another package of Skittles, you know?" Jacob says to him. "You don't have to eat the ones off the floor."

Mayor Dick pops another one in his mouth. "My tongue has been in far worse places. A little bit of gym floor never hurt anyone."

"Quality men at this Book Boyfriend Auction," Jacob says. Then he gives me a soft smile, a smile I've only ever seen him give me. "I'm sure it will go fantastic."

"I'm going to check in with the guys at the door," I say. "If you need anything, just holler and I'll come running." The guys all give me nods of understanding, and I head back into the gym and toward the doors. Giovanni is with me, just checking things out. "Good evening, guys," I say as I walk up to Scott, Alejo, Tim, Brian, Gabriella, and Dominic. "You can take your seats now, if you want, so you get the best ones."

"Who…was that?" Scott asks. His gaze is locked on the doorway to the green-slash-equipment room.

"Who was…who?" I ask. "My brother? My very married brother?"

Scott shakes his head. "Not any of those younger guys. The silver fox. The one who exemplifies the word *distinguished*. The man who has to be an absolute freak in the sheets. The one who looks kinda like Rizz but twenty years older."

"The silver fox?" I ask, at a loss for what he means. When I glance back toward the doorway, it suddenly clicks. "Mayor Dick?"

"His dick is the mayor?" Scott asks, incredulous. "I've heard of dogs and cats becoming mayors, but a dick…that's gotta be some dick…"

I roll my eyes. I can't tell if he's being serious or sarcastic. "*His name* is Dick. And he's the mayor. Hence, Mayor Dick."

Tim elbows Scott. "You always wanted to bang a politician, Shadow."

I shake my head, trying to loosen the thoughts running rampant there. Like, if he knew Mayor Dick was Jacob's dad, would he still want to go for it?

"Take your seats," I tell them. "I'm going to tell Braden and Kellan to let people come in now." Thankfully, they head past me and toward the front row. I then go through the doors and am met with a sea of people. The place is *packed* and Braden and Kellan are valiantly keeping the crowds in control and at bay. "Woah," is all I can manage to say.

"Thank God you're here," Kellan says. "The crowds are getting restless."

"You can let them in," I tell him. "And thank you for helping out with this."

"Of course," Braden says, coming up on my other side. "Anything for our neighbor's…*friend*."

Kellan drops his mouth open. "I thought we weren't allowed to sass him anymore."

Braden gives him a playful shrug. "I'm allowed to break the rules now and then."

I roll my eyes. "Well, I'll leave you to it." I turn on my heel and head through the gym, toward the green room to check in on everyone, with Giovanni hot on my heels behind me. It almost feels like he's my bodyguard and not Jacob's. When I get to the green room, Mayor Dick is still searching the floor for Skittles, and Jacob is chatting casually with Chad about Petey the Parrot. The rest of the guys are sitting around flipping through things on their phones. "Alright, guys, we're starting in five minutes. Listen for your name to be called and come out on the stage." They give me smiles and nods and Jacob gives me a heated gaze.

As I head back into the gym, I find my heartbeat kicking up a notch, and begin flitting about the quickly-filling space like my entire future depends on how this night goes. When I circle past Jacob's teammates, I overhear one of them say, "Yeah, but how long can he stay here? His entire life is down in Miami. Why the hell did he buy a house?"

I glance back at the green room door. Questions like that have been dogging me lately, questions that only have the answer that Jacob's time here is limited and he'll be going back to his real life in Miami any day now. While it's not new information to me, I can't help but wonder how soon it's going to happen—and what will I do when it does?

I'm pulled from my thoughts when some of the local business community comes over and introduces themselves to me. Thankfully, they mention their stores too, which I find easier to track than the names of people.

"Thank you for coming," I tell them. I continue around the room, greeting people and shaking hands. Pretty soon, the auction start time rolls around. I make my way to the stage at the front of the room and tap the mic a few times, quieting the chatter and pulling their attention to me.

"Good evening, everyone," I say. There's a moment of feedback that makes everyone wince, and then I continue. "Welcome to the Book Boyfriend Auction!"

The crowd claps and cheers, and one person shouts, "Bring out the men!"

"Because we all know a good book boyfriend loves animals, I want to remind you that tonight's proceeds are going to a variety of animal charities. We originally were going to donate only to the Frosty Bottoms Humane Society, but since the turnout is so good tonight, that gives us enough money to spread to other organizations too, like the downtown cat shelter and the wildlife rehabilitation farm just outside town." The audience claps and cheers at this.

"And for the auction," I say, bringing us to the reason why everyone is here tonight, "we'll bring out our leading men one at a time. I'll read their character bios and why you should love them, and then we'll bid on a dinner date at The Twelve Inch Italian, complete with romantic candlelight and roses."

"Bring out the men!" that same voice from before shouts.

"Bring out Jacob!" another voice shouts.

"Alright," I say, "let's begin!" I know if I delay any longer, this crowd will get increasingly restless, and it might not end well. I pull out my phone for the bios written up by the men. I haven't had a chance to review them before now, so I hope they're okay. "Up first, we have everyone's favorite local politician, Mayor Dick. Dick, come on up here."

The crowd politely applauds as Mayor Dick comes from the green room and out onto the stage. He waves his hand to the crowd in a very mayorly fashion.

"Mayor Dick is the man of your dreams," I say, reading what he'd written for himself. "When he's not rescuing kittens from trees or reading to kids at the local school, Mayor Dick can be found chopping wood like a lumberjack." What the hell did I just read? I mean, I don't know Mayor Dick that well, but I know this is all codswallop.

I glance back at Mayor Dick, who's to my left and slightly back. He's posing with flexed arms that seem to strain at his suit's sleeves. I think they're repurposed shoulder pads to make his biceps look bigger.

"Start the bidding!" a voice shouts, one that sounds spectacularly like Scott's.

"Right, uh, let's start the bidding," I say.

"One hundred!" Scott shouts, standing up.

"Um, one…one hundred," I say. "Do I hear one-fifty?"

"One-fifty!" a voice shouts from the back.

"Two hundred!" Scott shouts.

"Two hundred," I say. "Do I hear two-fifty? Two-fifty? Going once…going twice…sold!"

"Yes!" Scott shouts.

What the hell just happened? I can't focus on thoughts I don't want to think and instead move the show forward.

"Up next we have Chad. Chad, come on out here," I say. When Chad struts out from the equipment room, I start reading his bio. "Super successful and basically a local celebrity, Chad runs the Bottoms Up bar. He's the center of the local queer community and can be the center of your heart if you win him tonight." I look up at the crowd. "Would anybody like to start the bid? One hundred?"

On cartoons where they have crickets chirping during absolute silence…? That could happen right here.

"Let's try an easier opening bid," I say. "How about fifty?"

Again, crickets.

"I'll do fifty!" a voice shouts.

I look around for the bidder, and it takes me a few moments to realize that voice came from slightly behind me. I turn and see Lucas there, waving his hand at me.

"I have fifty," I say to the crowd. "Do I hear seventy-five?"

"Seventy-five!" Lucas shouts.

"You're already in the lead," I say into the mic. "You don't need to—"

"One hundred!" Lucas shouts.

"Sold!" I say before he can bid even higher. "Enjoy your dinner date…with your husband." I shake my head slightly. "Up next, we have the husband of man number two…Lucas! Lucas, please take the stage." When he does, I read his bio. "They say that beauty comes from the inside, but book boyfriend Lucas has the whole package—a beautiful inside and a gorgeous outside. And if you're the lucky bidder tonight, you can see both his outsides and ins—I can't read this in public."

Before I can open the bidding, Chad storms up beside me and grabs the mic.

"One hundred. Final offer. Bidding is closed." Then he races across the stage and takes Lucas in his arms and kisses him deeply, bending him backward like Lucas is swooning in his arms.

"Um…moving on. Book boyfriend number four is Tony! Tony, come on out." When he comes to the stage, I read from his bio. "The secret to a good pasta sauce is to let it simmer nice and slow and long." That's…that's it. That's all he sent me. "Tony, what is this?"

"Nothing more attractive than a man who can cook," he says.

I exhale long and deep. This is a frigging disaster. How I already have four hundred dollars raised and seven hundred tickets sold, I'll never understand. "Let's, uh, let's start the biddi—"

"Fifty!" a woman shouts in the back as she stands up.

"One hundred!" a man on the other side of the room shouts.

"One-fifty!" a third person shouts.

It keeps going like this until it reaches six hundred and fifty. There are wild cheers when a tall, skinny man at the back of the room makes the winning bid.

I proceed forward with the firefighters, Andrew and Frank. They wrote intros more or less in line with what I was hoping for and they brought in respectable amounts of seven hundred and eight-fifty. The firefighter fantasy is alive and well in Frosty Bottoms.

"Bring out Jacob!" a man shouts from the back.

"We want Jacob!" another man shouts.

"I want to have his babies!" a woman shouts.

"No, I want his babies!" the first man shouts.

"We're going to take a short intermission," I say very loudly into the mic. This absolute desert-like thirst for Jacob is starting to get to me. Would any of it change if they knew I was with him?

A few people boo the decision for an intermission, but eff them. I need a moment.

"We'll pick up in ten minutes with our main attraction," I say. Then I switch off the microphone and step back into the shadows for a moment.

Thankfully, the crowd disperses a little bit—they start talking to each other, a few make a beeline to the washrooms, and a few get up and wander. I see a bunch of them looking toward the back of the stage, to where there's a hallway leading to the green room; the other men have come out of there, so it doesn't take much for them to figure out that Jacob is in there.

I look over at the door too. The door is closed, and Giovanni is standing just outside of it, arms crossed over his muscular chest. It's him and his glower that's preventing people from just going up to the door and yanking it open.

This is somehow worse than people coming to the store to find Jacob. That was at least random people spread throughout the day over several days who just decided to stop by. This is seven hundred people who purchased a ticket exclusively to bid on a date with Jacob. Perhaps the only one here who doesn't have that intention is Leora—I spot her in the middle of the crowd, and she gives me a soft smile that seems to lessen my unease a little bit.

Then I notice Gabriella coming up on the stage toward me. "Hey," she says, "the event seems to be going well."

"Yeah," I say, wishing that this conversation and the entire evening was already over. "I'm a little surprised at the turnout. I mean, I sold seven hundred tickets, but I guess I didn't realize what seven hundred people looks like."

She looks out at the crowd too. "People really love Jacob. But they better enjoy having him here while they can; he'll be signing his new contract any day now," she says. When she turns back to me, she gives me a glance up and down. "So, is your boyfriend here?"

"My who?"

"Scott says you have a boyfriend, I was just wondering if he was here. I'd love to meet him."

"Oh, uh, right," I say. We had implied that to Scott so he'd hit on me less, but I hadn't thought of what to say or do if this exact situation were to come up. "He's here somewhere," I say. "He likes to keep a pretty low profile."

"I get that," she says. "Being in the public eye as a couple means you're constantly analyzed and assessed. Although I guess you two wouldn't have that problem in this small town, unless your boyfriend's some secret celebrity."

I chuckle, then say, "No, he's a pretty normal guy."

She looks past me, in the direction of the back hallway where the guys have all come from. "I was looking for Jacob, is he back there? I've been trying to talk with him since we got here and he keeps avoiding me."

"He is," I say, but then I quickly add, "but we're starting up again in a few minutes, so there's not really time to talk."

She bites her lip, looking disappointed. "Desperate times call for desperate measures, I guess." She says a few more things, and then thankfully she heads off the stage to go and sit with the guys again.

I let out a long exhale, but it does nothing to release the tension in my chest. Everything is tight and stiff there. I turn and head toward the side of the stage to go find Jacob. I nod at Giovanni as I walk past him, and then he blocks the entryway so no one can follow.

I hear Jacob's voice before I find him. The green room door is closed, but he's talking loudly. I don't mean to pause and eavesdrop, but I hesitate before putting my hand on the doorknob.

"I haven't figured it out yet," he says. He's on a call with someone, based on the fact that I don't hear a reply from anyone. "I don't know when I'm coming back."

A cold twisting feeling is tearing up my gut. I knock on the door to let him know I'm here.

"Linley, I gotta go, I think I'm being auctioned off. I'll call you later, okay?"

I open the door right as he ends his call.

Chapter Twenty-Seven
What Am I Supposed To Do?

   **Jacob**   

Before I can argue anymore, I see the door opening, and my favorite face peeks inside before walking in. "I gotta go," I tell Linley. I sigh, putting my phone in my pocket and smile at Edward. I really want to hug him. I haven't been able to touch him all day, and we're finally alone. There's no lock on this door, though. I can't try anything right now. "Sorry, stuff is just crazy. Is it my turn?"

Edward is holding a hand on his forehead and nodding. I've never seen him look so upset.

"What's wrong?"

He shakes his head at me. "Jacob, everyone is waiting for you. You need to go out there. I don't think it really matters what I say."

"What are you talking about?" I ask leaning in closer to him. "Did something happen? What's wrong?"

"I'm fine," he says unconvincingly, then turns and reaches for the doorknob. "I just—it's nothing."

"What is it? I can't go out there until you tell me what's wrong." My heart is beating so fast. He's not even looking at me.

"I just, how am I supposed to be okay with all of this?" he says, turning around to face me.

"All of what? The date? I don't have to do it. I only agreed to do this for you. I'll happily sign a check over to the charity and make myself look like an even bigger asshole than normal if that will make you happier than me going out there, because trust me I don't want to do this."

He's just looking at the floor, his whole mood is off. I've never seen him like this.

I step closer to him. "Look at me," I say softly. "Is that what you want me to do? I'll do it. Just tell me what you want. I don't care what anyone else wants."

"I'm a background character, Jacob. You're the main character; the background character does not end up with the main character. That's not how it works."

"I assume this is some book thing that I don't understand. But in my world, you are the main character. I only see you. You're all I think about. I might not be able to show it in public, but I—I always want to have you near me."

"I'm just gonna say it. How much longer do I have before you leave? Everyone has been asking you all day when you're going back home, and I haven't asked you once, because I'm too afraid of what the answer is gonna be. It's a given to everyone else that you're gonna just leave—so what does that mean for me?"

"Please don't look at me like that. Don't look at me like I'm out of reach when I'm standing right here."

Gio opens the door, and shouts inside. "You guys need to hurry up! That crowd is getting restless. Your dad is having a rough time out there on stage, he's doing knock-knock jokes. He was not made for theater. People are starting to complain."

Edward turns and walks out of the room past Gio. "Oh, no. I can't afford to give people refunds if they start asking."

I follow behind him, unsure of what I'm supposed to do. "Edward, wait, do you want me to just buy myself?"

"No. I have to auction you off. That's what people paid for."

What the hell am I supposed to do? I didn't do anything wrong, did I? I think I'm gonna puke. He's walking so fast, and he's just mumbling to himself. His little ears are all red, probably because he's so upset. But I didn't even say I was leaving. I didn't say anything.

"Shit," he mutters, before stepping on stage. "I didn't have you fill out the boyfriend profile."

I walk behind him, feeling the shittiest I've ever felt, and smile at the crowd. I can hear people shouting at me and cheering but his words from a minute ago are echoing louder than any of that.

My dad speaks into the mic and gives me a pat on the shoulder. "Now, the real prize is here! Better pony up, people. Who knows the next time our town will have a celebrity available for auction!"

Worst fucking thing he could've said.

Edward's posture sags at my dad's words, while he takes the mic. "Thank you, Mayor Dick. Now, up for auction is the person—"

People are being so loud that Edward has just stopped talking. He gives the crowd a smile. "I know you're all excited, but I can't auction him off if you don't let me speak."

The crowd continues shouting, but all I hear is him.

My dad comes back on stage and takes the mic from Edward's hand. "If you don't want more knock-knock jokes, let the man auction him off."

At that, the crowd quiets down, and Edward starts again. "Thank you, Mayor Dick. Alright, I can do this," he says, shakily into the mic.

If I bid on myself, he'll probably be really pissed at me. I asked him if he wanted me to so many times, and he said no. I have to just let this happen. Damn it. I've never had to show so much restraint in my life. I just want to hold him.

"Now, finally up for auction is the perfect book boyfriend, Jacob Rizzo. Jacob will—" He looks at me and freezes up. I didn't hear how this went with the other guys, so I'm not sure what he was planning on saying.

"No one cares! Five hundred dollars!" someone shouts.

"Five thousand," another one yells.

Edward taps the mic to quiet the crowd. "Now, wait, there's a method, if you all start shouting, I—"

"Six thousand!" another voice calls out.

I'm not even making eye contact with whoever is doing the shouting.

With all these people in here, the voices and bids are just overlapping at this point.

Edward shrugs his shoulders. "Go ahead, bid it out amongst yourselves. You're not listening to me anyway," he says.

"We get sex too, right?" a voice shouts.

I turn my head at that and make eye contact with the person I think asked the question.

"No," Edward says. "Whoever asked that, the answer is no."

"Ten thousand, and he can have sex with me if he wants!" a person in the front offers.

The people here are getting a little too excited, and I can see Gio is getting antsy. I take a few steps further back from the front of the stage.

"Why am I doing this?" Edward mumbles, a little too close to the mic. I don't think anyone else aside from me heard that, though.

"Twenty thousand," a person in the back shouts.

Edward holds his head. "Excuse me? Twenty thousand?"

"Fifty thousand," a familiar voice says.

"Fifty thousand?" Edward repeats looking at Gabriella.

She gives him a nod and a smile.

"Fifty thousand, any other takers?" he asks. After a few seconds he sighs. "Sold."

Wait, what? I cannot fucking believe she did this. Now I'm not only being forced by her father but also by her. There are reporters alongside the rows taking pictures, so I have to keep it together. Marco is definitely gonna see any pictures that get posted. Gabriella is walking over cheerfully, as if she did nothing wrong. I feel uncomfortable—there are too many people around, and the reporters that were along the side of the rows are moving in closer toward the stage. Gio quickly stands beside me, blocking a few people who were getting just a little too close. Once Gabriella reaches me, she gives me an innocent smile and points at the cameras. I force a smile, while screaming on the inside.

When I look to the left around Gio, I notice that Edward isn't standing there anymore. Damn it, where did he go? I need to get to him before I have to go to this dinner.

"Gio, where did he go?" I ask, while craning my neck.

"Who are you looking for?" Gabriella asks me.

Gio holds his hands out. "I don't know. I think he left that way with his brother. He was talking to the mayor a few seconds ago, but I don't see him now. I need to get you out of here. Let's head for that back exit."

"Let's get this over with," I say, looking at Gabriella.

"Oh, come on, it could have been so much worse," she says with a giggle. "You can't be that pissed about me buying you. It's your fault, anyway."

Before I walk outside, I scan the room for Edward, and I still don't see him. Damn it. I have to fix this. He needs to know that I'm not going anywhere without him. He needs to know that the reason I don't know when I'm going back is because I was waiting to talk to him first.

Gio holds the passenger door open for Gabriella, and she sits inside. "Oooh, I get to ride in your car. Feels kind of special to be in here."

Once Gio closes her door, he gives me a disapproving look. "You gotta be careful tonight. She's gonna tell Marco if you treat her badly. Show her a nice time, then you can—"

"He's pissed at me, or upset, I don't fucking know, Gio. He was all upset before the auction when you walked in there. I can't go out to dinner with her when I know he's somewhere feeling bad about things. What am I supposed to do?"

"I heard most of it through the door. He's just scared. Fix the situation with her, so you can fix the situation with Marco, then as soon as the dinner is over, we'll see how you feel. But just be a good date. There are gonna be cameras everywhere. Also, I heard Scott is going on a date with your dad, so you might see those two there."

"Hilarious." What a nightmare that would be. I can't even imagine something like that happening.

He pushes the seat forward so I can climb into the back. "I'm not kidding. Scott really won him in the auction."

Tony's place is just down the street from the community center, and thanks to the police blocking off the back entry lot, we were able to make it here surprisingly fast. I text my dad, hoping that Gio is really just screwing around.

Dad, tell me you aren't on a date with Scott.

I'm sitting at the bar at Bottoms Up and I feel miserable.

After the auction, it had gotten crazy busy in the gym, and I lost track of where Jacob was. I eventually found his dad and asked him if he knew. Apparently, he was sure he'd seen Jacob and Giovanni duck out an emergency exit with Gabriella in tow. I was hoping to talk to him, but I guess his celebrity status made that difficult.

So I followed Chad and Lucas. Instead of going to The Twelve Inch Italian for their prize dinner, they came here to Bottoms Up. I sat here at the bar and they disappeared into the washroom together.

I check my phone for the time and see that they've been in the men's room for a good ten minutes now. Their new jock employee had seen me come in, but I guess since I came in with his boss, he thought I was being taken care of, so he didn't come by for my drink order.

Since my phone is in my hand, I pop over to the social media apps and search Jacob's name. I see dozens—hundreds—of photos and videos from tonight, of him on the stage, him and I beside each other, and Gabriella scoring the winning bid. He looks dazzlingly handsome in each and every picture.

The men's room door swings open, and Chad and Lucas come out, hand in hand, with Chad wiping his mouth. They both go to the handwashing sink and wash up.

"What can I get ya?" Chad asks as he comes up to me, drying his hands with a paper towel.

"Something strong. Something stiff," I say.

"I can help you with the first thing. Seems like Jacob's the better option for your second request." Chad whips up a quick cocktail with what I realize are heavy pours. He slides it across the bartop to me. "Hey…are you okay?"

I pick up the glass and take a swig. It burns as it goes down. Perfect.

I take a quick glance around to ensure that no one is within earshot. "I just auctioned off my, well…Jacob to someone else. And not just anybody else, to Gabriella. She's been trying to talk to him in private since she got here and I have no idea what she wants from him."

"Have you told him how you feel about him?" Chad asks.

"I did. It came out as this word vomit where I think I made him feel bad for having responsibilities. I wish I hadn't done that."

Chad picks up a rag and starts wiping the counter down. "What did you tell him exactly?" When I do my best to recite my words, he says, "Yikes." He tosses the rag into a bucket of soapy water. "When I asked if you told him how you feel, I didn't really mean about the situation, I mean about how you feel for him. Have you told him any of that?"

I try to think back over the past several days. "Maybe not in so many words." My gut twists with anxiety and other uncomfortable feelings. "I've never gotten this serious with a guy. It's new territory for me."

Chad chuckles. "Before Lucas came along and seduced me, I don't think I saw a guy more than twice in a row. It was new to me too."

I glance down the bar toward Lucas, who's helping another customer and laughing as they talk to each other. "Well, it seems to have succeeded."

"Edward, what do you want most with Jacob?"

I don't even have to think about it. The answer slips from my mouth effortlessly. "I want to be where he is."

"You need to tell him that. If you share the same desire to be together, then everything will fall into place."

This is all helpful, and it makes me feel a little less miserable, but I'm still super unsettled by everything. I don't think I'll feel settled until I have Jacob again.

"How much do you know about this punch?" I ask him.

"I know it happened, I've seen the clip. He apologized the other day, though it seemed a little hollow. Beyond that, not much," Chad says. "Wait…have you not seen it?"

I shake my head. "It hasn't come up other than acknowledging it happened."

"You should watch it," Chad says. He waves to someone down at the other end of the bar. "I'll be right back. Don't go anywhere." I watch as he darts down the length of the bar and shares a friendly laugh with someone as he whips up a drink for them.

I'm suddenly aware of a presence beside me. Some part of me—a big part—hopes it's Jacob. But when I look, it's someone else. He puts his beer on the bartop and leans against it. "How's your night going?" he says with a smile.

"My night is over," I say, shoving myself to my feet. I give Chad a wave as I leave, and it looks like he wants to flag me down to make me stay, but I can't be here any longer. Every second I'm thinking of Jacob and what he means to me and the fact that he's across the street with Gabriella and that he's going to go back to Miami and that I'm just Edward, the bookstore owner, the boy who gets dropped before things get too serious, the one who's good for a quick lay but not good enough to keep for a long time.

When I shove through the door of Bottoms Up and into the chilly night, the cold air fills my lungs. Snow has started falling—the heavy, wet kind. The miserable kind. I don't even look across the street to Tony's place. Instead, I turn down the street and start walking toward Chad's apartment.

   **JACOB**   

Once Gio parks and we get out of the car, Gabriella walks close beside me. "Feels like we should hold hands," she says, nudging me. "People on dates hold hands."

"No. Definitely not." Images of Edward training me on what not to do on my date are flashing through my mind. I can feel myself smiling at the memory.

She waves to a person taking a picture of us and whispers, "I'm just kidding. Sheesh. You're so uptight."

Walking into Tony's restaurant, there are tables roped off like there were the other night. I don't actually see my dad and Scott, so maybe someone was just kidding around with Gio. I wonder what Tony is gonna do, though? He was up for auction, so does he just bring someone here to eat, or does he take his date somewhere else?

The hostess shows us to our table, and Gio takes his place a few feet behind me. I lean back in my chair and look at Gabriella. "50K, for what? I don't know what you want to talk about."

"Jacob," she says looking around. "Doug won't talk to me, and neither will you. I know whatever he said had to do with me. Can you please just tell me what he said?"

The same employee from earlier comes back over. She looks pretty nervous but gives me a polite smile. "Sorry, I forgot to take your drink order. I think I was supposed to do that," she says. "I can also take your food order if you're ready. The kitchen is crazy, so the sooner you get the order in, the better."

"He never drinks when he's out, but I'll have a glass of wine," Gabriella says. "Anything red. I don't know what I want to eat yet."

I'm not going to bother looking at the menu. I just want to get out of here. "I'll have a water, please. I don't think I'll be eating anything."

Gabriella chuckles and looks the menu over. "$50,000 and you're not gonna even eat with me? What a waste of money."

I smile up at the server, remembering that there are cameras everywhere. She isn't wrong, it was a waste of money. Can't imagine how she doesn't know what Doug said to me. He's in love with her, so I don't know why he wouldn't tell her what he said. It's not like he could have heard it from anyone else.

Gabriella is chatting with the server about a few things on the menu, but I can't even focus on whatever she's talking about, because my eyes are drawn to the Christmas tree by the front of the restaurant. Edward was so cute with that tree last night… I need to speed this pretend date along and get to him.

"Now, where were we," Gabriella says, once the server leaves. "Just tell me what he said. I know you too well, and there's no way you were defending me, so what could he possibly have said?"

Our table is near the back of the restaurant, but I still need to keep my voice down. The last thing I need is for people to hear this conversation. "Be so for real with me right now. You're honestly trying to tell me that your best friend hasn't told you what he said?" I cross my arms leaning back into my chair. "There's no way he didn't tell you."

She leans forward across the table. "Jacob, he has not spoken to me. He won't answer my texts, or calls. I am telling you the truth. I even went to his house and stood outside his door for like thirty minutes that night. He didn't even open the door for me."

"What have you told him about your relationship with me and the rest of the guys?"

"I have no relationship with you—aside from being friends…I mean, he knows I sleep with Brian and Scott sometimes. I don't know. Why? Did he say I said more than that?"

I honestly can't tell if she's lying, but I tend not to trust people. The server quickly drops off Gabriella's wine and my water, then heads to another table. I take a sip of water, and before I decide what to say to Gabriella, the door opens, and my eyes almost fall out of my head. I nearly choke on my water at the sight of my father walking in with Scott. "You have got to be fucking kidding me," I say, wiping my mouth with a napkin. Could this day get any more screwed up?

"Jacob, I'm not kidding. I will call Doug right now on speaker and ask him whatever you want. Sure, he probably won't answer but if I tell him I'm with you, he might." She follows my eyeline and smiles at Scott, giving him a wave. "Can't believe Shadow is gonna bang a politician. He must be so excited. That mayor is kind of sexy, he's got a whole daddy vibe—"

"Stop, please. Just stop."

Scott waves at me from a few tables away, and my dad is just avoiding looking this way. That's probably for the best. I'm definitely doing a shitty job of hiding my feelings right now, based on the way Gabriella is looking at me. Okay, I can't do anything about my dad and Scott. I have to just leave whatever that is alone and hope my dad doesn't screw my best friend. I rub my temples and down the rest of my water.

If I want to get to Edward, I have to deal with this. "I got clipped twice, and the first time he told me I deserved to stay down for what I was doing to you. I let that one slide because I figured he was just confused or maybe heard some stupid rumor. It was late in the game, and everyone knows how he feels about you, plus he's always an ass—so it wasn't out of character. But the second time, I took an elbow to the chest before Carter tripped me, then Doug pressed his cleat into my arm and said, 'I wonder how Daddy is gonna feel when I tell him that you and the rest of the team have been using his precious daughter as a fucking beard. Can't wait to see you all fall.'"

Her mouth drops open but just for a moment. "I absolutely never said anything like that to him," she says, then grabs her phone from her purse. Looks like she's texting someone. I have no idea who, though.

Now, I want a drink. Still can't believe I let him bait me like that.

"Okay," she says, placing her phone down. "I have never ever told him about what happens with the team and other guys. And as for you, you've never asked me to cover for you, so I think that should have told you right there that I didn't tell him. Still, he couldn't know that I play beard—God, I hate that word—for the team, unless someone told him. Jacob, if my dad finds out about this…"

"Why do you think I left? I'm about to sign the biggest contract ever given to a soccer player, and that's not gonna happen if your dad thinks I'm using you—and what about the guys? Their careers would all be in jeopardy too. Your dad might trade them all, who knows? He already told me this morning that I needed to straighten things out with you."

Gabriella's phone is ringing on the table. She holds her pointer finger up to me, then answers it. "Hey, thanks for calling me back."

I have no idea who she's talking to, and I don't really want to listen to her conversation, but we're sitting at a tiny table. I hear Scott's laugh across the room and shudder at the thought of my best friend banging my father tonight. Why does he have to be so bad at keeping secrets? I should be able to tell him stuff and not worry about the whole world finding out. If he goes to my dad's house, there are pictures of me all over the place. My dad has to be smart enough to remember that, right? For some reason, all I can do is picture him completely forgetting and walking inside his house with Scott.

"Hey, I'm gonna step outside real quick," Gabriella says. I give her a nod and pull my phone out of my pocket. There's a reply from my dad.

He keeps talking about taking me back to your place. I don't know how to get out of it. What am I supposed to do?

Oh my God. This day could not get any worse.

No. Do not go to my house. I don't care what you have to do, but don't go to my house.

I watch as my dad pulls his phone out. He gives me a quick glance over his shoulder then looks down at his phone and shoves it back into his pocket. This is too much for one night. I hope Gabriella gets back soon; I just want this date to be over. How could Doug have known about anything if she really didn't tell him? The guys are way too careful to let anyone else find out. I guess someone they hooked up with could have said something, but that's doubtful. There's an unspoken code, and I really doubt someone would have said something, they'd be outing themselves, too, especially since they only do that with other players in the league. When I look back toward the door, I see Gabriella walking in, she gives me a tight smile and discreetly gestures with her phone toward Scott.

"What? Why are you pointing at Scott?" I ask as she sits down.

She sips from her wine and shakes her head. "That was Doug, he says hi. Kidding, he hates you more than ever, but he did tell me who told him about the whole thing. One guess." She tips her glass back, finishing her wine off.

I look toward Scott then back at her. "No fucking way. He wouldn't." Who am I kidding? He absolutely would, just not on purpose. And this is such a big secret that he must have been really drunk, and why tell Doug, of all people? How would that have even happened?

Gabriella giggles, looking around the restaurant. "You're joking, right? You know that out of everyone he can't keep a secret. Look at him over there with the mayor. We're gonna hear all about everything that happens between those two. Wouldn't even matter if that guy has him sign an NDA."

How am I supposed to keep calm right now? She's absolutely right, and I don't want to hear or think about that happening. I need to get Scott alone, so I can find out what he said to Doug. This also doesn't help my situation, because the fact is that Doug still knows.

"I tried to get Doug to promise that he wouldn't say anything to my dad, but he wouldn't agree. He said if you don't want him to say anything, then you can ask him yourself."

"Ha! No. Honestly, Doug can say whatever he wants. If Scott is the one that told him, then Scott should fix it. I never asked you to cover for me, so at this point let Doug say something to your dad. If I'd known it was Scott that told him, I probably wouldn't have left. Would have still punched him, but I probably wouldn't have left." For a split second I think about what would have happened if I hadn't left—and I think of Edward. I wouldn't have met him, I wouldn't be here...

I don't care about any of this stuff with Doug. I can deal with Scott later; right now I want to go be with Edward. I have to try and wrap this up without making her feel like I'm rushing her out the door. I look over my shoulder at Gio, and he quickly comes up behind me. "I gotta get up, need to hit the bathroom," I tell him.

He drops an eyebrow at me. "Gimme a minute. Hang tight." I watch as he makes his way down the small hall that leads to the men's room, but that's as much as I can see from here.

"Jacob, you can't be serious. My dad will destroy Shadow, and the other guys. You're talking about half the team." She looks completely flustered holding the sides of her face. "He's gonna be so pissed."

"Maybe *you* should talk to your dad. Don't let Scott do it, or me, or anyone else. I mean, this is really between all of you guys anyway. It doesn't have anything to do with your dad, but yeah, he's gonna be pissed. Maybe less if you tell him that you actually have fun, though. I don't know. If

Doug makes it sounds like they're all using you, then it's definitely not gonna go well."

She's looking down at her phone almost in disbelief. "You know, he only called me back because I told him I was out with you. I can't believe this was the reason why all of this happened. I mean, I knew it had something to do with me but couldn't figure out what. I didn't think it was this. Why would Scott even have told him? Scott is only motivated by two things, ass and food. How would this have even come up?"

Gio gives me a nod from the hall and walks toward me. "I'll be back in a minute," I say to Gabriella and head his way. I did not miss the feeling of so many eyes on me at once. I really don't need to use the bathroom, but I do need to talk to Gio.

"All clear, don't take too long," he says, pushing the door open for me.

Since there's no one inside the bathroom with me, I blurt out, "Scott was the one who told Doug about Gabriella and the rest of the guys."

"Could have guessed that," Gio says, looking to the left. His eyes widen slightly, before he looks back at me. "Ah, shit, speak of the moron, he's on his way over. You want me to stop him?"

"Fuuuck," I groan. "No. Just let him in but if my dad comes this way don't let him in here. Wait, did he see me get up, or was he coming in here to—" I cover my mouth. He couldn't have been coming in here to do stuff with my dad.

"He sees me standing here now," Gio says. "I'm sure he got up because he saw you get up. Don't kill him. I know you're pissed but—" He turns to the left toward Scott. "How can I help you?"

"Just need to talk to Rizz really fast. Can I get in there before my date gets up and follows me in? That mayor is sexy, I have the feeling he—"

I reach forward, pulling Scott into the bathroom by his shirt and close the door. "Don't finish that sentence. I am going to kill you and not just because of my da—the mayor."

Scott looks confused once I let go of his shirt. "You pulled me in here, I thought maybe that was a sexual pull. You haven't lived until you've screwed around in a bathroom," he says with a glance toward a stall.

"Shut up." His body jerks back a few steps when I shove him. "How the hell could you have told Doug about Gabriella playing beard for the team?"

"What? What the hell are you talking about?"

I don't really want to do this with him in here, and I really need to get to Edward. "Bro, listen, I need to go, Gio won't be able to block the bathroom off for long. Talk to Gabriella about it, but I can't—I don't have time to deal with this right now. Figure out what you said to Doug and then you and her are gonna have to come up with some kind of a way to deal with it. I need to go."

"No," he says, stepping in front of the door. "Is that what happened? Doug said something about Gabby and me, so you punched him?"

"No, not exactly. He was being a dick and threatened to tell Marco that all of us were using her. He also stepped on my fucking shoulder, but yeah, I left because I couldn't chance Marco taking his word on it, and I had no idea what kind of evidence he had. Marco has seen me out enough times with you guys that I'd be guilty by association, right? So has the media, so the best thing for me to do was to leave until it blew over. Now, if I want a contract, Marco says I have to tell him what Doug said."

"Move it along," Gio says against the door.

"I'll tell him," Scott says. "I don't care. What's he gonna do? Throw me off the team?"

"Yes. That. That's exactly what he's gonna do. Are you actually stupid?"

"Rizz, he's not gonna do that. We don't even have a coach right now, you think he wants to rebuild the team, too? Plus, you haven't signed your new contract. He's gonna be way more interested in making sure his little golden boy signs his deal. If I talk to him before you sign, he's definitely not gonna let me go."

I don't really know what to say to him right now. He's not exactly wrong, but the look on his face is telling me that he doesn't feel too confident. "You don't seem like you actually believe that. I think Gabriella should do it, though. I mean, yeah, all of you, but really, it's her dad and whichever one of you came up with this idea... Wait, whose idea was it for her to start doing that? I just remember it happening, but can't remember how you guys all decided."

"Gabby's. She didn't want to be left out of stuff when we were all hanging out. I can say that with one-hundred percent certainty. Definitely her idea. What the hell does Marco think, though? He thinks we all take turns banging his daughter? Isn't that worse than hooking up with guys?"

How can he be so naïve? "You *are* all banging his daughter. What are you talking about?"

"Don't say it like that," he says with a shove. "We're not married; we can do what we want. No one is doing anything wrong. If you're not in a committed relationship, then it's just sex, man."

Just sex... For some reason hearing him say that triggers something in me. "Listen, I need you guys to figure it out. Text me later and let me know what you decide. I have to go."

"Wait, I'll just tell you after my date. He's being weird about me going back to his place, but he's also being weird about going to your place. Did you make all of these small-town people afraid to be around you?"

Shit, my dad. I can't tell Scott about him. This will blow up in my face if I do. "Don't bring him to my house. If he says he doesn't want you to go home with him, then just back off. You don't have to have sex, man."

Scott laughs loudly and fixes his hair in the mirror. "I'm definitely doing that. You know I can't resist a daddy."

"Scott, I'm not screwing around. Don't bring him to my house. Text me later, I have to go."

Gio opens the door with a look on his face.

"Wait," Scott says, "What if I don't tell him it's your house? I can just—"

"No. Absolutely not. He could be someone's dad, he's so old, man. I'm not playing around. No means no."

Chapter Twenty-Eight
They're Both Naked

My hair is wet and my coat damp when I finally come up to Chad's building and let myself inside.

"Spank me!" Petey squawks. Other than the parrot, the apartment is quiet. They've left the Christmas tree on, the lights casting a glow throughout the room.

"Hi, Petey," I say.

I throw my coat to the floor and sit on the couch, starting up Chad's TV and pulling up the YouTube app. "Jacob Rizzo punch," I say into the remote. A dozen screencaps pop up in the search results with pages more of results. They all have titles in big, bold fonts with words like *soccer's bad boy*.

I click on the first search result and watch. I tune out the person narrating because he's sensationalizing it. I know he is. Jacob might be cold to people, but he doesn't have a temper. I watch, entranced as the confrontation between Jacob and the ref is replayed over and over, each time ending with Jacob punching him.

I switch to a different video that shows me the whole thing. Jacob gets tripped by someone on the opposite team, and he's down on the ground. The ref comes over and exchanges words with Jacob; they're clearly not happy with each other. I don't know anything about soccer, but I feel like the guy that tripped Jacob should have gotten in trouble, but he didn't.

The game continues, and the video does a little time cut to a few minutes later and another player trips Jacob. The ref comes rushing over again and again refuses to do anything about the player clearly intentionally tripping him.

And then—wait...

I pause and zoom in. This ref, he must be the guy named Doug. Is he... Doug has his cleat digging into Jacob's shoulder. It's just on the edge, so it's easy to miss, but to me it's clear as day. He's hurting Jacob. I return the zoom to normal and hit play. He leans in close and says something to Jacob. I can almost see the angry spittle flying from Doug's mouth as he says whatever he's saying.

Jacob launches to his feet, and the ref stumbles back a few steps. There's a tense standoff between them—and then Jacob charges at Doug, right as Doug is pulling a yellow card out.

Then Jacob punches him. He goes down on the ground, knocked out cold.

Jacob's teammates run over, pulling him back from the unconscious ref. Another ref comes running over. This one has a red card out and is screeching his whistle, then Jacob gets kicked out of the game. I feel a need to know what the ref said. How could he have evoked such anger from Jacob?

I back out of the video; I don't want to see that anymore. The screencaps underneath this video are more of Jacob, but not of the punch. I click on one of them; it's a highlight reel of his greatest plays.

The video takes me through a list of his top ten moments. The strength, skill, and athleticism he displays is amazing. I know he's fit, and that as a professional athlete, he has skills and does impressive things, but I was not prepared for what I'm watching now. He's kicking the ball all over the place, across the field with his teammates—I recognize Scott and Tim as the ball gets passed to them, and I see Brian in the net.

But more than anything, what I learn from these videos is just how deeply passionate he is about soccer. The overwhelming joy on his face when he scores a goal is something that warms my heart.

How could I ever try to keep him from this? I feel bad now for confronting him. He's going to go back to Miami, yes, there's no other option. Not only does he just simply love what he does, but he has a contract and commitments—this is his job.

The video ends, and it rolls into another, this one about the team as a whole, with most clips focusing on Jacob. I sink into the couch and watch him, feeling both admiration for his skill and talent, and sadness at how I talked to him and what I said.

My thoughts keep returning to what Chad asked me—have I told Jacob how I feel? What *do* I feel? We started as sort of friends, and now we're…well, we're more than friends. We're definitely more than friends with benefits too because those benefits don't usually include the deep feelings I'm feeling for him. Like, I haven't put words to those feelings yet, but they're, like, serious feelings. Jacob is always saying he wants to be near me, and that's how I feel, I just want to be where he is. He makes every day a little brighter, every moment a little more joyful.

So what does this mean?

"Oh, God, Petey," I say. "I think I effed that one up. I've read this book before—now he'll go to Miami and I'll never see him again."

"Asshole! Asshole!" Petey squawks.

There's a knock at the door.

I shove myself to my feet and cross the apartment. "Be nice to the visitor, Petey," I say over my shoulder.

"Be nice. Be nice," Petey repeats. "Be nice."

"You're going to scare people off," I tell him.

Then I open the door.

I don't know who I expected, but I certainly hadn't expected Jacob. His hair and coat are dripping wet from the heavy snow, and his cheeks and nose are reddened from the cold.

My heart skips a couple beats as I take in the sight of him.

   # JACOB   

The door opens, and I see him. Only one word comes to mind. Mine. He's mine and I need him to know that. I need everyone to know that.

"Jacob, what are you—"

I crush his lips with mine, pulling him in by his waist, kissing him harder, deeper than I've ever kissed him before. His hands are quickly tangled in my hair, his tongue twisting wildly against mine, until I pull back, holding his face in my hands, slowly brushing my thumbs across his cheeks. We're locked in an intense emotional stare, both still panting from our kiss. I move my lips closer to his, staring into his eyes. "Do you want to be my boyfriend?" The words whispered against his lips like a fervent prayer.

He nods at me, then kisses me, pulling my body the rest of the way inside the apartment, while our mouths collide, and he presses the door shut.

I slide a hand up his back gripping a fist full of his hair, licking, slurping, panting, taking in every drop of air he breathes out between kisses. My fingers clench tighter, pulling his head back, through our kiss, while walking him backward down the hallway.

His hands are fumbling, roaming across my chest, while we nearly stumble into his room, our mouths never separating, our kiss too desperate, the need between us too strong. I close the door behind us while he pulls at the buttons on my shirt. "Fuck me, Jacob—please," he begs. His legs hit the side of the bed, and he's pulling me toward him. I untuck my shirt, and he moans, pressing his body closer against mine and I—I'm gonna give him what he wants. I've never done this to anyone before, but with my hand in his hair, I bring my mouth in front of his, licking across his mouth, kissing him quickly, before dragging my tongue up his throat. Using my thumb I stroke his Adam's apple, slowly. "You're mine now...all mine," I whisper.

He whimpers, looking at me, eyes drunk with lust, his throat vibrating against my finger.

My grip tightens around the back of his neck. "Say it. Say you're mine."

He presses his lower half against mine, grabbing at my belt. "Yours, all yours," he moans, loosening my belt, then pulling my pants down, before sticking his hand inside my briefs.

My cock is throbbing, but I want more than just his hand, and after two days of not being inside him, I can't wait much longer. I turn his body, pulling his ass against me so he's facing the bed. Wrapping my arms around him from behind, I quickly strip him from the waist down, then pull his shirt off, and my own. "You're wet," I whisper in his ear, gripping his cock. "Was it…because I did this?" I ask, wrapping a hand around his throat, pressing my dick between his ass cheeks.

He lets out a tiny squeak, leaning his head back, allowing me to grip his throat tighter. "Fuck—Jacob," he whimpers, voice cracking.

While squeezing his throat, I rub the head of his cock. "So much pre-cum, it almost feels like you came for me already," I whisper, my grip tight on his neck, and my own cock beginning to leak.

His pulse quickens against my fingers, and his throat moves while he moans. "Mmm, fuck me. Choke me and fuck me, please—" he begs, placing his hand atop mine, squeezing tighter.

"Filthy. Little. Mouse," I whisper beside his ear, my fingertips pressing tightly against the smooth skin of his throat. "Bend over for me."

Edward climbs onto the bed, lifting his ass in the air. "There's lube and condoms in that small drawer," he says looking over his shoulder.

"Don't need that," I say, grabbing the small bottle of lube and a condom out of my pants pocket. "Made a stop on the way here." He raises his ass higher, while I squeeze the lube out and start massaging his hole. "You're so tight." I rub and slide my fingertips around, teasing him before slowly stuffing a finger inside. "Look how tight you are after not having my dick for two days—we can't let this happen again. I can't fuck you, if you don't loosen up for me."

"Mmm," he moans, reaching back, spreading his ass open. "I can take it. Give me more."

I pump my index finger inside of him slowly, before slipping a second finger inside. Two fingers in, and he's still too fucking tight for me to go inside. I finger him faster, stretching and spreading then tear the condom open with my teeth, sliding it on while fucking him with my fingers. I slather more lube on his hole slipping some inside before covering my dick with it. He's nice and open now, and so fucking sexy. "Fuck, I could come just from looking at you like this," I say, aiming my cock at his entrance. I slide it around the outside, teasing him, pressing just the tip inside, then circle his hole, before pulling out again. I love the way his breath hitches when I take it away, there's something about it that turns me on. His hips shift backward, his body is begging for more. Slowly, I drive inside, keeping a hand on his back.

"Nnngh—Ja—cob, fuck, you're so thick," he cries out when my crown finally slips inside.

I cover his body with mine once I'm fully buried, and grip his throat again. I whisper beside his ear, "This is what you want? You want me to fuck you like this?"

"Fuck, yes, choke me," he begs.

I squeeze his throat and fuck him just like he wants, and it's so damn hot with my body sealed against his like this. I'm grinding deep while keeping pressure on his neck. He's panting, I can tell he's close.

"Jacob, I'm gonna come, I'm gonna fucking come—"

My balls tighten, and I feel myself ready to explode. "Come for me," I growl. "Come for me while I choke you, baby—" I squeeze his throat tighter and thrust into him again and again. His body stiffens and his hole tightens on my cock, and before I realize what's happening, we both come.

I stay atop him for just a few seconds, trying to catch my breath, panting beside his ear, before pulling out, and standing next to the bed. The trash can across the room catches my eye, and I quickly toss the condom out and kiss him on the cheek when I come back around the bed.

He looks up at me, sweaty hair strands sticking to his face. "Boyfriend?" he says with a grin.

"My first one ever," I answer, smiling at him before grabbing my briefs off the floor. "Where is the bathroom?"

Edward rolls onto his back, still fully naked, rubbing his reddened neck. "It's down the hall, I'll come with you, but you need to cover up just in case Chad or Lucas come home early. Wait, you don't have any extra clothes. Is Giovanni coming back for you?"

"Ah, I told him I'd let him know when I was ready, but a lot of stuff happened tonight, and I don't really want to go back to my house with everyone. I can rinse off then we can go there if you want?"

He scoots to the edge of the bed, looking up at me. How is it that just being close to him makes me forget the rest of the world? I'd completely forgotten about anything until he mentioned Gio. I hold his face in my hands and kiss him softly, then place a kiss on his throat.

"You choked me," he says, pumping his eyebrows at me. "I didn't think sex with you could get any hotter, but damn, that was the hottest sex ever." I run my fingertips through his shaggy hair, ruffling it a bit. "Did it feel different for you?" he asks.

"Well, yeah. You're the first person I've ever wanted to keep and just knowing that you agreed to be mine, made it feel different. I was kind of nervous coming over here, but the truth is that everything feels different with you. Everything feels better with you, and nothing matters outside of you." That probably sounded so stupid, but it's the only way I can explain it. "The choking was hot, so that felt different, too."

"I, um, I—I feel the same," he says looking up at me. "I think that was just more emotional than I expected it to be. Not what you said, what you just said was really nice, but I mean the sex. The sex was—it felt like we were submitting to each other. But in a way that I can't explain. It was like a trust thing. I've never felt that before."

His big brown eyes continue to draw me in deeper and deeper. Whatever I feel for him is getting stronger. I lean down and kiss him gently, then press my forehead against his. "I do trust you," I whisper, while stroking his cheek. "And I *am* submitting to you. I don't take the word boyfriend lightly. When I said I wanted you to be mine, I meant it, but it goes both ways, I'm yours now, too."

"I have to keep reminding myself that you're real…" he says before standing. "And we are both still very naked. Do you want to borrow some of my clothes? Most of my stuff is in the suitcase at your house, but I still have a bunch of clothes here."

Damn, I only have my suit, and I can't sleep in that. I watch as Edward rummages through the drawers in the tall brown dresser on the opposite side of the room. I didn't think this through. Maybe we should just go back to my place? I really don't want to, though. If we stay here, it will just be us, with no one else around. I have so much to talk to him about, and I won't be able to do that at my house. But, still, this is his brother's place, and I feel kind of weird about it for some reason.

Edward walks toward me smiling, holding a pair of underwear and shorts in his hand, partially blocking his dick from my view. "Do you want to sleep over? You said that you didn't want to go back to your place. You could stay here with me. Chad and Lucas won't even know, since your car isn't here. Plus, I was kind of depressed earlier, so when they come home it's not like they're gonna bother me."

I don't know how Gio would feel about that. And I really should try and talk to the guys in the morning. Now that Scott and Gabriella know what happened, I probably should try and clear the air with the rest of the guys.

He's tilting his head walking toward me; he must notice the indecision on my face. "Let's take a shower and you can think about it," he says, tugging on my hand.

I follow him outside of the room, and even though he said no one was home, I still look left to right before stepping into the hall.

The bird squawks loudly, making me jump. "Pretty boy, pretty boy," he says, moving side to side in his cage.

"That was the nicest thing I've ever heard come out of his beak," Edward says, before we head into the bathroom. He turns the water on inside the small shower and pushes the curtain aside for me after stepping in. It's much smaller than I'm used to, but that just means I can be closer to him. He grabs a washcloth and squeezes bodywash on it, then turns toward me. "Mmm, my boyfriend is very sexy," he says, scrubbing my chest, before squatting down to clean my dick.

"Wow, not wasting any time," I joke. He's scrubbing so diligently with a huge smile on his face, it's cute but it's also already turning me on. My dick is getting harder by the second. "You're like a sexy little cleaning mouse," I say, threading my fingers through his wet hair. "Wait, weren't there mice that cleaned in one of the classic cartoons?"

He giggles in front of me, scrubbing my legs. "Mice that clean? I don't know what that would have been, and I have to ask, were those mice distracted by muscular thighs and a delicious dick when they cleaned?"

If someone could come from just a look, I'd be coming from the look he's giving me. "Don't look up at me like that," I say, playfully gripping his hair. "You're way too close, plus all the touching—well, you can see what's happening. But this shower is too small for any positions that are coming to mind."

He pushes on my thighs, moving me directly under the showerhead. He's just staring at my cock as the water runs down it, rinsing away the soapy bubbles. It looks like he's ready to pounce on it. I hold my arms out wide, moving the shower curtain to show him the lack of space. "Look, I can't move you around in here, there's no room."

Edward grips my dick and kisses it. "We can have more fun later, then," he says before standing.

"Insatiable, huh? Why does that turn me on? Is that weird that you wanting to go again, only ten minutes after, somehow is making me harder?"

"Seems normal to me." He scrubs his body down quickly, then slides past me to rinse off. "We shouldn't do anything in here anyway. I've lost all track of time. If you're sleeping over, I should get you back in the room before Chad and Lucas get home. Even if you aren't sleeping over, we should hurry. Can't imagine my brother seeing you like this. I'd never hear the end of it."

On the way back to Edward's room, he grabs a clean set of sheets from the hallway closet. "I'll have to try and wash those other sheets in the morning. Hopefully without Chad or Lucas noticing," he says, then pulls me into his room.

We quickly replace the sheets with clean ones, and I slip into my briefs, then lie on his bed beside him. The bed is really uncomfortable, but once Edward's head hits my chest, I feel warm and cozy. He pulls the heavy red comforter up, tucking himself against me. I don't wanna go home tonight.

He's tracing the muscles on my chest, running his finger along my tattoos. "I'm sorry for making you feel bad at the auction. I was just freaking out about everything. I shouldn't have jumped on you like that."

"You didn't say anything wrong. You were scared, it's okay. I just had a lot to consider, and we hadn't really talked about it, so even though everyone else was making it sound like I'd definitely go back, the truth is that I wasn't really sure what I wanted to do."

His finger has stopped moving, I can tell he's still feeling really unsettled. "So, did you decide what you want to do?" he asks, timidly.

"Hmm…yes and no. I decided one major thing, which is that I'll do whatever I have to do, to be where you are. And what I mean is that I don't want to force you to do anything, or have to make you move things around, I want to be the one doing those things for you. I just—I need you near me." I feel his body relax against me, along with a quiet exhale that felt much heavier than it sounded. "For the contract, well, it hasn't been signed yet and Marco wants me to tell him exactly what Doug said, before we move to formal negotiations."

"Can he do that? Force you to tell him what someone said? Feels like he shouldn't be able to. What does that have to do with your contract?"

"He's the owner of the club, so, yeah, he can do whatever he wants. But if he doesn't sign me, someone else will. I have a year left on my contract, and he doesn't want me playing a whole season with other teams trying to sign me. It sounds cocky, but I'm the best player in the league, there's no way he won't sign me. I do want to respect him, though, just because of what he's offering." I sigh, rubbing his arm. "He wanted me to get on a jet tonight."

He lifts his head, looking at me in shock. "The owner of the team asked you to get on a jet, and instead of doing that, you're here with me?"

"The only negotiation I was interested in tonight, was getting you to agree to be my boyfriend—which worked out perfectly. Definitely didn't want to get into contract talks with Marco, or talking about Doug and that whole situation."

"Can I ask you what Doug said? I hope you won't be mad, but I watched the clip of the punch and some other game clips, too. I could see that you were shocked by whatever he said before the punch, and I definitely noticed"—he kisses my shoulder and nuzzles his nose against it—"that he stepped on you, right here. Really pissed me off."

I kiss the top of his head, then lie back on the pillow. "Not my finest moment you saw there. It was stupid, he said something about the guys and me using Gabriella as a beard, then threatened to tell her dad, which would mean the media would find out. But mostly he didn't card anyone that was taking cheap shots at me all night, then dug his cleat into me, so I was already pissed. With the Gabriella stuff, I just panicked, afraid for my teammates and my career. I've never used her like that, but the others do—they all have some understanding about it. Anyway, I thought Gabriella was the one that told Doug, so I've been ignoring her since it happened, well, I ignored everyone, not just her." I exhale, covering my head with my forearm. "Turns out that Scott was the one that told Doug about their arrangement. That little schmuck was the one who told him everything."

"I knew it had to be something bad for you to do that. So, what are you gonna do? I feel like Marco, even though I don't know him, is gonna be really mad if you tell him the truth. I don't know what father would want to hear that."

"I don't know. I told Scott and Gabriella that they needed to deal with it. I can tell him a little, but I would never out anyone."

Edward jolts, sitting up. "Wait, what happened with your dad and Scott? I can't believe Scott actually won him. They were at the restaurant when you were there, right? That was what everyone was supposed to do."

"Unfortunately, they were there. I have no idea what happened. That's part of the reason I don't want to go to my house. I told Scott not to bring him back to my place, and I told my dad not to go there. I have no idea if either will listen to me. But, as evidenced by him running his mouth to Doug about the big team secret, you can see that he can't be trusted. The whole world would know that my dad is the mayor by sunrise."

I need to shift the conversation to us. I want to tell him what I'm planning to do and just hope that he's okay with it. I have all these plans and thoughts but none of them matter if he doesn't want them.

"So, about us…" I say. "I don't know exactly what I'll say to Marco about the stuff with Doug, but I want to tell him about you." I feel his body tense up and I rub his arm, trying to get him to relax. "I don't want to hide us, or you. I can't stand the thought of you feeling like a secret or wondering if what we have is real, I was so upset today at the thought of you being scared to lose me. I couldn't take it, I laid into Linley a few times and pushed Marco aside until I could talk to you first. I don't want you to feel like you aren't the most important thing to me, and in order for me to do that, I'm gonna have to stop hiding who I am, but if that makes you uncomfortable—"

"It doesn't," he interrupts. "I just don't know how I'm worth it. This is your career. I saw the people at the games going crazy over you, I saw commercials with you, so many things. There's so much pressure on you. Is a guy from Twilight Hollow that owns a little bookshop really worth all the trouble?"

"I'm gonna keep working on getting you to realize how much this 'guy from Twilight Hollow' means to me," I say with a chuckle. "You don't cause me trouble. I need you near me. Besides, you're my boyfriend now. I can't hide the way I feel for you any longer."

"That makes me really happy. I don't want you to hide it, but I would understand if you needed to. His hand moves to my abs, teasing the small line of hair underneath my navel. "So, are you staying the night? Or are we going back to your place?"

"I want to stay," I answer, taking his hand in mine and kissing it. As much as I want to shove his hand down my underwear, I need to take care of a few things first. "I have a bunch of stuff I have to do if I'm gonna spend the night. I was a dick today to Linley, and Gio is pretty worried, so I need to try and call them both, fill them in on what I want to do. I should have Gio stop by with some stuff, it's getting late though, so I don't really want to ask him to come back here."

He smiles at me softly, before his eyes widen. "Oh! I just realized something! When I moved in here, Chad and Lucas bought me a bunch of bathroom stuff in case I didn't have any that first night."

I watch as he walks across the room and out of the bedroom. I need clothes, not really bathroom stuff, besides we just took a shower. What is he even talking about?

"Here we go," he says walking back inside the room waving a new toothbrush at me. "Still in the packaging. You can have this one. Unless you're planning on Giovanni bringing you your own stuff."

"Sweet. That's perfect, thanks. Now," I say, sitting up against the headboard. "I'm gonna make a few phone calls, and then we can do whatever you feel like doing. But I have to actually focus, so don't feel bad when I lock in on these conversations. Shouldn't take too long."

"Hands off until the phone calls are over. I can do that," he says, grabbing a book with pink pages off his nightstand. Can't say I've ever seen a book with pink pages. He tosses a pillow from the top of the bed down near my feet, then flops on it. "Safer for me to be down here, away from your chest and other parts."

This is fine. It's better that his face isn't directly beside mine when I'm trying to have business conversations. Although, his ass is on full display now inside those gym shorts—it's so squishable and fuckable. Damn it, I really want to bury myself in there. I pat his ass cheek and give it a squeeze, resisting any other urges, then call Linley.

About an hour has passed since the second conversation with Linley started. Gio was a pretty quick call, he let me know that Scott hadn't made it back to my place yet, and even though he wasn't a fan of me staying the night here, he agreed to let it go in exchange for me never bringing up what happened in Cancun again.

But Linley is scrambling a bit, she's trying to get things set up quickly, she'd like me to get to Miami as soon as possible to clear the air and start negotiations. Since Marco is also hiring a new coach, all the potential candidates are asking if a new deal has been signed with me, which he, of course, can't lie about.

Linley pauses for a moment, then asks me the same question she's asked no less than three times. "Are you sure you want to use the word boyfriend? You can just say you're seeing someone. Boyfriend sounds so—serious. You haven't had any relationships in the public eye, maybe we just start with you guys going out to a few places together, then we have the talk with Marco. How about that?"

Edward peeks over his shoulder after hearing me groan into the phone, and I give his ass a reassuring pat. "I have told you so many times already. Yes, I am going to call him my boyfriend because that's what he is. No, I'm not going to try it out and see how it goes. I already know it's going to work out, and I really don't think Marco is going to have a problem with it. I don't know why you do."

I hate that he's listening to all this, but I also don't want to hide anything from him. Conversations like these will be a part of my life as long as I'm playing soccer. I really should stop rubbing his ass though, my brain may be pre-occupied with this conversation, but my dick is a different story. He's just happily reading his book while Linley reminds me one more time that she thinks this is a bad idea. "Jacob, listen to me, Marco is a businessman, he does not care about your feelings, he cares about whether this will affect your game. He cares about whether you're going to be focused, and what is going to take priority. No one is worried about you telling him you're in a relationship with a man, I'm worried that he won't like the idea of sharing you, and that will make you less valuable. 'Nothing will ever come before soccer'—that's what he wants to hear. That's what your sponsors want to hear, that's what fans want to hear. I can't promise you that this decision to announce a relationship won't affect your value. Do you understand that?"

"I understand. But I feel like being honest is more important at this point, and the truth is that I can't say what everyone wants me to say."

She sighs into the phone. "Alright, I'll let Marco know you can meet with him tomorrow. Maybe plan to stay a few days, bring Edward with you. Don't bring him to the negotiation, of course, but maybe just bring him here, so he can see how he likes it. He should get to see you in your natural environment versus what he's been used to."

"Ah…I'll talk to him about it, but I think he's gotten a pretty good glimpse already, thanks to you."

"You're joking!" she says through laughter. "Alright, listen, we'll do this your way, but if the bottom line gets affected tomorrow, I'm pulling you out of there. Just don't do the thing you do, where you become unreasonable. I'll message you as soon as I hear from Marco. He said Gabby was calling him just a little bit ago, so I'm wondering if she's spilling the tea… What a clusterfuck this has turned into. Should have been the easiest deal in the world…"

"Okay, thanks," I say, cutting her off. "Let me know when you hear from Marco."

I reposition myself on the bed, moving beside Edward and kiss him on the cheek. "Sorry you had to hear all of that. This is gonna be wild."

He rubs my back and leans his head against my shoulder. "Thanks for wanting to do all this for me. Do you know what time you're gonna have to leave tomorrow? You'll probably miss the party," he says with a slight pout.

"Don't know yet. I want to go, though, so I'll try my best. I'll know more when Linley hears back from Marco. She wanted me to bring you along tomorrow, but it's like she forgets that you just opened your store and you have your own responsibilities. I don't want my job to get in the way of your shop."

His eyebrows raise and he pulls his mouth to the side looking down at the book. "I could—I could go, if you want me to."

Of course I want him with me, but negotiations can take hours, sometimes days. I'd feel bad leaving him alone during all that time. It would be nice to bring him home with me and show him around, but I feel like it would be better to wait until after the deal is signed.

"Hmm," I say, nuzzling against his cheek, kissing it. God, I love the way he smells, and the feeling of my lips against his skin. "I want you to go with me, just not tomorrow. Your store is gonna be really busy, and Marco might be in a bad mood and drag shit out. Once everything is settled, we can take a trip there together."

"I'd like that," he says, scooting in even closer.

I squeeze his ass with my hand while using the other to prop my head up on the pillow beside him. It's so perfectly round and juicy, and so very close to me. With the way his shorts are hugging his ass crack, I really can't help myself and start to drag my finger up it, slowly dragging it back down, stopping over his hole, teasing him with just a little push.

Without taking his eyes off his book, he reaches back, placing his hand atop mine, pressing my pointer finger against his warm hole.

Giving him what he wants, I press harder, teasing his rim, softly licking his earlobe. "You just gonna read while I play with you?"

"Nope," he says, quickly closing the book. Within seconds, he's pinned me underneath him, strong tattooed arms over my head while he licks my neck. He's rubbing his cock against mine through the fabric of his shorts and my underwear. He kisses and licks down my chest before releasing his hold on me, moving his hands to tug my underwear down.

I flip our positions, gripping the sides of his ass and pull his shorts off, exposing his thick, hard cock, then straddle him. He's hot and sexy beneath me, grabbing at my dick, rubbing it against his. The friction is too much, the sensation is driving me crazy—his cock is leaking, and mine is too, but it's not enough. I climb over him, grabbing the lube and a condom from the top of the nightstand, and toss both beside him, then swipe two fingers across his tip. My fingers are covered in his precum, sticky and wet, he's sticking his tongue out flat, and it's so hot. I'm not gonna feed him this just yet. I lick across his tongue, moaning, then slide a hand under his neck, gripping the sides of his throat.

"Mmmnn—fuck," he moans.

I squeeze tighter then bring my fingers above his tongue, he's lifting trying to get them in his mouth. Sliding my hand up the back of his head, I press my cum-covered fingers into his mouth. He's sucking and licking all over them, and my cock is ready to burst from the sight, so desperate, so needy. "So fucking thirsty. You like the way I make you taste?"

He nods, while his tongue moves all around my fingers, sucking them, licking in between them.

"Your cock is begging for it. How about your sweet little hole?" I ask, pulling my fingers from his mouth, and rubbing his asshole. "Mmm, what a good little mouse," I whisper, swirling them around his rim, before grabbing the lube and quickly coating his entrance and my fingers with it. He's still loose from earlier, so I shove two fingers straight in, pumping and swirling. He's grinding down on them, holding my hand, using it to fuck himself. It's the hottest thing I've ever seen.

"Jacob—haah—fuck me. Fuck me, please," he begs, while shamelessly ramming my fingers into his ass.

"I'm gonna need these," I say, pulling my fingers back, ripping the condom open. Minutes later I'm pounding into him from behind, thrusting as hard as I can, so hard that the headboard is knocking into the wall, but I can't help it, he's slippery and open, and the sight of his hole swallowing my cock is so fucking delicious. I love when I can slide in and out like this, slamming my weight against him. He's gripping the sheets, panting, his back is sweaty, and it's so fucking hot. I slow my pace, still burying myself inside of him over and over, trying to find the spot that makes him squeak. I'm grinding around, moving my hips in a way that drives him wild, while clutching a fistful of his hair.

The tiniest of whimpers escapes him and he moans, "Ja-cob, right there, nngh."

I'm so close to coming, just a little more, but—I hear a squeak that didn't come from him…and keys jingling?

"Oh, wayward brother! We're home to cheer you up!" Chad's voice calls out.

"Oh, fuck, my brother's home," Edward whispers.

Holy shit, holy shit. My eyes shift to the door that isn't locked and I quickly pull out, then grab Edward by the waist, pulling him backward. The two of us lie against the pillows and I tug the comforter up and we slide under the covers just as the bedroom door opens.

"Honey, we're home!" Chad shouts, flinging the door open with

Lucas beside him. His eyes nearly fall out of his head when he sees me. He smacks Lucas on the chest. "Holy shit!"

"He's naked," Lucas says, dropping his head. He pulls on Chad's arm, urging him to leave.

I pull the cover up a little higher. Not easy to give him any shit when I'm sitting here with a condom on my dick inside his apartment.

"They're *both* naked," Chad says. "To think, we came here to cheer you up and you two were here doing that. We even closed up a few minutes early."

"We weren't doing anything," Edward says, straight-faced.

Chad giggles at that. "Do we look stupid to you?"

"We weren't doing anything," I say, giving Chad and Lucas a shrug. "Just had my shirt off because I felt like it. It was warm in here."

Lucas and Chad fold their arms, looking above the bed. "You were definitely having sex. You might as well admit it. You're one hundred percent caught," Lucas says.

"How can we be caught doing something we weren't?" I ask. Damn it, my dick is really uncomfortable now. I need to get this condom off and get out of this bed.

Chad points above our heads. "First of all, it smells like sex in here, which is hot because, well, look at you, but also not hot because of my brother. But yay for him. Second, there are two little birds that hang on the wall above that bed. They are no longer there, and the only way those birds wouldn't be there, was if the headboard shook them loose off the wall."

Edward and I look up and see the two empty nails. "We could have died!" Edward shouts. "Where the hell are the birds?"

"This proves nothing," I say matter-of-factly.

Before I can grab onto something the mattress drops to the floor. "What the hell?!" I shout.

"You broke our bed!" Chad shouts, while Lucas is laughing uproariously behind him, practically on the floor.

Edward is holding in a laugh, while I pull the comforter back up. "Still proves nothing. But I will pay to replace this for you."

Chapter Twenty-Nine
Back In
Twilight Hollow

Edward

"Edward," a voice says. It pulls me from a dream. It was a very good dream. It involved Jacob saving me from a dragon. "Edward, wake up." It's Jacob's voice, I realize. It's gentle, so it's not an emergency. I crack my eyes open and see him sitting on the bed beside me, looking all energetic and wide awake.

"I don't want to go to the gym," I mumble. "I'll just be out of shape if it means I can stay in bed." I roll over onto my side and pull the blanket up over my head, swallowing me in darkness again.

Before I can fall blessedly back to sleep, his hand is on my hip, rocking me. "Edward, it's important. And it's not the gym."

I don't emerge from my blanket cocoon, but I say, "What time is it?"

"Four."

"*Four?* Are you literally insane? Let me sleep."

"Edward," he says, shaking my hip again. "It's really important."

I groan really, really loud, then flip the blanket down. Jacob has a smile on his face. "Are you leaving me for Miami already?"

He shakes his head. "That's not for a few hours. We need to do something first. But…"

"But what?"

He takes my hand in his like he's about to ask me something serious.

"Gio has clothes for me and he's parked out front. I feel really weird about leaving the apartment and coming back inside without anyone knowing."

"You…woke me up…so you can get clothes from Giovanni? At four in the morning? My brain clearly isn't working. Maybe I need coffee."

"Your brain is working fine. So…can you let me out and back in?"

I yawn really long, then say, "Yeah, I can do that. Then we go back to sleep."

"No," he says, "I want to take you somewhere."

My bottom lip sticks out with a pout. "But I don't want to go to the gym."

He kisses my forehead. "We're not going to the gym, but where we *are* going is a surprise, so I can't tell you. And we need to do it now, before I go to Miami."

I very reluctantly get out of bed and almost immediately regret it. The apartment is cold, and I'm shivering as I open the door briefly so Jacob can grab the clothes from Giovanni. Thankfully, Chad and Lucas had put a sheet over the birdcage for the night, so Petey isn't screeching profanities at us. While Jacob gets dressed, I step in the shower for a quick rinse and to brush my teeth. When I get back to the bedroom, he's still sitting on the mattress—which is on the floor with the broken bedframe scattered around it—smiling at me and dressed immaculately. I throw on some clothes and we head out of the apartment. There, Giovanni is waiting for us with Jacob's car.

"Please tell me you have the heat on in there," I say as we approach the car.

"Nice and toasty warm," Giovanni says.

"You're a saint." I climb into the back seat when he opens the door for us. And Jacob climbs into the back with me. "No front seat?"

"This is important," he says. Then he takes my hand in his. "Besides, it's four in the morning. Who in their right mind would be up at this time?"

When Giovanni gets into the driver's seat, he shifts the car into gear and pulls away from the curb. I yawn and lean my head against Jacob's shoulder. He shifts our bodies so he can put his arm around me and hold me close.

"Are you comfortable? Are you warm enough? We can turn up the heat," Jacob says.

"I'm fine," I say, snuggling against him. I can't help but yawn again. "It's so early…"

"I know," he says. It's about now that I realize I'm touching him in Giovanni's presence. He seems fine with us, of course, but Jacob and I have never touched each other with anyone around. But before I can ease back and put that familiar distance between us, he leans back into his seat a bit more, inviting me to snuggle a little closer. He's so comfortable to lie against, and he smells good too.

I'm not aware that I've fallen asleep until Jacob jostles me. "Hey, we're here, I think…"

I rub the sleep out of my eyes. It's still pitch black outside. "Where's here?"

"Look around," Jacob tells me.

We're parked in a parking lot somewhere, barely lit by a struggling street light. This place looks *very familiar*, but I can't quite place it. There's a building to our left and a bit of a wooded area to our right.

"Wait," I say. "Are we…are we at the Burger King in Twilight Hollow? Why did you bring me here?"

He gives me a smirk and says, "We are." Then he undoes his seatbelt so he can turn and face me. He takes my hands in his again.

"Again…why did you bring me here?"

He leans forward and kisses my forehead softly. "You have so many bad memories of this place. I wanted to give you a new one. I don't know how to do this boyfriend thing yet, but one of the first things I want to do is to let you know that this place was never good enough for you, and all the bad shit that happened is in the past. So, now, I'm gonna give you something else to remember when you think about this place."

I glance toward Giovanni, who is doing his best to ignore us. I lean forward and whisper to Jacob, "We can't do *that* with Giovanni right here." I chuckle as I say the last few words, while also getting a bit hard at the thought of him railing me again.

"Definitely no sex in the car," Giovanni says, "and it's way too cold for me to get out and give you privacy. No, his idea is much stupider than that."

"It's not that stupid," Jacob says.

"I'm not fending off bears for you."

Jacob rolls his eyes.

"What are you gonna do?" I ask Jacob. My mind is spinning with all sorts of possibilities of what he has in mind, and half of them have me chuckling.

"Bears are hibernating right now. Plus, we're in town," he says to Giovanni. Then he wiggles his eyebrows at me. "I assume it's just back there?" he says, pointing to a little road that goes into the trees. It's not an official road with pavement or even gravel, it's just two tire tracks worn into the dirt with grass growing between them.

"Yeah," I say. "It doesn't really go very far, just kind of around a couple trees where you're out of sight of everyone and everything."

Giovanni shifts the car back into drive and leads us down that tire-beaten path. In no more than a handful of seconds, we're completely cut off from the Burger King. We're right in the middle of town, but totally secluded from it. Giovanni shifts into park.

"What are you gonna do?" I ask him, laughing again. "You can't, like, burn it down."

"It's a stupider idea than that," Giovanni says.

"Yeah, I'm not doing that, even if I very much want to," he says. "I'm doing this…"

He pushes the seat forward and lets himself out of the car, then leans his head back in. "I'll be right back," he says, grinning.

He closes the door and turns around, approaching the big tree beside the car, his breath frosting the air. Then he…unzips his pants?

"Is he…" I say.

"Pissing on the tree? Yes," Giovanni says. "That camera on the back of the Burger King damn well better not reach back here or Linley will have my head."

"It doesn't," I say. "I worked here in high school and figured it out when people would drive behind the building and just disappear for twenty minutes at a time." I watch as he absolutely definitely pisses on the tree. Then he seems to shake the last few drops out, stuff it in his pants, and zip up. I cover my mouth as I laugh, then I say, "This is wild!"

"This is still the stupidest idea he's ever had," Giovanni says.

Jacob hurries back to the car and yanks the door open, but before he can come in the car, Giovanni holds a packet of wet wipes out to him. Jacob takes one and wipes his hands down, and before he can ask what to do with the wet wipe, Giovanni holds out a little trash bag. Then Jacob clambers into the back. His foot catches on something, and he falls onto the seat beside me. I help him roll over and sit upright, then he leans close and kisses me.

"What was that about?" I ask. His eyes are sparkling with triumph, and his joy is infectious. "We drove all the way here for…you to take a piss?"

"It's not just any piss. I'm pissing on all of *them*," he says.

"Who?"

"All the men that treated you poorly, like you were less than important and like you were disposable. No one is going to treat you like that again," he says.

That makes my heart swell with joy. He did that for me. We went on this whole little field trip for me so he can show me what he feels for me.

"I love it," I tell him.

"Gio," Jacob says, "take us back to Edward's place, and then take me to the airport."

"Yes, boss," he says. He carefully backs out of the woods. He then pulls into the drive-thru for Burger King. "You need to get your boy some breakfast after dragging him here at four in the morning. And you need to get me a coffee."

"Deal," Jacob says, passing his credit card forward to Giovanni. "Your coffee can be your tip for watching over Edward while I'm gone."

"He's not going with you?" I ask.

"No, he agreed to stay and make sure everything goes okay with your store and with the team at my place. Besides, I have the rest of my security team there."

"Don't get me started," Giovanni says, glaring at Jacob in the mirror. "If one thing goes wrong, I'll have Barry's ass."

Jacob and I both laugh at his phrasing.

"Not like that," Giovanni says, "you know what I mean."

The drive back to Frosty Bottoms goes a little faster than I'm used to, likely because of the limited traffic at this hour.

When we pull up in front of the apartment, I shuffle away from Jacob, returning those several inches of space between us. The world is starting to wake up, and there are already people out and driving about.

"Come here," Jacob says, tugging me close again.

"But the people…"

"I have tinted windows and I just want to give you a quick kiss."

I open my mouth to say something, but he dives in and kisses me on the cheek. It's sweet and I love it, and it has me glowing when I finally climb out of the car and head into the apartment. It's not until I'm in and the door is fully closed that Giovanni pulls away from the curb to take Jacob to the airport. I watch through the peephole as his car disappears.

When I turn around, I find Chad standing there with his arms crossed and wearing a housecoat over a pair of pajama bottoms. "First, you break my bed, and now you're in and out at all hours," he says. He's trying to play the part of a stern parent or something, but can't hold onto his scolding act, as a smile soon appears. "Where were you anyway?"

I laugh at the memory of it. "He took me to Twilight Hollow. To the Burger King."

"Why on Earth would he…wait…*that* Burger King?"

"You know it?" I ask.

"I was passing through town several years ago and needed some boner-servicing and a local showed me the place." He waves his hand dismissively at the memory. "You're avoiding the question. Why'd you go there? And please don't leave out any inches—I mean, details."

I walk past Chad and sit on the couch. "It's nothing like that. Last night we had a feelings conversation and he was following up on that this morning. Like, making a statement."

"A statement…" he says, skeptically, "with his dick?"

"No. Well, yes, in a way. But no." I stop and make myself start over. "He's heard me mention the Burger King a few times and the types of men I'd go back there with. He wanted to…erase my memory of those guys. He showed me what he thinks of those guys."

Chad pinches his eyebrows in confusion and skepticism. "I feel like you're leaving out details, but it's too early to pressure you for them."

I stand up from the couch. "I can maybe give you details later," I say, "for now, though, I need a little more sleep. Sorry for waking you."

"You didn't wake me; I tend to get up pretty early, even though I go to bed super late. I'll put on some coffee so it'll be hot and ready for you when you get up."

"Thanks, Chad," I say. Then I head to the bedroom and close the door behind me.

I take a moment to assess the damage we caused. The broken bed frame needs to be replaced, and a lot of cleaning needs to happen. I start picking up some of the larger pieces and putting them in a neat pile against the wall.

Then after moving another large piece, my hand freezes. Underneath that piece is my BBL. I put down the piece of wood and pick up the notebook, sitting down on the mattress to look at it.

I flip through the pages and see the list of all the different things that book boyfriends did to care for their love interests, and I see the random scribbling of names of past guys who did one or two or sometimes three things before disappearing or breaking up with me.

I close the notebook and lay back on the mattress, resting it on my chest. Jacob has shown me so much care and affection. The things he's said and done might not be on my BBL, but that doesn't make them any less important, and there are things on the BBL he hasn't done, but those don't really matter anymore. He makes me feel like I'm seen and that he cares for me and likes me—that's what's important.

Plus, he pissed behind the Burger King for me.

No one has ever done that before or even attempted anything else of such significance. He's removing the hold those lame guys from my past have on me. He's freeing me from that past. And that's more caring than anything else in here.

I push myself to my feet and cross the room to the trashcan. I toss the BBL in there without a moment of hesitation. Then I throw more trash in there to bury it. I'm done with that. I have Jacob now, and I'm never letting him go.

After I do that, the doorbell rings, and I head out of the bedroom. Did Jacob forget something here?

When I reach the living room, Chad is already opening the door. I don't see who it is, but before either he or the visitor can say anything, Chad closes the door in the person's face.

"Who was that?" I ask.

Chad's face is red with frustration as he turns around. "A charlatan," he says, walking past me.

Chapter Thirty
Don't Ask Him

EDWARD

"A charlatan?" I echo.

"Wait," a new voice says. I see Lucas has woken too and just came in the room. "Your dad is here?"

"Your dad—our dad is here?"

"Chad, you have to let him in," Lucas says.

Chad is on the far side of the room, standing in the doorway to the kitchen and facing away from us, just shaking his head. "I have to do no such thing."

"Don't be ridiculous," Lucas says, approaching the door and opening it. "Bertrand, come in."

"Lucas, my favorite son-in-law," Dad says.

"Your only son-in-law," he says, then adds almost as an afterthought, "for now."

"Hi, Dad," I say. I get to see Dad as often as I get to see Mom, which is to say not very often. Like Mom, he travels for work, though I've never been entirely clear on what he does. I know he was involved with a multi-level marketing scheme at one point and always went to conferences.

"The son that talks to me," Dad says. He comes in and opens his arms wide, and I go in for a hug. "It's really good to see you, Edward."

"It's good to see you too. It's been so long since we've seen each other."

"Oh, it can't have been that long—didn't I see you on your birthday?"

"Three years ago," I say, wincing.

"No, not that birthday. I mean the one where I got you tickets to that boy band or something."

"Uh, My Chemical Romance isn't a boy band, but, yeah, that was three years ago." I hug him again. "But it doesn't matter, I'm just so happy to see you."

"Can I get you a cup of coffee?" Lucas asks.

"I'd love one," Dad says as we break from our hug.

We sit on the couch in the living room. Chad has moved from the kitchen doorway and is now facing us with his arms crossed. Lucas comes back into the room with three cups of coffee, handing one to Dad, one to me, and keeping the third as he sits down on the chair next to Dad's side of the couch.

"I love what you've done with the place," Dad says to Lucas.

"Thank you," he says. "Chad seems happy to let me play housemaker and decorate. It's much better than the plain walls and Ikea furniture he had before." He gives Chad a look that I interpret to be a little inside joke between them.

"And how have you been, Chad?" Dad asks.

"Fine," Chad replies, quickly shutting his mouth again.

Dad sighs. "Will you sit down? You're like a gargoyle over there."

Chad hesitates for a moment, but then he comes and sits in the chair on the other side of the couch, the one near me. He sticks out his lower lip in a pout.

"Well, I'm here because your mother called me," Dad says to me.

"Yeah? About what?"

"I think you know what. A certain young man I've been seeing all over the news, who I thought I might see while I'm here." He looks around. "Jacob isn't here, is he?"

I shake my head. "You came all this way to meet my boyfriend?"

"Boyfriend?!" Chad shouts. But when he makes eye contact with Dad, he looks away, like he didn't just have an outburst.

"I didn't know you were dating him," Dad says. "Though your mother made it pretty clear that's where it was heading."

"It only became official last night," I say. "And it's kind of secret for now, so this is the first anyone's heard of it." I glare at Chad, the source of much of the town's gossip.

"That's good," Dad says. "Your mother will be happy to hear the update. But to answer your earlier question, I was already in the area for a business deal when your mom called, so I thought I might as well stop by and see you in person."

I used to deflate a little bit whenever Dad would tell me that he had other priorities, but now that I'm older, I'm just happy with whatever in-person time I can get with him.

"What's the business deal?" Chad asks, speaking voluntarily for the first time, albeit in a critical tone. I give him a bit of a scolding look. "You here to see a man about a horse?"

Dad chuckles. "Not quite. I've got a buddy with an overstock of designer handbags that he wants to sell me for cheap. I can turn around and sell them for ten times the price. Quick money."

"Son of a bitch."

"Excuse me?" Dad says.

"Oh, that was Petey," I say. I point at the bird cage on the other side of the room, with a sheet draped over it.

"Oh, right, I forgot about Petey," Dad says. "May I take his sheet off?" Lucas nods.

Dad gets up and crosses the room, gently lifting the sheet and folding it neatly. "Good morning, Petey."

"Morning, whore. Morning, whore. Awrk!"

"Always a pleasure to see you too. Anyway…" Dad says, coming back to the couch. "I wanted to ask how you were doing, since your shop has been getting all that media attention."

I smile and sip my coffee, then say, "It's been going really well. The media thing is a little weird, but it comes with the territory when you're around a celebrity like him, and it's brought a lot of foot traffic to my store."

"Dating a celebrity is hard," Dad says, and Lucas nods knowingly.

"After all, I'm married to a celebrity with your mother being a world-renowned travel writer."

I give him a tight smile, then say, "I'm not sure it's quite the sa—"

"She travels the globe!" he exclaims, interrupting me. "She's won writing awards. She's been a panelist on travel TV networks, for God's sake. I know exactly what you're feeling with that media pressure." He wipes his forehead, and he might…be sweating? From the thought of my mom being a "celebrity"?

"Yeah, it's, uh, it's something, isn't it?" I say.

"But the important thing is that I love your mother. We get through all this craziness together because we prioritize each other."

From different countries? I think. But I don't say that out loud.

Dad puts his hand on my shoulder. "I also came here on a mission from your mother; I'm here to visit your shop and take pictures."

"Really?" I get this swell of excitement in my chest. "I need a shower but we can go right after. I need to do some cleaning before we open since it's been so busy lately."

Dad agrees, and I head to the bathroom. Through the door, I can hear Dad and Lucas talking, and even Chad chiming in now and then, seemingly at least partly over whatever that charlatan thing was about. Twenty minutes later, we're walking through the streets of Frosty Bottoms. When we reach downtown, I take him to BJ's Cookies first.

"I haven't eaten yet, so a snack is necessary," I tell him.

"But cookies? The dad in me says this is a bad idea."

The door jingles as we enter, and I introduce Braden and my dad to each other. We order coffees and breakfast cookies packed with raisins and nuts.

"Are we seeing you tonight?" Braden asks.

"Tonight?" I ask. "Oh, the masquerade at Bottoms Up?"

"Besides my nonna's party, which I know you've also been invited to, the masquerade is *the event* of the season."

"I think we will," I say. "Hopefully, Jacob makes it back in time."

The corners of Braden's mouth twitch into a smile at the word "we".

"I think Kellan's going to stop by later. He has something for you," he says, giving me a wink.

"Should I be excited or afraid?" I ask.

Braden laughs. "With Kellan you never know, right? But in this case, I'd say excited."

He hands our coffees and cookies over, and we wish him a good day. When we exit the shop, I stop us on the sidewalk.

"That's it," I say, pointing across the street. I'm not often over here on this side of Main Street, so seeing it from this perspective is impressive. This is *my shop*. It's bright and colorful, even with all the lights turned off.

"It looks great," Dad mumbles through a mouthful of cookie. I hold his coffee as he pulls out his phone to take a few pics—and while he has it out, he snaps a couple selfies of us—then he texts them all over to Mom. She immediately replies with heart emojis. Dad tucks his phone back in his pocket and says, "I bet you make a fortune here."

"Pfft. There's no money in books, Dad. I just do it for the love of stories. Come on," I say. "Let's get inside."

Thankfully, there aren't any Jacob fans already waiting outside the store, though I'm sure they'll be here soon enough. Part of me wonders if they'll trickle off now that the auction is over and there's no chance to buy him, but then I remember the screaming fans in those videos I watched. He'll always have people searching for him.

"Wow," Dad says, "it looks even better on the inside."

"Thanks. Jacob really made this vision come to life."

"Jacob, eh?" he says, giving me a look before returning to checking out the store. I follow him as he walks over to a hammock chair and sits down in it. A moment later he stands up. "I forgot how easily I get motion sickness." He inhales deeply and then exhales. "Now that it's just you and me, your mother has some ques—I would like to know some more about Jacob." He pulls out his phone and very woodenly reads, "Tell me how you two met and started dating."

I sit down in one of the non-hanging chairs, and he takes the seat opposite me. I break off a piece of my breakfast cookie and swallow it down. "We started as sort of friends because we were always talking to each other on the phone when he was working on my shop." At his confused look, I add, "He was working as a contractor before word got out that he's here. So this was one of his jobs." I then explain to him the unfolding of our blossoming relationship.

I know he's reporting this all back to Mom, and I didn't give her the fullest answers before, so hopefully this will satisfy that writer side of her.

"Cool," Dad says. Then he looks at his phone again. "When can we meet him?"

"Um…as my parents or as fans?" I ask, wincing as I say it.

"Can it be both?" he asks me. "I've watched a number of games and followed his career a bit. But if he's the man who makes you happy, I want to meet him for that reason first and foremost. The soccer fan thing is just a bonus extra, like a gift with purchase on the shopping channel."

"I'd love for you to meet him, as long as you don't make him uncomfortable. Like, don't ask him to sign a bunch of memorabilia that you'll sell." Dad nods in agreement, even if he seems a bit reluctant. "Things are busy right now with opening the store, so when things calm down I'll see how Jacob feels about it and maybe we can set something up."

"Maybe…we…can…" Dad says as he types it in his phone, "set…something…up."

"Does Mom want to know anything else? Or, sorry, do *you* want to know anything else?"

Dad reads something on his phone again, but then he turns it off and shoves it in his pocket.

"This isn't one of her questions, but if I'm reading your mother right, and I can read her pretty damn well, she's worried about you and just wants to know that you're okay. Getting together with a man like Jacob has to be challenging in unexpected ways."

"It is," I acknowledge, "but it's going well, Dad, and I'm fine. Jacob is going to tell the team owner about us today and we'll see how that goes and how he feels about his star player being in a relationship that might sometimes distract him from soccer. After that, he wants to tell the team about us." Thinking back over the past few days, I doubt that the team would have a problem with it, at least the team members that I've met.

Dad leans forward, elbows on his knees, hands clasped together. "Do you care what they think? Does Jacob care?"

"No, I don't. He doesn't." I sigh. "It might make things more difficult if any of them have problems with Jacob having priorities other than just soccer now, but, no…it doesn't change anything between me and Jacob."

"Good, I'm glad to hear it," Dad says. "As long as you're supporting him and he's supporting you, that's all that matters."

I take another bite of my cookie. "Are you sure there isn't anything else Mom wants to know?"

Dad waves his hand dismissively. "Your mother can just call you for the rest."

We finish off our coffees and cookies, and he then helps me mop and sweep. By the time we finish up, there's already a line-up outside the door.

"I didn't realize romance books were this popular," Dad says as he looks out at the people. Some of them have their faces pressed against the glass. I'm going to have to wash the windows soon with all the handprints and nose prints.

"They're here for Jacob," I say, "probably hoping he's hiding in my back room."

Dad looks toward the back room. "He's not, though, right?"

"No, he's not," I say, trying to keep the edge of exasperation out of my voice. I'm glad he wants to meet Jacob, but I don't want it to turn into the fan scenario it seems to be bordering on.

"Ah, well, next time then," he says. "I, uh, I should probably head now, Edward. I have to see a man about designer purses in an hour and it's at least a forty-five minute drive from here."

I give him a hug. "Thank you for coming. I'll see you sooner than three years from now, right?"

"Of course," he says, "though I still think you're wrong about that being three years."

"I have a tattoo to commemorate that concert. I know the date."

Then we head to the front door. I let him out and let in the hordes. I hear Jacob's name murmured and whispered among the crowd, but so far, no one has outright asked if he's here. The first hour or so continues much like this—people coming in with only a small fraction of them genuinely looking for books.

After a while more of this, the bells on the door jingle, and a familiar face comes into my store with a big paper gift bag in his hands.

"Good morning, Snowflake Princess," I say to Kellan.

He gives me a royal bow. "And good morning to you, loyal subject." He comes up to the counter and puts the bag up on it. "Congratulations on last night. That was way bigger than anyone expected and must've made you feel so good."

My face warms with a blush that I hope is subtle and he doesn't catch on to, because my first thought was that he somehow knows about the railing of a lifetime I got last night. But when the memories of sex pass, I realize he means the auction.

"When I planned it, I was hoping for a couple hundred bucks for charity—certainly not tens of thousands of dollars." I chuckle nervously. "I hope I haven't set a precedent for next year."

"Oh, of course not," Kellan says. "This year is an anomaly. The goal isn't to be bigger and better every year, the goal is to have fun and live in to the Christmas spirit. So…did you have fun?"

"I did, I really did." On the night-of, I likely would have said that fun was not part of the evening, but looking back and from the perspective of where I am now with Jacob, the evening had a lot of fun built into it that I could have easily enjoyed if I was in the right frame of mind.

"Speaking of fun evenings…you're going to the bar tonight, right?"

I glance across the street to Bottoms Up. At this time of day it's fully locked up and the lights are out.

"The masquerade, right? I'm planning on it, and so are Jacob's teammates."

The excitement is clear in his voice. "Are you bringing your… friend?"

"Um…" I glance around, ensuring no customers are in earshot. "Keep your voice *super chill and discreet*…but I think you mean…my boyfriend."

If the gleam in Kellan's eyes had a sound, it would be the loudest of screams.

"Your…b—" He bites back a squeal.

"I think he'll come," I say, speaking before he can actually squeal. "But I can't promise anything yet."

Kellan takes several deep breaths, trying to calm himself. Then he puts his hands on the gift bag and says, "Maybe this will help sway things in that direction."

I try to peek in the top of the gift bag, but some tissue paper has been shoved in, and I can't see what's beneath it. "And what's that?"

He pushes the bag in my direction. I pull out the tissue paper, and what's beneath it appears to be a mass of black and white and yellow feathers, all glittery and shiny. When I lift out the item, I see they're two masks, with intricate beadwork woven into the feather design.

"These are *gorgeous*," I say. "We would be penguins."

"Some penguins mate for life," Kellan says. Then, with a wink, he adds, "They're also insatiably horny."

"Where did you get these?" I angle the mask toward the window and the added light so I can see more of the careful detail work that's gone into it.

"Braden's nonna makes our masks every year and she likes you a lot so it didn't take much convincing to get her to make a set for you and Ja— your *boyfriend*." Again, he almost squeals. I give him a stern look to lower his voice. "Sorry," he whispers.

I look at the masks again. "Leora made these?" My heart warms at the thought. "I'll have to give her some free smut next time she's in." I carefully place the masks back in the bag.

He waggles his eyebrows. "She's been telling me all about the porn you've sold her."

"It's not porn, they're romance books."

"I read a chapter, it was like balls-to-the-walls sex. I think the dialogue was all gasps and moans. If that's romance, then I need to read more romance."

I wave toward my bookshelves. "Take your pick. Maybe you'll learn something."

The door jingles again, and the ever-present murmur of the crowds kicks up a notch. I look to see who it is—Jacob's friends have all come in, with Giovanni and Dominic in tow. In the rest of the store, people are pulling out their phones and snapping photos, but no one seems brave enough to go up to them.

To Kellan, I quickly whisper, "He hasn't told his friends yet, so keep that between us."

He gives me a nod with a twinkle in his eyes.

"Hey, guys," I say as they come up to the counter.

Scott extends a hand in greeting, and I shake it. "We're prowling the downtown today looking for masks," he says, "and we thought we'd stop by and check out your place and see Rizz's handiwork ourselves."

"I really love the colors," Gabriella says, "so much pink and purple. It's beautiful."

"Thank you. Jacob wasn't too sure about my choices but he trusted me. I'm glad he did." I then point out some of the features of the place. "He installed all the bookcases, and those hanging chairs too. Before him, this place was an empty lifeless shell."

Brian heads to the nearest bookshelf mounted on the wall and gives it a little tug. He raises his eyebrows and says, "Seems Rizz knows what he's doing."

"Sorry to interrupt," Kellan says, with sparkling eyes, "but did you say you're looking for masks?"

Scott looks at Kellan, then back to me, almost as if questioning who this is.

"Scott, this is Kellan. He owns the candle shop next door and he's the town's Snowflake Princess. He's also friends with my brother, the owner of Bottoms Up, and Jacob's neighbor."

Scott grins and shakes Kellan's hand. "Yeah, we heard the masquerade is banging, so we want to check it out. I want to see Frosty Bottoms's wild side before we head back."

"Do you know where we can get masks?" Tim asks.

Kellan nods. "There's a party shop around the corner there, they stock up on masks at this time of year, specifically because of the masquerade. Just tell them the Snowflake Princess sent you."

"Oh, yeah?" Tim asks. "They'll give us a discount or something?"

Kellan shrugs. "Probably not, but they'll know I got to talk to you and that's the coolest part of everything today."

"I want to look around a bit before we go," Gabriella says. "I should pick up a few things for the long drive south."

"Have a look around," I say. "You'll find little signs on the shelves to help direct you to the different genres and heat levels."

"Heat levels?" Brian asks. "It's a book about kissing, isn't it?"

Gabriella laughs and takes Brian's hand in hers, patting the back of it. "My sweet summer child. Let's go educate you on what's really in these things." She leads him across the store, straight toward the spiciest section I have. I bet she saw the little sign with five chili peppers as soon as she came in.

My phone buzzes in my pocket with a text. I slip it out and see it's from Jacob. *Just landed. I'll let you know when I'm heading into the meeting.*

I reply with a kiss emoji.

When I shove my phone back in my pocket, I look up and find Kellan watching the team and their security with wide-eyed amazement. Then he turns to me and says, "Who ever thought Frosty Bottoms would be the epicenter of hot sports guys? Did you hear that Mayor Dick went out with Scott last night? That's gossip I haven't followed up on yet."

I sigh because I know how much Jacob disliked the Dick and Scott thing. "Kellan, don't you have a store to run? You're forever here or at BJ's or running around town."

"My cousin is watching the shop for a little bit," he says.

"But doesn't she watch the shop always? And you're only there for a little bit?"

"Running a store is a lot of work."

I want to give him some sarcastic reply, but I bite my tongue. "The main event for the Snowflake Festival is Monday, right? You must be excited."

There's a slight panicked look in his eyes that disappears almost as soon as it appears. "Super excited! There are no problems whatsoever. Everything is super peachy. It's gonna be amazing."

I cross my arms and glare at him. "What is it?"

He sighs and almost seems to deflate. "Santa Claus called to give me a heads up that Mrs. Claus is sick, so there's a chance she might be absent—but even worse, there's a chance he might catch whatever she has by Monday."

"I'm sure it'll be fine," I say. "Monday is still a long way away—"

"It's forty-eight hours," he says, interrupting me.

"Which is still a long way away. That's a lot of time for Mrs. Claus to get better and just because his wife is sick doesn't mean he will be too."

He looks defeated as he says, "Maybe. We'll see. I've floated the idea of being substitute Santa past a few people, but I've had no bites yet." When Gabriella comes back toward the desk, Kellan plasters a smile on his face. As Snowflake Princess, I'm sure the pressure is on to create a perfect day.

"Found some good books?" I ask as Gabriella places a small pile of them on the counter.

She glances at Brian. "We did."

"Some of these are his, aren't they?"

She rolls her eyes. "He's too embarrassed."

Brian remains quiet, but his face is bright red like a tomato.

I ring the books through the register—the filthiest books I have in the store, books that might even make Leora blush—and then put them in a bag for discretion.

"I'm gonna ask him," Scott says to Alejo. It's one of those hushed whispers of two people disagreeing but not wanting to make a scene.

"No, man, don't do it. It's none of our business," Alejo says.

"But he might know. And Rizz is my best friend and I have a right to know. I'm gonna ask."

"Don't," Alejo warns.

"You can't stop me, I'm gonna ask—" He cuts off when he realizes we're all looking at him. I cross my arms and wait for him to say what he's going to say. He steps closer to the register. "Edward...you're Jacob's friend here. Do you know where he went last night? He didn't come home. And, of course, Giovanni won't tell me where he went."

I shake my head. "He texted me this morning, that's all I know. That and he's planning to be at the masquerade tonight."

Scott comes closer and lowers his voice even more. "Hopefully, he doesn't think I slept with the mayor. He told me not to bring him home, so I didn't."

I shake my head again. "I don't know what he thinks."

"But it's weird, right?" Scott presses. He turns to his friends and says, "He didn't come home. We all think it's weird, right?"

"We don't think it's weird," Tim says. "*You* think it's weird. And now I'm wondering if you're weird."

"Oh, come on! It's weird that he didn't come home."

"We all agreed before we left that you weren't going to ask," Tim says. "Rizz would be pissed about you asking Edward what happened. He won't like you being in his business. But here we are."

Scott turns back to me. "Does he have any other friends here? I thought you were his only friend. I mean, it's not like he found someone and had a hookup or something." He points to Gabriella. "He didn't even come back after the date with Gabby."

"And he didn't even tell me where he was going," Gabriella says. "He barely talked to me last night."

"So you know nothing?" Scott asks me. "Really?"

I shake my head, feeling bad for lying to Jacob's friends but also knowing he wouldn't want them to know where he was—at least not yet. "Sorry."

Scott sighs. "Alright. Well, thanks anyway."

We all give Scott a moment more in case there's more of an outburst. When there isn't, Gabriella holds the bag of books up and says, "Thank you. We'll see you tonight at the masquerade."

"I look forward to it." I give the team a wave, and they head out in search of the party shop Kellan had mentioned.

When it's just Kellan and I again, I see his eyes are wide and his mouth is open. "Oh. My. God. The drama. Braden's gonna love this gossip."

"You don't have to tell him everything," I say.

"Oh, I do. He might not want to hear it, but I'll be bursting with this till I let it out with someone, so it might as well be him." He looks out the window and watches as the team crosses the street and walks away. "It's so cool," Kellan mutters.

"What's so cool?"

"You know a bunch of guys from the team, like, casually, you hang out with them."

I let out a soft sigh. "They're just people, you know?"

"Edward, there are people and then there are *people*. Those people are *people*."

"That made zero sense."

Kellan's smart watch dings with an alert. "Ah, I have to get across town for a meeting with the mayor for final planning details for the Festival. And gossip on him and Scott."

"So…you're still not going to your store…the business you own and run?"

"No time!" he says as he hurries out the door.

A little while later, the crowds seem to thin out considerably. My phone buzzes with another text from Jacob: *Marco pushed the meeting back a couple hours which I'm sure is some sort of dick power move. Do you have privacy for a call, by any chance?*

CHAPTER THIRTY-ONE
I NEED HIM

Of course! I text back. *Lemme shove all these people out the door!*

As luck would have it, the last person in the shop is heading out at that moment, so as soon as the door closes, I lock it and flip the sign for lunch then hurry into the back room.

Closed for lunch. Call me!

No more than half a second later, my phone is ringing with a video call. When I answer it, I'm greeted by Jacob's gorgeous face.

"Hello, handsome," I say.

He chuckles. "Hello, little mouse. How was your morning?"

"It was interesting! It started with a surprise visit from my dad," I say.

"That's cool. Did you have a nice time with him?"

"I did. And it turns out he's a big fan of yours—I had no idea he'd ever watched a game of soccer in his life."

"I look forward to meeting him someday," he says.

"I'd like that. Anyway, after he left, your friends were all here. They wanted to check out your work…and they also asked me if I knew where you went last night."

"Ah." He fiddles with something off camera, likely just distracting himself as he processes what I said. Then he looks at the camera again and says, "I can't believe they asked you that."

"That's okay. I told them you'd texted me this morning, saying you were going to Miami and you were planning to go to the masquerade."

He gives me a smile. "Thank you. Sorry to have put you in that awkward spot."

"It's no problem, really." Wanting to change the subject to something other than his friends, I ask, "Where are you?" I can't see much of the background around Jacob's head, but I do see glimpses of walls in a very spacious room.

"I'm at home for a bit. Well, my house in Miami." He stretches his arm out a bit to give me more of a view behind him. He spins around slowly, showing me what looks like a *massive* living room. It's almost the size of his entire house here in Frosty Bottoms.

"It looks gorgeous," I say.

"Maybe, but it feels empty for some reason. I don't remember it feeling like this before." He walks through the house and swings his phone around a few more times, giving me glimpses of his kitchen, what looks like a video gaming room or home theater, and the entry foyer. "But my favorite room is up there."

"Oh, yeah? What room is that?"

"My bedroom," he says. The phone shakes around as he goes up the stairs and down a hall, taking me into his bedroom. He flops down onto the bed, holding the phone above him. "I'm so pent up, I'm just gonna lay here until it's time to go."

"That bed looks comfy," I say.

"It's comfortable, but it would be better if you were here beside me."

I feel a tug at my heart when he says that; he's only been gone a few hours and I already miss him. It's weird looking at his bedroom thinking that he has this whole other house there.

"I wish I was there, too. I could help with you feeling so pent up...maybe release some of that tension."

"Yeah?" he says with the hungriest grin I've ever seen on his face. He flips over so the phone is resting on the bed and he's above it. The view is exactly what I see when he's on top of me.

My cock is already throbbing at the sight of him. "Mmmhmm, but, Jacob…I'm in the store."

"You said you're on lunch. The door is locked, right? You're in the back room?"

I can feel the heat rising in my body, making me feel flush and warm. "It is, and I am." I let my hand slide down to my crotch, and I grope myself through my pants.

"Edward…" Jacob says, his voice low and sultry. "I want to see you… All of you."

God, this man turns me on so much. I'll do absolutely anything he asks.

I prop the phone on the shelf in front of me and then push the chair back to give me some room to stand up. The lighting in here is actually complementary for once, highlighting the parts of my body and face that I love best.

"Take your clothes off," he says. I hesitate, looking around the room, and he says, "You locked the door. No one is gonna come in."

I quickly strip off my clothes.

"Tsss, you're fucking sexy… Your body," he growls, looking at me.

"Are you getting naked too?"

"For you, little mouse? I'll do anything." The camera shakes as the bed jostles from him tearing off his clothes.

"I want to see more of you."

"What do you wanna see?" he asks, holding the phone over his face.

"Everything…" I'm already finding it hard to breathe, just looking at him.

He hovers the phone over his gorgeous abs, slowly moving over the delicious ripples of muscles, down the line of hair leading to his thick hard cock. "One sec," he says.

He props his phone up on something—maybe his clothes—and sits against the headboard. His cock stands tall and proud between his legs. Fuck, I need that in me—mouth or ass, doesn't matter, as long as it's in me.

"God, Jacob…" I say, squeezing my cock, urging it to calm down. I'm gonna come before we even start.

"Your hand is already on your dick… Good boy," he says. "You like touching yourself?"

I nod, slowly stroking myself. "But, I like it better when you do it."

"We'll do it together," he says. I watch as he spits in his hand, making eye contact with me before gripping his cock.

"Fuck," I breathe out. I want him to spit in my mouth, to spit on me. I stroke myself faster imagining it.

He's stroking at the same pace, eyes locked on me. "Yeah, exactly like that. That's so good…"

I keep rubbing, but with my other hand I fondle my balls, lightly tugging at them. "I need you, Jacob," I moan. "I need you inside me."

"Fuck, I need that too," he says, then bites his lip.

His hand is moving faster and mine is too—I can feel my orgasm building, watching his hand sliding up and down his cock, just imagining it's inside my mouth.

"More," he says. "I want you to come for me."

I find my hand moving faster up and down my dick, my grip getting tighter. "I'm already so close."

"Mmm…I like that…when you're close, it makes me fuck you harder, makes me drive in faster, deeper, makes me want to come in that perfect little hole…"

"More… Tell me…" I beg. My breath starts to quicken, and I feel my heart racing, while I pump my hand faster and faster.

"I want to come so deep inside of you that you taste me for days, fuck you so hard you can't walk, make you scream my fucking name…"

"Ngh…Jacobbb…" My body spasms as all my muscles tighten and it's like a star explodes in my core and energy and light and heat fly out from me. I lose my sight temporarily. And when I blink and it all starts coming back and the rush of endorphins subsides, I see my cum splattered all over the floor and the shelf in front of me, even on the image of Jacob on the phone.

"Fuck…" Jacob moans, jerking himself faster, harder, and leaning further back into the headboard. A few moments later, cum flies up from his cock, splattering across his abs and chest. He lets his hand fall to his side as he gulps in breaths of air.

"You make me want you…" he says, breathless. "I want to be with you, wherever you are. I just wanna hold your hand."

"I want that, too. I want my boyfriend here with me," I say, still a bit in shock that this perfect man covered in cum is mine.

"I'll be there as soon as I can," he says.

We end our call shortly after so he can go and clean up and head to his meeting with Marco. I get dressed and pull out my cleaning supplies to make this back room spotless again. And when all evidence has been sanitized away, I head out into the store, finding a line-up of people waiting to come in.

   JACOB   

My phone vibrates loudly when I step out of the shower. I glance down to see Linley calling but send her to voicemail until I can get dressed. I almost forgot how big my closet is here, well I forgot how big everything is really. Why *does* it feel so much bigger? Maybe bigger isn't what I'm feeling?

I grab my navy suit out and walk back inside my bedroom, looking around while dressing. It's gorgeous outside, and the sky is so blue. I'd gotten used to the constant gray skies of winter in Vermont, so the sunlight coming in through the window feels amazing. I really love the view here, I forgot how nice it is to be able to look outside at the ocean. It's so peaceful and calm, I can't wait for Edward to see it.

I turn away from the window, and take a deep breath, while grabbing my phone, but before I can call Linley, I see a text from her.

Meeting starts in an hour. I'll see you there.

I chuckle looking down at my phone. Now that I'm fully dressed and staring at it, I can't believe I just did that with Edward, that was my first time having phone sex. I don't know if he noticed how many times I almost dropped the damn phone, but he was just so sexy, that I started fumbling. I don't think he noticed, though. On the plus side, I'm definitely much more relaxed now. Oof. Thinking about him covering his phone in cum makes my balls tingle a bit... I need to get out of my bedroom. I can't stand in here and think about that anymore, or I'm not gonna want to leave for my meeting.

Since I have a bit of time before I head to Marco, I should take a walk outside to check on the pool and maybe the boat, too.

Everything is so bright and open here, there's so much space. Walking downstairs, I feel like the staircase is longer than I remember. Or maybe it's just taking longer to reach the bottom? I hesitate on the last step, looking around at the large foyer. Empty, it feels empty—that's what this feeling is. My house in Frosty Bottoms isn't even a quarter of the size, and lately there have been all kinds of people in it, and when the team wasn't there, Edward was there. Is this how I'm going to feel any time I'm away from him? No, that's ridiculous. I'm sure it's just because I haven't been here in a while.

I disarm my security system and step outside. There's a nice breeze coming off the water today. I glance down at the pool, everything looks good—the cleaners have done a good job keeping up with it. Don't know why I was worried about that, but with it being an infinity pool, I was kind of nervous, because there are so many extra steps to take.

"Jacob Anthony!" my mother's voice shouts from behind me. I turn to see her closing the slider door behind herself. "What are you doing here?!" she shouts, coming toward me with a large beach bag tossed over her shoulder.

"What am *I* doing here?" I ask. "I think you're saying the wrong thing. I live here, the question is, what are *you* doing here? Did you come here to use my pool? You have your own pool. No wonder the guys have been taking good care of it." I smile at her, and she hugs me tightly, smelling strongly of bananas and coconut. I look down at my suit once we separate. "Ah, is that sunscreen I smell?" Damn it, now I'm gonna smell all fruity.

"It's tanning oil, actually." She whacks me with her bag. "Yes, I'm here to use your pool. It's so much bigger than mine. I've been checking on it a few times a week…and maybe using it. The question is, what are *you* doing here? I didn't know you were coming home. When did you get here?"

"I'm not really here, just here for negotiations, then headed back to Vermont. Hopefully, just a quick signing of papers. Marco already acted like a jerk, though. Wanted me here first thing this morning, then pushed the meeting off. I'm leaving in a few minutes."

She places her bag down on one of the lounge chairs beside the pool and crosses her arms looking at me. "Why wouldn't you think to tell me this? I saw you last night on the news with Gabby. I know you're not interested in her, so why did she pay $50,000 to go out with you? So desperate for a rich girl."

"She wanted to know what happened with Doug, so she paid to basically corner me into telling her. Come to find out it was Scott that told him what happened."

"Che idiota! What is wrong with him? Now look at what a waste of time this has been. All the effort you put into protecting him and the team and yourself—and he was the one who did it? I'm gonna smack him when I see him—after I ask him if he slept with your father, of course." She puts a hand on my shoulder reassuringly. "Your father said they didn't, but the day I believe your father again, will be the day my mother disowns me."

"I don't want to hear about Dad and Scott. But, honestly, I'm not upset about Scott telling Doug. Sure, he was stupid for doing it, but because of that, I met Edward and I'm finally happy. I've never met anyone like him… I actually asked him to be my boyfriend last night, and I'm gonna tell Marco about us today."

She sits down, dramatically holding her chest. "Boyfriend? Jacob, listen to me. You've never been in love, these are big feelings you're having but you certainly don't mean to tell me that you're going public with a relationship? Your career, honey… People love you because you are available, if you become unavailable, things are gonna change. Besides, he was like a scared little thing at your house when I met him, and I've seen him on the news, how is he gonna handle all of this? And what's he gonna do when you move back here? You'll need to be back here permanently in a few months, what then? You haven't thought this through," she says.

"Don't. Don't tell me how to live my life, or try to tell me what's best for me. I'm done listening to what everyone else thinks is best." Jamming my finger against my chest, I continue, "I know what's best for me, and what's best for me is him. I don't care what you, or anyone else thinks about it. Call it first love, call it infatuation, call it whatever you want, but the fact remains, I'm doing this with him, and I don't give a shit what anyone else thinks of it."

She looks a bit taken aback by all of that, which is fine by me. I suspect the next conversation will go the same, so I really don't care.

"Jacob, take a breath. I know you haven't felt this way for anyone before, but really look around you, look at what you've built, everything you have. You can't throw it all away like this."

For some reason, I feel so angry I could cry. "Mom. I don't need any of this, this house, this life, anything here, but I do need him."

She sighs, looking around. "Well, if that's how you feel about it, I can't really stop you." She stands and squeezes my face, giving me a pensive look. "I do want what's best for you. If you think this is what's best, then I don't have any right to try and stop you. I just hope you've thought it through."

"I have. I want to be near him, and I'll do whatever it takes to make it work. I want to be the one that makes him happy. I just—I want to hold his hand, Mom. I don't want to hide him."

"Alright, alright," she says, lightly smacking my cheek.

My phone is vibrating in my pocket, and I pull it out to see that the car is here to take me to Marco's. "I gotta go. If Marco drags things out past this evening, I'll be back, otherwise I'll talk to you soon."

This conversation with Marco and Linley has been going in circles for what feels like hours, but the giant clock on the wall tells me it's only been an hour.

"I don't have a problem with you being in a relationship. I have a problem with that relationship getting in the way," Marco reiterates for the thirtieth time.

"It's not going to get in the way," I reassure him, yet again. "You want me to say nothing is going to come before soccer, but can *you* say that soccer comes before everything? I was eighteen when I said that. Of course, Edward will, in some instances, come before soccer. I'm just being honest. But I do think it's kind of stupid to have to say it out loud. It's not like I'm gonna be missing games, or practices. Your wife and kids come before soccer; it doesn't make you any less invested in the club."

He leans back in his chair pillowing his hands behind his head. "Well, speaking of family, I'm glad we got that business about Gabriella straightened out. If you would have just told me that you weren't involved, I would have spared you. There was no reason to keep it all a secret when you had nothing to do with it. Of course, Scott and the others might not have been so lucky. Still though, the punch, that can't happen again. It was like you didn't even remember you were part of a team. That's the part that makes me nervous. What will happen if someone says something about your boyfriend? Will you forget that you're part of a team? That this is your family, too?"

"No," I say firmly, bringing a small smile to Marco's face.

It's quiet inside the office, and aside from the strong smell of his cologne, it's good being back here. There's a tinge of excitement at knowing that I'll be playing soccer again soon, and I already feel better just from telling him about Edward. Saying the words out loud was really so freeing.

Linley has been pretty quiet for the past thirty minutes. She doesn't like the fact that I'm laying it all on the line here, but really, I'm not asking for much. I can tell she's getting ready to crack though. She crosses her arms and leans forward in her chair. "Marco, respectfully, he came here because you asked him to, first thing in the morning, and he's gonna hop back on the jet as soon as this meeting is over, does that sound like he's putting his new boyfriend before his obligations? Does that sound like someone not committed to this team, or this family that you've built? He'll have spent eight hours on a plane today, just because you asked him to, just because he wanted to respect you, and be honest about what was going on. I don't think the boyfriend would have wanted him doing all that. Think about it."

I kind of want to correct her and say that Edward was in full support of this, but it's not the time. Especially given the change in Marco's posture.

He gives her a smile of approval and turns the contract papers toward me. "Sign them," he says with a grin.

We've already gone over them, so the smile that covers my face at this being over, is one that can't be contained. I have a boyfriend, a new thirty-million-dollar contract, stake in the club and things honestly have never felt better. I sign my signature on the line, sounding out my name as the pen glides across the paper.

"Done!" Marco says, clapping, then stands to shake my hand.

I stand across from him and give him a smile, while shaking his hand in return. "Thank you for trusting in me. I won't let you down."

"Ah, I know you won't," he says, coming around the desk. "But don't forget you need to finish off that community service. You have a good three hours left, so make that work." He points to Linley. "Pretty sure she fudged some numbers but let's get one more thing on the books before we announce your deal. I have a few candidates dropping by for coaching interviews, and I'd like to be able to tell them you saw it through."

"I can do that," I say, smiling at both him and Linley.

He pats my back and squeezes my shoulder. "Good. We want the golden boy of soccer back on top. No punching people or doing anything crazy."

"Oh, are we adding things on?" I ask facetiously. "I *should* tell you I pissed in the back of a Burger King this morning, but I won't do anything like that again." I reach for the doorknob, giving him my thirty-million-dollar smile, and add, "Also, I'm going to a masquerade party at a gay club tonight, but I'll behave. Thanks again," I say before walking out.

Chapter Thirty-Two
His Boyfriend Is Me

   JACOB   

After another four-hour flight, which I may have slept all the way through, and quickly getting dressed at home, Gio pulls us in front of Edward's brother's place.

"Alright, superstar, you ready for this? After you bring him out here, you've got only about ten minutes before the world sees you holding hands with someone. Not too late to change your mind."

I grab the bouquet of flowers I brought for Edward off the back seat and shake my head at Gio. "I'm not gonna change my mind. I just wish I had a different mask to wear, since I wore the wolf one at Halloween. Lowkey hoping he wears the same one, though. You have no idea how cute he looks in his mouse mask." Thinking of Edward in his mouse mask quickly brings back all kinds of feelings, but I have to remind myself that I absolutely cannot have sex with him in the bathroom again.

"I don't know how a grown man could look cute as a mouse, but whatever makes you happy. He's gonna love those flowers, though. I don't even like flowers, and I like them."

"Yeah, I'm so lucky that you were able to pick them up. Alright, be back in a second," I say, stepping out of the car. My breath frosts in the air on the way to the door. Why do I feel nervous all of a sudden? I ring the doorbell and take a step back. I can't wait to see him.

The door opens and Edward smiles brightly at me, backing up so I can come inside. "What—How? Are those peonies?" he asks. "I mean, hi, you look really good. I saw you this morning, and yet, you're here now and you're hotter? And holding my favorite flowers?"

The look on his face was well worth the begging I had to do to get Gio to pick these up. I pass him the flowers, then nod at him, kissing him quickly. Our tongues touch, and I can feel the heat spreading throughout my body. I missed him and I've only been gone since this morning. The taste of him, I want it permanently stained on my lips.

With my hands on his waist, I squeeze him lightly and pull back. "We should really get going. If I don't stop kissing you, we won't be going to that party."

His cheeks are red when we separate; it's the cutest thing I've ever seen.

"I love peonies," he says, turning toward the kitchen. "Where did you even find them? They're not even in season." He's rummaging through cabinets looking for something.

"Pretty boy! Pretty boy," Petey squawks.

"Petey, you better stop flirting with my boyfriend!" Edward shouts, still looking through cabinets. "I wonder why he doesn't say the really dirty stuff to you?" He giggles, then pokes his head out of the cabinet, looking at me. "So, where did you find the flowers?"

"Ah, I asked Gio to see if he could help track down a place that had them. We finally found one, I guess the florist has them imported a few times a month. We got lucky that he'd just received a shipment. If I'd known for sure that Marco wasn't gonna drag the negotiations out, I would have ordered them this morning, but I wasn't sure how things were gonna go."

"Found one!" he says, pulling out a tall glass vase from a cabinet. "Thank you for going through all that trouble. I've never had anyone bring me flowers before," he says while filling the vase with water. "I can't believe you remembered my favorite flower, and these are so bright and beautiful. The pink is the prettiest pink I've ever seen."

"Of course I remembered your favorite flower. That was one of the first things you told me. We were talking about different shades of pink for the shop, and you said, peony pink was your favorite, which led to you realizing there were a bunch of different shades of pink peonies, then into telling me peonies were your favorite flower."

He gives me a smile when he turns the tap off and sets the vase up on the counter. "That's right, I remember that. I felt so stupid after that conversation. You were making me nervous in all kinds of ways. Especially your morning voice, those early morning check-in calls, your voice was all gravelly and grunty," he says with an overexaggerated shudder.

"Gravelly? I remember thinking how cute you sounded, it's funny to think you were nervous all those times. Sounded pretty confident to me."

"Well," Edward says, "I wasn't. But, I actually have a surprise for you, too. Well, it's not my surprise so I can't take credit for it, but it's still a surprise."

He walks toward the living room, and I follow behind him. "I'm intrigued, what is it?"

"Ta-da," he says, holding up two very fancy looking penguin masks. "You like them? Leora made them for us."

"Leora? That's Braden's nonna, right?" I take the mask from his hand and rub my fingers on the bright yellow feathers. "She just decided to make them for us? Or you asked her to?" I'm a bit stunned, even though I shouldn't be, people here are always doing nice things for each other without being asked to. There are no ulterior motives with the people in Frosty Bottoms, everyone really goes out of their way to help everyone else. It's completely different in Miami, I don't even know any of the other people in my neighborhood. But that's more of a security thing. People in the neighborhood know I live there, but I prefer to keep to myself.

"Kellan asked her to make them. He said he had a feeling about us. Not that it was very hard for him to figure out, of course," he giggles moving in for a quick kiss.

"Well, I'll have to thank her and Kellan too. Macaroni penguins are my favorite, so this is actually perfect," I say.

"I didn't know they were macaroni penguins, but Kellan did say something about them mating for life." He pumps his eyebrows at me, then grabs his coat off the couch, tossing it over his arm. "Giovanni probably has the heat on, so I doubt I'll need this, but I should bring it just in case," he says and opens the door.

When we get out to my car, Edward hesitates as I reach for the door handle. Not sure what that's about. He's looking around the car like he's lost something. "What's wrong?" I ask.

"Giovanni is usually holding the door open for you. I was just surprised not to see him. Is it too cold?"

"Ah, this is our first date, I want to be the one opening doors for you."

He hangs his head back dramatically. "You're not real," he jokes. "I must be in a coma somewhere."

I swing the door open and watch his cute little ass climb into the back seat. I climb in behind him and smile at Gio.

"Hi, Giovanni," Edward says. "Thank you for hunting down the flowers for me. They're gorgeous."

Gio gives him a smile and a dismissive wave, while he backs out. "Technically, *he* found them, I just drove there and picked them up, and negotiated with the florist, which was way more intense than you would expect. But your boyfriend wanted to make sure you had your favorite flowers for your first date, and he's nothing if not determined when he decides to do something for you. You don't wanna know how much he paid for those," he says, shaking his head. "Not that it matters to him. Wouldn't catch me spending that much money on a first date, I can tell you that."

"Alright, alright, we get it, you're cheap," I say, patting Gio's shoulder from the backseat.

Edward's mouth moves to the side like he's deep in thought. He opens his mouth to say something, but doesn't, instead he pats my leg and buckles in.

I'm too curious to let that go. Besides, I want everything to be perfect for him, so if there's something he needs, I want him to be comfortable saying it. I cover his hand with mine. "What were you about to say?"

"Nothing, it's just, you said this was our first date, and Giovanni just said it too, but I always thought *Elf* was our first date. Was that not a date? It was the first place you invited me to."

"No," I say, shaking my head. "Well, yes and no, but it wasn't the same, you weren't my boyfriend, and we couldn't even hold hands. Besides, if you're going by that logic, the night your store opened would have been our first date. I invited you to my place, remember?"

He crosses his arms shifting in his seat. "Actually, by that logic wouldn't Bottoms Up have been our first date since I invited you into the bathroom?"

"What?!" Gio shouts.

My head drops at that, and I chuckle. "Nothing, it's nothing. We just hooked up in the bathroom there before we knew each other."

Gio's body tenses and he points in the mirror. I can almost see the heat coming off him. "Edward is like family now, I'm not holding this in. You little shit! Do you know how worried I was about you? And I told myself there was nothing to worry about because the one thing I know about you is that you're not going out, getting in trouble anywhere, and somehow you were banging guys in bathrooms?" He shakes his head at me. "I think it's time I finally kick your ass."

"Woaahh," I say. "One guy. This guy, and we've already talked too much about this. That was private." I turn to Edward who is still giggling at Giovanni's outburst. "And you can call any of those things our first date, because you are the boss, but *I* am going to call this our first date because I've never asked anyone on a proper date before. You're also my boyfriend now, so this feels more like a real first date."

He lays his head on my shoulder. "I'm so happy to be with you. I don't care which one we call our first date."

Gio is still shaking his head at me when he pulls into a parking spot behind Bottoms up. "Stay close to me, okay? I hate this whole idea. Look at this place," he says, gesturing to the parking area around us, full of cars and people. "And definitely no bathroom business. Don't forget that Marco told you to behave."

"I'm not planning on making a huge scene," I say, while putting my mask on. "It'll be fine. Besides, we're just two gay penguins at a gay bar."

Edward puts his mask on and squeezes my hand. "If you don't want to do this, you don't have to," he says softly. "We can still be boyfriends even if you decide you don't want to tell everyone while we're here."

I know he's being serious and that was very sweet, but I can't help but laugh out loud. "I can't take you seriously, I mean, you're cute for saying that, but the little feathers on top of your mask are just flipping around from the heater blowing on it." We both giggle a bit at that, then decide to step out of the car.

I don't feel too nervous walking through the parking lot holding Edward's hand, but I can tell that he and Gio both are. *Should* I be more nervous about this? No, that's ridiculous. I'm just telling my friends that I found someone I really like, what's there to be nervous about?

The doors are wide-open, and people are pushing past us while we walk inside, with Gio leading the way. I don't see the team yet, but I know they're already here. There are so many people in full costume, which feels weird since it's a masquerade. A Christmas masquerade is a weird idea anyway, but I'm pretty sure I just saw someone dressed as a pink flamingo, complete with a pink feathered bodysuit. Maybe the masquerade idea just morphed into this sort of second costume party. The music is so loud inside and there's barely any room to move.

"This way," Gio says. "Doritos told me they blocked off the end of the bar and a few tables for the team."

Edward squeezes my hand tighter, and I change my grip, threading our fingers together. We approach the bar from the side, and I see Scott sitting at the bar behind a roped off area, there are two empty seats to the left of him, and Gabriella and Brian are sitting on his right. I don't see Tim and Alejo yet. What the hell are those white feathery masks they're all wearing? Maybe they're swans?

I pull Edward along with me, and Gio opens the roped off section, moving the little red velvet rope to the side. "See? Where the hell is this clown?" Gio asks, looking around. "Got the owner's daughter over there, the goalie, Shadow—who knows where the other two are, but common sense would tell Doritos to stay here. Drives me crazy," Gio grumbles.

Now that we're walking past the barricade, people are starting to stare, it's almost like one by one they're realizing that it's me behind this mask. Chad smiles brightly at us while we're walking up to the bar. He's wearing a very large lion mask, but the bottom half of his face is visible. Gabriella notices me before Scott does, she's tilting her head to the side looking at me. Scott turns his attention toward her, and Edward and I walk beside him, standing on his left.

"Well, well, well," Chad says. "Who do we have here?"

I'm not sure why he's talking like that, or why he's shirtless in December, but Edward and I give him a wave. Edward hops on one of the empty stools beside Scott, leaving the one next to him for me.

Scott spins to the left, looking me up and down. He sips his drink then laughs, I don't think he's noticed that I'm holding Edward's hand yet. He's probably having a hard time seeing—I know that I sure as hell am. "Was not expecting you to show up in a penguin mask," he says. "Where did you find that?" He leans back, looking around me at Edward. "He has the same one? Did you guys buy them together? They look handmade."

Edward loosens his grip on my hand, seemingly trying to give me an out if I need it, but I'm not taking it. I squeeze his hand beside me, just waiting for Scott to notice. "One of the locals made them for us. Kind of amazing because I didn't even tell her I liked macaroni penguins."

I don't know how much he's hearing because he's not really reacting to anything, so he's either in a bad mood or he's just not adding anything up yet.

Chad is leaning across the bar talking to Edward; I can hear him ordering a drink.

"Do you like our masks?" Scott asks, leaning his head next to Gabriella's, which makes Brian lean forward too.

"What are you supposed to be? Swans? Or ducks?" I ask.

"Cranes!" Gabriella shouts. "Like the team, hello?"

I chuckle at that. "Of course you're Cranes. I was so confused wondering why you would all be wearing swan masks."

"Nothing to be confused about, what we're dressed as makes sense," Brian says. "One of the bar owners is dressed like a gazelle and the other one, well, he's there," he says, pointing at Chad. "He's a lion, and a couple times we've seen the two of them all over each other. Not sure which one is the predator in that relationship." He lifts his beer for a drink and shifts his gaze back to the bar.

"Your penguin masks are so cute!" Gabriella shouts. "Don't you just love this place? Reminds me of Dirty Peaches back home. Peaches is bigger, but this is a really nice place. Oh! and there's a costume contest and a dance contest tonight, Shadow says he's not entering. He's too upset about his failed conquest."

"Shut up, Gabby," Scott says playfully.

Gabriella rubs his back and leans on his shoulder. "Aww, poor Shadow didn't get to fulfill his dream of banging a politician." She lifts her head looking at me. "The mayor wouldn't give it up."

Oh, thank goodness. I didn't even bother asking my dad what happened when we texted earlier because I knew for sure that within five minutes of being around Scott, I'd get the full story.

Scott smiles looking over his shoulder. "You know, when you pay for someone at an auction, there's an unspoken rule that you get to sleep with them. I don't know what his deal was, wouldn't even let me touch his dick, couldn't get him to kiss me either. I'm sure he's at least somewhat open to guys because he was kind of flirting with me but then, I tried to—"

Aaaand he noticed that I'm holding Edward's hand. There it is. Scott pulls his mask off, eyes wide and gestures animatedly toward our hands. "What, what, what?"

"Are you stuck?" I ask him.

"What the hell are you holding his hand for? You can't be—you're not—are you? Oh my God, are you?"

I pat him on the shoulder. "I'm gonna need you to use your big boy words if you want to have a conversation, buddy."

Gabriella and Brian are whispering through giggles.

Scott takes an overexaggerated breath in, making a calming motion with his hands, when he exhales. "Why are you holding his hand?" he asks through a fake smile.

I look down at our clasped hands, then turn to Edward, who has just been chuckling the whole time. "Boyfriends hold hands, right? I thought we were supposed to do this?"

Edward nods, with his gorgeous white smile showing.

"Boyfriend says we're supposed to hold hands, so we're holding hands," I say.

Gabriella is shaking Scott dramatically. He appears to be frozen in place with the dumbest look on his face.

"What do you mean?" Scott asks.

I shrug at him. "Boyfriends hold hands."

"What do you mean?" he repeats.

Edward tugs on my hand and I lean in close to hear him. "I think he's having trouble processing," he says. "Just be nice to him. He *was* just rejected by the mayor last night, now he's finding out that his idol—I mean best friend, has a boyfriend. That's probably rough."

I nod at him, then turn back to Scott. His mouth is still wide open and he's just staring at the two of us. I put a hand on his shoulder. "Are you okay, for real?"

"No," Scott says. "I don't understand. His boyfriend is you?"

"Yes. His boyfriend is me."

"*You* are his boyfriend? You said he had a boyfriend… That boyfriend is *you*?" he asks.

"Scott, we're together. This is my boyfriend, Edward." I lift our hands up showing him.

Lucas makes his way over standing across the bar in front of us. His mask is amazing, there are big horns coming off it. "Edward, Jacob, nice masks," he says, then points at the two of us like he's realized something. "Oh. My. Gosh. Jacob and Edward! It's like the gay *Twilight* remake!"

I giggle and Edward shakes his head. "Other than the names being the same, there aren't any other similarities. Definitely not gay *Twilight*."

Lucas points at Gabriella. "She said her name was Gabriella, that's kind of close to Bella…"

"Have you even seen the movies?" Scott asks, suddenly pulled from his trance. "Gabriella isn't interested in either of them. Other than the names, there's nothing else similar."

"Well," Lucas says. "At our Halloween party, Jacob was dressed as a wolf when he met Edward, so there's that."

Scott's mouth drops open looking at me. "You dressed as a wolf? For a Halloween party at a gay bar? Was it the mask from my *Twilight* party?" He rubs his temples, then picks his mask up from the bar. "The betrayal… Wait, how did you end up at a Halloween party? And how did you, of all people, approach a guy at a bar? You're never interested in anyone. What the hell?"

"Grindr," Lucas says.

I hang my head back and cover my mouth, looking at Edward.

"Thank you, Lucas," Edward says.

"Oh my God," Scott mumbles. "I don't even know you anymore. Gone for a few months and you're a different person… I tried to convince you to use Grindr so many times and you said you would never…you said you would *never*, Jacob. How did this happen?"

Edward laughs loudly, then turns to me. "Now, this is one I actually want to hear the answer to," he giggles.

"Ahhh, not you, too?" I say looking at Edward. "I don't know, Scott. I was really stressed out and like you said, you were always trying to get me to use it. And I mean, I guess it was just fate, I don't know. Edward wasn't even living here yet, so it couldn't have been anything but fate." I continue recapping our relationship up to this point, and Scott listens, completely engrossed in the story.

Once everyone is caught up, I smile at Edward squeezing his hand tightly.

Scott shakes the ice around in his drink. "Never have I ever heard someone describe a hookup in a bathroom so eloquently. 'Twas fate that you railed this man in the bathroom," he says, raising his drink.

We all giggle at that, and Gabriella leans forward. "Hey, Edward, I'm sorry about paying 50K to go out with your boyfriend last night. That was probably uncomfortable. I wouldn't have done that if I knew you were together."

Edward scoffs a bit. "I wasn't worried about it. He had the option of you long before he knew me."

Brian lets out a laugh at the end of the bar. "And here I thought Rizz was rude!"

I thought it was pretty funny, but Gabriella's mouth is wide open, and she looks a bit unsure how to respond.

Edward leans forward looking at Gabriella. "Was that rude?" he asks innocently. "I didn't mean it to be. I was just being honest."

"Uhhh, it was a little rude, yeah," Scott chimes in. "I mean, he technically had the option of anyone in the world before he met you, so no reason to make Gabby feel bad about it. I feel bad about it, though. You're hot, but damn, you got my best friend holding your hand in public, calling you his boyfriend… I don't know how you did it, but good for you. I tried many nights to cross that bridge but I was refused entry every single time." He looks around the bar. "Speaking of, do you think Dick is here? He told me last night he was gonna come. I wanna take one more shot at that before we leave tomorrow."

Disgusting. The thought of him wanting to have sex with my dad is absolutely disgusting. I'm sure my dad is here, but since I can't say he's my dad, I'm just gonna pretend I have no idea who he's talking about. "Who is Dick?" I ask.

"The mayor, man. You must be close with him since he helped keep your secret the past few months. You probably have his number saved in your phone. Can you just text him?"

Chad taps the top of the microphone from behind the bar. "Alright, everyone, first up is the dance contest, so, all contestants, this is your five-minute warning to get to the middle of the dance floor. Anyone not dancing, we'll need you to move back so that everyone can see the contestants. Five-minute warning," he repeats.

Lucas takes the mic from his hand and places it on the bar, wrapping his arms around Chad's waist. "You're not dancing here tonight," he says.

"No, I only dance at home and I would never *dance* at someone else's house," he says looking at me. "But maybe Jacob wants to show off the moves he used that broke the bed last night," he jokes, sticking his tongue out flat.

"What?!" Scott shouts. "Whose bed did you break? You had a foursome? With his brother?!"

Edward spits his drink out. "No, God," he chokes out through coughs. "What the hell, man?"

I feel a hand on my shoulder and before I can turn to see who's touching me, Gio removes the hand. "Don't touch him," he warns. "I'm gonna need you to back up."

"Woahhh, it's me, Giovanni," my dad's voice says. I turn and see that my father is the very same pink flamingo I saw when I walked in.

Damn it, I don't even want to look over at Scott. This is so awkward. I was feeling so relaxed too, well I was before the—wait, why have I been so relaxed? This whole thing has been a trainwreck. Edward squeezes my hand, and I instantly realize why I was feeling so relaxed. It's because he's been holding my hand this whole time. He hasn't let go once. I smile softly at him, and squeeze his hand back.

"Sorry about that, Mayor Dick," Gio says. "Can't have people touching him. Even if you are the mayor. Lucky I didn't tackle you."

Scott stands beside me, it looks like he's pretending he doesn't know my dad is standing right there. He's just stretching his arms out, obviously trying to show off his muscles. "Oh," he says, feigning surprise. "I didn't see you there, Dick. I love your costume."

My dad looks at me, then turns to Scott. "Thanks, I like to go all out for these parties. I'm actually needed on the dance floor, though. So, I'll see you around. Good to see you, Mr. Rizzo," he says, turning away from us.

Scott sits back down defeated and throws his hands up. "See? What the hell was that about? How can he not be attracted to me? Also, with you guys wearing masks being right next to each other, there's a real similarity in the eyes. Weird. I noticed it last night too. Obviously, he's nicer than you, but you do kinda look like him."

Edward pats the stool beside him, urging me to sit down. I move the stool closer toward him and take a seat. Behind us the dance contest is starting, and we all swivel around.

Tim and Alejo finally join us with Dominic following close behind.

"Before you talk to Rizz, he has a boyfriend now, and it's him," Scott says, pointing to Edward. "I know you're both shocked, but yes, Edward is Jacob's boyfriend. They're together now."

"We're not surprised. Picked up on that a few times," Tim says. "You don't pay attention to people, do you?"

Scott looks around confused. "What do you mean? Of course I pay attention to him."

"Be serious," Alejo says. "Shadow, come on, he was at his house at five am for the gym, he came out to dinner with us, the guy literally stopped by the park to talk to him. Also, Tim and I were pretty sure we heard Rizz talking to him in his bedroom the night we all went out. Why do you think we were telling you not to bother asking Edward about him not coming home last night?"

I guess we weren't being as discreet as we thought. Scott is just staring at me with that dumb look on his face again.

"Oh, Mayor Dick, with the moves tonight," Chad says into the microphone.

There are too many people crowded around the dance floor. I can't see anything from where I'm sitting, not that I want to anyway.

Lucas has a bottle of vodka in his hand. "Let me make you guys a celebratory drink," he says standing in front of Edward and me. "White Russians." He pours the alcohol into two glasses along with the other ingredients then slides them over.

"Jacob doesn't really like to drink," Edward says, to which Scott nods in agreement.

"Wait, Lucas, what are you saying we should celebrate?" I ask.

"Your relationship, of course. We didn't get to celebrate last night since Edward forced us to leave after the bed breaking debate."

I reach for the glass and nudge Edward's toward him.

"Are you really gonna drink that?" Scott asks.

"Of course I'm gonna drink it. It's to celebrate my first boyfriend." I lift the glass and tap it against Edward's, then take a sip. Whoo, that's strong. I smile at Edward. "Wow, it's been so long since I had vodka. I should have warned you before I drank that, but vodka usually makes me kind of goofy."

"Goofy?" Scott asks. "When did that happen? Man, now I'm gonna have to get a boyfriend, too."

Tim and Alejo approach the bar, sitting on the stools that Brian and Gabriella were sitting in. I didn't even notice that they left. "Back to the matter at hand," Tim says, looking down the bar at me. "When are you coming back to Miami?"

Edward smiles at me, then sips the rest of his drink. He doesn't look nervous at all. I know he's okay with this conversation now.

"Not sure, honestly. Marco wants me to come meet with the new coach when he signs him, but he hasn't decided on one yet. I plan on bringing Edward down there soon so he can check everything out. Don't know which will happen first." I finish off the rest of my drink and slide it next to Edward's empty glass.

"I'm speechless," Scott says. He swivels in his seat looking out at the crowd. "Ugh and this freaking mayor, treating me like I'm not hot enough for him. Give me his number," he says, elbowing me.

"No! Let it go, man. He's old, who cares if he doesn't want you."

"Jacob!" a voice I can't place calls out. I feel a hand on my shoulder, and Gio quickly removes it.

"Son of a bitch," he grumbles. "You can't touch him! I don't care if you know him."

Two people touched me tonight. I'm gonna give him so much shit about this later. Now is not the time, though.

"Apologies, Apologies," the tailor says.

"It's fine," I tell him.

Edward spins in his chair to see who I'm talking to. "Oh! I remember you, Chester! The suit looked really good when he wore it last night."

"Ah, yes," Chester says. "They covered the whole auction on the news last night." He looks me up and down and gestures to my body. "When you have a canvas like that, it hardly matters what kind of paint is added to it." He chuckles at himself. "But I'm here about the corset. How did it fit? You like?"

"Corset?! Scott shouts. "Rizz! A corset? For you or him?"

"Shut up, Scott. I'm not answering that."

"I will," Edward says. He's looking at me like he's seeking my permission.

I shrug at him and hold my hand out. "Be my guest."

"The corset is for me," Edward says. "But I haven't gotten a chance to wear it yet. Hopefully soon. Tonight?" he asks, rubbing my leg.

I don't get embarrassed easily, but I'm sure that if this mask weren't covering my face, everyone would see how red my cheeks are. His hand on my leg, and the thought of him in that corset is doing things to me. I absolutely can't get hard in this bar right now…and yet, it's happening.

Scott, once again, is sitting there in shock.

"Oh, wonderful!" Chester says. "Well, if either of you would like to model it, or maybe a joint modeling session, my partner and I would love that. We're looking for someone to use in a few ads. Oh, but that probably would be frowned upon because of your career, I suppose."

"Don't think that's even on the table. He's only just decided to come out of the closet today," Scott says.

Edward pulls his head back at that and tilts his face looking at me. He looks so cute in his little penguin mask. "Technically, he *has* been out of the closet, he just hasn't been in a relationship, right? More so that it didn't come up because he wasn't interested in anyone else. Am I wrong?"

This vibe coming off him is insanely sexy. I don't know if he's feeling more confident because we're officially together, or because something changed in him now that people know we're together, but this self-confidence is crazy attractive. He's just saying how he feels without holding back, and that's such a turn on.

"No, you're not wrong, baby," I say. Oh.My.God. Did I just call him baby? I think I may have said it once during sex, maybe, but…but…it just slipped out. Wait, he's smiling at me, maybe he liked it?

A chorus of cheers and claps mercifully pulls everyone's eyes from me. "That does it!" Chad says over the speaker. "The winner this year is Mayor Dick, beloved by all and banged by many. I don't know if he's offering bathroom sessions tonight, but we all know where his office is and how much space there is under his desk on Monday, if not!"

What's worse? What's worse? Calling your new boyfriend baby or hearing your boyfriend's brother talk about what a slut your father is? The latter probably. Maybe.

"Monday is a city holiday," my dad says, taking the mic. "I would like to thank all of you for coming out tonight, always a pleasure to be here. A special shout out to the men from the Miami soccer team." The guys raise their drinks in salute from the bar. Except for Scott, of course, who is just pouting at this point. "It was nice to have Mr. Rizzo here to ourselves for a while, but he certainly looks much happier over there with his friends."

"With my boyfriend!" I shout over. "Happier with my boyfriend!" I shout again, holding our clasped hands up. Edward squeezes my hand tighter and leans his head against my shoulder. The crowd cheers, and my father smiles brightly from beneath his ridiculous flamingo mask.

Chad takes the mic back from my dad, and I feel Edward's lips graze my ear, along with the tickle of a feather on my cheek. "If my brother says something stupid, I'll make it up to you tonight."

"Has he not already?" I say turning toward him. This is the closest our faces have been since we got here, and as much as I like the penguin masks, they're definitely hindering my ability to kiss him right now. That's probably for the best, though. Holding hands in public is one thing, but people will really go crazy if I kiss him.

"We'll head into the costume contest in about an hour," Chad announces. "For now, we can do some open mic karaoke. Anyone that's interested can go see that sexy little gazelle at the bar. No funny business, though. I'm looking at you, Mayor Dick."

Edward's chin is propped on my shoulder, and I turn toward him. "Does that count? He did talk about my dad... Seems stupid to me."

"Doesn't count. That was pretty tame. The night is young, though, and I see Kellan and Braden over there. If they end up coming over, my brother is bound to say something stupid."

Scott is just mumbling to himself while drinking something blue and frosty looking. "Corsets, boyfriends, penguins…what's next? Dancing on the bar?"

Edward looks at me and bites his bottom lip. "Now, *that*, I would pay for."

I grab the drink that's in front of him and down it. No idea what that was, but it was strong. "Lucas!" I shout down the bar, hopping off my stool. "Can I hop up here?"

"Jacob, don't! You do not want to hop up on the bar. Stop playing, you know you're not gonna do it," Edward says, giggling.

"He's not going to hop up on the bar," Scott says. His eyes widen. "Wait, are you? Bro, are you?"

Lucas is walking toward me with the mic in hand. Am I really gonna do this? Well, if I am, I can't wear this mask, that's a quick way to bust my ass. Mask in hand, I turn to Edward. "Do you think I won't do it? You said you wanted me to."

"What song do you wanna sing?" Lucas hands me the microphone, then wipes the bar top down with the towel.

"He's not gonna do it," Edward says, pulling on the mic. "Jacob, be serious."

Gently, I lift the mask off his face and smile at him. "Watch me. My boyfriend said he wanted me to do it, so I'm gonna do it," I say, lifting myself onto the bar.

The crowd beneath me is cheering and whistling, like this is completely normal behavior when this is actually insane for me to do.

"Jacob!" Gio shouts moving toward the edge of the bar.

A song I recognize from the nineties starts to play, but I can't quite place which group it is. Somehow my brain knows the lyrics. Edward is looking up at me smiling, while pretty much everyone else is taking pictures with their phones.

The words leave my mouth effortlessly, and before I know it, I'm singing to Edward in front of an entire room full of people who are singing along with me. The smile on his face and the feeling in my chest are both worth whatever reaming that I'm gonna get from Linley and Marco tonight.

People are waving money at me, catcalling me down the bar, but I'm only up here for one person, and he's…waving money at me, too?

"Get up here, little mouse," I say, reaching a hand down.

Edward looks side to side a bit hesitantly, then lifts himself up onto the bar, standing beside me.

Fuck it. Let everyone see this, too.

I pull him in close and kiss him deep, and hard, running a hand up through the back of his hair, while the other is wrapped around his waist, holding the mic. Our bodies are pressed against one another, our tongues, moving wildly, while the alcohol mingles between us. He tastes so sweet, my boyfriend tastes so sweet… "Jacob," he murmurs, slipping off my mouth.

I pull back, breathless, and press my forehead against his, kissing him once more. I lift the mic between us. "Before I hop down, I want to introduce my boyfriend, Edward, he owns Hot for Plot, the bookstore across the street."

Edward smiles and waves bashfully, then tucks himself against me, wrapping his arms around my waist. Keeping an arm around him I talk to the crowd, "I just want to thank everyone in the town for being so supportive and helpful over the past few months, I'm not quite ready to leave Frosty Bottoms just yet, but I'm truly grateful for the way the community embraced me."

"Take your pants off!" a voice shouts.

"Take it off, take it off, take it off," the crowd begins to chant.

Edward pulls the mic from my hand. "He is not taking his pants off, and he's not impregnating anyone either," he says giggling. A few people let out a couple of boos but most are just laughing or clapping. He passes the mic to Lucas and takes my hand in his, and together we hop off the bar.

"Let's go try out that corset," he whispers to me.

CHAPTER THIRTY-THREE
A TREE FOR YOU AND ME

 EDWARD

We, in fact, did not use the corset last night.

We hurried home shortly after that. If Giovanni weren't in the car with us, I would have ripped Jacob's clothing off him then and there, just like in my favorite book, *Taxi Cab of Lust*. Between dancing on the bar and publicly claiming me, I was ready to be defiled by this man in every way possible. When we finally reached the house, Jacob and I ran into the bedroom, we'd torn each other's shirts off, and tugged his pants halfway down. I was digging around in the closet for the corset when we heard the noise of the team coming in.

"Damn it," Jacob had muttered, pulling his pants back up. We both put our shirts back on and went out into the living room to join them.

The team was chatty, and we ended up staying up with them for a few hours.

When we all finally broke and went our separate ways to sleep—and I didn't need to leave and then sneak in the window this time—I followed Jacob into his room, and we closed and locked the door.

Even though it was incredibly late, he fucked me hard. So hard, I had to bite the pillow to stop from squeaking.

Now we're all awake and looking a little worse for wear—us for what we did, but the rest of the team for their late night at the masquerade. I'm not quite walking right today.

Jacob's friends are heading back south, so they're home in time for Christmas. The house is a flurry of activity as they all pack up their bags and try to straighten up behind them.

"Have you got everything?" Jacob asks the group. They're all standing by the front door with a collection of backpacks and small suitcases on the floor around them.

"We do," Scott says. Then he turns to the others and says, "I think?"

Everyone takes a moment to double-check their bags, and they all chime in that they've indeed packed everything.

"And if you forget anything, I can get it sent over to you," Jacob says. "Or bring it when I go back to Miami."

Scott gives Jacob a little pout. "I know you're coming back soon, but I'm gonna miss you."

"We're all going to miss you, buddy," Tim says.

Scott gives Jacob a hug, and Jacob half hugs him back.

"I'm glad to know he's had you here with him all this time," Scott whispers to me when he hugs me. "I'm only a little jealous, now." He gives me a playful wink.

When all the goodbyes are done, I sidle up beside Jacob and put an arm around his waist, and he puts an arm over my shoulders. We follow the group out onto the front step and watch as they load up their van. We wave goodbye one more time as Dominic turns on the vehicle and drives away.

After they turn the corner and are out of sight, we step back into the house.

"Finally, we're alone…" I say, pulling Jacob closer to me and planting a kiss on his lips.

He kisses back, hard and hungry, but when he breaks from the kiss, he says, "Well, almost alone. Gio's still here."

"Oh…" I say, my smile fading. "Right."

He kisses me again. "He doesn't care. He'll ignore us."

"It's hard to ignore you when you're so loud about it!" Giovanni shouts from the kitchen.

Jacob giggles and rests his forehead against mine. "It's fine, really," he tells me.

"I'll get used to it."

"Besides, it'll be different when you visit Miami," he whispers. "He'll be in the guard house. So you can make all your little mouse noises and he won't hear a thing."

I look up at him. "I can't wait to see your place in person."

"You'll love it, I know you will. I want you to feel comfortable there."

My heart flutters at that, and I feel a bit lighter too. We haven't really talked about what our plan is, but I know Jacob wants to bring me to check out Miami sometime after Christmas.

"Come on," Jacob says, taking my hand in his, "let's get some coffee in you and then figure out what we're gonna do today. I have a few ideas."

He leads me into the kitchen and then brews me a cup, using a machine that I think Giovanni had set up when he moved in. Giovanni is sitting at the island with a coffee of his own.

"I'm so glad Doritos is gone," Giovanni says. "He's like walking chaos."

"I thought he was alright," I say. "Seems like a nice guy."

"I'm not saying he's not nice," Giovanni says, "just that he doesn't bring his A-game to the job. When you're protecting guys like your boy here, it's a full time commitment."

I look to Jacob and find him wrinkling his nose. "What's that smell?" he asks.

I inhale deeply. "I'm not smelling anything. But I don't have the greatest sense of smell."

Giovanni inhales deeply too. "To be honest, boss, all I smell is Doritos."

"The chips or the man?" Jacob asks.

"The man. He has a certain greasy smell to him, like he doesn't use soap."

Jacob inhales deeply again. "Ah, that's it…but it's not just Dominic. I can still smell Scott's cologne." He sniffs again. "Everywhere. God, it's gonna take forever for that to go away."

I breathe deep one more time, and I think I can smell what they're pointing out.

"That man never truly leaves a place," Giovanni says. "His body may be gone but his smell isn't."

Jacob waves his hand in front of his face. "Who do I call to deodorize the house? Do you think I can get a cleaning company this close to Christmas?"

"They might charge higher rates for a rush job," Giovanni says, "but it'd be worth it."

"Um..." I say, interrupting them, "couldn't you just open the windows?"

Jacob shakes his head and looks at me. "Wouldn't all the bugs get in?"

"It's December, you don't need to worry about that," I say. "You don't open your windows in Florida?"

"The windows at my place don't open; they're as big as this wall."

"Well, with these, you just leave them open until the smell is gone."

"You can do that?" Jacob asks.

"There's no law against keeping them open."

I put the coffee cup down on the island and walk to the window at the wall behind Giovanni. "You just"—I open the latch and lift the window up—"do this. And then you open at least one window on the other side of the house so fresh air blows through." They watch as I go to one of the living room windows and open it. Instantly, the breeze passes through the house, bringing in the crisp cold air of winter. "But since it's December you don't want them open too long because it'll make the house too cold."

When I return to the kitchen, Jacob says, "I didn't know my boyfriend was a genius."

"I don't know what I'm more shocked about—that you didn't know you could just open the windows for this or that your windows are the size of this wall," I say.

"Things are different down there," he says, while filling his water bottle and taking a sip. "What do you want to do today? We have that party at Leora's tonight, but we still have the whole day ahead of us."

"Hmm…well, I—"

"Wait!" Jacob says, interrupting me. "Before you say anything else, you said the other day you wanted to get a tree. What do you think about doing that today?"

"When did I say that?" I ask. I have literally no memory of it, but if he says I did, then I must have.

"You were, uh…tipsy when you said it at Tony's the other night."

I laugh at that. "Well, if I start asking for Christmas trees when I'm drunk, then I guess I don't get too wild." I peek around the corner to the living room. "That'd be perfect! When your mom was here, she said—"

"I still can't believe he met your mother and survived," Giovanni says, shaking his head.

"I think she might like him," Jacob says.

"Based on what?" Giovanni asks.

"She let him help make dinner."

Giovanni looks stunned.

"Anyway…she said this place needed a tree and that kind of stuck with me. Besides, Christmas is two days away and it doesn't look like it in here, aside from the cabinet ribbons and a few other things. And—I'd really like to have a real tree for our first Christmas together."

"We'll buy a real one today," he says. "And I'll need a stand and probably some more decorations. I only had enough for that small fake tree."

I love the fact that he'd already thought this out. I can't even remember saying it to him, but he was planning to do this for me, just because I said I wanted it when I was drunk. He's the most thoughtful man I've ever met. I put down my coffee cup and smile at him. "It'll be a nice date with just the two of us."

"And me," Giovanni says.

My smile falters. "I forgot you have to come."

"Way to make a guy feel welcome."

"I meant to say I'm looking forward to us having a nice date with a third wheel tagging along."

Giovanni narrows his eyes at me. "I think you're getting too comfortable with me."

"He means it in the nicest way possible," Jacob says to Giovanni.

"Ohh…okay. I'm totally unfamiliar with 'third wheel' being used in a positive sense," Giovanni says deadpan. But he gives me a wink to know he got that I meant it as a friendly poke and not an insult.

A little while later, the three of us bundle up for a chilly morning in Frosty Bottoms and then head out to Jacob's car. He sits in the back with me again while Giovanni drives us around.

"Where to?" Giovanni asks.

"There's a Christmas tree lot out by the community center. Let's go there," Jacob says.

No more than fifteen minutes later, Giovanni pulls into a parking spot on the street in front of the lot. He gets out and pushes his seat forward so Jacob and I can get out, then he follows us, staying close behind as we wander through the trees. They're all bound in netting, so it's hard to tell the shape, but a lot of them look lush and green.

"Do any stand out to you?" Jacob asks.

"I think I keep getting drawn to that one," I say, pointing at a tall one in the corner of the lot, leaning against the fence.

"I was eyeing that one too," he says.

We walk toward it, holding hands, with my shoulder bumping into his with each step, and our shoes crunching in the snow under our feet.

A guy that works here seems to have picked up on our interest because he heads our way. "Good evening, fellas, looking for a tr—holy shit, it's Jacob Rizzo."

I wince at how loud he was, then glance around, but it seems we're his only customers at the moment, so there are no rabid fans (other than him, I guess) to spoil this moment. Jacob seems rather unaffected by the whole thing.

"Sorry," the man whispers. Then at a normal volume, he says, "Did you find a tree you like?" He still looks like he's brimming with excitement though.

"We're looking at that one," Jacob says, pointing at the tree that drew us forward. "We'll take it."

"Wait," I say. "I used to Christmas tree shop with my grandparents; you don't buy a tree without examining it." To the guy, I say, "Can you cut it open?"

He grins. "Of course. I was going to suggest that anyway." He pulls out his box cutter—which I see makes Giovanni come and stand beside Jacob—and with a quick slash, the netting falls away. He reaches into the tree to grab the trunk and shake it out. A moment later the branches all fall into place.

Holding Jacob's hand, I lead him around the tree. "And you want to see it from all sides to make sure there are no bald spots or anything."

The tree looks gorgeous on the front and sides, but we both stop when we reach the back. There's a big gaping hole like someone had cut a bunch of branches off.

The worker comes around to see what we're looking at. "Oh, yikes," he says. "This is not the tree for you. Here, let me put this one down." He leans it against the fence and dusts his hands off. "Maybe I can help you find the perfect tree. What's gonna make you the happiest? One that's really full and thick but might be a bit shorter? Or one that's got some real length to it, though it might be a little on the skinny side?"

I glance at Jacob, and I see he's working as hard as me to not bust out laughing.

"It all, uh, it all depends on how it's used, right?" I say. "How it fills the space and all that. Jacob, do you prefer a, uh, *girthy* but stubby tree to fill your room? Or one with length but on the slender side?"

"I feel like I'm the wrong one to answer that question. That's more of a you thing."

"Girth. Girth all the way," I say.

"Perfect," the tree guy says, seeming to totally not be getting the dick innuendos. "I have one over here that I've been hoping goes to the right home." He leads us across to the opposite corner of the lot and pulls a thick tree out from the line-up against the fence. "I opened this once for a family with a small house and they said it was beautiful but far too wide for their small living room." He slices the net open, grabs the trunk, and shakes out the branches.

"This one is definitely wider," I say. "And it's really filled out on the front."

I follow Jacob as we do a circuit around the tree. "It seems full all around," he says as we return to the front.

"Your living room is large enough to hold it," I say. "I think it would look really good in that corner by the window."

He looks at me with a warm smile. "You're right." To the employee, he says, "Sold!"

"Perfect," the man says. "Do you need any supplies like a tree stand or lights?"

"Definitely a tree stand," Jacob says. "I should have enough lights at home."

"Great! We've got stands by the checkout. Follow me." He leads us to the checkout desk, and while we're there, he pushes the tree through a netting machine to wrap it up again. From a little shack, he pulls out a simple metal tree stand and hands it to me.

"How much?" Jacob asks, pulling out his wallet.

"A hundred for the tree and twenty-five for the stand, but for you I could do everything for seventy-five," the man says.

"No discounts, I'm more than happy to pay full price. Thank you so much for your help." When the man sets up the machine, Jacob taps his card on the reader.

Jacob takes the tree, and suddenly looks at it with concern. "How are we getting this home?"

"You usually tie it to the top of your—oh…" I say, "you probably don't want it riding on the roof of your Mustang, scratching it and getting sap on it and making it smell like pine."

"No, it's okay," he says. I can tell it's not a hundred percent okay, but he's trying to hide it. "Getting this home is important."

"I don't mean to intrude," the man says, "but my shift ends in a couple hours when my brother gets here. I've got a truck and could easily drop it off at your place. No charge; I'm just happy to do it for you because your games bring my family such joy."

Jacob agrees and gives the man his address, and says if we're not home by then to please leave it by the front door.

We pile back into the Mustang, and when we're all buckled in, Giovanni says, "Where to, boss?"

Jacob looks at me. "We still need decorations. Any suggestions of where we might go for those?"

"I don't know the town as well as you," I say. I think back over the past week of all the businesses I've seen and heard about. "Oh, wait…that antique store where we bought those ornaments from. They had a lot of Christmas stuff and prices seemed decent."

"Oh, right," Jacob says, snapping his fingers. "Dusty Balls, right?"

"Yes, I think that was it," I say.

"This damn town and its damn names for everything," Giovanni mutters as he pulls away from the curb.

"I still can't get used to the names here," I say, more to Jacob than to Giovanni.

"The way almost everything has a sexual double entendre?" Jacob asks.

"Bottoms Up, Dip Your Wick, BJ's Cookies, The Twelve Inch Italian, Pump 'N' Go, and Sticky Bunz are just a few of them," I say. "I guess I expected the stores to be more Christmas themed, not so much butts and dicks themed."

Jacob shrugs. "You named your place Hot For Plot, that's not sexual."

"Are you serious? You think Hot For Plot isn't sexual? It's got hot right there in the name."

He gives me a kiss on the cheek. "Well, I've discovered that you look cute when you get a little hot over books."

"Wait…what did you name your contractor business? Now that I think about it, I only remember seeing your dad's name when I paid you online. Is there an actual business name?"

He looks slightly embarrassed, but then he says, "I just called it Jacob's Contracting and Fix-It."

"That's not too bad," I say.

"But all my signage says 'expert erector, licensed and insured.' I realize now what it sounds like, but at the time it seemed so harmless."

"Expert erector, licensed and insured," Giovanni repeats from the front seat. "Are you crazy? You're never leaving my sight again."

Jacob holds his hands up in surrender. "I'm not planning to run away or start a business again. Once was enough." Then he whispers to me, "Though doing that led me straight to you, so it worked out well in the end."

"Alright, you two, we're here," Giovanni says, pulling to a stop on the street in front of the store.

We exit the car and walk up to the building. "Ohh…this is cute," I say, pointing at a pink bench just outside the door. "This matches the pink in the store perfectly. I should get this and maybe put it by the low-level bookshelves."

Jacob whispers into my ear, "If we take it home, you propped up on your hands and knees would put you at the perfect height for railing you from behind."

"I don't think it would match your house, though," I say, not playing too much into him, "so at home we'll have to keep using the bed."

We giggle and then head into the store. The Christmas ornament section has gotten bigger since we were last here. We start digging through stacks of boxes, occasionally pulling one out that might be promising, with Jacob shaking his head at most of them.

"What about this one?" I ask, lifting the lid off a box filled with naked Santa ornaments. I close the box and put it back. "Never mind. How about these ones?" I open the new box, revealing brightly colored ornaments.

"Those are cute," he says.

I look in the box again. "I think what's drawing me to them is that they look a lot like my grandparents' ornaments."

"Oh, we're definitely getting these ones then," he says. He grabs a second box of the same ornaments. "Your face lights up when thinking of your grandparents, so I want these happy memories floating around as much as possible."

"You mean it?" I ask. I'm a little floored that he'd bring in my grandparents as a reason for him to buy ornaments for his house.

"Of course," he says.

I then notice he's holding an ornament in his hands. It looks like a blown glass classic-looking elf. He dangles it in front of his face to look at it in the sunlight coming in through the window.

"Whatcha got there?" I ask.

He looks at me with a smile. "I've always been drawn to elf ornaments, not really sure why. This little guy is cute and I think I want to take him home."

I step closer to him and rest my head on his shoulder. "I think he'd look perfect."

"You're right, this will be perfect on our tree," he says. "I think we have enough ornaments between these and what we have at home. What else do we need?"

"You said you have lights, right? I think the only thing missing would be garland," I say.

"Used garland?" he asks. "There's something weird about that."

"Can I help you gentlemen?" a voice asks behind me. I turn around to see the older woman who staffed the checkout desk when we were here last. "Oh, Jacob, it's good to see you again. And, you're Edward, right?"

"We just bought a tree," Jacob says, "but I don't have a lot of decorations, so we're fixing that problem. We're wondering if you have garland?"

"I do," she says, turning around but not taking a step. "Right here." She pulls out several packages of garland.

"Oh, I thought they'd all be used," Jacob says. "These look like they're unopened."

"The used stuff gets all tangled and dull looking. For the new stuff, people buy it and don't use it and eventually donate it here, so we've got quite the selection."

"What do you think?" I ask, holding up several packages of gold garland. "It would probably go really nicely with those ornaments."

"Sold," he says.

The lady leads us to the register and rings our purchase through—and we also buy the pink bench sitting out in front of the store and arrange to have it delivered to Hot for Plot—and soon we're back in the car and heading to Jacob's place.

"I can't wait to decorate the tree," Jacob says. "I've had housekeepers do it the last few years and it was my mom doing it before then. I think the last time I decorated a tree was when I was probably ten years old."

"Aww…" I say, "little Jacob decorating a tree sounds cute. We didn't really do it much because my parents were always travelling, but I helped my grandparents whenever I could. They'd always throw on some Christmas music and my grandma would bake cookies while my grandpa and I got the tree put together."

"Gio," Jacob says, leaning forward, "can you take us to Stuff Your Face Hole? We need to get some groceries."

"You got it," Giovanni says, putting his blinker on for the next intersection.

"We need groceries?" I ask.

"We're making Christmas cookies."

"But…can you even eat them?"

He kisses my cheek. "They're to make you happy more than anything else."

A few minutes later, we're parked at the grocery store and climbing out of the car. It's crowded here.

"Wow, so many people," Jacob says, pulling his beanie down a little further. "Wasn't expecting that. I normally get my groceries delivered."

I take his hand and pull him through the crowd. Giovanni follows as close as he can.

"I don't know what you have at home, so we'll have to get everything." I take him to the baking aisle and in Jacob's arms, I stack bags of flour and sugar, as well as packages of baking soda and vanilla. "Come on, we need butter and eggs still."

"Why are there so many people here?" he asks.

"It's a Saturday and it's the weekend before Christmas. Everyone is getting their weekly groceries, plus whatever they need for Christmas dinner," I say. "Eggs have to be by the dairy, which is where we'll find the butter too."

"How do you know what we need for cookies?" he asks. "Do you have a recipe memorized?"

I laugh. "No, I don't, but these are basic baking ingredients. If you have these, you can make basically any kind of cookie. I was thinking of some sugar cookies, which will need all of this." When we get to the eggs, I pull out a carton and check that none of the eggs are broken, then go further down the aisle for the butter.

"Oh, candy canes," Jacob says. "I want some for the tree."

"I think I saw some back by the mandarin oranges in the fruit section." We cross the store and come up to the candy cane display and find Kellan and Braden standing in front of it, sorting through the boxes.

"They have to have them," Kellan whispers to Braden.

"They might not. I don't see them very often. Remember, last year's were some special mistake order Rachel had; she didn't get them here at the grocery store." He holds up a box. "What about these ones? Would they do?"

Kellan looks at them and shakes his head. "Nowhere near big enough." He walks around to the other side of the display, looking through the boxes on that side. "There are other kinds over here. Still not seeing the right ones though."

Braden goes around to that side, but before he looks at candy canes he finally spots us standing beside them. He elbows Kellan.

"Why are you elbowing me?" Kellan says.

"We're not alone," he says out the side of his mouth.

Kellan suddenly looks up at us like a raccoon caught mid-theft. "Uh, hi," he says. "Hi, neighbor. Hi, neighbor's friend." He puts down a box of candy canes.

"Nope. They're boyfriends now, remember?" Braden says to Kellan.

"Hi," I say. Jacob just grunts something vaguely like a hello.

There's an awkward silence, then Braden asks, "Looking for candy canes?"

"Yeah," I say, stepping forward and picking up a box. "Jacob bought a tree today, so we're decorating it when we get home."

"Oh, that's cute!" Kellan says. "It'll be your first Christmas together. Our first Christmas together was special."

Braden glances at the ingredients in our hands. "Are you baking something?"

"Cookies!" I say. "Sugar cookies, most likely."

"You, uh, didn't want to order them from a bakery? Like a cookie shop that might be having a sale right now?"

I give Braden a smile. "Just recreating some traditions. My grandparents baked cookies while decorating the tree."

"That sounds sweet," Braden says. "Do you have a recipe? If not, I could text you a good one."

"That would be amazing, thank you," I say.

"Speaking of thank you," Jacob says, speaking up for the first time since we ran into them. "We wanted to thank you, Kellan, and Braden's nonna, for making our masks for last night. It was very generous of her." After he says the words, he visibly clams up.

"I'll pass the thanks on to Leora," Kellan says. "She talks about Edward and the store constantly, so it wasn't a hard sell to get those masks made. I think she already wanted to make them but was waiting for someone to ask."

"We'll be sure to thank her in person at the party tonight," I say.

"Yes, we'll see you there too," Braden says. Then he says to Kellan, "Come on, let's leave these two to shop and go find that special cat food for the boys for Christmas."

"Before we go," Kellan says, "can I have a hug?" He opens his arms wide, inviting Jacob in.

Jacob shakes his head.

Kellan rolls his eyes but he giggles too. "See you boys tonight."

They give us a little wave and then hurry off in search of cat food, but as they walk away, I distinctly hear them saying something about the size of candy canes.

"What the heck was that candy cane stuff about?" I say as I watch them.

Jacob puts his hand at the small of my back. "I have no idea. And I'm not sure I want to know."

"Anyway…" I pick up a box of rainbow colored candy canes. "What about these ones?"

"They're perfect," he says.

"I think that's everything…ready to go?" We turn and head toward the cash registers, Giovanni close behind.

Chapter Thirty-Four
Say It Again

Giovanni turns the corner and takes us into Jacob's neighborhood. A few minutes later, he's pulling up the driveway.

"The tree is here," I say, pointing to the front door as we pass it and enter the garage.

"Perfect," Jacob says.

We get out of the car and go through the garage, dropping off the cookie ingredients, Christmas ornaments, and garland on the kitchen island. We then head to the front door and open it.

"That really is a massive tree," I say.

"But it'll be perfect in here," Jacob says.

I look at him with a smile. "You're using that word a lot today—perfect."

He wraps his arms around my waist and kisses my nose. "How could I not? Everything about this day has been perfect. We have the tree, the ornaments, the cookie ingredients…and you as my boyfriend. What more could a guy ask for?"

I want to say something dirty that he could ask for, but I see Giovanni standing nearby, so I keep my mouth shut.

I'm pretty sure Jacob can read my mind, though, because his eyes go dark with lust. It's only there for a moment because it quickly fades and we pull the tree and stand into the house.

"Let's set the tree up first," I suggest, "and then we'll make the cookies and come back to decorating the tree. That would give it time to settle into place first. What do you think?"

"You know what I want to say, right?" he says.

"Perfect?"

"Perfect."

We set up the stand where we want it to go, and then, with a pair of scissors, we cut open the netting around the tree. The branches all fall down at once, nearly knocking me over, but Jacob catches my arm just in time, while holding the tree with one hand.

"Thank you," I say.

While Jacob turns the tree inside the stand, I get down on the floor on my back and scoot underneath it, adjusting the screws so the tree stands straight and tall.

"Is it stable?" I ask.

"Hang on, scoot back, I'm gonna let go."

I see his feet back up a couple steps, and the whole thing sort of tilts to the side. He rushes forward to catch it before it all comes down.

"Let's try again," he says. I loosen all the screws, and he rotates the tree a little bit. "I'm holding it as steady as I can."

I start tightening the screws again. My wrists are getting cramped from all the twisting motions and the confined spaces. "How about now?"

He lets go and backs up a few steps. "Looks good!"

"Looks crooked," Giovanni says.

"What?" Jacob says.

"Come look from this angle."

I watch as Jacob's feet move around to where Giovanni is standing. "Oh." Then he comes to the tree, and it jostles slightly as he grabs it again. "Can you loosen the screw closest to the wall? It has to angle that way a little more."

I loosen that screw, and then he tilts the tree in that direction. I tighten the opposite screw and then he lets go once more and backs up. Then I watch his feet circle the tree as he looks at it from all angles.

"How's it looking?" I ask.

"Hmm…one more thing," he says. Then he gets on the floor and starts crawling under the tree with me.

"Jacob, there are tree needles all over the place," I say, nudging his shoulder to stop him from sliding under. "Plus there's sap and the floor is already sticky."

"So?" he says. "I'll be here with you, that's what matters."

"But your shirt will be dirty. Jacob, no."

But he doesn't listen. He comes completely under the tree with me.

"That's my cue to go upstairs," Giovanni says. His footsteps recede and climb the stairs.

"Hi," I say. He pulls me close and kisses me hard. "What's that for?"

"Ever since I saw you scoot under here, I knew I wanted to kiss you under the tree."

"Then do it again. Kiss me some more."

He pulls me close again and our lips lock and our tongues caress each other's. I push my legs forward and intertwine them with his. He reaches around me and grabs my ass, pulling my crotch into his, making me feel how hard he is. I'm just as hard as him.

"Mmm…Jacob…" I moan.

"Edward," he breathes out.

He dry humps me, rubbing his hard bulge against mine, as he nibbles his way down my neck.

"Jacob…" I moan again.

He kisses his way back up my throat, coming to my mouth again, kissing my lips. "As much as I want to do this now…we should make those cookies and decorate the tree…"

"You're such a distraction," I mumble into his mouth. "Maybe we can play after decorating? Don't make me wait till after the party."

"Edward, I wouldn't last through the party if we waited that long."

I snuggle up against him, resting my face in the crook of his neck.

"Just a moment more before we make cookies." I inhale deeply, breathing in his scent.

After my boner starts to soften a bit and the moment has passed, we shuffle out from under the tree. Jacob gets up first and holds his hand out to help me up, and when he does, he pulls me in for another hug and kiss.

"You are covered in needles," I say. I can feel them under my hands, stuck all over the back of his shirt. "And they're even in your hair."

"You've got them too," he says, sensually rubbing his hands down my back. "It was worth it for that kiss, though."

When we part, I try to brush the needles off me, and he tries to get them off him. When most seem gone, I pull out my phone and see that Braden had sent me his sugar cookie recipe. We quickly get ourselves together in the kitchen with the ingredients and equipment and instructions.

Jacob giggles to himself.

"What?" I ask him.

Eyes bright with laughter, Jacob says, "Am I coming on these ones too?"

Deadpan, I look at my phone and say, "Cum doesn't seem to be on the ingredient list."

It doesn't take long for us to whip up the dough. Jacob doesn't have cookie cutters, and we didn't think to buy any, so we use a drinking glass and make them round cookies. We put the first baking sheet in the oven, and soon the house smells of fresh-baked cookies.

After a few minutes, I turn on the oven light and bend over to peek through the window at the cookies…and feel Jacob's hand on my ass. When I stand upright again, he leans back against the kitchen island. I step close, in between his legs, and wrap my arms around him, reaching up for a kiss.

After the kiss, I say, "You still have needles on you."

"And you've still got some in your hair." He plucks at my head, pulling some off.

"We might need to change and have a shower together," I say, "you know, so I can look at your back and you can look at mine."

"Such a naughty little mouse."

A few minutes later, we pull out the first tray of cookies and put the second one in. While we wait for it to bake, I lean against him, resting my head on his chest, listening to his heartbeat. I've never felt as secure as I do right now in Jacob's arms. We rest against each other like that until the timer beeps and the second batch of cookies is done.

I take the cookies out and then transfer them all to a wire rack. "We'll let these cool," I say, "and until then, we could decorate the tree."

Jacob picks up the boxes of ornaments and candy canes from the island, and I pick up the garland. "I'm so excited," he says, with one of the biggest grins I've ever seen on him.

After we put the boxes and garland in the living room, I follow him to the garage and help him pull out the plastic crate that has some of his other Christmas decorations. When we get that to the living room and open it, I see bundles of Christmas lights on the top, so we pull those out and start stringing them on the tree.

We hang the ornaments next, making it look colorful and vibrant.

"Here," I say to Jacob, handing him the elf ornament he bought today, "I think you should hang this one yourself. Probably right in front."

He takes it from me and hesitates. He reaches for my hand and takes it in his. "Let's put this up together." We step closer to the tree and, together, we hang the elf in the front and center. "I love it."

I snuggle into his side. "I love it too." In just this one day, Jacob has done more for me than anyone ever has, and for the first time, I feel completely at peace. Looking up at him, I say, "Thank you for this…for everything. This day was perfect. I couldn't have asked for more."

He kisses my forehead. "I'd do anything for you, little mouse."

We stay like this for a little while longer, both admiring the tree, then I say, "The last step is the garland."

He picks up one of the packages of garland and rips it open. We make quick work of hanging it on the tree. Because it's so large, we rip open the remaining two packages. But after putting the second string of garland up, the tree is fully decorated, and we didn't need the third one.

He goes to his coffee table and picks up the third strand of garland, giving it a little tug between his two hands, testing the strength of it. Then he looks up at me with eyes laden with lust.

   JACOB   

I grip the garland in my hands, stretching it. "This is really strong," I say, looking at Edward. He's told me so many times that he's down for anything I want to try out. I wonder if he'd be cool with me tying him up with this. He's putting a few candy canes on the tree, holding the box in his hand, completely unaware of the ways I'm planning to ravage him.

"Do you want to put some on, too?" he asks, holding a candy cane toward me.

Before I can ask him what he thinks of me tying him up, I hear my phone ringing from my bedroom. Since I changed the ringtone for Linley, I know that it's her calling before I even make my way over to it.

"You've been ignoring her all day," Edward reminds me. "You remember what happened last time, right? I know I'll never forget it."

"Ugh, yes," I say, tossing the garland over my shoulder. Edward follows behind me walking toward my bedroom. I throw the garland onto my dresser, and Edward puts the box of candy canes down.

He rubs my arm. "I'm gonna take a shower, okay?"

I kiss him on the forehead and pat him on the ass. "I'll be right here when you get out."

He giggles at me, turning toward the bathroom. "I'm starting to feel like we should skip this party…"

I'll have to ask him if he's serious when he gets out of the bathroom, because I'd much rather stay here tonight. I grab the phone and answer it, "Hello, best agent in the entire world. How are you today?"

"Why have you been ignoring me all day? Could it be because Marco gave you one very specific instruction, and you chose to flat out ignore it? Or should I say, *dance* all over it?"

"I'm gonna do the community service," I say, pretending not to know exactly what she's talking about. "The Snowflake festival is tomorrow, I'm sure there's something I can help out with. I didn't go back on my word."

"Oh, that's good news. Of course, it doesn't exactly make up for you singing on a bar, obviously tipsy. What were you thinking?" she asks with a hint of laughter.

"Are you pissed? Because it sounds like you're not pissed. I just wanted to do it, so I did it."

"Well, listen, I think that was stupid. Not the part where you told everyone he was your boyfriend, but the dancing on the bar thing, that was stupid. You could've gotten hurt. Anyway, that's not why I'm calling. You've got a ton of new sponsorship offers that I'm gonna need you to look over. The situation has changed now with the new contract, so it's up to you how many of these you want to take on. I'd suggest almost all of them, because that just means more money for me."

"And more work for me," I say. "Who are the potential sponsors?"

We switched to a video call about two hours ago, and at this point, I'm just completely exhausted. Edward has been asleep beside me since a few minutes after he got out of the shower. I want to lie next to him, but I've just been sitting up this whole time, since I haven't showered yet, and I'm sure there's still tree stuff in my hair.

I think everything from the past few days is catching up with me. Through a yawn, I say, "Yeah, let's negotiate those ten, and the rest we can talk about when I get back to Miami."

"And when will that be?" she asks.

I rub my finger against Edward's sleeping cheek. "I don't know. I'm thinking as soon as training starts, so pretty soon. I'm gonna bring Edward there for a visit, but I can't just expect him to pick up and move, so we'll have to figure everything out." I yawn again, this time feeling my eyes start to close. "I need to end this call, though. I'm spent. We have a party we're supposed to go to in a few hours, and I don't know how I'm gonna function if I don't rest first."

After we hang up, I carefully get out of bed and walk into my bathroom. I really don't feel like going to this party, but any chance to show Edward off is one that I'll gladly take. When he got out of the shower, I asked him if he really wanted to go, and he said he'd rather be woken up for sex than woken up for the party. So, I guess I'll decide what to do after I get out of the shower.

I take a quick shower and brush my teeth just in case I end up falling asleep for the night. It's only five o'clock, but I feel tired enough to just pass out.

Edward is in the exact same position he was in before I got into the shower. I text Gio before climbing into bed:

Hey, I think we're skipping the party. So, you can take the night off.
Sounds good. If you need anything let me know.

I turn over and lay my head on Edward's shoulder. The smell of the cookies is still on his skin, but the scent of the tree is hanging in the air. My perfect little boyfriend smells like Christmas.

"My Jacob," he murmurs, cuddling against me.

There's no telling how long we've been asleep for when I open my eyes, because it's so dark inside my room. We somehow switched positions, though, because Edward's head is on my bare chest, and my arm is wrapped tightly around him. I kiss the top of his head and rub his arm.

He shuffles a bit, looking up at me through sleepy eyes. "What time is it?" he asks. "Are we skipping the party?"

"No idea," I say, reaching for my phone. "It's eight o'clock, I told Gio we were gonna skip, but if you changed your mind, I can tell him we want to go."

"Mmm…I don't want to," he says, nuzzling against my neck, planting a few soft kisses on it.

"Is my little mouse hungry? Do you want me to make you something?"

He lifts his head, looking at me. "Not hungry but thank you. Are you…hungry?"

"Mmhmm, but what I'd really like before I eat, is to see you in that corset. I moved it, so it's hanging on the closet door. Don't want a repeat of last night."

He props himself up on his hands and straddles across me, rubbing up my chest, before dropping his lips on mine. He kisses me deeply, sucking on my tongue, while I squeeze his ass through his shorts.

"Go put that corset on for me," I growl. "Then we're gonna try something new."

His eyes are wide with excitement as he climbs off me, and walks toward my closet. He takes the corset off the back of the door and shuffles around the inside of his suitcase before heading into the bathroom.

My dick is already achingly hard from both our kiss and his cock grinding against mine. I stroke myself a few times under the covers, imagining all the things I'm gonna do to him. I see the garland on my dresser and decide it would be better to just bring it over here, so I'm not fumbling around when he comes out of the shower. The box of candy canes is sitting right beside the garland, and I have another idea—actually I just got two ideas at the same time. I pull one candy cane out and place it, along with the garland, onto my nightstand.

I don't want to make too much noise and have Gio come downstairs, so I creep quietly into the spare bedroom next to mine. I know there is a set of candles and new lighters in one of these boxes, and I'm pretty sure I didn't throw away the edible lube. Scott gave me all of it as a gift, and I laughed and said I'd never use it.

After checking three boxes with no luck, I decide that if the candles aren't in this box, I'll just give up on this idea. As I open the flaps, I smell the scent of vanilla and know instantly that I have the right box. I pull out the three glass candles and see the lube near the bottom of the box, along with the lighters. Once I have everything, I head back into my room, hoping that Edward isn't sitting in bed waiting for me.

Good, the bed is empty, and Edward is still in the bathroom. I kind of want to ask if he needs help with the corset, but I really don't want to interrupt whatever he's got going on in there. He'd ask me if he needed help...at least I think he would. I place the lube on the nightstand, and candles on the dresser, spreading them out evenly and lighting them one at a time. When the last candle is lit, the bathroom door opens, and my boyfriend is standing in the doorway wearing nothing but the black corset and a black jockstrap. I drop the lighter on the dresser and we lock eyes. "You look so fucking hot right now," I say walking over to him.

His face lights up, and he rubs his hands down his waist and turns a bit, giving me a peek at his juicy round ass and the straps just beneath his cheeks. "You like it?" he asks me with a wicked grin.

I pull his body against mine squeezing him by his tight little waist. "It's perfect. You look beautiful," I say and kiss his cheek. "Sexy," I say, and kiss the other. "Good enough to eat," I whisper beside his ear, sliding a finger down his ass, pressing on his hole. I thread my fingers up through the back of his hair, pulling his mouth into mine. I'm kissing him thirstily, desperate to taste him in every way possible tonight.

He moans, trying to keep pace with me, while I guide him toward the bed and he lies down. He looks up at me panting, when our mouths separate. "What are you gonna do to me? Da—" He sucks his lips in, looking like he regrets what he almost just said.

I grab the garland and straddle across him on my knees. Stretching the garland to show him how strong it is, I ask, "What did I say about holding things in? What were you gonna say?"

He smiles at me, closing his eyes. "I almost called you Daddy, but I remembered you said you didn't like it."

"Silly little mouse," I say, lifting his arms above his head. "Did I ever say that to *you*?"

"No. No, you didn't."

I lean down and kiss his hands, pressing them together while wrapping the garland around his wrists. Once they're secure, I look down at him, hands above his head and nearly start to leak at the sight. The tattoos on his arms, the corset wrapped tightly around him like a perfect little present, it's all so sexy. "Say it," I whisper, my mouth hovering close to his, "Let me hear it."

"Fuck, Daddy," he moans.

I trace my tongue along his lips, feeling his dick hard against mine through my thin sleep pants.

"Say it again," I command, then drag my tongue up the side of his neck, tasting the sweetness of his skin.

"Fuck me, Daddy," he begs.

"Not yet," I whisper beside his ear, teasing his piercings with my tongue. I kiss my way down the front of his corset. He lowers his bound hands, squirming beneath me, trying to touch me. "No," I say, pressing them back against the pillow. I continue kissing my way down, rubbing my face against his hardened cock when I reach it. The heat and hardness are too tempting. I wrap my lips around the head through the fabric of his jock. "Mmm," I moan with it in my mouth.

His broken little sounds are driving me crazy. I tug on his straps, pulling them down, exposing his thick cock. "Look at you, leaking for me already." I glide my tongue across his head, savoring the salty taste of his precum, swirling it around in my mouth before sliding my hand up to his throat and rising onto my knees.

My grip tightens around his neck, and his mouth opens in eager anticipation. I spit straight into it, and his eyes roll back, while his throat vibrates in my grasp. "Mmm—fuck—yes," he moans, while his sticky cock twitches.

"Such a good little mouse." I kiss him deeply, sloppily—fuck he looks so sexy in this corset, but I really want to take it off. "Do you know what I've been thinking about?" I whisper, moving my hand down near his dick.

He shakes his head at me.

"I can't stop thinking about you being turned on when we were first talking as employee and boss. I was just a worker, and you were"—I grip his cock—"getting off to the sound of my voice." My fingers tighten around him, and I rub the underside with my thumb. "Seems so dirty. Getting off to thoughts of the contractor."

He's panting, spreading his legs wider. "Haah—touch me more. If I can't touch myself, touch me," he begs, moving his hands.

"What were you picturing? Were you imagining a big strong hand…stroking you like this?"

"You—I was picturing you," he whimpers, while I move my hand painfully slowly, up and down his dick.

The corner of my mouth rises in a smirk, and I spit into my hand, drawing a moan from him. "Me?" I grip him once again, moving down in between his legs. Pressing one of his thighs up, spreading him wider, I bring my face above his dick and blow softly on it. "How could you picture me?" I drag my tongue slowly up his balls, all the way to his tip, then swirl my tongue around the head, licking his slit. "You didn't even know what I looked like."

"Haah—fuck—Jacob—nngh—you—the bathroom," he breathes out.

My eyes go wide looking up at him from between his legs. "You were jerking off thinking about the guy who railed you in the bathroom?" I stroke him long and slow, watching his chest rise and fall.

"Mmhmm," he moans through hooded eyes. "Please—fuck me—Jacob."

"Not yet," I say rising, onto my knees. "Flip over, I wanna see your hole."

He shows me his hands, still bound by garland, and I pout at him, then flip him by his waist, turning him onto his stomach. He pushes himself up onto his elbows and lifts his ass into the air, arching his back like a cat. It's incredibly sexy, and his tight little hole is right in front of my face. Fucking perfect. "How about back here?" I lick the underside of each cheek, squeezing them tightly. "Did you finger yourself imagining it was me?" I ask, tracing his rim with my finger before pressing on the center.

He's grinding back against me while I tease him, rubbing softly. "Yes…I did."

"Naughty." I slap both of his cheeks, then climb over toward my nightstand, quickly grabbing the lube and candy cane, then pull my pants off. My dick is so hard, I don't know how much more I can take. I unzip the corset, watching it fall against the mattress, and he exhales in relief.

"More," he begs. "More—I want more—spank me more—please, Daddy."

I bite the end of the plastic wrap off the candy cane and spit it out across the room, quickly unwrapping it. His ass is juicy and thick, perfect for spanking. I spank his tender flesh three times in succession—*slap, slap,*

slap. With each slap he whimpers and writhes, begging for more, over and over.

Reaching around, I bring the candy cane to his lips. "Lick this, then I'm gonna fuck you with it, make your hole taste even sweeter, then drink every fucking drop and feed it to you."

He turns to the side, sucking the cane in, then licks around it, grazing his tongue against my fingers. "What a filthy little tongue," I whisper, then bring the candy cane to my mouth and suck it before licking around his tight puckered entrance.

My tongue slips inside, and he whines, "Yes, more, more, eat me, Jacob. Eat me, then wreck me."

"Mmmhmm, I'm gonna," I say against his hole. "This lube is supposed to be fruit flavored, but I've never tried it before." I squeeze some onto my finger, tasting it first. "Mmm, tastes good. Let's try some here," I say, squeezing it above his asshole, watching as it drips down. "Fuuuck," I growl, swirling it around with one finger, holding the candy cane beside it. "This is smaller than my finger, baby—let's start with this, and if you're a good boy, I'll give you my cock."

"Yes, please—fuck—yes."

I slide the candy cane in easily, moving it in and out, watching his hole cling to it. I'm being careful not to fuck him too hard with it, but this teasing—I can't take it anymore. I pull the candy cane out and lick it, then wrap a hand around the front of his throat, hauling him upward toward me, with my chest flat against his back and my dick pressing between his cheeks—skin to skin—sweaty, sticky, and raw. I press the candy cane into his mouth, squeezing his throat, rutting between his cheeks, poking against his entrance, while he sucks the candy cane. I can't wait any longer. I toss the candy cane aside and tug at the garland, unbinding his wrists.

He pulls my face closer, turning his head, so our mouths connect, his tongue is massaging mine through desperate whimpers, while I jerk his cock from behind. "I want you to come inside of me, bare—but only if you want to," he says, panting.

Minutes later, after my fingers have loosened him, my cock is fully buried inside him from behind, and I'm riding him hard and deep. He's wet and warm inside, and I need to fucking come. Gripping his waist, with my fingers tight against his flesh, I pound him over and over, each thrust obliterating his prostate and my will to prolong my own orgasm.

He squeaks loudly, then cries out while he comes, clawing at the sheet so hard that he pulls it loose. "Ja-cob—Jacob—yes—yes—fuuuck."

I reach forward, pulling a section of his hair while his hole squeezes my cock through his orgasm, and I fuck him through it. A pleasure so intense rushes through me, exploding outward, and I come—deep inside my boyfriend's ass, yanking on his hair, while he moans loudly, and I do, too. Nothing has ever felt better. He rocks back and forth on my cock until every single drop is spent inside of him.

I release his hair, softly stroking my fingers down his neck, while I pull out. "Stay," I command, and I press my lips against his dripping hole, lapping around it. It's wet and salty, and I bury my face in it. His hole clenches, while I suck out my cum, not stopping until my mouth is full of it. "Mmm," I moan, pulling back.

He turns on his back, reaching for me and opens his mouth. I press my mouth against his and feed him my cum, holding his face in place, while he swallows my load thirstily, like he can't get enough. Our mouths stay entwined and the taste of our sex swirls between us, while our tongues caress each other, until the taste of us becomes one.

"That was—" I say, unable to find the right word in the moment, with my mouth so close to his.

"Perfect," Edward whispers, kissing me once more before I lie beside him.

Chapter Thirty-Five
Santa's Sexy Friend

We step back into Jacob's bedroom. We've just come from the gym—it was nice to work out with just the two of us. The gym had been totally empty, so we had tons of privacy to feel each other up. Now that we're back, we're sweaty and in need of showers.

Jacob lets me shower first, so I strip everything off, hop in, and clean off. When I'm out, he takes his turn.

When he's done, I'm sitting on the bed and watching him get dressed. After he pulls on some gray sweatpants, there's a loud banging at the door and someone rings the bell.

Jacob pulls out his phone and looks at the camera feed from his doorbell, then rolls his eyes.

"Who is it?"

He turns the phone to face me, and I see Kellan on the view from the doorbell's camera. "It's a Snowflake emergency!" Kellan shouts. "Open up, Jacob!"

"Come on," Jacob says, grabbing my hand and leading me through the house. When we get to the front door, Giovanni is there, and he looks like he's ready to punch someone. "Don't worry, Gio, it's okay."

Jacob yanks the door open, and Kellan is standing there.

"Jacob!" he shouts. He's in full panic mode. "I need your hel—wait, are you always shirtless at home? Is this what everyone is missing out on? And gray sweatpants too? Do I need to come knocking daily for this view?"

Though Jacob's back is facing me, I can tell he's rolling his eyes. "What do you want, Kellan?"

"I need your help or else the Snowflake Festival will be a disaster!" Kellan shouts. Pure panic is written across his face. "Jacob, do you still need community service?"

"How is this happening again?" Jacob says. "This feels familiar. But yes and no. Yes, because, yes, I do, but no, because whatever you're thinking of, I don't want to do."

"Santa is sick! I was hoping he'd be better by today, but he spent all night puking. The kids...the kids are going to be devastated with no Santa!"

I come up to the doorway and stand beside Jacob. "Kellan, calm down. Take a deep breath, in..." he breathes in "...and out..." he breathes out. "Now, Santa is sick...what do you need from Jacob?"

He looks at Jacob with big puppy dog eyes. "No one is willing to step in for the role of Santa. Could you do it?"

"Kellan, I don't really look like Santa," Jacob says. He pats his abs for emphasis. "And kids aren't fooled by a pillow under a Santa suit."

"Please? I need your help. You could be Santa's helper, maybe?"

I get sudden visions of Jacob dressed as a skinny Santa and making the entire town happy. Community service hours or not, this is something I want to see him doing. It's a memory I know we'll both cherish for years to come.

"He'll do it," I blurt out.

Giovanni looks at me. "Who says he will?"

"Please?" I ask, giving Jacob a smile.

Jacob sighs and hangs his head. Then he looks at Kellan and says, "Fine, I'll do it."

"Yes!" Kellan says, jumping and clapping.

"But on two conditions," Jacob continues. "One, I'm not wearing Santa's old outfit. No way am I putting that thing on after he's worn it for however many years. So I need you to get me a new one. And, two, Edward has to be my helper and he'll need an outfit too. A sexy little elf one would do the trick." He looks at me with a grin.

He might think he's one-upped me, but I just kiss him on the nose. "This is exciting!" I say.

Kellan promises to get our costumes for the day and then quickly goes over the plan. We have to meet near the community center in an hour to get ready and ride the carriage to the festival grounds. We'll go up on stage, and he'll meet all the kids and promise to pass their messages on to Santa.

"Thank you!" Kellan says with a squeal. "Can I get a hug before I go?"

"No," Jacob says.

"Well, can't blame a gay for trying…again." With a wink, he turns and runs to Braden's truck, which is idling on the street with Braden at the wheel. "Off to find your costumes!" he shouts, then jumps in the passenger seat and the truck screeches away.

Jacob closes the door and looks at me. "I'm volunteering to be Santa, huh?" I can tell he's not mad at me, and likely secretly loves the idea.

"You'd look cute in red and white," I say.

"And you'll look cute in green and white, or whatever color your costume ends up being," he says.

Giovanni rolls his eyes and sighs. "You two never stop. I'm going back upstairs. Call me whenever this love-fest is over."

Jacob and I laugh as Giovanni turns and leaves, then we head back into the bedroom for Jacob to finish dressing.

"This is…a bigger deal than I expected," I say.

Jacob and I (and Giovanni) are standing in the parking lot at the community center. In the middle of the parking lot is a horse-drawn carriage, two horses, and a sleigh being pulled along behind the carriage loaded with fake presents. There are so many people here with all the volunteers dressed as elves and what looks like a high school marching band.

"Which is the thing you fixed?" I ask.

Jacob points at the sleigh with presents. "It's that side panel there. I cut it and then Braden and Kellan painted it."

"It looks fantastic," I say, "you're really good at what you do."

We're interrupted by the sound of the marching band warming up.

When it quiets down again, Jacob says, "I knew Christmas was a big thing here, though I didn't realize it was this intense."

"You've never been?" I ask.

He shakes his head. "Though my dad lives here, I was always with my mom, so this is all new to me."

A truck comes screeching into the parking lot, and before it comes to a full stop, Kellan flings the passenger car door open and comes running toward us with a large plastic bag in each hand.

"I brought your costumes!" he shouts when he's halfway toward us.

When he comes skidding to a stop in front of us, he hunches over with his hands on his knees, the bags resting on the pavement, huffing and puffing. He pushes himself upright and he's swallowing lungfuls of air. "I need…to go…to the gym…more. Or at least…on the…treadmill." Then his eyes light up as he looks at Jacob. "Maybe I could join yo—"

"No," Jacob says.

"One of these days I'll break through that wall of yours," Kellan says. He then holds up the bags. "For both of you. Oh, wait." Then he crosses his arms, switching the order of the bags. "Now, it's right."

I take the bag from him, and inside is a green and white elf costume. Jacob pulls his costume out of the bag and it's a red and white Santa suit.

"I'm still Santa's friend or something, right?" Jacob says.

"Right!" Kellan says. "There's no beard or wig and no pillow for your tummy. You're just Jacob, the absurdly fit friend of Santa. I tried to find a costume that had a little cutout to show off your abs, but no luck."

"Thanks, Kellan, I guess," Jacob says. "I'm just going to put this on top of what I'm wearing since it's so cold out today."

Jacob and I quickly tug our costumes on, layered over our clothing. We both take off our coats and use the costume top as a coat. It's surprisingly warm once I have it all on and done up. Jacob looks at me with a big grin.

"You're such a cute little elf," he says.

"Can I get a picture of the two of you?" Kellan asks. Jacob agrees, so we stand side by side. Kellan holds up his phone to take a photo, but then says, "Look more relaxed. This isn't a prison photo."

Jacob slings an arm around my shoulders, pulling me in close, and I put a hand on his stomach. We're both laughing and then he kisses my forehead. That's when the camera flash goes and Kellan takes a pic.

"Oh my god," he says, "you two are freaking adorable. Here, I'll text it to you, Edward."

A moment later, my phone chimes, and I pull it out of my pocket. The picture from Kellan is super cute. I forward it on to Jacob so he has it too.

"I love it," he says as he looks at my screen. He kisses me on the forehead again.

I set that photo as the phone background and then shove it back in my pocket. "So, what's the plan from here?" I ask.

Kellan leads us to the carriage. "You two will ride into town square in here. When you get there, just follow the lead of the volunteers. You'll recognize them in the bright pink beanies. They'll direct you up onto the stage. I'll introduce you as Santa's helper, and the kids will all come up and tell you what they want for Christmas. And then you're done and can just enjoy the festival. Sound good?"

Jacob looks at me like he's uncertain, but when he sees the smile on my face, he smiles too. "That'll work."

"Good!" Kellan says. "I want to ask for a good luck hug but I know what the answer will be, so you'll get a good luck thumbs up. I have to hurry to town square, I'll see you there!" He then runs out of the parking lot and down the street toward the festival grounds.

Jacob opens the door of the carriage. "After you, my sexy little elf."

I climb into the carriage and then Jacob climbs in after me, sitting beside me on the bench.

And then Giovanni climbs in too.

"We should have gotten an elf costume for you too," I say.

"Over my dead body," he says. Then to Jacob, he says, "Respectfully, boss."

"We'll plan better next time," Jacob says, "and get you a costume too."

Giovanni's eyes go wide with fear, making both Jacob and I laugh.

A short while later, volunteers in pink beanies round everyone up and the parade starts. The marching band leads everyone out, with kids dressed as elves coming up behind them. And then the horses start walking, pulling us all forward. After a few minutes, we turn onto Main Street, and the crowds start appearing along the sidewalk. Jacob waves on one side, and I wave on the other. Giovanni has his arms crossed and is assessing threats.

The crowds get thicker as we get closer to town square, and soon the pace of the parade slows and the carriage comes to an eventual stop. People are cheering loudly and whistling, and a lot of them are singing carols too, which seem to be led by a choir on risers next to the main stage.

"Wow," I say, "this is even bigger than I thought it was when I first realized it was bigger than I thought it was."

"All this for Christmas?" Jacob asks.

"Get in the spirit, boss," Giovanni says.

Volunteers open the carriage door and bring a staircase up to it. Giovanni gets out first, looking out on the crowd and searching for any dangers. Then Jacob comes out and the screams get louder, and then I follow behind him.

I see Kellan on the stage with a glittery tiara. I point him out to Jacob, and we walk toward the stage, waving at the fans as we go. I'm sure ninety percent are cheering for him, but I'm reveling in it too.

When we get up on the stage, Jacob turns and waves to the crowd, who scream louder now. They eventually stop screaming and Kellan steps up to the microphone.

"Good morning, Frosty Bottoms!" Kellan shouts into the microphone. A wave of cheers rises in response. "We got a little bit of bad news this morning, Santa has the flu. But, thankfully, Santa's good friend, Jacob, is here to save the day!" The crowd screams even louder. "We'll start with Jacob meeting all the children, so, children, please line up at the stairs at the end of the stage and we'll let you come up and sit on Jacob's lap one at a time."

The choir starts singing carols again as the crowds move. I take a moment to look around; there are food trucks all over the place, lots of photo opportunities, and some of the businesses have set up little stalls with gifts to buy and games to play.

When I look toward the end of the stage to the stairs where the kids will come up, I find hundreds of people…and they're not all kids.

"Children only," Kellan says into the microphone. "If you're an adult, please stand aside."

"What if I pay?" a man shouts.

"What if my kid will only do this if I sit on his lap first?" someone else shouts.

I stomp over to Kellan and grab the mic from him. "Children. Only. Children. Only. Any adults in line get coal in their stocking. Children. Only."

"What if I'm young at heart?"

"Children. Only."

Thankfully, Braden approaches the line and starts making the adults leave so the line is only kids. With that problem solved, I hand the mic back to Kellan and go and stand beside Jacob, who is now sitting in the Santa chair. Giovanni is on Jacob's other side, ready to tackle someone if need be.

The first kid comes onto the stage and sits on Jacob's lap. It's a cute moment where the girl is shy, but Jacob makes her feel comfortable, and then she tells him what she wants for Christmas. After a few more exchanged words, she hops off his lap and runs to the other side of the stage.

The next kid comes and sits on Jacob's lap. Over the next couple hours, Jacob has a conversation with each and every kid. The parents are all standing in front of the stage, getting pics of their kids on Jacob's lap.

When every kid has seen Santa's helper, Jacob stands up and stretches. Kellan speaks into the mic and thanks Jacob, and the crowd applauds and cheers. We head backstage and quickly take off our costumes and fold them neatly for Kellan, then we head offstage and into the crowd, with Giovanni right behind us.

"That was fun watching you do all that," I say.

He chuckles. "It was surprisingly more fun than I expected it to be."

"Is it your cheat day? I feel like you've earned a greasy snack."

He looks at the food trucks around the town square. "Mini donuts?" he asks.

"Deal."

When we get in line for mini donuts, I realize Leora is in line ahead of us. "Merry Christmas," I say to her.

She turns around, and her face brightens when she sees me. "Edward! Jacob! It's so good to see you both!"

"Enjoying the Snowflake Festival?" I ask.

"Oh, immensely! It's so much more fun when I'm not the Snowflake Princess. Retiring and passing the tiara to Kellan is the best thing I've ever done. I get to just enjoy it and not work it." She reaches out and pats Jacob's arm. "And you did amazing as Santa's helper."

"Thank you," he says with a smile. "We should apologize for missing your party last night, but we were just a little too exhausted from everything going on."

"That's perfectly fine," she says. "Plus, I've been young and in love before, I know there are other *priorities* for your time."

Jacob blushes but changes the topic by saying, "We also want to thank you for those amazing macaroni penguin masks. They were perfect."

"So perfect," I echo.

"You knew they were macaroni penguins! I'm thrilled to hear that. I was worried you weren't going to realize they were the monogamous type. I got a lot of teasing for that from my boyfriend." She points toward a group of men playing a ring toss game. I have no idea which one is her boyfriend, but given how active and youthful Leora is, I imagine her boyfriend is the one without completely white hair.

"Macaroni penguins are my favorite," Jacob says, "I recognized what type it was right away."

"Oh, fantastic!" she says. "Edward, I'll be stopping by after Christmas to see what new smut you've got for me. I'm reading so much more these days. Your store has really reignited my passion for books."

"Perfect, because right after Christmas I'm expecting a shipment of the rest of the *Debriefing the Lawyer* series. You're going to love how it all ends," I say.

"Oh, I can't wait!"

We continue chatting with her as the line moves forward, and after she gets her mini donuts she hurries over to her boyfriend. We pick up our order and walk around, checking out the different things set up for the festival. Thankfully, the crowds mostly leave us alone; perhaps they got their fill for the day watching Jacob interact with all the kids.

As we walk, I can't help but sink into the feeling of a new me that Jacob has brought out, especially in these past couple days. I've long put others first and learned to not speak up about my wants and needs and desires. It was just how life treated me, and I went along with it. It became who I am.

But now…now, it's different. Jacob wants to know what I feel. He wants to meet my needs and desires. And I know that he's not going to disappear like all the others have done. Jacob is here to stay. Well, to stay at my side, maybe not in Frosty Bottoms, though that's a conversation we haven't quite had yet.

It's a conversation I'm ready for, though. As crazy as it may sound, if being with Jacob means moving to Miami with him even though I just started settling in here…I'd do it. Jacob means the world to me, and I like who I am when I'm with him. I'm a better person because of him. He'd tell me I've always been that better person and, yeah, he's probably right, but it's him and his desire for me that lets me bring out my full self without shame or worry or fear.

"Everything okay?" Jacob asks, giving my hand a squeeze.

"Yes," I say, leaning my head on his shoulder. "Everything is just right."

After we've had our fill of the Festival, we make our way back to the community center where Jacob's Mustang is parked and head home.

   JACOB   

Edward is nestled up against me on the couch, and we're watching *Home Alone*, while drinking hot chocolate at his request. I kind of wish we'd gotten matching Christmas pajamas, but that's an idea that I'll have to use next year. With Christmas Eve being tomorrow, I guess we could still get them if he wants to. "Would you like matching Christmas PJs?" I ask him.

"That would be fun. I've never matched with anyone before, that sounds cute. I always love those commercials where they show the family all happy at Christmas and they're all wearing matching pajamas, even the pets have them."

"After we visit your brother tomorrow, we can see if there are any matching sets at any of the stores."

He giggles at me. "Jacob, you can't go to stores on Christmas Eve. It will be pure chaos there, worse than the normal chaos that follows you in public places."

While we were in the shower, Braden dropped off a tray of cookies to thank us for helping out today. Gio had to grab them for us, he said Braden told him he wanted to drop them off alone, just in case I happened to answer the door shirtless again.

Edward leans forward, grabbing another cookie off the tray, and takes a bite. "Mmm, this one is better than the last one!" he says excitedly, holding it toward my mouth.

"Baby, you've said the same thing about the last five cookies," I chuckle. "Every single one is better than the last one?"

"Try it," he says. "It's a cheat day, so nothing counts. That's how cheat days work."

It does smell delicious, and every one has been really good. I take a bite of the chocolate cookie, and my mouth is quickly filled with the taste of marshmallow and caramel. "Mmm, oh okay, this one is better than the last one."

"Mmm, gooey marshmallow filling. It kind of tastes like a brownie, right?"

"Mmhmm, it does. I'm glad he brought them over."

He snuggles up tighter against me. "Today was really fun. I felt bad for Gio, though. Do you think he gets tired of it? Having to be on alert all the time?"

"Yeah, I'm sure he does, at least with the way things are here. This twenty-four-hour stuff really isn't fair for him. Gotta be completely draining worrying about so many things constantly."

"Yeah, I can relate to that," he says, tracing the tattoo on my forearm. "In a different sense though. The feeling of worrying about something every minute of every day is exhausting. I kind of felt like that my whole life, always worried about something…" He threads his fingers with mine and looks up at me. "Until you. But now, I feel safe and cared for and the thought of worrying about you not wanting me or me not being good enough—it just seems so stupid now. I've never met anyone like you, I've never had anyone that made me feel so wanted and secure. You've just— made everything better."

I stroke his cheek with my thumb, staring into his big brown eyes. "That makes me so happy. You—you make me so happy. I can't remember a time before you, that I felt like me. I don't ever remember feeling anything outside of soccer. For the first time, I feel like my life is my own, and I'm not just going through someone else's plan for me or doing what society expects of me. With you, I feel like I'm finally living, and life is not just soccer, it's not just meal plans and exercise and competition, it's you and me—together—holding hands just like this." I lift his chin and kiss him softly, then squeeze him in tighter, pulling the thick gray blanket up higher.

"Now that I'm not, like, afraid of losing you, I feel like we should talk about the thing that I screwed up talking about last time."

"What are you talking about? You've never screwed anything up."

"When do you think you need to go back? You know, to Miami?"

"I'll need to go back when Marco hires a new coach just for a quick meet and greet, like I told you, then I'll need to be there for training before the season starts. But after Christmas, I was thinking if you wanted to, we could make that trip and see how you like it there. Not to move, but just to check it out. I don't want you to feel any pressure, though. You also just opened your—"

"I want to go," he says, interrupting me. "I'll talk to Kellan and see if there's anyone local that's looking for extra work that can help with the store. He's never at his shop anyway, so if I ask him to, I'm sure he could keep an eye on the place for me. Plus, my brother and Lucas are here. Depending on the hours, I'm sure one of them could help out in the morning. Besides, everyone says this place is like a ghost town after Christmas is over. Yesterday, I looked at the sales coming in through the website and they're pretty high. In-store sales are high, but the numbers online are much higher. So, once I get a feel for after-Christmas foot traffic, I might find I don't need to be open as much. And I'm not—" He cuts himself off and sits up straight looking at me. "I'm not attached to this place, Jacob—I'm attached to you."

"I'm attached to you, too, little mouse. Let's talk to Kellan and your brother and see what they say. We'll make a plan to go next week and if that doesn't work out, we can play with the dates a bit."

"That sounds perfect. I have to ask something though, when you took the jet the other day, was that your jet or like a team jet?"

"Pftt, I'm rich, but I'm not that rich. Well, I kind of am but I don't have my own jet. I have a boat, though, it's pretty dope. I can't wait to take you out on the water."

His eyes go wide and he looks at me like a deer in headlights.

"What? What's wrong? You don't like boats?"

He puts a hand on my leg, shaking his head. "I don't know how to swim. I never learned." He covers his mouth. "What am I gonna do?"

I refuse to laugh at my boyfriend, at least that's what I'm telling myself, but Edward's facial expression tells me I'm not doing a very good job at hiding how adorable I think it is.

He shoves me playfully. "Don't look at me like that. I can learn. It's not funny," he says, fighting back a smile.

"No, baby." I pull him back against me, wrapping my arm around him, and kiss his cheek. "It's not funny. I was just thinking…I'll have to get a baby gate set up for you, because I have an infinity pool, you'll float right out into the ocean if I'm not paying attention."

He giggles against me while I stroke my fingers through his hair. "I'll teach you how to swim. After all, you taught me how to feel."

"Still saying the sweetest things," he murmurs, nuzzling against my chest.

I want him beside me, not just now, but forever, I think.

EPILOGUE
THE WOLF
AND THE MOUSE

   JACOB   

Two years later

"You two are like fish!" I shout at Edward and Darcy when I step outside onto the patio. Our new puppy, Darcy, might like the pool even more than Edward does.

Edward swims over to the side of the pool, looking up at me, his gorgeous white smile shining brightly in the sun. He sticks his tongue out at me, showing off his tongue piercing. "If my husband weren't so sexy, I wouldn't have to cool off in the pool so often."

I smile at that. We had sex about an hour ago, and he decided to take a swim afterward, while I tied up some last-minute business before our Christmas break officially started.

Darcy paddles to the side and climbs out of the pool, using the steps. He looks so cute running toward me with his little blue life preserver on. I squat down and pet him, mussing his face between my hands. Labs really are the cutest little puppies. "You wanna get out of the pool now? Or you wanna go back in? Your Uncles Chad and Lucas will be here soon." He shakes his fur out and gets my pants and face wet. "Ahhh, Darcy." I wince, wiping the water from my face with the inside of my sleeve.

"Don't take his jacket off yet," Edward says. "I'm not ready to get out."

I pick Darcy up, since I'm already wet and walk over to Edward. "We're on vacation, baby, you don't have to get out. No calls, no appearances, nothing but you, me, and Darcy for the next week." The puppy is whimpering in my arms, squirming for me to put him down, I assume because he wants to get back in the water with Edward. "Such a little traitor," I say, placing him down.

He hops into the water beside Edward, licking his arms, when Edward scoops him up. "Aww, Daddy didn't forget Uncle Chad is coming today," he says to Darcy. "I know he didn't, because he just told you about it thirty seconds ago," he chuckles.

I hang my head back looking up at the sky. "Of course I didn't. I just don't know why we told them to come on Christmas Eve. We wanted to have a sunny, relaxing Florida Christmas this year and somehow it morphed into Chad and Lucas staying with us for five days."

Darcy wiggles out of Edward's arms and swims toward the stairs again, running toward me once he's out of the water.

"See," Edward says, "he's not a traitor, he loves us both." Using the edge of the pool, he pushes himself up out of the water, and climbs out.

There are towels for both him and Darcy on the lounge chair. I grab his towel and wrap it loosely around his shoulders, squeezing him tight. He kisses the side of my neck softly, rubbing his tongue ring on it. I grip his shoulders and pull back. "No, no, no—your brother will be here any minute. We can't. Insatiable. After two years, still so insatiable."

He giggles at me, while Darcy sits in between us looking up. "Come on, Darcy, Daddy says we have to go inside now." He takes the puppy's jacket off and dries him with the other towel, while holding him in his arms.

"It was kind of your idea to invite them," Edward says when we walk inside. "I take full responsibility for your mom, and my parents, but you can't pretend you didn't invite Chad and Lucas to stay with us."

He's not technically wrong. We were sort of opposite snowbirds last year, so once the season ended, we went up to Frosty Bottoms the week of Thanksgiving and spent the holidays there. This year, Edward wanted to spend our first Christmas as a married couple in our home in Miami, but Chad and Lucas were pretty down about it.

"Technically, yes," I say walking upstairs with Edward following behind. "But only because when you told them that we were staying here for Christmas, they were all bummed out. Remember, they started talking about getting coverage for the bar and making plans. How could I not invite them after that? Besides, I know you like the board game tradition on Christmas Eve. I won't accept anything outside of a perfect Christmas for my husband."

When we walk into our bedroom I point at him and add on, "That does not include tomorrow when our parents are here. All bets are off tomorrow. I'll do my best, but I have no idea what they'll be like. They were so loud when they got together at the wedding."

"Well, yeah, but your dad was there, and he won't be here tomorrow, so it should be a little less...exhaustive." He walks into our en suite bathroom, quickly stepping inside the shower to rinse off.

My phone rings loudly from inside my pocket, and I sigh. "Damn it. No one is supposed to be calling me."

"It's probably just Gio, don't get all worked up," he says.

I look down at my phone and see that Edward is right, because he's always right. I accept the call. "What's up, Gio?"

"The brother-in-law and his husband are here. I'm gonna let them through," he says.

"Alright, thanks. If I don't talk to you after your shift, make sure you stop by around dinner time tomorrow. You could, you know, stay for dinner with the rest of the family."

"Dinner with your mother? On Christmas? I'd rather pass another kidney stone, but thank you. Not to mention your husband is gonna try to pull that calling me Gio crap, I don't wanna sing that song again. I let him call me that once at the wedding, and now he thinks every special occasion means he can say it."

I look at Edward as he steps out of the shower and grin. "Aww, he thinks of you as family, too. I'll let him know if you stop by tomorrow, that you said it's okay if he calls you Gio again. Okay, byeee," I say, and end the call.

"They're here," I say looking at my husband, delicious and still soaking wet from the shower. This man knows what he does to me when he's standing in nothing but a towel, and he knows damn well I can't do anything about it. My eyes flick to his lower half, and I pull him in close, squeezing him tightly against myself. "Maybe we can pretend we aren't home," I say, kissing the side of his still-wet skin. I can't even count how many times we've had sex at this point and, still, seeing him like this, holding him tight—the need to be one with him burns stronger than ever.

Holding one hand on his towel, keeping it closed tight, he strokes my cheek with the other hand and kisses me quickly. "I love you, but no. And we need to get dressed!" he says excitedly. "The driveway is long, so we have a few minutes, but we have to hurry."

"Ahh, okayyy," I say, dramatically dragging myself to the closet. I hang my arms down with a slouch and slink inside.

Edward giggles and follows me inside. "Oh noooo, not Zombie Jacob, put him away."

He calls me Zombie Jacob whenever I don't have the energy to do something and have to force myself to do it anyway. He usually offers me something good that peps me up.

"What will it take to bring back my perfect husband?" He perches his chin on my shoulder. "How about tonight, after everyone is asleep, we can have hot tub sex, and you can mark me under the moonlight like a wolf?"

"Yes. That. I want that," I say, straightening my posture.

Edward giggles, flipping through his side of the closet, and I quickly grab a shirt and shorts from my side.

While we both get dressed, I can't help but stare at him. I love him so much. I'd do anything to make him smile. "Baby," I say and take his hand in mine. "I love you, and even if you didn't want to have crazy wolf sex in the moonlight, I'm actually really happy your brother is here, because I know how happy it makes you."

He kisses me softly. "I love you, too, and I think you're actually kind of happy that he's here despite what you say."

The doorbell rings and we make our way downstairs. "Eh…maybe a little," I say with a smile.

EDWARD

I'm so excited. I've been looking forward to Chad and Lucas coming to visit ever since the idea was first tossed around. They were so generous to let me stay with them in Frosty Bottoms when I first moved there; I hadn't known Chad all that well before then and really got to know him much better over my time in the town. Every time we fly back, we make sure we have a good visit with them and spend some time at the bar.

I open the front door of our house, and Chad and Lucas are there, wearing designer sunglasses, tropical shirts, and far-too-short shorts.

"Little brother!" Chad exclaims. He pulls me in for a hug, and after that, he holds his arms out to Jacob, but Jacob shakes his head at him. "Still no hug? Kellan got one!"

"That's different. Kellan helped us find staff for Edward's store," Jacob says.

Before we left Frosty Bottoms for Miami, Kellan stepped up to make sure the store could run with me being here in Florida for most of the year. I manage the business from a distance and we usually fly up whenever Jacob has a long weekend.

"It's so good to see you," Lucas says, hugging me, then he offers Jacob a handshake.

"We're so glad you could both come," I say.

Chad looks at me quizzically. "When did you get a tongue ring?"

"About six months ago." I stick out my tongue to show it off. "Jacob loves it."

Jacob pumps his eyebrows at me.

About that time, Darcy comes running through the house to see all the commotion. Chad squats down and scritches both sides of Darcy's neck. "And who's this cute friend?"

"This is Darcy," I say. "He was a little birthday present from Jacob."

"Darcy?" Lucas asks. "As in Mr. Darcy from *Pride and Prejudice*?"

"The one and only!" I say. "Mr. Darcy was always so caring and loving to Elizabeth so it felt like the perfect name."

I notice that Chad isn't paying attention; he's gawping open-mouthed at the inside of our house.

"Wasn't he a bit rude to her?" Lucas asks. "At least in the beginning?"

"No," I say, "it was a perfect relationship."

Lucas lowers his eyebrow. "I think you're misremembering that or romanticizing it or something."

"Holy shit this place is huge," Chad says, interrupting our debate. "I knew this place was big, but I didn't know it was *this big*. How big is that tree? It must be ten feet."

"It's eleven feet, but who's counting?" Jacob says.

"Do you want a tour?" I ask.

I take them through the house and show them the different rooms, including the guest bedroom they'll be staying in. I had forgotten that they hadn't seen the house yet. They'd flown down for our wedding, but because we then took off on our honeymoon right away, that didn't leave much time for houseguests to come and visit.

"How many bedrooms do you have?" Chad asks.

"Eight bedrooms," I say, then I rattle through the rest of the list people like to know, "and we have seven bathrooms, a game room, a home theater, and a party room. And my favorite is the little book nook that Jacob built for me."

"Do you have a home bar? I could whip up some cocktails later."

"In the game room," I say. "I think it's pretty well stocked; we don't drink much since Jacob is on a strict diet plan."

"But I could have something today," Jacob says. "It's cheat day, and Christmas Eve, so the rules don't really apply."

I lead them through the patio door to the back.

"Oh my God, you have an infinity pool?" Chad asks, clearly

astonished, as we step out the back door. "And it flows into the ocean? Edward, I had no idea your place was this fancy!"

"It doesn't *actually* flow into the ocean," I say.

Then Chad points past the edge of the patio. "And is that your boat?"

"It is," Jacob says. "We could take her for a spin after everyone leaves tomorrow maybe?"

"That'd be amazing," Lucas says.

I then lead us to a table and chairs next to the pool, overlooking the ocean. Jacob dips into the house briefly and comes out with a bottle of wine and four glasses. He pours some out for each of us, then sits beside me and takes my hand in his.

After we finish our wine and just enjoy the late afternoon sun, we head back inside. It's tradition to play board games on Christmas Eve night, and I'm thrilled we get to host this time.

Before heading to the game room, Jacob and I change into our matching Christmas pajamas and tug an identical pair onto Darcy. Chad heads straight to the bar and whips up some cocktails for us as we set up for a rousing game of Monopoly.

"Add extra pineapple to Edward's," Jacob says, giving me a smirk.

"And Jacob's too," I add.

Chad tilts his head at us, confused. "I didn't peg Jacob as a sweet drink lover."

"Only on special occasions," Jacob says.

Some time later, the drinks are drained, and Chad and Lucas are fighting over whether a player can or cannot continue to collect rent while in jail.

After an evening full of games and fun and laughter—and that one argument—Chad and Lucas head off to the guest bedroom on the opposite side of the house to tuck in for the night. I'm with Jacob in our bedroom, snuggling against him on the mattress with my head on his chest.

"I had a wonderful day," I say. "I'm so glad they could come and I'm really looking forward to your Christmas morning pancakes."

"Christmas morning pancakes? How are those any different from the pancakes I normally make you, baby? I just made you some this morning."

"Those were Christmas Eve pancakes and I loved them, but Christmas morning pancakes are the most special."

Then he chuckles so low it makes his chest vibrate. "I can definitely deliver on Christmas morning pancakes in bed, but I believe you promised me something for tonight."

I look up at him. "Oh? I don't remember any promises…"

He quirks an eyebrow upward. "Maybe we should head to the hot tub and see if that refreshes your memory." Then he howls like a wolf.

I laugh at that, but I also get incredibly hard knowing the railing I'm about to receive.

I kiss his nose and then get off the bed. "Wolves are hunters. You're going to have to catch me if you want to claim me."

I bolt out of the room, heading down toward the hot tub. He comes running after me, howling like a wolf. He's a faster runner than me, so he catches me just before I reach the hot tub. He wraps me in his arms and whispers into my ear, "I love you, Edward."

"I love you too, Jacob," I say.

While our story may be chaotic at times, there's one thing I know for certain—my Jacob and I will live happily ever after, hand in hand.

About the Authors

Cameron D. James and Cali Kitsu are besties who couldn't wait to team up to bring you another smutty Christmas book, set in the perfectly festive town of Frosty Bottoms.

Cameron is the spicy gay romance pen name for Craig, who is publisher at Deep Desires Press. He also writes queer young adult romance as Dylan James.

Cali is executive assistant at Deep Desires Press, and an author of both spicy gay romance and gay young adult romance.

You can listen to both of them on the *Cali & Craig Talk…* podcast, where they talk about books, butts, and everything in between.

When they're not writing or podcasting, these besties can be found baking, playing *Stardew Valley*, or chatting over some coffee.

Also By The Authors

Cameron D. James
Cookies, Candles, and Cute Butts for Christmas
Books, Balls, and Cute Butts for Christmas
New York Heat
Silent Hearts
Autumn Fire

Cali Kitsu
Cookies, Candles, and Cute Butts for Christmas
Books, Balls, and Cute Butts for Christmas
Froderick, Gay Son of Dracula
You Can Call Me Cooper
You Can Call Me Cooper: Author's Cut
Only My Husband Calls Me Cooper
Vincent & Sivan: Book 1: Rum-Soaked Awakenings

MORE FROM FROSTY BOTTOMS

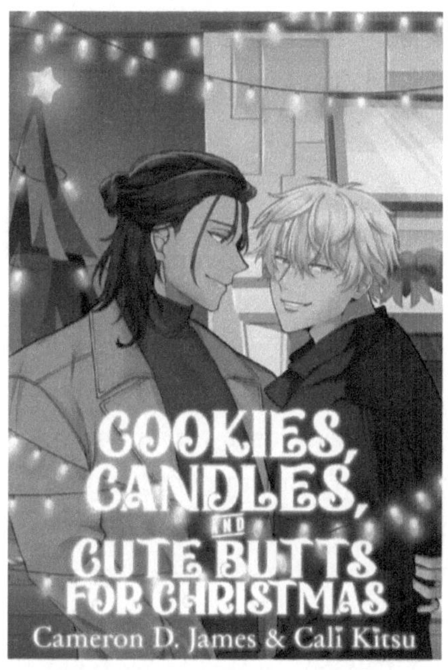

Cookies, Candles, and Cute Butts for Christmas
Cameron D. James & Cali Kitsu

It's gonna be a hot Christmas in Frosty Bottoms, when Braden, the new hunky veterinarian strolls into town, but this gorgeous man is no stranger, and he's no longer a vet. He's coming back to Frosty Bottoms to bake cookies and dip his wick in Kellan, the local candlemaker, who happens to be his childhood best friend.

Kellan knows Braden is coming back to town and taking over BJ's Cookies and he's unsure how to feel about it. They have a past; Kellan felt something but then Braden moved away.

Sparks soon fly when Braden reunites with Kellan, but they want different things. Braden is only interested in a relationship, while Kellan is only looking for hookups. With mishaps galore, including over-excited family, unrecognizable otters, and motorboating a muscle chest, everyone and everything seems to be pushing the two men together.

When the initial ice between them melts, it's not long before more than cookie dough is being rolled out on Braden's counters…and a certain bottom is getting frosted.

More from Cali Kitsu

Vincent & Sivan: Book 1: Rum-Soaked Awakenings
Cali Kitsu

Vincent & Sivan is an explicit, best-friends-to-lovers, dual gay awakening, adult MM romance novel.

Vincent and Sivan, sons of the world's most powerful pirates, are to be named captains this year, an honor for when they turn twenty-one. Under their fathers, they will rule in the modern age of pirates where the seas are at peace and long gone are the days of pillaging and plundering.

Best friends since childhood, they couldn't have more opposite views on love. Vincent wants to settle down with the right person, despite pressure from his father to marry once he's named captain. Sivan, however, finds the idea of love and marriage laughable.

Reunited after months apart as their fathers' ships patrolled opposite ends of the seas, Vincent and Sivan share a bottle of rum in the ship's storage room. A moment of curiosity steeped in hidden desire, filthy with lust, leads to a very hot and heavy night of rum-soaked awakenings…

But no one can know about this, no one can find out, or their promotions as captains, and the trust of their fathers, may be altogether shattered.

Vincent and Sivan are thrust into a world of secrets and betrayal, as their crews now face a long-buried threat when those determined to bring back the old ways of pirates emerge from the shadows.

Mⓞⓡⓔ ⓕⓡⓞⓜ Cⓐⓜⓔⓡⓞⓝ D. Jⓐⓜⓔⓢ

Autumn Fire
Cameron D. James

True gay love is a fairy tale. No matter what everyone says, that's what Dustin firmly believes. As he starts his first year of university, Dustin is happy in the closet, where he can meet his gay needs secretly through anonymous hookups.

But when Dustin has his first hookup of the university term, with a muscular dark-eyed jock in the library men's room, he can't help notice the deep and immediate connection he feels, one that seems almost like love. It's over as quickly as it begins and, as all anonymous hookups go, Dustin never expects to see him again.

The term gets difficult, especially when his math class begins. Dustin destresses with more hookups, but they don't sate him the way they used to, and he finds he cannot stop thinking about his start-of-term encounter. Soon, his academic needs outweigh the sexual, and Dustin caves in and gets a tutor.

Attractive, well-built, dark-eyed…and a jock, his new tutor, Kyle, is none other than his anonymous hookup from the men's room. Fate seems to have connected him to the man of his dreams.

Or maybe not, since Kyle is even more in the closet than Dustin is.

9 781997 726197